Library Media Center
Delavan-Darien High School
Delavan, Wisconsis

MH   Hamilton, Julia.
HAMILT   Other People's Rules.

200638

DATE | ISSUED TO

MH   Hamilton, Julia.
HAMILT   Other People's Rules.

200638

D1266128

Other People's Rules

Other People's Rules

Julia Hamilton

Library Media Center
D... ...on High School
L...... WI 53115

St. Martin's Press ≋ New York

This novel is entirely a work of fiction. The names, characters, and incidents portrayed in it are the work of the author's imagination. Any resemblance to actual persons, living or dead, events, or localities is entirely coincidental.

OTHER PEOPLE'S RULES. Copyright © 2000 by Julia Hamilton. All rights reserved. Printed in the United States of America. No part of this book may be used or reproduced in any manner whatsoever without written permission except in the case of brief quotations embodied in critical articles or reviews. For information, address St. Martin's Press, 175 Fifth Avenue, New York, N.Y. 10010.

www.stmartins.com

ISBN 0-312-26627-8

First published in Great Britain by HarperCollins*Publishers*

First U.S. Edition: November 2000

10 9 8 7 6 5 4 3 2 1

For Cherry Moorsom

Other People's Rules

PROLOGUE

Later on he would become a symbol for all that was wrong with Thatcher's Britain, the man who had had everything and thrown it all away, a corrupter of youth, a disgrace to his famous name. But before the shame and horror of the case had connected him in everyone's mind to the fate that befell Katie Gresham, before that Ivar Gatehouse was a man whom everyone had always wanted to know: as handsome in middle age as in youth, he was brilliantly married, exceedingly rich, the possessor of an ancient title and worshipped in the way the caste-ridden British worship the aristocracy, even at the end of the twentieth century.

An earl at the centre of a trial such as this has all the right ingredients for the climate of barely concealed enmity that now exists between the different castes that make up British society, not to mention the rise of Scottish nationalism with its fostering of cherished socialist nostra such as the return of large estates like Ivar's to the 'sans culottes' or 'the people', whoever the hell 'the people' are these days.

The trial is taking place in Dumfries Sheriff Court, a late nineteenth-century edifice constructed out of the red sandstone that is the depressing hallmark of Dumfries architecture. Every

3

morning whichever family members are attending that day pass through the pompous pillared portico and into the entrance hall with its black and white tiles, its uniformed attendants, the tall mahogany doors that lead into the various courtrooms; it is the kind of place where you would expect to find the Ivar Gatehouses of this world presiding gravely over the misdemeanours of others, not on trial for murder themselves. Claudia has refused to be smuggled in the back, saying it is cowardly. And so she comes with Ivar each morning, head held high, chin up, dressed as always in her ravishing clothes, and the crowd falls silent, respecting her dignity and the way she does not invite pity but behaves like a true aristocrat.

The Greshams arrive in their chauffeur-driven car, Pauline in the black she has mostly worn since her only child vanished all those years ago, still beautiful, although the slope of her shoulders betrays the ruin within, followed by Michael in one of his perfect Savile Row suits, haggard and glamorous, waving casually to the hordes as befits a star who has never lost his ability to work a crowd, whatever the circumstances. As with Claudia and Ivar, the onlookers fall almost silent as they pass, knowing that *Hello!* magazine is happening in front of them.

The rabble outside – there are many unemployed owing to the collapse of farming in the locality (you can buy a sheep for less than the price of a packet of crisps at Wallets Marts in Castle Douglas) coupled with the fact that global chaos in the money markets has brought about the closure of the Japanese electronics factory on the Annan road – seems mesmerized by the fact that Earl Gatehouse is on trial for this terrible killing. The proceedings are extensively reported every day in the national as well as the local press; there are American film crews from CNN (Katie Gresham was, after all, the Milo heiress) and chic black-clad arty types chattering in French or Italian whilst they handle microphones and camera equipment. Dumfries, for about the only time in its entire history, is at the centre of the universe.

Passing in front of this almost silent crowd, Ivar never

4

appears to register when his name is shouted by a photographer or the occasional insult such as 'Paedophile' or 'Child molester' is hurled by one of the industrialized riff-raff (reared on the poisonous diet of the red-top press).

In fact, Katie Gresham was not a child although she was officially under-age for sex; she was some way off sixteen when the affair started but so sophisticated and used to getting her own way that she could have passed for twice her actual age. The locals, for all their millennial technological sophistication, are still feudal in feeling when it comes to Earl Gatehouse. They are horrified and fascinated at the same time. They can't really believe what is happening.

If the gutter press had its way, however, he would be sent from this place and hanged by the neck until he is dead. Not since Lord Lucan went on the run in the early seventies, leaving the blood-soaked body of his children's nanny on the darkened basement stairs, has there been such a sensational case in Britain.

PART ONE

At about the same time as Pauline was marrying Michael, my parents were students at Oxford: my father, Harry Diamond, was reading languages at Merton and my mother in a short pleated skirt and knee-high boots was immersed in English Literature at St Hilda's. They were married by the end of the next year after graduating; he to go on to post-graduate work, she to teach in a girl's school, and to write. I was a mistake. They didn't want children, not then anyway, having neither the money nor the inclination to waste valuable time changing nappies and getting up in the night, and I was always aware, however scrupulously loving they were towards me, that I had somehow spoiled something by arriving when I did.

When my father was killed in a car crash, my mother, Jane, became a house-mistress at a girl's school called Wickenden Abbey, near Banbury. It meant free accommodation and free education for me, and holidays in which she could work at her writing and I could maunder about on my own at Wickenden under the indulgent gaze of the flunkeys who maintained the building and grounds.

Wickenden was one of those schools you could stay at your whole school life, entering at four and leaving at eighteen as a perfectly formed Christian feminist with liberal ideas

9

and a strong sense of one's 'duty' to the community. It had been founded in the twenties by three teachers from Charlton Priory, clones of Miss Buss and Miss Beale, with the same ideals: education for women with a strongly Christian service ethic and it was to this school that Ivar and Claudia Gatehouse decided to send their only daughter Sarah Anwoth (*Lady* Sarah Anwoth) in 1979, the year we both turned sixteen.

Sarah had been a pupil at a convent somewhere down the road from Wickenden (the Gatehouses were a recusant Catholic family), but had not flourished in the care of this particular set of nuns (there had been several) and so had been removed by her father, who didn't give a damn whether his daughter went to a convent or not as long as she was a success. Ivar's Catholicism was like everything else in his life: it had to fit in with Ivar, if not, too bad, or tough shit, as Sarah would say; her swearing was one of the reasons the nuns at Holy whatever-it-was thought it would be better if she were educated somewhere else.

I was assigned to Sarah as her 'house-mother', a Wickenden custom whereby new girls were looked after by someone who already knew the ropes. We all knew who she was, of course. Susie Fenwick had a subscription to *The Tatler* (not the kind of magazine Wickenden girls were supposed to read) which was passed round the house study (the room where we all met for assembly and did our prep) and we had seen pictures of Sarah's glamorous parents Earl and Countess Gatehouse at race meetings and dances and in the royal party at Ascot: Ivar exchanging a joke with the Queen Mother, Claudia and Princess Margaret murmuring to one another. Claudia Gatehouse also had another life as a painter, apparently, and every now and again reverent articles about her would appear in magazines or newspapers, as if being a countess as well as a painter was some kind of a miracle.

I had a picture of Sarah in my mind before I met her, compiled from having read too many school stories when I was younger: she would be aloof and rather snooty and say 'yah' a lot. In fact she was garrulous and untidy and instead of arriving in a chauffeured car found her way to the school in a taxi picked up at the station.

'Where are your parents?' I asked, as I showed her upstairs to the dorm we would be sharing with three other girls.

'Pa's speaking in some debate and my mother's in Morocco,' said Sarah. 'They're never bloody well there when I need them. Tom and I always have to get ourselves to school and back. I bet your parents brought you down by car, didn't they?'

'My father's dead,' I said. 'My mother's the house-mistress here.'

'Shit,' said Sarah, 'I didn't know. Fuck, I'm sorry. How tactless of me.'

'It doesn't matter,' I said laughing.

'Is she a martinet?' asked Sarah, lugging her case up the back stairs.

'Not really, but you'd better not swear so much. They're very down on it.'

'Just like the fucking nuns,' said Sarah loudly. 'It makes you worse, don't you think?'

'Were you expelled?' I asked curiously as we pushed through the fire doors into the wing where our dorm Silver Lime (known as Slime) was.

'Not exactly. They couldn't officially expel me because Pa's a Knight of Malta. It's very posh if you're a Catholic,' she said, seeing my look of bafflement, 'nuns are very keen on all that. I was definitely a disappointment to them.'

'Did they want you to be a nun?' I asked, knowing from history that aristocratic girls were sometimes put in nunneries if they were difficult, although I had no idea that it was still going on.

'Some fucking hope' said Sarah cheerfully, heaving her suit-case on to her bed, 'I hate all that crap. I'm just going to sit around all day painting my nails and going out to lunch like Ma does.'

'I thought your mother was an artist,' I said.

'She is when she has the time between parties or people coming to stay or staying with other people. It's a fucking nightmare.'

'What's she doing in Morocco?'

'Having a sex change,' said Sarah. 'No, actually, she's staying with someone who has a house there, to do some work, or that's the theory. What happened to your father?' she countered suddenly, taking me by surprise. I liked her directness. Most people pussy-footed round the subject.

'He died in a car crash when I was seven.'

'Do you miss him?'

'Not really. You forget. Sometimes I don't think about him for days or even weeks.'

'I suppose that's what would happen,' she said, considering me gravely, 'you just have to learn to bloody well cope.'

We became friends immediately. When Sarah was sent up to the headmistress for keeping Dubonnet in the Ribena bottle in her washing cubicle towards the end of her first term, I was asked by my mother to keep a more careful eye on her. 'Her family consider you to be a good influence,' she said, flapping a letter at me. 'They want you to go and stay in the holidays. Would you like to do that?'

I find it hard to remember a time when I was a stranger to Sarah's family, when I was not in one way or another hypnotized by them. What was it in me that made me so susceptible to them, so much so that the time before I knew them seems to belong to another life, not my own, as if contact with them changed me chemically into something different, something unrecognizable?

Sarah had already mentioned this invitation to me and I had accepted. I knew or thought I knew that my mother would like it because she could then do what she thought of as her 'real' work, that is to say writing, not marking essays and chasing up lazy or sluttish girls about their untidiness, their lack of work, or, as in Sarah's case, their drink problem. Without me there she could retreat into her ivory tower.

I had been to the Gatehouses' London house with Sarah at half-term. We had taken an early train and then a taxi to Eaton Terrace – Sarah was very good at getting herself about, unlike a lot of girls whose parents appeared to exist only in the role of chauffeurs – where she had let herself in to the house with practised ease. We found ourselves in a wide hallway lined with what looked like Picasso drawings. To the right was a huge drawing-room containing several enormous sofas upholstered in dark red damask; over the fireplace a landscape painting hung on chains, dominating the room. On a chair by the door someone had left a bag and a fuchsia pink silk scarf printed with a pattern of scent bottles. Sarah picked it up and sniffed it.

'Why are you doing that?' I asked. Later, when I had put two and two together I realized that she knew perfectly well that the scarf belonged to one of her father's teenaged mistresses. I think she was jealous. Ivar had, after all, been molesting Sarah for years by this point, and in the twisted way in which these things work, she cleaved to him even though he tormented her, much as the battered wife returns to the batterer.

'No reason,' she said, turning her back on me. 'What's the time?'

'Nine-thirty.'

'Look, let's go out and get some coffee,' she said, 'we can come back here later. Quick, before anyone knows we're here.'

'I thought your parents were here,' I said.

'Sssh,' she said in a whisper, and I followed her down the Picasso-lined passage and out of the front door which she pulled to gently behind her. We went to a café in Sloane Square and ordered coffee and croissants.

'What was all that about?' I asked.

'One of my sisters was there with a boyfriend,' she said, not meeting my eye.

'So?'

'Good Catholic girls aren't meant to have sex before marriage,' she said in a deadpan voice, so that I wasn't sure whether she was joking or not. From what I had heard of her two elder sisters, Davina and Louise, scruples about sex didn't seem to concern them particularly.

'But you –'

'Look, let's just order the bloody breakfast, shall we?' she said in a way that led me to believe that she didn't want any more questions and that if there was something here I failed to understand then she wasn't going to enlighten me.

When we went back to the house in Eaton Terrace just before lunch, Ivar Gatehouse was there with Tom, his only son, and Louise, the sister next in age to Sarah. Davina was the eldest and was working at *Vogue* and going to parties, whilst Louise was at Bristol University reading English and also going to parties. Louise was the one I liked the best, although my friendship with her was never more than lukewarm. Davina was a perfect stereotype of what you would expect a rich earl's daughter to be: silly, vain and snobbish. She never liked me: I was an outsider in every sense, and took up space merely as a friend of her crazy kid sister. The three girls were physically very similar, blonde and scrawny, with pale blue eyes and fine thin hair that Sarah always grumbled she could do nothing with, although it looked all right to me. When she was in London she invariably nipped into Michaeljohn where Tamas, who did Claudia's hair, would do hers too. It was just one of the many things she took for granted and never gave a thought to. One of the things about being rich is that you never have to think about money or getting an appointment with Tamas at Michaeljohn.

Ivar was lounging on one of the damask sofas but got to his feet when we came in. He was about fifty then but didn't look it; like his daughters he was tall and thin, but dark; his face was angular and distinguished, handsome in its way, but it was not a kind face. As Sarah introduced me I could feel his gaze fall on me, sum me up, dismiss me, his interest falling away as swiftly and chillingly as a cloud crossing the sun.

'Hello, brat,' Louise said to her sister, 'escaping from prison, are we?' Sarah, as the youngest, was regarded with indulgent amusement by her older siblings who found her outrageous behaviour hilarious. Louise turned to me and smiled: 'I hear you're Sarah's minder,' she said, stubbing her cigarette out. 'You'll certainly have your hands full. The nuns couldn't compete.'

'Shut your head,' said Sarah, who had just discovered this phrase and enjoyed using it as often as possible.

'Your language!' said Louise admiringly. 'I think it's money down the drain, Pa, that posh school. You should have sent her to Kirkcudbright Academy.'

This was a 1500-strong comprehensive in the county town a few miles from Gatehouse Park, described by Sarah even then as being full of girl gangs and lippy youths who all looked as if they had razor blades up their sleeves. Sarah would have survived, of course. She would have survived anywhere; she and Tom, considering their background and upbringing, were fantastically adaptable and had already developed a tough, chippy, ever so slightly wild-child way of leading their lives.

'And this is Tom,' said Sarah, ignoring her sister, 'the Chosen One: the Hope of Nations, aren't you, Tomo?'

'That's me,' said Tom, who had also got up when we came into the room. He was still at Eton then, dark-haired and pale-skinned like his father, shy, clever and terribly screwed-up (going through a druggy phase), but with an intensely serious streak in his nature – he wanted at one point later on at the end of his first year at Cambridge to become a priest (he told me later he had read *The Seven Storey Mountain* and been stunned by it: Merton's story seemed to have some shatteringly exact parallels with his own). As personalities they couldn't have been more different; Tom was a throwback to his ascetic martyr ancestor, Gerald Anwoth, who died at the stake and is commemorated alongside St Edmund Campion and the other English saints at Tyburn Hill where the snooker-playing contemplative nuns of the order of the Sacred Blood of Jesus pray perpetually for their immortal souls.

At that point in his life, Ivar Gatehouse was almost but not quite at the pinnacle of his success; Mad Margaret had just swept to power and it was fashionable to be a Tory peer, particularly if you were, as Ivar was, very good-looking. He was front-bench spokesman for agriculture in the House of Lords, an important post to have in that place where thousands of square miles of agricultural land were owned by a handful of men, most of them elderly and at least half of them asleep. Ivar was anything but asleep. He had his ministerial job, his estate to run, a glamorous young family to oversee, not to mention management of his extensive and complex financial affairs; he also wrote articles, which the *Daily Telegraph* faithfully printed, about the perils of Euro-centrism, and the pernicious danger of EC subsidies which lulled farmers into a false sense of security; besides all that he was hot on ecology and the preservation of ancient buildings, having recently founded the Save Scottish Peel Towers Fund.

His good looks, his aristocratic lineage and his obvious ability in public affairs made him the darling of the gossip columns and the features editors of glossy magazines: reverent profiles of Ivar were printed every other month it seemed. Sometimes joint features appeared with Claudia wearing the beautiful clothes she had a passion for, in which the pair of them would discuss their 'working' partnership (thanks to Maggie's culture of enterprise the language of corporate management was already seeping into the area of personal relations): his politics and public profile, her painting and good works – there was something called The Gatehouse Trust, a Catholic charity which provided for teenage runaways, victims of abuse, etc., which was Claudia's especial responsibility. Perhaps there was a hint of a hollowness behind all this glamour, the barest idea of a couple who were altogether too glib about themselves, a stubborn gospel of joy promoted by worship of Mammon, but if there was I did not see it then and would not have recognized it if I had. I was drawn to their light like a moth to a flame. Ivar was like a man who thought he could walk on water and, believing in his own genius, managed the miracle for a few short years.

That Claudia knew of his affairs – that he came to a point where he could only get it up for young, dependent girls – and tolerated them in those days I only guessed at later. By 'tolerated' I mean she suppressed the knowledge of them. She was much younger than her husband and had been very much in love with him. The quest for perfect clothes, the brittle thinness, the almost desperate glamour were all bids for Ivar's attention. She wanted to be what she had once been to him: the girl-wife seeking protection, his accomplice; but the reality of life with Ivar, his rages and coldnesses, the outward carapace of his charm and ability that deceived people, meant that those times would never return. She knew too much about him. The depression that she had sufferered from since her teenage years was muffled by alcohol and sheer physical strength. In Scotland she was a *tour de force*: she gardened, hunted, shot, threw parties and had hordes of people to stay almost continuously. Her painting gave her the excuse she needed to vanish when strength and sheer willpower deserted her as, with the passage of years, they did increasingly.

In her mid-forties she was hospitalized with depression, vanishing quietly into The Priory for a couple of months (the time when Sarah had told me she was in Morocco). This crisis had been precipitated by her disastrous love affair with Bozzie Lovell, a Scottish neighbour, who was said to have wanted to marry Claudia, which was of course quite impossible as her husband would never consent to divorce her. Knights of Malta are not supposed to have those kind of marriages. They are supposed to go to Lourdes with the sick and the halt, wiping bottoms and learning true humility. But the affair with Bozzie, which had started as the quest for a little fun, an amusing something on the side, had become serious on Claudia's part. She had wanted to leave Ivar, but Ivar's selfish pride would never let her go. He thought of women as chattels, objects, to whom he paid considerable outward observance, but inwardly despised.

Why he was like that was a question I spent a long time thinking about when it was all over; in the end, I came to the conclusion that a wildly successful but remote father coupled with a submissive mother who never questioned her role had been, in Ivar's case, a fatal combination. His own good looks, ability and the position in life which he inherited were the extra ingredients that might ruin him – people indulged him because of them. He had the Anwoth temperament, people would say, just like dear old Sholto and Gawain, his grandfather and father, the fifteenth and sixteenth earls respectively. That's why they've all got on so well in the world. He might appear to be a cold-hearted bastard, but he's not really. All the Anwoth men are like that; it's in their genes. Gawain was just the same: charming if he liked you but remote bordering on rude if he couldn't be bothered. He was obviously proud of Ivar but never had a kind word for him. Not the best kind of way to bring up a boy of course, but what can you do? Just thank God for the playing fields of Eton.

One of the problems was that Claudia was beginning to tire of her husband's cold heart; once The Priory had cleaned her up and got her (temporarily) off the booze they turned their attention to teaching her how to deal with her difficult marriage; it was like putting dynamite into a playpen. Claudia had come home armed with jargon about tough love and empowerment and how not to be an enabler, language Ivar found revolting and despicable; to him it stank of the swampy, hormone-infested victim culture promoted by socialism, language he was in no mood to pay the slightest attention to. It was at about this time that he began to believe that he really could walk on water.

No surprisingly it was also at about this time that Ivar began to think about Katie Gresham. There were several reasons for this: Katie had turned into a self-confident, striking beauty of exactly the right age to attract Ivar; she was a challenge to him, being young, beautiful and rich with matching independence of spirit, not his normal kind of girl at all. She was also Pauline

Gresham's daughter and Pauline Gresham was the only woman who had ever refused him, as I was to discover by accident later on. I am convinced that that counted for a great deal. Ivar did not like being made a fool of and Claudia had done just that by cuckolding him with Bozzie (and then compounding her betrayal with a head shrink instead of having a chat with nice old Father O'Bubblegum who would tell her that all men were like that, my dear), but Bozzie at least lived in Ayrshire, a seventy-mile drive away, unlike Katie, the ultimate forbidden fruit, who was virtually next door. Sophia Bain was just a plaything – a young, well-connected fashion journalist (it was her scarf we had seen on the chair that day at Eaton Terrace – Hermès scarves were having a high fashion moment at that time – her perfume Sarah had recognized), one of a string of pretty girls aged twenty or under that Ivar slept with and gave presents to, invisible supports who kept his profile effortlessly airborne, and who talked him up constantly at parties and to People Who Mattered; perhaps it was at this point that Ivar was beginning to lose his grip slightly, the hidden Ivar colliding dangerously with the public man.

I remember Sophia Bain doing something at Gatehouse Park that I believed had vanished with the Edwardian era: she left before breakfast for unspecified reasons; the tame Catholic priest, Father Cottrell, drove her to Dumfries station; if he noticed the bruises on her arms he gave no indication of having done so; Ivar was usually careful not to hurt these upper-class girls where it would show. I met Sophia in the bathroom we shared very early in the morning. She was sitting on the edge of the bath crying softly. When I asked her what was wrong and how she came by the prominent bruises on her bare arms she simply shook her head and told me to go away. It was just an accident, she said, please leave, go back to bed. I was puzzled and alarmed by what I had seen but I didn't at that time connect Sophia's injuries with Ivar. Why should I? I was still dazzled by the glamour of my surroundings and the feeling that I was somehow living inside a story, that I had become through my friendship with Sarah one of the 'chosen', somehow special. As an only child somewhat given to fantasy, I felt at that time that Ivar and Claudia had, somewhere beneath the conscious surface of my mind, become the king and queen and I a member of the court. From where I am now I see this as natural given the circumstances of my childhood, but there was a time in my life, after what happened later, when I saw it as disgusting, a cancer that I wanted to cut out of myself; I was corrupted and for a long, long time I blamed myself.

My friendship with Sarah was a surprise to my mother who, for reasons of her own, did not altogether care for Ivar and Claudia Gatehouse. With her writer's nose for what lay beneath the surface of things, she smelled a sweet whiff of the corruption emanating from Ivar Gatehouse that I was too young to put a name to.

'You don't have to go if you don't want to,' she said, giving me one of her searching house-mistressy looks. 'Don't go just because you think I want to write. You matter much more than that.'

'But I do want to go,' I said, sensing difficulty where I had not expected it. 'Please let me go.' Her reluctance made me want it more than ever.

'If you're sure,' she said, frowning slightly, possibly at her own selfishness. She was the sort of person who always felt she ought to suffer a little if she was to get what she wanted.

'But why aren't you sure?' I cried. 'You're always telling me that you're sorry I'm an only child, so let me go and stay in a big family.'

'Mmm,' she said, biting her lip. 'I know. I'm sorry. I'm not making much sense. It's just that I'm not sure it would be a suitable atmosphere for you. They might turn your head,' she added, allowing herself to smile. 'Your father would disapprove.'

My father's family were Polish Jews who had come to London at the turn of the century and made good. Like me, he had been an only child, the son of a civil servant who was still alive and living in Golders Green in a drab little terrace house where he pursued his obsession of writing the history of his grandparents' village, a place a few miles south of Cracow with an unpronounceable name composed of handfuls of z's and x's that had been destroyed by the German Army within a week of their invasion of Poland in 1939.

'But he's not here,' I said angrily. 'He's dead. Why should he have a say?'

The dead were, surely, the dead? I was unaware then that the departed exert a pull on us as subtle and as invisible as spider's silk.

As a selfish fifteen-year-old, it never occurred to me to wonder why my mother hadn't remarried or ever even seemed to have a boyfriend or any kind of admirer; I just accepted things the way they were. I was too young to remember anything much of my parents' marriage other than a picture in my mind of my mother (my blue-stocking mother!) sitting on my father's knee and laughing. The feeling that accompanied this mental picture was, needless to say, one of jealousy. Much later when I was able to understand things better we talked about how happy her marriage had been but that she had been rash to marry so young, just at the start of her career. Her parents, a doctor and his wife from Kent, had disapproved of my father, a radical Jew boy full of revolutionary ideas, as they saw him; however, when he was killed, my grandparents had tried to help my mother, who had refused and still at that point refused their help. She had a younger sister, to whom she was not particularly close, who was married to a doctor and lived near my grandparents in Kent. This was the sum total of my family and what a boring deadly little family it seemed, especially in comparison with Sarah's.

I had seen photographs of Gatehouse Park; once a mere peel tower, it had grown over the centuries with a Georgian front here, a Victorian wing there, into a massive pile; I had fantasies of it being like Glamis with a secret chamber no one could find, full of ghosts and priest holes, and secret passages

Library Media Center
Delavan - Darien High School
Delavan, WI 53115

behind doorways painted to look like bookcases. I had just read Lampedusa's *The Leopard* before I went to Gatehouse Park and I was enchanted by the idea of Donnafugata, the Sicilian palace where the lovers Tancredi and Angelica wandered half blindly day upon day in the vast labyrinth of halls and staircases, forgotten sets of chambers; to me, the whole idea of a large house with uncounted rooms had a sort of mysterious perfection to it.

Even the Gatehouses' London house had an atmosphere of careless luxury that fascinated me: the deep sofas, the piles of cushions, the huge dreamy landscape over the fireplace that I only much later discovered was by Salvator Rosa, the pair of the one in the Wallace Collection. I had enjoyed the briefest taste of this life but I was starving for more. Salvator Rosa and Donnafugata seemed infinitely preferable to the cramped, musty sitting-room of my grandfather in Golders Green and his stifling routine, his pedantic scholarship, his obsession with the lost bloodlines of obscure families, and to that other world of school I knew so well: the baths with plugs choked with hairs, the squawking floorboards and dreary classrooms smelling of chalk and dust, the smell of cooking that lingered in the long corridor outside the dining-room, the ugly school chapel with its hideous modern stained glass and an altar which looked like something from the IKEA catalogue.

The end of term came, as always, appallingly slowly. First there were exams to get through, then the results and then, finally, speech day and freedom. Ivar came to speech day as guest of honour, sitting next to Miss MacMaster, the headmistress, on the platform. Claudia sat slightly behind him next to Miss Bateson, the head of the upper school. I examined her as closely as I could from a distance. She was fashionably thin and pale and weary-looking, but wore the very latest clothes, some of which I could swear I had seen in the copy of *Vogue* I had been reading in Smith's the week before. Even from a distance she had that inexplicably 'different' look that the very rich have. She sat very still whilst

Ivar talked about young people and the importance of politics in all our lives, especially the lives of women, and how we ought to think about careers as MPs. He was a polished speaker, deft and witty, with a good voice, and got a rousing cheer at the end from the girls and some of their mothers who thought him sexy and liked being addressed by a fashionable peer, especially one so beautifully turned out.

Afterwards, Sarah took me over to their group to say hello to her parents: close to, Claudia was even paler and thinner than she had appeared on the stage. I remember noticing that she wore a ring the size of a Glacier mint on her wedding finger and that she smelled strongly of some extremely expensive scent, but when she said, 'Hello, Lucy,' in a surprisingly friendly voice, as if I was exactly the person in the whole world that she wanted to see, 'we meet at last. Thank you for looking after my bad daughter,' I was completely won over by her manner. This was my first exposure to Claudia's extraordinary charm, her greatest weapon; like many exceedingly manipulative people she used it to get what she wanted, to solve the problem of wanting to be loved whilst at the same time getting her own way absolutely and utterly in everything, except with her husband. They were very alike in some ways. No expensive clinic would ever solve Claudia's problem with herself. Her astonishing charm was merely an outer casing. The inner Claudia, the 'true' Claudia was fractured and unhappy, perpetually at odds with herself.

I remember reading somewhere that couples are drawn together for reasons other than the obvious ones of sex appeal and charm and fun and that what binds people together just as strongly is the things they don't mention, the poisonous similarities: overweening ambition, an inability to be thwarted, the desire to control others.

Even Ivar smiled warmly at me, remembered my name, which surprised me, and shook my hand, saying how much they were looking forward to having me to stay.

'You must pray for good weather,' he said, 'there's nowhere

like the Stewartry when the weather is good; it's like the Mediterranean without the people.'

'What's the Stewartry?' I asked Sarah as we walked away.

'It's where we live, stoopid,' she said, 'I keep telling you. Over the border and turn left: it's an old name for the two counties of Kirkcudbrightshire and Wigtownshire. It was once a Stewart fiefdom, a kind of little principality. Don't worry,' she added, 'you'll love it.'

I went north the second week in July that year, taking a train from Euston to Dumfries. I had never been to Scotland in my life and had no idea what to expect other than heather and haggis and hills. I had of course some vague notion of Scottish history, a kind of Madame Tussaud-like line-up stretching from Robert the Bruce and the spider via Mary Queen of Scots with her head under her arm to Bonnie Prince Charlie who, for some reason, I knew for a fact had ended his life as a drunk in Rome. Where the Gatehouses fitted into this pantheon and why they had received a title and from which monarch or prime minister was a mystery to me.

Sarah had come to meet me with Tom who had just passed his driving test. Although it was July a cruel wind was blowing through the station; Sarah, skin and bone as ever, was wearing a coat and a long woolly scarf wrapped several times round her throat. But even if the weather had been tropical Sarah would have been cold. In all the time I knew her I never saw her warm; like some Victorian maiden aunt she was always complaining about draughts and chafing her hands and putting on more vests and socks.

'Did you bring your furs?' she asked. 'I hate this fucking climate. It'll probably snow soon. By the way, you do know my brother Tom, don't you?'

'Yes,' I replied, glancing at Tom who looked as pinched and chilly as his sister. His hands were plunged into the pockets of his jacket and I remember noticing that the sleeves looked too short for him and that the collar of his shirt was so frayed that it looked as if it had had an attack of mange. For the son of such a rich man he looked as if nobody bothered much.

'Hello,' said Tom, making a movement with his head. 'Car's out the front. Let's go.'

The car in question was an old half-timbered Morris Minor estate full of Mars bar wrappings and empty cigarette packets. A wall-eyed collie lying on the back seat got up and gave me a menacing look as Tom shoved my case in the back.

'What's her name?' I asked.

'Jip,' said Tom. 'Don't approach her. She's extremely anti-social.'

'Tom rescued her from a cruel farmer,' explained Sarah. 'I would have had him shot personally.' She began to walk away from the car across the forecourt towards the grim stone portals of the Station Hotel.

'Where're you going?' asked Tom, lighting a cigarette.

'Time for a drink,' said Sarah, 'come along, children. We can't throw Lucy to the lions without a drink first.'

The bar of the hotel was empty but for a man in a corner who was lingering over a pint and reading *The Scotsman*. We stood at the bar and ordered whiskies from a stout barman in a maroon suit who spoke in a dialect that might have been Urdu as far as I was concerned.

'What time's dinner?' Tom asked.

'Dunno; usual time I suppose.'

'Do we have company other than what's already on offer?'

'Bound to if they're in. Are they?'

'She was doing menus this morning with Heather.'

Tom and Sarah often referred to their mother as 'she' or 'her' or Ivar and Claudia together as 'they'; it was their way of depersonalizing their parents towards whom out of an instinct of self-preservation they affected a world-weary air of detachment. As the two youngest in the family they regarded themselves as separate, a mobile guerrilla unit whose principal aim was to avoid entertaining the numerous friends and acquaintances of their parents who came to stay in an

25

endless stream when the family was in Scotland. When they were younger, Sarah told me, they had tried to get the guests they particularly disliked to leave by whatever means they had at their disposal such as apple-pie beds, sewing up the legs of pyjamas, a crab placed under a pillow, or the simple expedient of unscrewing the numbers on the doors of the bedrooms when there was a particular houseful in order to cause as much chaos as possible.

It was quite a drive from Dumfries to Gatehouse Park. Jip was put on the front seat and Sarah and I sat together in the back pretending we were in a taxi and Tom was our chauffeur. I was on a beautiful high, a combination of the unaccustomed whisky, my freedom from the endless rules and restraints of school life, mingled with Sarah and Tom's peculiarly anarchic sense of humour. During that journey I had the strangest feeling of being aware of my life for the first time, as if from being merely alive I had at last begun to live.

The main road was choked with lorries on their way to the ferry at Stranraer so Tom took us a back way: an unmarked road that wound its way through boulder-strewn moorland and down into tiny dour villages with a single street of houses and a pub if they were lucky; the landscape was wild and empty, water glittered in pewter sheets where there was a loch or a swift glimpse of the sea. At one point we stopped at a place where a path led to a tiny white-painted chapel with tall windows whose plain glass panes glowed in the evening light. We stood in silence on the small promontory looking across the green hills towards the sea, the wind lifting our hair. I will never forget it.

'She's passed, don't you think, O Brother?' said Sarah as we climbed back into the car.

'What?' I asked. 'What have I passed?'

'A very serious test,' said Sarah, 'an initiation. You didn't speak. Anyone we take to the chapel who speaks is immediately returned to the station and then sent southwards to oblivion.'

'"Safe in the magic of my woods",' quoted Tom, who had

hardly spoken until now, '"I lay, and watched the dying light. Faint in the pale high solitudes, And washed with rain and veiled by night . . ." Rupert Brooke. So underrated.'

I caught his eye in the driving mirror and for a moment we stared at one another; then he ostentatiously leaned over towards Jip and began to talk to her in a low voice. Some of his words lingered in my inner ear . . . *faint in the pale high solitudes* . . .

'Wake up,' said Sarah's voice, 'we're here.' The car was passing slowly over an ancient stone bridge; to my left I could see endless marshes, tall reeds swaying in the breeze, and the broad sweep of a river; to my right there was dense woodland. The drive lay just ahead up to the left, a wide bend leading to open gates set within curved walls; beyond and to the right there was a lodge, pink stucco with the gothic window surrounds painted black; all the Gatehouse cottages and lodges were painted pink and black, it was the architectural version of your own racing colours. Next-door ('Next-door' in Scotland can mean anything up to a hundred miles away) Pauline had encouraged Michael to do the same with the Balmachie houses which were painted a pale pistachio-green with window surrounds in cream.

The drive seemed to wind on through the woods for ever, but eventually we came to a walled garden on our left and then, set back, a row of pink cottages with barge boards and painted gables; another series of bends took us at last to the house where a large number of cars were parked. I wasn't unused to big houses – Wickenden was the former home of the last Duke of London – but the fact that Gatehouse Park was even bigger and was still lived in by the same family who had been there since the sixteenth century made me feel dwarfed, Lilliputian. For a moment looking up at its numberless windows, its towers and crenellations, I wondered what the hell I was doing there. Inside, I could hear dogs barking and a commanding voice shouting at them to be quiet. I followed Tom and Sarah into a vast hall lined with row upon row of portraits of Anwoths.

Straight ahead of us the sound of a cocktail party was coming from a doorway by which stood two girls in black skirts and white shirts holding trays with glasses of champagne on them.

'Damn, bugger, blast,' said Sarah, *another* party. I thought so. Let's take some champagne and run. Come on. There's a really good film on tonight.'

'Your language,' said a voice, 'is enough to make a strong man weep.'

Sarah spun round to greet the speaker, a dark, handsome well-dressed woman in her early fifties, I guessed, wearing a black dress with lashings of pearls and very high heels.

'Aunt Marian!' said Sarah. 'I didn't know you were here.'

'And why shouldn't I be here? Good evening, Tom, how are you? Please introduce me to your friend.'

'Er . . . this is Lucy,' said Tom, shuffling his hands in his pockets.

'Lucy,' said Aunt Marian, 'how do you do. Do you have a surname?'

'Diamond,' I said. 'I am Lucy Diamond.'

Aunt Marian's eyes flickered almost imperceptibly as I repeated my surname. Diamond, I could see her thinking, Jews.

'Is your father Joe Diamond?' Joe Diamond was an eminent libel QC and always in the newspapers.

'No. My father's dead.'

'I'm exceedingly sorry to hear it.' Dismissing me, she turned to Sarah. 'Your mother's expecting you to join us, darling, you'd better get changed. The Annans are here and you know they never come out for anyone except your mother.'

'Who're the Annans?' I asked as we went up a broad staircase under the solemn gaze of Sarah's dead family. Tom, I noted, had melted away somehow, dematerialized like the Cheshire Cat.

'Duke and Duchess of. Complete crocks, both of them. He's in a wheelchair, she totters about on sticks being wonderful and wipes away his drool. We'll have to show up though, what a fucking bore it all is. Do you mind?'

'Of course not,' I said, wondering what she would do if I did.

'They can never be alone for a moment,' she was saying, 'it's always a fucking circus here. I'm sick of it, so's Tom. Davina likes it but Lulu thinks it stinks only she's old enough to pick and choose.'

'Is she here?'

'No, she's in Greece with some friends, lucky so-and-so. I think she's got a boyfriend they don't approve of, so she has to keep him away.'

'Why don't they approve of him?'

'He's not one of us, I suppose,' she said casually.

'What is he? Black or something?'

'God, no. He's just middle-class. That's a crime here, you know.'

'Where does that leave me then?'

'You're not a suitor,' she said. 'That's when the trouble starts. It's just like a racing stables; the bloodlines have to be right.'

'And have they got a suitor for you?'

'Too bloody right they have,' said Sarah. 'He's the grandson of the dribbling duke downstairs.'

'And will you marry him?'

I was amazed that one could still have a conversation like this in the late twentieth century; we could have been two girls on this staircase a hundred years earlier, when such things would have made more sense. I was a month off my sixteenth birthday then and knew nothing much about anything, let alone families like Sarah's, rich and powerful, for whom the bubble of privilege had not burst: no Labour government had unseated them with death duties (they were too well-advised for that), no Earl Gatehouse for at least a hundred years had taken to gambling or serious low life (the son of the last one to disgrace the family name had redeemed his father's pitiable folly by marrying an American heiress whose portrait by Sargent hung in the room where the party was being held). Ivar's father, Gawain, the sixteenth earl, had been a highly successful diplomat and then a tremendous war hero who had escaped from the equivalent of Colditz disguised, like Toad, as a washerwoman, saved by his ability to speak fifteen languages idiomatically; their family pride was thus utterly undented but they were quite clever enough to know that they must conceal this fact. Their publicity was brilliantly managed (Ivar was into spin before anyone had even thought of such a concept) – people admired Ivar principally because he was clever and hard-working and the fact that he was also immensely rich and grand was coincidental, the cherry on the cake. He spoke well in public, appearing the very embodiment of *noblesse oblige*, and he also gave the impression of being both relaxed and amused; *no side*, certain eminent people would say of him, *almost a humble man*; the fact of the matter was that Ivar was a brilliant actor. The majority of people simply had no idea that such ruthless considerations as his about birth and blood still existed, let alone were being put into practice. They thought all that sort of thing was over and done with. They were completely wrong, as I was discovering.

'Christ, I don't know,' said Sarah impatiently. 'He might be run over or something, or I might. *Carpe diem*, that's my motto.'

The Sargent painting was entitled 'Lady Creetown and her children' and was obviously painted in the room in which I was now standing. It took up most of a whole wall of the enormous salon I entered with Sarah and I was transfixed by it. In it, Lady Creetown (the wife of Viscount Creetown, eldest son of Earl Gatehouse) sits on an enormous sofa with her three children disposed about her, a boy on either side of her with the baby gambolling on the floor. Mary Creetown (née Pierce) was the daughter of the owner of Pierce Oil and Pierce Railroads, not to mention the Wall Street firm of Pierce & Pierce and was a young and pretty blonde whom Sargent (who famously didn't flatter his sitters) would have had absolutely no trouble in painting; in fact, she looked like the prototype for Sarah.

'Stop being such a tourist,' said Sarah, 'and come and say hello to my mother.'

'I like being a tourist. You resemble her.'

'Don't you start,' said Sarah. 'That's what everyone says.'

'I would be pleased if someone said that. She's so pretty.'

'She's dead,' said Sarah. 'I want to be myself, not the great-great-granddaughter of a Sargent painting.'

I said nothing but I thought with an unexpectedly painful jolt of my grandfather in Golders Green trying to trace living members of forgotten families who had died in the Nazi inferno of those first few weeks in September 1939, a people whose history had perished in flames.

Claudia, in lace and velvet, was sitting next to an old man in a wheelchair. A stroke had moved his mouth slightly to the side of his face and his wasted hands were twisted together in his lap, where a rug concealed his shrunken legs.

'That's the dook,' whispered Sarah, 'doesn't it make you believe in mercy killing? He ought to be put down really, it's not kind to keep him hanging on like that.' 'Wait till it's your turn,' I said, riveted by the sight of this – to me – *rara avis*. I'd never seen a duke before in the flesh.

'Here's Sarah,' said Claudia in a loud voice to the duke, getting up as she spoke. 'You remember Sarah, don't you, John?'

The duke smiled at Sarah, or gave what passed for a smile; I watched, horrified, as a string of dribble unwound itself from his mouth, but Sarah was equal to it. She sat down on the chair on the other side of the old man appearing not to notice the drool, and asked him how he was. Then she introduced me. When the duchess tottered over, Sarah kissed her and introduced me again.

'There, my darling,' said the duchess in her twittery voice, wiping her husband's chin, 'that's better.' Her old liver-spotted hand was thin, curved like a bird's claw with rheumatism, heavy with Annan diamonds; one of her rings was even bigger than Claudia's Glacier mint but much dirtier. Her fingernails had remnants of earth under them.

'We so love your mother's parties,' the duchess was saying to Sarah, 'Johnny won't come out for anyone else, will you, my darling?'

'He's so deaf,' said Claudia, taking my arm, 'that I almost wish he wouldn't; let alone all that slobbering. How nice to see you, Lucy. I won't ask you if you had a good journey because that damn train's always late, has anyone offered you a drink yet?'

'I won't, thank you,' I said.

'How demure you are. I believe the young should learn how to drink,' she said, signalling one of the girls with trays whom we had passed at the door.

I thought of the bar at the Station Hotel but said nothing. When the tray arrived I selected at random a glass of what looked like orange juice.

'That's Buck's Fizz,' said Claudia, 'just so long as you know. The first time Sarah drank it she went over the top and was sick all the way from the Jardine-Fullers at Thornhill. It was a nightmare. How's your mother?'

'Very well. Glad the term's over,' I said neutrally. 'Pleased to see the back of me, I think.'

'She needs a break, your poor mother, and we're more than glad to have you here,' continued Claudia, scarcely listening to my replies. I wondered whether this tête-à-tête was running along pre-ordained lines or was unscripted. 'How do you find Sarah? And Tom? By the way, where *is* Tom? I don't think I've seen him this evening.'

'I don't know,' I said, hoping this one answer would do for all her questions. 'I haven't seen him since we arrived.'

'Never mind that,' said Claudia, lighting a cigarette with a gold lighter which she slipped back into a tiny crystal-encrusted bag. 'You don't smoke, do you?'

'No,' I said.

'All my children have smoked since an early age. There isn't really anything one can do about it,' Claudia continued, 'the nuns tried to get Sarah to stop but she just paid no attention. Are you a Catholic? No, of course you're not, what a silly question. I wasn't, but I had to convert when I married Ivar. I felt a bit like Rex Mottram in *Brideshead* but Father Cottrell didn't seem to notice. Ivar said it didn't matter what I *felt*, apparently one's feelings are irrelevant even if they involve feeling doubtful, but just to answer the questions in the right way, so I did . . .' she paused for breath, while I sipped my Buck's Fizz, 'Sarah's had a rather ghastly report,' she continued, 'did you know?'

'No.'

'Well, she has. The Dubonnet saga went down very badly with the headmistress. Your mother was more lenient – at least she has a sense of humour, thank God – but Miss MacMaster was very harsh about her. She said she was "degenerate"! What sort of a word is that to use about a girl of fifteen? Sarah's naughty, but she's not degenerate . . . we're hoping you might be able to knock a bit of sense into her, help her keep her feet on the ground. Ivar thinks you're an excellent influence, and a good friend for Sarah. We're terribly grateful to you. There are really very few girls in this part of the world, other than Katie Gresham of course, Michael and Pauline's girl, and Katie already appears to be a member of the jet set at almost sixteen. That's not how we do things in Scotland, I'm afraid. We don't approve of vulgar display. Darling Michael used to know these things but he's forgotten. Ivar says he's contaminated by that ghastly world he moves in. I'm so glad Sissy isn't alive to see it all.'

'Is that *the* Michael Gresham?' I asked. Naturally, I'd heard of him, although I'd no idea until Claudia mentioned them as a family that they lived nearby. I was quite certain that Sarah had never mentioned it.

'Michael and my husband were brought up together,' replied Claudia, 'and, yes, he is *the* Michael Gresham, as you put it,' she added in tones of icy distaste. 'The Greshams' land marches with ours. Katie, their only child, is the same age as Sarah, only she's been brought up rather differently. Americans aren't as strict as we are with our children. They believe in giving them everything from an early age. Such a mistake. Not the way we do things here,' she repeated firmly, as if I were some rebellious piccaninny who was stepping out of line.

'Oh, I see,' I said nervously, longing to know more but realizing I'd somehow put my foot in it. How we *did* things in Scotland was evidently like this, I thought, looking round me: old money providing the foundation for the future. Gatehouse Park could in no way be described as shabby grandeur – the fabric of the house was in apple-pie order – but it was fixed and unchanging; this room looked much the same as it did a century before.

'I know you'll do your best, Lucy dear, to see that she behaves herself next year,' Claudia was saying, 'it's so important that she does well in her exams. Look, we ought to go in to dinner, let me introduce you to Sandy Carsluith. He can take you in. He's Johnny Annan's grandson, such a nice boy.'

Alexander Carsluith was fair and pink-cheeked and blushed when he was introduced to me. He had a head of tight blonde curls which made him resemble some esoteric breed of sheep, a long Roman nose down which he stared at me out of large pale eyes, and a slight lisp.

'So you're Sarah's friend,' he said, as we went into the dining-room where long windows looked west across endless lawns towards the sea. It was still quite light although candles on the long table had been lit; two statues of blackamoors either side of the door we had just passed through held their flickering candles hospitably aloft. 'Is this your first time up north?'

'Yes,' I replied, glancing behind me at a full-length portrait by Ramsay of Lady Gatehouse holding the hand of Lord Creetown. They were leaning against a tree with the same westerly background view of woods and sea that I had just seen myself for the first time. I loved paintings and I was as entranced by this one as I had been by the Sargent in the salon. It never failed to make Sarah laugh when I looked at the pictures in the house with such interest. 'You'll be like the old bags who show people round on open days,' she would say. 'You hear them talking about the pictures and the furniture as if they were the owners.'

'You just don't know how lucky you are,' I would reply, nettled by her comments. 'They only sound like that because they revere beauty. You're just a spoilt little rich girl who can't see what's in front of her nose.'

'I do love you,' Sarah would say humbly, 'you'll always tell me, won't you, Luce, when I'm being an arrogant bitch. She's always telling us we should know more about the pictures too, but then that's her field.'

'You'll have a lovely time,' said Sandy, glancing behind him to see what I was looking at. 'Can you reel?'

'Sorry?'

'Scottish dancing,' he said. 'You have to be able to do that here. I'll teach you if you like,' he added kindly, 'it's very easy once you get the hang of it. Rather heady stuff actually; gets into your bloodstream,' he added shyly.

'Does Sarah do it?'

'Of course she can do it,' he said, sounding doubtful, 'but she thinks it's funny to mob it up. It isn't, you know, and it spoils it for everyone else. Tom's just as bad. It'll happen after dinner here I should think, once my grandfather has gone home, although he may stay for the first dance. He used to love reeling when he was younger, poor Grandpa. When he was taken prisoner in the war he and his fellow officers made up a reel. We may dance it later. It's called the Duke of Annan.'

'Oh hello, Sandy,' said Sarah joining us as we queued for a plate at the long table where the supper was laid out. 'I hope you're looking after Lucy properly. She's my new best friend.'

'He's going to teach me to reel,' I said.

'Oh no, you're not,' said Sarah. 'She's mine. I don't want her turned into a performing monkey. There are quite enough of them here as it is. All these people in tartan trousers look as if they've come from a carpet warehouse.'

I looked round the room and indeed almost every man was wearing tartan trousers, including Sandy himself whose long thin legs were clad in a hideous clashing tartan of particularly virulent reds and yellows and greens. On his long thin feet he wore elaborately-laced old-fashioned pumps that made him look as if he had just escaped from one of the portraits on the walls.

'She's impossible,' said Sandy to me rather sadly, 'she always was.'

'He talks about me as if he's my nanny,' said Sarah to me later when we were upstairs in her bedroom getting undressed, 'but he's only two years older. He's so solemn and sensible and *boring*. I think he's the most *boring* person I've ever met.'

'And one day you'll end up marrying him,' I said, just to see what she would say.

'You only live once,' said Sarah, half listening, 'that's my motto, so we have to take advantage. *Carpe diem*. I already told you. I like Sandy but I can't imagine being fucked by him, can you?'

As I was trying to think of an answer to this, Sarah continued: 'And by the way, what was she saying to you tonight? I saw you two whispering away while I was talking to the dook.'

'She said you'd had a lousy report. She's worried about you.'

'She just says that,' said Sarah dismissively, 'she doesn't really care. Why should she care?'

'She is your mother,' I said.

'When she remembers she is,' Sarah answered. 'When she's not busy . . .'

'What?'

'Nothing. It's nothing. Just leave it.'

At this point in our friendship Sarah was always stopping dead when the faintest whiff of something disagreeable came up. Even then, very early on, I realized that something important was happening to me. I was becoming – had already become – a part of a family that was not my own. Other than my mother I didn't have a family around me. My mother was a good woman, a serious, decent, clever one too, but she was slightly remote; I didn't feel passionately involved with her in the way I was already beginning to with this family. I had relatives but I didn't have a proper family. I was being drawn into Sarah's world and I was glad of it, so infinitely preferable did it seem to my own mundane existence. I was starstruck. I had never met a duke before, even one who dribbled when you spoke to him, nor danced the Gay Gordons with a duke's grandson who, although he looked like a friendly sheep, was nevertheless an earl already. I didn't want to go back to dreary Wickenden after this to spend the endless empty days of the holiday trailing into Banbury on my own, moping about the shops and then waiting at the bus stop outside Boots for the bus home with the schoolkids and old ladies and the yobs. I had entered a different world and I wanted to stay in it for ever.

The Greshams were not there that first evening at Gatehouse Park. They were in America at their house in Connecticut or in the Bahamas (they owned an island, I forget which), but they were due to return for Katie's birthday on August 1st in honour of which a huge costume ball would be held at Balmachie House; the dress code was *Les Liaisons Dangereuses*, Katie's idea apparently. Gatehouse Park would be full to overflowing with guests for this swank party; there was even talk that Mrs Thatcher was coming and would be staying with the Gatehouses, but there was a problem about security and she never came after all, not that it mattered; all we wanted was to go to a party where the Stones were playing and where Michael Gresham would sing his signature hit song from the early sixties, 'Sweet Lola Dune', as he had promised to do.

When we were in bed (that first visit I shared Sarah's room – later on I would be given my own room) I told Sarah what her mother had said about the Greshams and asked her what she thought of Katie.

'She's really attractive,' she said grudgingly, '*really* attractive, but she acts like she's twenty-five not fifteen. Tomo lusts after her and so does Pa. He's always going on about how lovely she is; it makes me sick.'

'He's probably just being polite,' I said, puzzled by the venom in her voice.

'He isn't actually,' she snapped. 'He's not her father and he should lay off.'

'Why're you so upset?'

'Don't ask.'

'Why not?'

'Just don't,' she said. I realized I had strayed into one of Sarah's no-go areas and by this time I knew better than to continue asking questions. Curiously enough, however, the following Sunday one of the supplements, it might have been the *Sunday Times Magazine*, carried a long and richly documented feature about the Greshams which I pored over when Sarah wasn't looking: most of the images to start with were of Pauline Gresham in all the many different, but invariably well-documented stages of her life: the first at her father's (the billionaire Lewis Milo) Connecticut estate, Stanborough Farm, in riding clothes, holding her pony Johnson (they were one of those grand American families where even the animals had servants' names). The next picture was of Pauline at Radcliffe in the classic student uniform of the time: V-necked sweater and narrow pants, her rich auburn hair lying on her shoulders, a smile hovering around her generous, heavily-lipsticked mouth.

Then there was the breathtaking goddess at her coming-out dance in the Fifth Avenue apartment wearing a Balenciaga ball dress that looked as if it were made of spun sugar tied with gleaming ribbon. The coming-out dance led on in a natural progression of events to Pauline as a bride at her wedding to Tufter Saintsbury at Stanborough Farm taken a couple of years later in the late fifties. By then she was a Givenchy girl, simple and peach-perfect in his clean lines, her neck like the stalk of some exotic flower bowed down by the weight of the famous Milo pearls. I stared and stared at these pictures. She seemed so beautiful, but so remote, almost as if she were not human at all, but the text told another story: an earnest young woman endlessly involved in good works on a scale that few could match, almost all with the emphasis on children: hospitals, holidays, and educational schemes; there was money for research into female infertility too, something Pauline suffered from herself.

When Tufter Saintsbury died from a brain haemorrhage resulting from a bad fall whilst playing polo in Argentina, Pauline was left a childless widow of thirty. It was shortly after that she met and married Michael Gresham. In the photograph taken on their wedding day, Pauline was not in Givenchy but in a simple St Laurent shift with no hat (and no pigeon's egg pearls either), clutching Michael's arm; she looked beautiful but it was Michael in the full glory of his good looks who took my breath away in a denim suit and blue shirt but no tie, his blond hair collar-length, his handsome features chiselled, the epitome of emergent aristo coolth. They were fashionable, rich and talented. Michael's cult album 'Horseferry Road' had just come out and had already sold a million copies. The press adored this golden couple and there were several photographs of them taken at their house in London and at Balmachie, Michael's estate, only a few miles away from Gatehouse Park. There was one photograph of Katie as a baby and then a few blurred shots of a little girl on a yacht or at one of her father's concerts, hand-in-hand with her mother, a kidnap attempt having made the parents nervous of having their one and only and exceedingly precious child photographed. The final shot was Katie at fifteen by Snowdon. Sarah was right. She was beautiful. I gazed at her lovely face with envy: huge blue eyes, her mother's wide mouth, her father's blond hair and a figure to die for. Sarah was right in another way too; Katie's was not the face of a child. She looked young but there was something hard in that bold stare and something knowingly sexual about the way she sat with her legs crossed, so confident for one so young.

I remember ringing my mother at the end of ten days at Gatehouse Park and asking if I could stay on. She was in two minds about it. Either Miss MacMaster, the headmistress of Wickenden, had said something to her about the kind of company I was keeping or the ghost of my father had been haunting her, but she was distinctly uneasy.

'These people are so rich and rare, it worries me. You sound as if you're on a different planet. Ordinary life will seem *very* ordinary when you eventually return to it,' she said, when I had rashly told her about the forthcoming party at Balmachie.

'It won't. Please let me stay. Why're you suddenly in a twitch?'

'Sheila mentioned it,' she said, meaning Sheila MacMaster. 'She thinks Lord Gatehouse wants as much leverage as he can get over the question of Sarah. She doesn't think much of her, as you know. Says you're completely different material. She sees you as a future headgirl of Wickenden, you know. She has very high hopes for you.'

'It was Mac who asked Ivar to talk at speech day,' I said. 'She can't have her cake and eat it.'

'Eat her cake and have it, you mean?'

'You know what I mean,' I said impatiently. 'Why are the Gatehouses suddenly a bad influence? Sarah isn't degenerate, you know, she's just Sarah. She's naughty but she's not bad,' I added, finding that I was echoing Claudia.

'All right,' my mother said, and then there was a deafening noise and the line went dead.

When I rang back she said she had dropped the receiver. She did not add that this was but one of a number of symptoms that were worrying her badly and that in the next few days she would be going to Banbury General for tests to see what was the matter with her.

In fact Mac had been remarkably forthright to my mother

about the Gatehouses. She was a Scotswoman herself of humble birth whose politics were certainly left-of-centre and she disapproved of the smash-and-grab atmosphere generated by Maggie; having come from an underclass herself she knew what she was talking about; she also had a very Scottish aversion to Catholicism which she knew was unreasonable but which she couldn't help.

'There's something about that man,' she said, 'that I don't like. He's too smooth for his own good; so talented and yet somehow heartless. I feel it in my water. And Sarah Anwoth looks like a classic case of upper-class neglected child syndrome to me; everything money can buy and more but no one pays any real attention to her. Parents who are too busy doing their own thing to do any proper parenting. That's why Lucy is useful to them. If I'd known they would become such friends I would have turned her down flat. I almost did anyway. I should have listened to my instinct, but then he offered the Gatehouse Political Bursary and I was sunk. Just as he intended, no doubt.'

The bursary in question was a substantial annual prize awarded for the best essay to a girl who wished to go into political life (in support of any party except the Communists!). Mac had dreamed of such a thing for years. Ivar had obviously done his homework as usual; he was getting increasingly desperate to find a good school for Sarah and knew he would have to offer what amounted to a bribe to get Wickenden to take her. One of Mac's perpetual refrains was that there were too few women in parliament. What was the point of being enfranchised if we couldn't make a difference to the actual parliamentary process? There were issues pertaining to women that needed women to see them through the legislative process, and so on and so forth.

The Greshams of Balmachie were a nice old county family, nothing like as grand as the Gatehouses of course, but gentry in that place since time immemorial, at least since the sixteenth century when a Thomas Gresham had been given the priory of Balmachie for services rendered to the Regent Murray. They had pottered along marrying other local gentry for hundreds of years, quietly increasing their lands and improving their house when there was any spare money, which mercifully there had not been since the eighteenth century when another Thomas Gresham, who married an Anwoth girl, hired the Adam brothers to rejig his house; the result was the most stunning success, a kind of muted beauty that took your breath away. There were all the touches one might expect: a vista, a graceful colonnaded portico, local stone that had somehow weathered in the right way so that the house had turned a becoming greyish pink, not that in-your-face congested rouge of Dumfries sandstone; there was a loch where exotic black swans specially imported by Pauline from Australia swam and a folly where, when it was warm enough, Pauline and Michael gave supper parties under a chandelier filled with lighted candles, and busts of Roman emperors gazed sightlessly from niches in the walls; a quartet might be playing outside if there were any musicians staying, which there often were. Although a pop star, Michael loved classical music and had formed the Gresham Players who had made several distinguished recordings of baroque music. He had been encouraged in this by Pauline.

When Michael, aged sixteen, had inherited the estate from his father, the house had been run down in the charming but slightly worrying way of beautiful old houses in rural areas: sagging ceilings, rising damp in the basement, chimney breasts that leaked in all the bedrooms upstairs. The storms of autumn meant Michael's poor old mother Sissy had to run up and down stairs with buckets from the back kitchen into which the torrents of water drummed noisily.

Michael was not a satisfactory son. People felt for Sissy. He idled away his schooldays flunking his exams, doing nothing in particular except playing lead guitar in the skiffle band he had formed with other boys. His mother thought Cirencester

Agricultural College was the answer for a boy so spectacularly ungifted in any way that really mattered; she couldn't afford to send him into the Scots Guards, his father's old regiment, because there was no spare money to provide him with the private income necessary if he was to hold his head up in such a regiment and be a credit to his family name.

Michael went to Cirencester where he tore around the lanes in an old car he had bought somehow and practised his music in the farm cottage he had rented with a couple of other boys.

The next thing poor Sissy knew was that Michael had thrown in Cirencester and had gone to live in London. It was 1958 and he was hanging out in Soho and lodging with Lady Sadie McGowan, a bohemian grandee who had a large house in Tite Street, where, as Sissy confided to the bridge table, he was paying his way by playing his music at parties and meeting all the wrong kind of people. But after eighteen months of Lady Sadie, Michael's career took off; he was spotted at a party by a record producer and cut his first LP, 'Hanging Fire'. It was a sensation and Michael Gresham burst into the sixties along with the Beatles and the Stones. He was already a millionaire several times over by 1961. His standing with the bridge table improved immensely when he had the roof at Balmachie completely renewed (goodbye bucket duty) and bought Sissy a new Aga and a fridge as big as an aircraft hangar, which made her the envy of all her friends. When Sissy's Austin A30 collapsed he replaced it with a red mini to zip round the lanes of Kirkcudbrightshire in, one of the first to be seen in those parts.

In 1962 Michael married Pauline Milo Saintsbury, the heiress to the Milo pharmaceuticals fortune. Lewis Milo was a member of an old Hungarian family whose company was said to have supplied the Nazis with the chemicals for the gas chambers. His fortune was immense, even by American standards, and Pauline was his only child. Michael's family, who were all landowners or retired colonels (or both), disapproved, finding the presence of so much new money vulgar in a rather sinister way, but when

Sissy gave a party for the newly-weds at Balmachie, Pauline won the hearts of all the crusty old guard with her beauty and her exquisite manners; she spent hours talking to Sissy's Aunt Ettie who was deaf and difficult. Pauline also played an exceedingly good hand at the bridge table, which gained her numerous Brownie points in a society that thought highly of such pursuits. The locals noted that she was kind to Sissy and it was Pauline who had the lift installed when Sissy's arthritis got so bad that she found it difficult to walk upstairs. They also approved of her charitable pursuits and the fact that she adored gardening.

Katie, her mother's first and only child, was born the year after Tom Creetown. Poor Pauline, who had so much, could only have one child (and was lucky even to have the one apparently) owing to an undiagnosed case of endometriosis in her teens. Claudia and Pauline were friends but there was always a certain coolness between them. Claudia, as Ivar's wife, considered herself the First Lady of the Stewartry by hereditary right but Pauline and Michael's celebrity upset that old order of things, the hierarchical balance so carefully connived at by the locals; Michael's money was just about all right because he was who he was but Pauline's money was really just too much to comprehend. And who knew how it was come by? Money amassed so quickly could not be legal and there were stories circulating even then about Lewis Milo's relations with the countries behind the Iron Curtain, whom he was rumoured to be supplying with Western goods in return for fantastic concessions.

And the Greshams were not always there. They had a house in London, and apartments in New York, in Monte Carlo and elsewhere. They had an aeroplane and several helicopters. The old rhythms of the Season did not bind the Greshams as they did the Gatehouses, who were in London in the autumn, returning to Scotland for Christmas and for the shooting, the school holidays and the summer. Ivar was after all Lord Lieutenant and thus intimately linked with his native heath whereas it was sometimes only possible to tell where Michael and Pauline were by reading the international gossip columns.

Katie Gresham was an only child, just as her mother had been, and became the new Milo heiress at an early age, when her grandfather died in somewhat mysterious circumstances. Sissy was also dead by then and the bridge table was reticent about such matters, but it soon became known that Lewis Milo had died of a heart attack whilst making love to his mistress in the Hotel Georges V.

*

'Sissy would have hated that,' said Daphne Jardine. 'I'm glad she didn't live to read about all this.'

'She was always terribly worried about Katie inheriting so much money,' said Kath McCordle. 'Four no trumps.'

And with reason. There was a kidnap attempt when Katie had just started at Bedales.

'Why Bedales?' asked the bridge table. 'God alone knows. They only go to the lessons they want to go to, apparently. Two hearts.'

'No, dear, that's Summerhill.'

'Not that she'll have to earn her living,' said Eve Dunbar, 'so it won't much matter.'

'But no discipline, Eve dear. Three spades.'

*

Michael wanted to remove Katie from Bedales but she wouldn't let him. She had a bodyguard for a while whom she enjoyed giving the slip. Like a lot of people who grow up with security she found it a hoot. She was a bit of a rebel, was Katie; hardly surprising. After all, what else was there to do? The Gatehouses thought her spoiled as a child and unstable as a young woman. They muttered drugs and too much money, but she and Tom were friends. (And more than friends as I now know.) And sometimes Louise Anwoth stayed at the Greshams' house in London if Katie was there and vice versa.

The first time I saw Katie in the flesh was a few days before her party. It was 1979. She was going to be sixteen on August

1st but Sarah told me that Katie was already having sex with a boy in her year at Bedales. I was shocked which made Sarah laugh.

'But it's against the law!' I protested feebly.

'That's the whole point of going to bloody Bedales,' she said. 'You lose your virginity and get a bit of practice. I'm longing to lose mine, aren't you?'

I didn't realize until much later that this was a trick question.

I wasn't sure what I felt about it all, but it made me look at Katie Gresham with even greater interest. When we found her she was playing croquet with my friendly sheep, Sandy Carsluith, and a couple of girls who were at school with her. Her features resembled Pauline's but her gorgeous golden colouring was her father's. She had long pale hair and was lightly tanned from her holiday in the Bahamas. She was very tall, almost six feet, and I remember noticing that her left ear had a double pierce, very unusual in those days. Her eyes were the same startling blue as Michael Gresham's, drooled over by thousands of lovesick schoolgirls for the last twenty years.

'Hi Sarah,' she said, angling her mallet carefully as she made her shot, 'how are things?'

'You'll never get it through that way,' said Sarah grumpily.

'Watch me,' said Katie, as her mallet hit the ball a tremendous crack. 'Is Tom with you?'

'No. He's coming over later, he said. This is Lucy.'

'Hi Lucy,' Katie said, glancing round, 'meet Rosie and Ant. Do you want to join us?'

'I'd love to,' I said.

'We ought to be getting back,' said Sarah, 'we just came by because Ma wanted to get a cutting from Pauline.'

'Aw shucks,' said Katie, grinning at me and raising her eyebrows slightly, as if to say, 'See what I'm up against.' She treated Sarah's evident hostility with a kind of amused disdain, much to Sarah's annoyance. Rather to my surprise I found I liked Katie. Teenage girls are amongst the most savagely cruel beings on earth but Katie had seemed fun and relaxed, a damn sight more relaxed than Sarah anyway. I'd have liked to have hung out on the croquet lawn gossiping with her and her friends but it wasn't to be. She had the same knack her mother had of making people feel at ease without appearing to.

'I hate the way she patronizes me,' Sarah said, as we walked away. 'See what I mean?'

'You weren't very friendly,' I said mildly.

'Whose side are you on?' asked Sarah angrily, walking so fast that I had to trot to keep up.

We met Michael in the black-and-white tiled hall of the house when we went in, searching for Claudia. His hair was shorter than it had been in his heyday, he was wearing a pair of tatty jeans and a baggy sweater and his feet were bare, but his sex appeal was still as potent and as tangible as the heat from a five-bar fire. My heart lurched when I saw him, even though he was of my parents' generation. He was so famous and here he was in the flesh. I almost had to pinch myself.

'Hi sweetheart,' he said to Sarah in his rock star's transatlantic drawl. 'Who's your friend?'

'This is Lucy Diamond,' said Sarah, adding naughtily, 'a great fan.'

'Hello, Lucy,' said Michael, 'love the name. Was your mum a Beatles admirer by any chance?'

'I think it was just an accident of fate,' I said stiffly. The idea of my mother being a Beatles fan was risible but I wasn't about to say so.

'I like that,' he said nodding his head and laughing, 'an accident of fate. Maybe I'll call my next album that. Heh!' He seemed genuinely tickled but I felt obscurely that he was making fun of me. He padded off mumbling to himself and vanished through a swing door.

'Isn't he an angel?' said Sarah. 'I adore him. He was going to be my godfather, you know, but the Cardinal didn't approve. Michael wrote a song mocking the Pope and that was that.

Wouldn't it have been heaven to have had him? He might have given me a diamond-studded rattle or something.'

'Is he into all that?'

'No, of course not. He's one of us, don't forget, although he's good at pretending not to be, and Pauline's the epitome of restraint. You know how water can sometimes be so hot that it seems cold? Well, Pauline's like that. She's so rich she can seem almost poor.'

'Never has any money on her, like the Queen?'

'That sort of thing. You haven't met her yet, have you?'

'No.'

'Oh, you'll like her. Everyone likes Pauline except Claudia. Claudia,' she added, pretending a haughty tone, 'has reservations, except when she wants something of course.' Sarah's cynicism about her parents still took me by surprise. 'She says the Milo money is tainted. They helped Hitler massacre the Jews, you see; Lewis Milo supplied the Nazis with the stuff they used in the showers, at least that's what she says.'

'Is it true?'

'WGF,' said Sarah, jumping down the steps.

'What does that mean?'

'Who gives a fuck.'

Before we went home that day – two or three days before the actual dance – Sarah took me to meet Pauline who was in the marquee with the celebrated decorator, Rosa Richardson, who had recently arrived to stay at Gatehouse Park. Claudia was still plundering Pauline's walled garden, her pride and joy. Rosa Richardson was a grey-haired, steely-eyed, exceedingly shrewd and rather formidable fifty-something with a grand manner whose speciality was stately homes; she was doing the Chinese Room with Claudia at Gatehouse Park (which hadn't been touched since the eighteenth century) and also had a scheme, I forget what, with Pauline whose life, among other things, was filled with schemes involving decorators. It was one of the penalties of owning so many houses. They were discussing the fine-tuning of what seemed to me the most

48

breathtaking flower arrangements I'd ever seen. The marquee was striped in pink and white but lined inside with muslin (what Pauline called 'toile') which gave a gauzy, misty effect; lilies and other flowers that I couldn't name were twined round pillars and every table had a centrepiece of pink and white rosebuds designed by Katie. Sweet sixteen could not possibly have been made sweeter.

'Hello, darling,' said Pauline to Sarah, turning round as we came in. She was wearing camel trousers and a camel sweater the sleeves of which were pushed up. On her feet were a pair of old loafers with the backs trodden down. Working clothes, she called them, except Pauline's working clothes were all designed by Calvin Klein. Her auburn hair was pulled off her face in a ponytail and she didn't seem to be wearing any make-up or even any jewellery. She must have been in her late forties then but I remember distinctly that her casual beauty was quite shocking, more so in the flesh than in photographs. She had large hazel eyes, flawless skin and those even, white American teeth that are one of the hallmarks of real money.

'Hi,' said Sarah breezily, 'I wanted you to meet my new best friend, Lucy.'

'Hello New Best Friend,' said Pauline, in her sweet way, holding out her hand, 'what do you think of the flowers? Any suggestions?'

'They're gorgeous,' I said obediently, but Sarah wasn't having any of that.

'It smells like a church,' she said.

'Too strong do you think?' asked Pauline distractedly. 'I guess some people don't like it or it gives them hay fever or something.'

'By the time everyone's in here the lilies will have to compete with scent and food and smoke,' said Rosa, 'no one will notice.' She gave Sarah a look which said plainly, 'Shut up, you little tosser.' She thought Sarah was uppity and that someone should make it clear she was out of order.

'And of course,' Sarah continued undaunted in a conversational voice, 'the pollen stains your clothes irrevocably.' She was teasing Pauline, knowing it was making Rosa angry. It was quite deliberate.

Rosa took Pauline's arm and led her away into the centre of the tent. I heard her say, 'Darling, no one's going to be leaning against the pillars and anyway you can't *do* a tent this size without those damn Stargazers. Actually, I adore them and I adore the smell.'

'She's such a bloody bully that Richardson woman,' said Sarah, 'poor old Pauline likes to fuss; after all, she hasn't got anything else to do, has she?'

'I suppose not,' I said. 'I thought the flowers were amazing. And she's a dear.'

'Pauline? She's all right. She shouldn't let herself be pushed around; everyone does it from the Richardson hag to Katie to Michael. If I had her money, I'd make sure everyone did exactly what I wanted.'

'Yes, you'd be a real old tartar, I'm sure. You probably will be when you're old.'

'Thanks a bunch,' said Sarah.

Later on that evening when we found ourselves going ahead of the others into the dining-room at Gatehouse Park, Rosa took me aside.

'Your friend is a menace,' she said. 'I'd spent the last forty minutes persuading Pauline that the flowers were a *tour de force* and then Sarah comes and tramples all over my efforts deliberately. It's the calculated insolence of it all I can't stand. You should tell her.'

'Perhaps you should tell her,' I said rather daringly.

'That's not the way things are done here,' she said, 'I should have thought you knew that. This is a house where you have to whisper things in people's ears, like a court, in the hope that what you say will reach its target indirectly.'

'I haven't been here very long. I'm just a guest, like you.'

She missed the submerged insolence. What I thought of her

did not register on the scale of the things that mattered in her life. I was just some nincompoop schoolfriend of Sarah who should be damn well singing for her supper instead of behaving as an accomplice to a rude young person.

'What I don't understand is why Ivar and Claudia don't rein in those two younger children. They get away with murder and nobody seems to do a damn thing about it. I hate rudeness in the young more than anything. Mark my words, Lucy. Those two are going to come a cropper if they don't look out. They're spoiled. That's what it means to be spoiled – not to care whether you upset other people because you can only think of yourself and your own self-gratification.'

'Sarah's not like that,' I said uncomfortably, knowing that Mrs Richardson had a point.

'You don't think so now because you're besotted with this family and their house and their whole way of life, but wait a few years and then you'll see that I'm right. The Gatehouses are very grand and very rich but they are not invincible. Things that have been built up for centuries can come down in months, believe me, I've seen it happen.'

There was a place at Gatehouse Park, a bathing spot that was like something out of a dream to me. If you walked over the lawns that I had seen from the windows of the dining-room on my first evening you came eventually to a sloping path, whose verges were overgrown with tall grasses, cow parsley, giant hogweed and leggy buttercups, and which slowly, windingly took you down to the edge of the estuary where, in a fit of inspiration, Ivar's great-grandfather had built a glass and wood bathing box on stilts with steps down into the sea when it came frothing in. This was a treacherous coast with capricious tides and currents and quicksands that could envelop man or beast in an instant. The cream-painted wood of the hut was decorated at the top with a frieze of dancing maidens in gossamer robes with circlets on their heads perpetually advancing into an art deco wave that broke ornately over their feet. Inside, there were

Library Media Center
Delavan - Darien High School
Delavan, WI 53115

cubicles for changing and old-fashioned wicker chairs called bundlers for lounging in when the sun was warm but the wind was cold. For the rare fine days there was a verandah all the way round the hut where swimmers and bird-watchers alike could wait for the tide to turn and the sound of the advancing sea. Pulled up on to the bank was a rowing boat with a clutch of old bamboo-handled shrimping nets lying in the bottom.

'Do you like shrimping?' Tom asked me.

'Never done it,' I said.

'You'll love it,' said Sarah. 'Shrimping is cool. We'll take her tomorrow, eh Tomo?'

Late in the afternoon of the day before Katie's dance, the houseparty at Gatehouse Park came down from the big house to swim. Katie was there too with her Bedales friends and her father who had driven over from Balmachie in the safari Land-Rover that had been on the cover of 'Desert Days'.

From my vantage point I could see Michael Gresham standing at the other end of the verandah with Katie, although I couldn't quite hear what they were saying. It was a beautiful evening; the huge clear sky was full of light even at this time of day; Michael, talking to Ivar and Rosa Richardson, had his hand on his daughter's bronzed and gleaming shoulder and I remember noticing that she was almost as tall as her father. Sarah was sitting between that group and me on the steps of the hut sulkily watching the tide come in but Tom was playing French cricket on the flattened grass with Ant and Rosie and their shouts and laughter kept making Katie turn her head to see what they were doing. I could see that she wanted to join them but I could also see that she was enjoying being the centre of attention. She was saying something and her father was laughing, even the austere Mrs Richardson was smiling; only Ivar, facing me, was not smiling but watching Katie with fierce intensity. I was afraid to move for fear his burning gaze would consume me too. I was amazed at how unguarded his expression was. He looked as if he wanted to devour Katie. And I could see why. Her wonderful figure, with its long shapely legs and a beautiful slender waist was exposed to best advantage in a skimpy white bikini of the kind I would have given my eye teeth to get away with. Her pale hair fell down her back like a waterfall. When she turned round her eyes were piercingly blue in her tanned face. She was sixteen going on twenty-six or even thirty. Ivar wanted her. It was written all over him.

At this point, Tom came bounding up the steps, grabbed Katie and attempted to throw her over his shoulder in a fireman's lift. The whole scene broke up and dissolved in a kaleidoscope of shrieks and yells.

More young people appeared; two or three of Tom's friends from Eton who were staying and a couple of girls whom Sarah knew from Wigtownshire came to swim and to stay for a barbecue. The grown-ups vanished up to the big house after a while for drinks and dinner while Tom and Katie were busy making a barbecue with bricks and wire; when the last grown-up had gone, Katie rolled a joint and passed it round.

'Do you smoke?' she said, offering me the joint.

'Not really,' I replied, hesitating.

'Go on,' she said, 'you'll like it. Do you good, won't it, Tomkin?'

'The world of good,' said Tom, winking at me. 'Our job this summer is to corrupt Lucy thoroughly before she goes back to her innocent life in the deep south.'

'That shouldn't be too hard,' said Katie, watching me. 'Look, she's a natural. Well done, Lucy!'

She liked Tom a lot, that was obvious, and he liked her too. That was also obvious. I was jealous. I found Tom very attractive not only for his rather Byronic good looks but because he was always kind to me. I was more than a little in love with him myself by then. Later on, when we were all fairly stoned, I was aware that Tom and Katie had vanished from the circle round the fire. When they came back, what seemed like hours later, they looked dishevelled and slyly happy.

*   *   *

It was just before that time that the man who later became known as the 'Falkirk Abductor', Jock Kettle, started snatching young girls – not very small girls but teenagers. He liked them, so he told the police, just at that moment between girlhood and womanhood; the season, if there is such a thing, between spring and summer. He was all the more sinister because he was an educated man (a former lecturer in modern history at Falkirk University) and a brilliant liar. The second young girl had been taken that summer of 1979. Kirsty Carson, aged fifteen, had been out for a bike ride by herself on the road that led past the entrance to her father's farm, Kilmuir Mains, near Ayr. Kettle had come by in his battered old white Transit van and taken her, just like plucking a flower. Bike and all, bundled into the van. She was never seen again.

The next morning at breakfast Kirsty Carson's abduction had made the front pages of the newspapers, a personal note in the annual publication of crime figures. 'She was fifteen,' said Sarah, 'our age. Imagine! And it's not all that far from here either. Vanished. Just like that.'

At the other end of the long table, Ivar looked up. 'She's probably run away,' he said. 'The papers love sensation, especially in the Silly Season.'

'The police are certain it's an abduction,' said Sarah looking down at *The Times*. 'There's a link with another girl who vanished six weeks ago, they say.'

Sarah shut up after that but she became obsessed with Kirsty Carson for some reason and often mentioned her to me. The fact that the lost girl was the same age seemed to haunt her. Much later on, I figured that Sarah's obsession with people vanishing was to do with her parents and the way they conducted their lives. She felt insecure and was sensitive and intelligent enough to know that one or both of her parents might vanish. After all, love affairs were a way of not being present and their mere existence opened the door marked 'Exit' in a marriage. And as I was to discover, she knew much more than she should about all that.

All very well, as Rosa Richardson had said on another occasion, to behave in that Edwardian way if you live all the rest of your life to match. 'This place is like Brideshead without Nanny,' she said to me when we found ourselves alone together one evening the following week. 'Modern children know too much, even in a vast house like this. No wonder young Tom's going to the dogs and Sarah shows every sign of following him.'

'She's not,' I said defensively, wondering at her presumption in discussing the children of the household (where she was after all employed) in this frank and unflattering way.

'Awfully sad not to be able to let your children roam,' Sir Anthony Sinclair was saying. He was a very important civil servant who was using Gatehouse Park as a resting place on his way north to shoot grouse on August 12th. The Gatehouses knew everyone who was important in all kinds of circles, belonging as they themselves did to the small group of people who wielded power, made news, governed the country or represented it abroad.

'We have the sixties to thank for that,' said Lowell Stein, a friend of Ivar's who ran a high-profile lobbying outfit. 'All the old barriers swept away.'

'People like Michael, you mean,' said Rosa Richardson in her deep voice, lifting a silver cover off a dish and then replacing it. 'Who's eaten all the sausages?' she asked, glancing over her shoulder. 'I say, Lowell, they're not for the likes of you, you know.'

'Possibly not,' said Lowell smoothly, 'but they are very good.'

The night before Lowell Stein had also asked me if I was any relation to Joe Diamond but when I had said I was not he had not dismissed me in the way that Sarah's Aunt Marian had, but had proceeded to question me closely about my friendship with Sarah; how many times had I been to Gatehouse Park, what my mother did, what I wanted to do, and what did I think of it all here. When I was reluctant to answer his last question he said, 'Oh come on, Lucy, you can tell me. After all, we're the outsiders in this joint, you and I.'

I shrugged. At that point, I didn't want to admit my outsider status but simply to lose it. I wanted to be a member of this club so badly that the need practically paralysed me and I certainly didn't want to associate myself with Lowell Stein's palsy-walsy stuff. To my hyper-critical eye he lacked polish, his clothes were wrong, even his accent seemed dodgily plummy as if he had somehow assumed it along the way together with the tasselled loafers, the loud chalk-stripe suits, the shirts that shrieked 'hand-made'. Even his gold cuff-links seemed too bright and I found myself repelled and at the same time mesmerized by the way his abundant hair poked out of his cuffs and his nostrils and threatened to boil over the collars of his shirts.

'He needs electrolysis,' said Sarah, watching him swim the night before. 'Honestly, Luce, he's like a bloody gorilla or an orang-utan minus the orange bottom.'

'Who is he?' I asked.

'One of Pa's gang, I suppose,' she replied. 'He's a lobbyist, whatever that is. A fixer. Someone who does things for people in return for favours.'

'What things?'

'Christ, I don't know,' she shrugged. 'Gets rid of inconvenient obstacles, people, whatever, schmoozes his way around the House of Commons.'

'What are the favours?' I asked.

'Being here, for a start,' said Sarah. 'He likes being asked to stay because it makes him feel part of the inner sanctum and he can boast about it to his pals. She can't bear him,' meaning Claudia, 'but then she is a frightful snob. She daren't say anything to Pa because he's so useful. When she was caught drunk-driving last year it was Lowell who made it all right.'

'How did he make it all right?'

'Search me. That's his job. But the press never got hold of it and that was because Lowell knows how to control what Pa calls the flow of information. Or stop it altogether.'

Our costumes for the dance were supplied by a firm in Manchester which sent a van full of the sort of clothes that would have delighted the Marquise de Merteuil and the Vicomte de Valmont up to Gatehouse Park for us to choose from.

'It's all right for you,' wailed Sarah on the morning of the dance, as we struggled in and out of dresses with hooks and eyes and lacing in inconvenient places, 'you've got tits. I'm just a bloody washboard.'

'Tits are all very well in theory,' I said, 'in practice they're a bloody nuisance.'

At that point, I certainly had tits: I was small and curvy, a round pale face in the mirror with thick wavy dark hair in a ponytail, a retroussé nose, not my father's schonk (luckily for me), dark eyes; politely, I could have been described as voluptuous, in truth I was plump but not quite fat. I had a body shape genetically programmed to get me through a bad winter on the steppes, but being a child of my times I yearned to be like Sarah. I admired and envied her aristocratic boniness: her wafer-shaped shoulderblades that could be seen under tee-shirts, the tiny baby swellings that passed for breasts; she was all knees and cheekbones, so thin that one felt she could be folded in half like a fan. I adored her look of fragility, the way she was always wrapped in scarves and shawls because she felt the cold; to me, she was the princess in the fairy story, the princess and the pea, and I, in true fairytale style, was her devoted fool.

We chose wigs with jewels looped through the frozen curls, and wore pink satin shoes with cuban heels embroidered with flowers. Years afterwards when I could bring myself to think about this part of my life this scene seemed like some remnant of an Edwardian dream come alive again: the vast house, the dressing-up box, the tableaux we were posed in by Ivar in the salon before dinner so that we could be photographed. Before we had come down, Tom, Sarah and I had rustled away in our silks to have a joint. I was reluctant for some reason to do this, but Sarah persuaded me.

'Come on Luce,' she said, 'we need all the help we can get this evening. They're all guzzling vodka out of their tooth mugs as we speak, believe me.'

'Anaesthetic is a social necessity,' added Tom, who was lounging on one of the beds in our room.

'But they don't mind you drinking,' I said.

'They knoweth not what they think,' Tom replied, 'as long as it impedeth not their fun, as long we do not in the wayeth get. Thou shalt not be found out is the Eleventh Commandment and the one most pertinent to our gathering tonight,' he continued in a parody of his housemaster's voice, making us giggle. Tom was a brilliant mimic and had developed a highly comic rolling dialogue most of which took the form of supposed pillow-talk between his housemaster Trevor and his wife Teresa.

There was a room on the attic floor Tom and Sarah, in their deliberately perverse way, liked that some Victorian Anwoth had used to house his collection of flora and fauna. The panelling was tongue and groove that had once been white but had now faded to a creamy yellow and the specimens were placed on shelves running right round the room. The Victorian ancestor had clearly been a little strange: the specimens were mostly freaks of nature: organs with monstrous growths on them like dry rot, a tiny human hand with a sixth finger, a baby bird with no feathers and three heads attached to its stringy neck. We smoked one joint and then began drifting round the room staring into the jars.

'You know,' said Tom, 'I just wonder where the hell he got half these things from. He must have known some good grave robbers.'

'Rich Victorian gent seeks body parts,' said Sarah. 'You could do anything then if you were so inclined and you had lolly. Nothing's really changed. You still can.'

'Still can what?' asked Tom, who was leaning against the table only half listening.

'Do anything you like if you're rich enough.'

'Like what?'

'I dunno: sex, drugs, rock'n roll,' said Sarah.

'Yeah, so?'

'So, nothing.' Sarah shrugged. I glanced at her and noticed that there were tears in her eyes. She put her hand to her cheek, a gesture she invariably made when feeling vulnerable. Already, I knew all these things about her. On the way downstairs I asked her why.

'It doesn't matter,' she said, '*de nada*.'

'You were crying,' I said, 'there has to be a reason.'

'Not this time.' She shook her head so violently that her wig tilted. 'It's the dope; it goes straight to the conning tower.'

Afterwards, when the dance at Balmachie had been reduced to a series of glossy photographs in *The Tatler* (*Hello!* had not then been born) the events of that evening were already engraved in my mind as dense and marmoreal as a bas relief, or as clearly etched as the nymphs entering the frozen wave in the frieze at the bathing hut.

To soothe Pauline, Rosa Richardson had got hold of a flunkey to take out the stamens from all the lilies entwined in such profusion together with orchids and tulips around the pillars of the magnificent marquee. This was really the job of the florist wing of the party-planners but Pauline was in a state and Rosa, as a close friend of such an important person, took charge as was her wont and was late back to Gatehouse Park to change into her costume.

'We can't leave until Rosa's ready,' I overheard Claudia say to Ivar before we left for dinner at Balmachie. They were talking outside the door of the loo where I had taken refuge in the library corridor beyond the salon.

'Why the hell isn't she ready now?'

'She had to help Pauline at the last moment. You know how Pauline panics.'

'The woman's a complete half-wit,' said Ivar impatiently.

'You say that about everyone,' Claudia replied. 'Every woman is a half-wit to you.'

'I don't think this is quite the moment to start a fight,' said Ivar, moving away, with Claudia following him. I could hear the rustle of their clothes and the soft thump of the door swinging shut behind them as they went into the hall.

Without knowing it I was already deeply intrigued by the Gatehouses' marriage. I was not the child of a writer for nothing and Lowell Stein was clever enough to identify a good case of outsider syndrome when he saw it; I was part poor little match girl, nose pressed to the glass in wonder, but also part nosey parker making mental notes. There were things that puzzled me about the Gatehouses, mysteries about them that were like clues to a plot I still lacked: there was that Hermès scarf on a chair in the London house, and Sophia Bain's sudden disappearance; I could not forget Ivar's eyes on Katie Gresham the evening before and now this evening there were Sarah's tears that I knew instinctively were serious and sprang from some deep wound, but the full extent to which my friend was damaged was still not clear to me and would not become clear for some time. I was also still frightened enough of Sarah's Olympian parents not to want to be discovered eavesdropping, even if unintentionally, in a downstairs lavatory.

Dinner was tables of ten in the marquee; we were not seated by age but all mixed in together. I found myself sitting between a Tory peer, who paid me not the slightest attention once he had read my place card, and a well-known political journalist who did the same, who talked to one another across me throughout dinner, but I told myself I didn't care, that I would rather watch and listen. The waiters and waitresses and party overseers were also in costume; a string quartet (the Gresham Players) played in the hall, another in the tent; certain rooms in the house were allowed to be used for the elderly to sit out the dancing if they did not like being in the marquee, but there was no access to the upstairs of the house. Security men patrolled the grounds with walkie-talkies and there were police on the

Kirkcudbright road and marksmen on the roof, or so Tom drunkenly told me, in case someone tried to take a pot-shot at one of the numerous important people attending the party, ranging from the American ambassador and Mrs van Hoyland (who were staying the night before going on to Balmoral by helicopter the next day) to politicians, rock stars, aristocrats and a famous writer who had just been awarded a Nobel Prize. Ivar, splendidly handsome in a flowered silk swallowtail coat with a matching waistcoat, danced the first dance with Pauline alongside Michael and Katie. The band was playing swing, some hit song from the forties, and everyone clapped as they took to the floor.

'Pretty girl, Michael's daughter,' said the peer whose place card read 'Viscount Strathdial' to the journalist. 'One of the great heiresses of her generation. My God, if I had my time again I'd go for her. Get the roof done and everything.'

'Several roofs,' said the journalist who was in the process of getting drunk. 'They do say she's a bit of a goer.'

'What? The little Gresham girl?' Lord Strathdial was rather shocked by this.

'Oh, they start young these days,' said the journalist, pouring himself some more wine.

'Well, look at the mother. Pauline's still in pretty good nick, wouldn't you say?'

'Remarkable,' replied the journalist who was called Peregrine something. 'She obviously drinks at the same fountain of youth as Ivar Gatehouse.'

'Yes, Ivar always was a bit of a bloody boy wonder. Enormously gifted fellow. Gets it from his father of course. Gawain Gatehouse was the same.'

'But there's something a little reckless about Ivar, don't you think?' said Peregrine Thing.

'You have to be reckless in politics, my dear, it's a positive asset. Courage of your convictions and all that.'

'I wonder,' said the journalist. 'I hear all is not well in the state of Gatehouse; that Lady G has an amour and that Ivar himself isn't all he might be in that department.'

'Ivar's just got a touch of WHT, that's all,' replied Lord Strathdial, 'wandering hand trouble, don't we all. Mrs T. adores him, the *on-dit* is she fancies him and he flatters her. Tells her she's a wow, that sort of thing. Consequently, she won't hear a word against him. I hear he's destined for great things. As for Claudia, she's a marvel, an absolute marvel. Shoots like a dream.'

'So she's not going to leave the boy wonder then?'

'My dear, she can't. They're Cattolicos. They don't believe in divorce.'

'They merely have another name for it,' said Peregrine lighting a cigar. 'They say Bozzie Lovell's broken-hearted over her. He's got money. He could keep her in the style to which she is accustomed.'

'Bozzie Lovell's going nowhere. Nice chap and all that, but he's no Ivar. Being with Ivar is like riding the comet's tail; price she has to pay for all the excitement.'

At this point Tom, sent by Sarah, came to claim me. People were dancing now and the original formal pattern of the party was beginning to break into groups as people table-hopped talking to friends.

'Good time?' enquired Sarah.

I shrugged my shoulders. 'So-so.' I did not want to discuss what I had heard as I could still hardly believe my ears. 'How about you?'

'Boring,' she said. 'My wig hurts. There's a disco in the basement if you're interested. Sandy will dance with you, won't you, Sandy?'

The sheep acquiesced politely but looked glum. 'I'd hoped there would be some reeling,' he said.

'Oh, for God's sake!' exclaimed Sarah tipsily. 'There's more to life than dancing bloody reels.'

*

Rosa Richardson, surveying the marquee and the people therein from behind one of the flowering pillars, said to her friend Antonia St Lucia that she really thought Ivar Gatehouse should take his hand off Katie Gresham's bottom in such a public place.

'You can't get near anyone's bottom in these damn costumes,' replied Antonia, searching in her tiny clutch bag for her cigarettes and lighter. 'An amorous encounter in this would take some time.'

'I'm sure they didn't bother to get undressed,' answered Rosa, 'that was their secret.'

'How is life at GP?' asked Antonia, drawing on her cigarette with relish.

'Fraught,' said Rosa. 'Too much going on as usual.'

'I was really referring *au mariage*,' said Antonia. 'People are talking. Who's the girl sitting next to Sarah? I don't know her face.'

'Lucy Something. A schoolfriend of Sarah's.'

'Pretty little thing. Too plump at the moment, but she's definitely got something. Sandy Carsluith certainly seems to think so.'

'Sandy's hopelessly smitten with Sarah, always has been, but she's going through a bad patch, together with that brother of hers, Tom. Neither Ivar nor Claudia appears to notice.'

'Can't you say something?'

'Darling, I'm just the hired hand. No one's communicating properly, if you know what I mean. Claudia's all over the place doing a hundred different things at once. Every time I get her to sit down so that we can go over the archive notes for the Chinese Room the telephone rings or someone claims her attention or she remembers something she must do before lunch. It's infuriating.'

'Her way of coping perhaps?'

*

I was in one of the Portakabin sets of loos when I heard two girls creaking up the steps in their finery. They were chatting and giggling and one or both of them was smoking a cigarette.

'Dotty Finch said he did that to her,' said one, 'spent the whole dance staring at her tits.'

'Ivar's always been like that,' said the other girl whom, after a moment, I identified as Katie Gresham.

63

'Don't you mind?'

'Not really. I told you, he does it to everyone. He made a pass at my mother years ago when she had just married Dad and he'd just married Claudia.'

'What did your mother do?'

'She told Dad. There was a bit of a fight about it I think, quite a nasty scene; Dad's the jealous type although you'd never know it. He made Ivar apologize. There's this kind of old rivalry between them you see. They were kids together and Ivar was incredibly posh and rich and clever and Dad's family were broke; then Dad made it big and married Mum and suddenly we were posher and richer than the Gatehouses, maybe not as posh but a lot richer. I think Ivar still bears my father a grudge; he tries to hide it but I can tell.'

'I wouldn't like Ivar Gatehouse to bear me a grudge,' said the other girl.

'Oh, Ivar's nothing; he's a pussycat really,' said Katie. 'He eats out of my hand. He does whatever I tell him.' She snorted with laughter as she said this and I wondered just how many joints she had smoked.

I meant only to wait until they had gone but I must have fallen asleep due to the combined effects of the joint and the champagne. When I came to, the best part of an hour had passed. I went in search of Sarah and found her after a long time lying on a sofa alone in a back sitting-room.

'What are you doing in here?' I asked, looking down at the remains of tears on her cheeks. 'Have you had a row with someone?'

'Dadda sent me in here,' she said, 'he told me I was drunk.'

'Where's Tom? Why isn't he looking after you?'

'He's with Katie somewhere,' she said, shrugging. 'I mean . . . I dunno . . . maybe they're dancing.'

'I'll find Tom and he can take us home.'

'He's a bit out of it,' she said, 'not much use in the driving department.'

Eventually it was Rosa Richardson who drove us home

in Claudia's Mercedes estate car whilst Sarah slept against my shoulder. Tom did not return at all but slept under the billiard-table at Balmachie as an uninvited guest. Nobody noticed he was missing until the next day when a hunt was launched and a sleepy and extremely dishevelled Tom was hauled into the tent where a lunch party was in full swing to the accompaniment of much laughter.

When we eventually got to bed it was almost light and I found myself unable to sleep. It was one of my first experiences of the kind of hag-ridden night that I was to grow so familiar with, the inevitable outcome of partying. The events of the evening went round noisily inside my head like a carousel and the things people had said muddled themselves in my thoughts. I was deeply disturbed by what I had seen and heard but I was also titillated. All the gossip, drink and excitement (and a certain definite feeling of threat) had entered my bloodstream like a bacillus. I had come so far from my own boring, little world – I felt myself becoming one of them – how could I ever go back again?

Rather soon, as it turned out. A telephone call a couple of days later from Sheila MacMaster informed me that my mother was terribly ill. Mac did not say on the telephone that my mother was going to die, she saved that for when she met me at Euston.

'She has cancer of the pancreas,' Mac told me. 'The prognosis is poor, I'm afraid. The doctors say six months. We agreed, your mother and I, that I should tell you the truth and not fudge things. I always think it's for the best.'

I looked down at my hands and then out across the station concourse towards the towering buildings of the Euston Road. I was dimly aware that an announcement was being read out over the Tannoy system and that I did not really feel anything but a kind of numb loneliness. Mac was wearing her holiday clothes, a flowered skirt and a plain blouse, desert tan stockings and dreadful off-white sandals with a pattern of dots in them that looked as if it had been made by a skewer. I felt ashamed to be seen with her and then ashamed of myself for such uncharitable thoughts.

'Your aunt and uncle and your grandparents have been informed,' said Mac. 'Your grandparents, that is, your mother's parents, are coming from Kent to see her this afternoon. Your father's father has already been. Your grandparents want to see you, Lucy, they're going to wait for you at the school when they've been to see your mother in hospital.' She looked at me and waited. 'Did you hear me, dear?'

'Yes.'

'There's a great deal to discuss,' she went on as we walked towards the Underground, 'but it would perhaps be best if you went to live with your Kent grandparents.'

'And leave Wickenden?' I asked in sudden terror.

'I'm afraid we're very low on bursaries at the moment. Obviously, you would have to see out your GCEs, but after that it may be time to move on, Sarah dear. Go to a sixth form college, get to know your grandparents better.'

'I don't want to get to know them better,' I burst out, walking away from her as fast as I could towards the ticket machines.

My mother was in a room by herself in the hospital. She looked shrunken and forlorn in the high hospital bed. Someone had brought her some fruit and a plastic jug contained some garish-looking flowers in day-glo colours.

'Aren't they hideous?' she said, following my gaze. 'Simon brought them.' Simon was my Golders Green grandfather.

'Have you had a nice time?' she asked, as I turned back to her from the flowers. But I couldn't answer her question in this setting and I was angry with her for pretending to be normal when she was dying. Even now I felt she was holding me at arm's length.

'Why didn't you tell me you were so ill?'

'Because I didn't know myself. I suspected something was wrong but I didn't want to think about it.'

'You should have told me,' I said, and then because I couldn't think of anything else to say we fell silent.

'Don't be angry with me,' she said.

'I'm not.'

'Mum and Dad came,' she said trying to sound bright. 'They're at Wickenden waiting for you. I expect Sheila told you. They want you to go back with them to Tenterden. I thought it might be a good idea.'

'I'm not going back with them.'

'Lucy, try to be reasonable. It's the middle of the holidays. I'll be in here for another week or so. You can't stay on your own at Wickenden. Sheila's going away in a few days' time to the Lake District with Ruth.'

At this point, Sheila poked her head round the door. 'Better be getting back,' she said, 'we don't want to keep your grandparents waiting too long.'

'Who's going to look after you when you come out?' I asked.

'Mum and Dad have offered.'

'And when term starts?' At fifteen you can only think of yourself. I was aware of prison doors closing round me.

'I'll stay there. It's easier. There's a good hospital in Ashford.'

'Oh Mum,' I said, and the tears broke past my stoniness in a flood. I put my face in my hands and wept. I wanted to fling myself into her arms but she looked so fragile I was afraid I might hurt her.

I felt her hand stroking my hair. 'I'm sorry too,' she said. 'We were just going along so nicely, weren't we.'

My grandparents whom I did not remember ever having met were in Mac's sitting-room having tea that had been brought up to them by Doreen, a Scots girl with mild Down's syndrome, one of a number of such people whom Mac employed to do the menial tasks in the school. They got up awkwardly when I came in, not knowing whether they ought to kiss me or keep back out of respect for my teenage status and my grief.

'I'll leave you alone,' said Mac. 'You've all got some talking to do.'

'This is a terrible blow for you,' said my grandfather Nigel, the retired GP, who was fond of cricket.

'We hope you know that we're behind you,' said Norah, his wife. 'Your Auntie Jenny sends her love. She's near us, you know, with the two little ones . . .' she broke off to rummage in her handbag for the photographs of Sam and Abby, my little cousins, who were the source of her joy.

'I don't think this is quite the right moment, dear,' said Nigel, embarrassed by his wife's enthusiasm for life over death, for grandchildren seen as opposed to unseen.

'I'm sure Lucy would like to see pictures of her family,' said Norah, 'here they are. Aren't they lovely?'

I stared at a photograph of two small children under a Christmas tree. One, presumably Abby, was holding a Barbie doll by the hair, and the other, presumably Sam, was lying on his back on the floor having a tantrum. In my mind's eye I saw the Sargent picture of Lady Creetown and her children. I handed the photograph back.

'They're looking forward to meeting you,' said Norah. 'Your Auntie Jenny was wondering whether you'd be able to sit for her; she says it's getting harder and harder to find reliable girls.'

I didn't have to pack a bag. I simply removed my small suitcase from Mac's car and put it in the boot of Nigel's Cavalier. I went to say goodbye to Mac in her room.

'It's for the best, my dear,' she said, noting but not responding to my air of sulky gloom. 'You'll be back here at the beginning of term. Possibly your poor mother will have stabilized by then. These things do happen, you know. We'll just have to pray for a miracle. And you're lucky to have a family to take care of you. They seem like kind folk, Lucy. I know there were problems with your mother but it's up to you now to make it work. I have great faith in you, Lucy. Always remember there is nothing you cannot do if you put your mind to it.'

*　　*　　*

Tenterden was a pretty old Wealden town with rosy brick buildings, tea rooms and dress shops called 'Pamela' which sold the kind of clothes people like Norah wore to ladies' night at the Rotary Club. I hated it on sight. I knew a noose when I saw one. Nigel and Norah lived at Badger's Holt, one of the new housing estates tucked out of sight of the Georgian high street; there was an L-shaped living-room with a dining area at the end, and French windows to a garden lovingly tended by Nigel when he wasn't watching the cricket. The room was dominated by a large framed photograph of Jenny and Roger's wedding with Jenny encased in what looked like a giant meringue. Underneath this photograph hung matching pictures of the twins at their christening. I knew as soon as I set foot in this house why it was that my mother had got away and had never returned although it was not from this house but another like it that she had fled. The atmosphere stifled me, the routine drove me mad. I had not realized how genuinely unconventional my mother, with her complete lack of interest in domestic minutiae, was until I spent time at Badger's Holt. Meals with my mother in the holidays had really been picnics. She took her food into the room she used to write in or ate with me at the table in the kitchen of her flat but we didn't talk, we both read our books, sometimes with our feet on the table.

The day after I arrived in Tenterden Sarah rang me up.

'How did you get this number?' I asked.

'Mac gave it to me. I got her just as she was going out of the door on her hols. She wasn't too thrilled and made sure I knew it. Couldn't wait to get to her lesbian love at Grasmere, I suppose.'

'How on earth do you know that?' The thought of Mac with no clothes on and in bed with a woman was astonishing.

'Pa told me. He makes it his business to know these things. How's your poor *madre*?'

'Not very good. Still in hospital. That's why I'm here. I can't really talk,' I said, watching Norah's large bottom through the door as she vacuumed the hall and stairs.

'Pa says your mother should be in a different hospital, not Banbury, one in London. He knows the specialist for her kind of cancer, the leading man in his field. He's going to get her moved.'

'How?'

'I dunno. Same way he always does.'

'Has he told Mum? She's quite stubborn. She doesn't like being told what to do.'

'Oh come on,' said Sarah, 'it's in her best interests.'

Naturally, my mother's stubbornness was no match for Ivar's iron will. She was moved at the end of the following week to St Thomas's Hospital in London. Nigel and I drove up to London together in the Cavalier to see her. As we walked down the immensely long corridor towards Edith Cavell Ward where my mother was to be found, I was astonished to see Ivar Gatehouse walking towards us deep in conversation with a tall thin man whose white coat and air of concentrated calm proclaimed him a big cheese of some kind.

'Ah Lucy, there you are,' Ivar called out, spotting me at the same moment. 'I hoped I'd catch you. This is Professor Tompkins who's looking after your mother. He's got some good news for you. And you must be Lucy's grandfather,' Ivar continued, holding out his hand. 'How do you do. Ivar Gatehouse.'

'Pleased to meet you,' said Nigel. 'I'm very grateful to you, Lord Gatehouse, for all the trouble you've taken over Jane. I couldn't have done it and I used to be in the trade.'

Don't thank me,' said Ivar warmly, 'thank the good professor here. He's the one who got Jane a bed. This is his fiefdom, not mine.'

As Ivar spoke, I dismissed my former impressions of him as a snobbish, slightly aloof, rather alarming figure and was filled instead with a kind of amazed gratitude that he should bother with us. What after all were we to Ivar? Why should he do anything for us? And yet, here we were, me and Mum and Nigel, beneficiaries of Ivar's willingness to take the time and the trouble to solve a problem which meant that my mother and my life with her (and how I prized it now I had so nearly lost it) had a chance (a better chance anyway, judging by the expression on the professor's face) of continuing in the same way for a little longer. For the first time in days my heart lifted; there was light again and hope in the air. Somehow hope had swiftly evaporated at Badger's Holt.

'Well,' said Nigel, 'we're very grateful, really we are. What are her chances?' he asked, turning to Professor Tompkins.

'Fifty-fifty. But we've got a new treatment we're pioneering here that's already had some excellent results. Jane's agreed to join the programme, but we'll have to keep her here for some weeks and then somewhere nearby. I don't want her coming in and out of London from Kent or Oxfordshire. A commute like that adds hugely to patient stress.'

Nigel, poor Nigel in his blazer and his cricket club tie, his Tuf shoes, looked suddenly crestfallen. 'Oh, I don't know', he said, shaking his head, 'how we'd find a way round that.'

'My great-aunt's flat in Evelyn Gardens is empty,' said Ivar. 'She died six months ago, poor old Dolly. It's old-fashioned but comfortable. We were going to let it, but there's no rush. She's left it to Sarah for when she's older. Sarah was always her favourite. She used to say that it was hard being the third girl in the family. She should know. She was the third girl in her generation.'

'That's amazingly good of you,' said Nigel. 'I really don't know how to thank you. Jane will feel the same.'

Jane did not feel the same, but kept it to herself at that particular point. She was only human and she wanted the best chance she could lay her hands on, but she never doubted that Ivar had a motive. She had something he wanted and that something was me.

Towards the end of August, she was allowed out of hospital.

Nigel and I went with her in an ambulance to Evelyn Gardens, where Great-Aunt Dolly Anwoth had had a large flat in a red-brick Edwardian block. The lift was the old-fashioned sort with an inner and an outer door; there was panelling inside and a mirror, what Aunt Dolly would no doubt have referred to as a 'looking glass'. It was that kind of a building: old-fashioned but plush; the public areas were richly carpeted in a discreet dark red and the panelling in the hallway shone with polish. The porter at the desk managed to be both deferential and kind and insisted on taking my mother's arm as we walked towards the lift at the back of the entrance hall.

'Yes,' he said, 'we miss Lady Dorothea. A great lady she was, always doing charity works. Used to spend a lot of time at the cathedral, loved that place she did. The Cardinal used to come and have a drink with her quite often in the evenings. She worked at the homeless hostel down the road until she was in her mid-eighties. "I've been so lucky, Ted," she'd say to me, "born with a silver spoon in my mouth. You have to give something back, you know." Pity they don't all feel the same, really. Oh no, she was a great lady, a truly great lady.'

'Lord Gatehouse has lent us her flat,' said my mother, 'I expect he told you.'

'Just like his auntie, you see. Believes in putting something back in return. It's a family tradition. Very proud of her grand-nephew, she was, Lady Dorothea. He'd have been prime minister if they could've got him to renounce his title, she used to say, like that Quentin Fogg.'

'Hogg,' said my mother. 'You mean Quintin Hogg.'

'But he'd never do that,' said Ted blithely, pressing the lift button. 'And there's some of us that doesn't mind.'

'He must be lonely,' remarked my mother, as we creaked and swayed our way up to the fifth floor.

'Verbal diarrhoea,' I said.

'That is a truly repulsive phrase, Lucy,' said my mother. 'I suppose you picked it up from Sarah.'

'As a matter of fact, I did.'

Nigel helped us settle in. I was to stay with my mother until term began again. She would report to the hospital and there was also a district nurse. Ivar had offered private nursing but my mother had felt obliged to refuse.

On our second or third night in Evelyn Gardens when my mother, who slept a good deal, had already gone to bed, Ivar dropped in, having rung up from Ted's desk downstairs to announce himself. When I answered the door, he was wearing one of his magnificent suits made by Mr Boland in Artillery Row, having just attended a committee meeting in the House of Lords about some aspect or other of the new Agriculture Bill then being drafted. It was the first time I had ever been on my own with him and I knew that he could tell I was nervous.

'Lucy,' he said, 'hope you don't mind. Just thought I'd see how everything was. Is your mother up?'

'No. She gets really tired in fact. She's usually in bed by eight.'

'Any chance of a cup of tea?' he asked.

'Yes, of course. Come in.' I led the way down the long corridor towards the kitchen which was at the other end of the flat with a window that overlooked the well.

When I carried the tray into the sitting-room he was lounging in an armchair reading an old copy of *Country Life* left over from Aunt Dolly's day.

'That's kind,' he said, getting up as I came in. 'How are you managing on your own? I know your mother's around but you're doing most of the work.'

'It's OK,' I said. 'We're used to camping out together. We do anyway in the holidays.'

'What do you do in the day,' he asked, 'when your mother's seeing doctors or having treatment?'

'I go to galleries or museums, something like that.'

'So you're quite an academic sort of person, would you say?'

'I suppose so. I've always liked reading. And I like going to galleries. I was practically born in the Ashmolean.'

Ivar laughed. 'Tell me, Lucy,' he said, 'your father was an academic, wasn't he?'

'Yes. He'd just been made a Reader in Linguistics at St Clement's when he was killed.' I wondered how he knew about the father I could scarcely remember.

'Your mother's had quite a time of it then, one way and another?'

This seemed so patently obvious to me as to need no reply.

'How do you see your future, Lucy?'

'I want to go to university and then I want to go into academia like my dad, or the law. One or the other.'

'I admire that very much. I like people with ambition,' he said, stirring his tea. 'Of my two elder daughters one is reasonably intelligent – Louise – and one is not – Davina. Who is actually very dense, but as she's pretty she'll be all right. She lives in a very stupid world, Davina, the world of surfaces and froth which she takes for reality. Stupid women are a curse on humanity; without intelligent discourse . . .'

He stopped himself there. I said nothing. Some sixth sense told me I had better pretend I hadn't heard him say that.

'Sarah is the one who concerns me the most. She is very, very clever, we've always known that, but she wastes her time and my money.'

I waited for him to continue, still not knowing what was expected of me at this point, although at the same time I was gripped by what he said about Davina; his ruthlessness intrigued me and this unexpected intimacy was curiously flattering. This was an early taste of knowledge as power and very heady it was too. Just as he had intended it should be.

'You don't want to betray your friend,' he said, 'I like that. But how can we get her to concentrate?'

'We're coming up for O-levels,' I said, 'she'll have to concentrate a bit harder. We all will. It's easier if everyone's trying to do the same thing. She's only been at Wickenden a term anyway.'

Ivar put down his mug. 'Miss MacMaster has said that there

must not be another lapse of discipline,' he said. 'If there is, Sarah's out. Will you help, Lucy?'

'If Sarah wants to do something it's difficult to stop her. How do you propose that I do that?'

He smiled. 'I know I can rely on you to do your best,' he said, getting to his feet. 'I must get back. Poor old Barry's waiting in the car.' Barry was his chauffeur. 'I've got some papers to deal with before I can go to bed. What are you doing on Wednesday?' he asked.

'Nothing as far as I know.' Wednesday was my birthday but Mum and I hadn't planned anything definite. The chemo she was having made her feel pretty ropy and we agreed that if she felt up to it we might go out for a meal.

'It's your birthday, isn't it?'

'Yes.' Again, I wondered how he knew.

'I'd like to take you and your mother out to lunch. Perhaps you'd like to meet me at the House of Lords. The food is fairly filthy but you might like to look round.'

'I'm not sure Mum's up for that. She's not very strong.'

'Well then, Lucy, I'm sure she wouldn't mind if you came on your own.'

'I'd love to.'

'That's settled then. Come to the Peers' Entrance and ask for me.'

I'd been to the House of Commons on a school trip from Wickenden and seen Mrs Thatcher before her landslide victory berating Jim Callaghan like a school matron telling off a naughty boy, but I'd never been to what the peers themselves called 'the other place', with its miles of red carpets (as opposed to the workaday Commons green), that Puginesque fantasy world of soaring stonework and deepest leather comfort where the (mainly) elderly inheritors of hereditary power dozed away government time before awaking for a division or a drink in the bar with its astonishing views of the Thames. I pushed my way through the revolving doors and came face to face with a charming flunkey dressed in dark blue and gold who enquired of me whom I might be meeting and then asked me to sign a visitors' book whilst he located Lord Gatehouse who he had reason to believe was in the Whips' Office, either that or the Library.

I stood to one side watching as peers came in and out, greeting the elegant footmen before hanging up their coats on their very own pegs like good boys. It was a little like school, I thought, with everyone knowing his place and a place for everything, but stately and splendid and unbelievably archaic. I wondered what my father, if he were alive, would have to say about all this.

A figure came swiftly down the broad stairs to claim me. It was Ivar. He looked strangely animated for this slow and shuffly place, with a look of purpose about him as if his intelligence somehow created its own force-field that resisted the magnetic decline all around.

'Apologies, apologies,' he said, kissing me warmly on both cheeks. He smelled delicious in an unostentatious sort of way of something subtle and no doubt madly expensive. 'I got held up. Come up and have a drink and then we'll go in to lunch. Lowell's going to join us for the drink but we'll ditch him for lunch. I hadn't meant him to be here at all but there was something he wanted to discuss with me urgently.'

Lowell Stein was seated under one of the great windows overlooking the terrace and then the Thames. He leapt to his strangely dainty feet when he saw us approaching.

'Well, Lucy! What a surprise. I hear it's a big day for you today. Many happy returns.'

'Thanks,' I said, hoping I wouldn't have to kiss him.

'I'm very sorry to hear about your mother. How is she?'

'A bit better, I think, but it's hard to know until she's been assessed.'

'Well you're looking good,' he said, nodding approvingly, 'very good indeed. Lost a bit of weight, have you?'

I felt like saying, 'Mind your own bloody business,' but refrained. 'A little, maybe.'

'Suits you, my girl, suits you good. She looks great, doesn't she, Ivar?'

But Ivar merely smiled and asked me what I would like to drink.

Poor Lowell, when I look back I can see that he was trying to warn me off in his own way. We were fellow members of the same tribe and he felt protective of me. I had no father to fight my corner and my mother, as he knew, was powerless to protect me. Without knowing it, all unwitting, I had walked into the lion's den.

When Lowell had gone or had been got rid of, depending on which way you looked at it, Ivar took me into lunch pointing out various figures as we went. 'There's the Duke of Norfolk,' he said, 'premier peer of England. Wonderful man with a great sense of public duty. Catholic, of course. Also a Knight of Malta. The thing is, Lucy, that he knows that privilege brings with it responsibilities. It's the people who don't realize that who bring the rest of us into disrepute.'

'Something your Aunt Dolly knew about too,' I said, recognizing to my delight Frankie Howerd lunching with some distinguished-looking corpse, 'according to Ted.'

He laughed. 'He's a decent fellow, old Ted. Talks too much, but that's not a crime. He adored Dolly and was wonderful to her when she was failing. The management wanted to get rid of Ted last year, said he was past his prime, but I made sure he stayed on. His own wife isn't too well and he needs the money. He's good at his job too even if he is a bit slower than he used to be.'

One of Ivar's skills was weaving references to his personal philanthropy into the conversation so subtly that you scarcely noticed. All this talk of protecting and saving and giving back made me feel safe and unusually confiding.

'He's a darling,' I said, 'and terribly kind to Mum as well.' It felt very grown-up to be discussing the merits of our good and faithful servant Ted with Ivar, as if we were on the same level.

'There's Harold Wilson,' Ivar continued in a lower voice. 'You're too young to remember much about him, luckily for you. He's lost his marbles now, they say, gone completely gaga; probably the only answer when you caused as much damage as he did.'

We both laughed.

We were seated at a table by a nice old Irish maid called Kathleen whom Ivar introduced me to.

'It's her birthday, Kathleen, so she'll want something special,' he said.

'That's nice, dear,' said Kathleen, 'how old are you?'

'Sixteen,' I said.

'Oooh, and I had you marked down for eighteen, at least,' she said, laughing as if she had made a great joke.

'Her mother's ill,' said Ivar, 'but Lucy's at school with Sarah and is a great friend of hers.'

'How is Sarah?' said Kathleen. 'Lovely girl she is, Sarah, very naughty. She told me the nuns had expelled her.' She shook her head with mirth. 'A very bad girl she is.'

'Making a fresh start now, we hope, Kathleen,' said Ivar. 'Lucy's keeping her in order for us, aren't you, Lucy?'

'Doing my best,' I said. The monster gin I had had in the bar had slightly gone to my head.

'Now, Kathleen. What do we avoid?' asked Ivar.

'I wouldn't have the chicken, my Lord,' said Kathleen, 'me and Agnes didn't like the look of it. But maybe the veal or the calves' liver. The young lady might like a steak. She looks as if she needs feeding up.'

Halfway through lunch, Ivar produced a maroon box wrapped in a bow with the name Aspreys on the lid.

'A little something,' he said, 'with love from us all.'

'For me!' I was thunderstruck. Inside was a very simple but heavy gold chain, the kind you could wear by itself. I had never had anything half so luxuriously gorgeous in all my short life.

'Life hasn't been much fun for you lately,' said Ivar, 'and

you're at the beginning of your adult life now, Lucy. Many happy returns.'

Impulsively I leaned across the table and kissed him, which caused a bushy eyebrow or two to rise at adjoining tables.

'Some people have all the luck,' muttered a patrician voice, 'but Ivar Gatehouse has more than most.'

*

'Is that one of Ivar Gatehouse's daughters with him at that table over there?' asked Annette Donald who was lunching with Lord Nevele (Cosmo Nevele, the famous social arbiter), who knew everyone and everything.

'No, no, no. All those Anwoth girls are blonde and thin, like their dear mama, not a dark, juicy morsel like that one. She doesn't look English whoever she is. A new face, darling. Must be if I can't place her. Terribly young though. Is she his new bit, do you think? Rumour has it he knocks them about a bit, you know.'

'Who told you that?'

'Tanya Bain. Sophia came back covered in bruises from Gatehouse Park but wouldn't say how she came by them. Refused point-blank. Tanya was all for going down to the police station but Sophia wouldn't hear of it. Simply refused to discuss the matter.'

'Rosa says he was terribly spoiled by that sweet old mother of his. She says Ivar was adored but never properly checked when he was a little boy. Now he thinks he can walk on water.'

'Gina Gatehouse could never say boo to a goose,' said Cosmo, 'that's why Gawain married her; no one else would have put up with him: away all through the war . . .'

'That wasn't exactly his fault, darling.'

'The unofficial version,' said Cosmo, 'is that Gawain made a balls-up and that's why the 54th were captured so wholesale.'

'Do you believe that?'

'Gawain was a vain old thing, awfully keen on himself. There's probably some truth in it. They're all arrogant, the Anwoths, it's in the blood.'

*

After lunch, Ivar asked me if I wanted to sit below the bar and listen to a debate but I told him that I ought to get back to see how my mother was.

'Quite right,' he said, as we went down the stairs, 'you can come any time you want to a debate, just let me know.' He handed me a card. 'This is my private line at Eaton Terrace. Ring me if there's anything at all you need.'

He insisted on coming out with me until a cab was found, embraced me fondly and then shut the door. 'Give my love to your mama,' he said, waving me off.

At Evelyn Gardens my mother was sitting in the kitchen sipping a cup of tea.

'Good time?' she asked, observing my flushed face.

'Brilliant,' I said. 'Absolutely brilliant. He gave me this. Look.' I searched in my handbag for the Aspreys box to show her.

'That must have cost a fortune!' she exclaimed in horror. 'Oh dear me.'

'Why "oh dear you"? Aren't I allowed to be given things by anyone except you?'

'It's not that,' she said quietly. 'I don't understand why he's doing this. Letting us be here, expensive presents . . . it's almost as if he wants something from us.'

'What on earth could he want from us?' I asked angrily, knowing that my disdainful tone of voice would wound her and not caring, but I was hurt that she assumed it was not on merit alone that we were the recipients of Ivar's generosity.

I wanted to believe that it was my charm and good looks that were working the miracle, not some *quid pro quo* for Sarah's wellbeing at bloody Wickenden. I was coming into Ivar's orbit bit by bit and his enormous lustre had already dazzled me. My poor mother, knowing her power over me was fading, didn't know what to do or to say.

'Why can't you just accept his generosity without thinking there's an ulterior motive? If you were so bloody worried, why did you let us come here in the first place?'

'Because we didn't have much option,' she said quietly. 'I knew you'd rather be here and selfishly I knew I certainly would. My mother's twittering is enough to drive anyone mad.'

'I still don't see what I've done wrong.'

'You haven't done anything wrong,' she said, 'just be careful, that's all. Ivar is used to getting his own way. People with his kind of money and status invariably are. He's not a very nice person, Lucy, not underneath.'

'I find it astonishing,' I said pompously, 'that you allow yourself to be here if that's what you really think.'

'You see,' she said sadly, 'I think he's already got to you.'

That autumn Tom was in love with Katie Gresham. He kept his Morris Minor somewhere in Slough and drove down to Bedales at weekends to see her. It was his first attack of serious love. According to Sarah, her parents were worried that it was affecting his schoolwork.

'What about Katie?' I asked. 'Is it affecting her work?' We were sitting in the props cupboard – a favourite place for secret chats and cigarettes – amongst scenery for a production of *Salad Days* which had been put on at the end of the previous term.

'It doesn't matter if *she* concentrates or not,' said Sarah, grinding out her cigarette butt under her heel and putting the tell-tale evidence in her pocket. 'After all, she's the bloody Milo heiress. All that loot will tinkle into her coffers for the rest of her life.'

'Well, Tom's not exactly going to starve either.'

'No,' she said in an impatient voice which made her sound extraordinarily like her mother, 'but he has to work. Pa won an exhibition to Cambridge. Tomo's got to do the same or better.'

'What happens if he doesn't?'

'He will though,' she said stubbornly. There was a silence and then she said, 'He's really clever but that doesn't mean

81

anything to *her*. She's a siren, one of those people who doesn't mind wrecking other people's lives.'

'They're just going out together,' I said, 'what's the big deal?'

'She's really promiscuous. I hate her. She's still sleeping with the boy at Bedales and there's poor old Tom all over the place about her.'

'How do you know?'

'Milla Bilton-Lynes told me last week when I went up to that Scottish Peel Towers thing. She says Katie's well-known at Bedales for being a bit of a tart; she likes taking people up and then discarding them when she's bored.'

'So? That's Tom's problem, not yours. Don't get involved.'

I couldn't understand why she seemed so upset about Katie and Tom. It was only later on that I worked out that what was upsetting Sarah was not so much to do with Katie and Tom as to do with Katie and her father; she knew they were sleeping together but couldn't bring herself to tell me and of course she was jealous. Katie was usurping her position every way she turned.

'What?' I got up suddenly and switched the light on. We had been sitting in the dark. As I suspected her cheeks were wet with tears.

'What is it?' I asked, coming over to her and squatting down beside her. She looked dreadful in the way that very thin blonde people can: her skin was dry and blotchy-looking and her hair, which had a greenish tinge from too much swimming in our chlorine-infested indoor pool, was full of electricity during this cold snap and clung to her scalp.

'I can't tell you,' she said, wiping her nose with the back of her hand. 'You wouldn't understand.'

'Try me.'

She shook her head miserably. 'I can't tell anyone.'

If she had told me then what was going on I don't think I would have believed her. It was, as she said, quite simply beyond my comprehension; and she was in it very deep through no fault of her own, helplessly impaled; it occurred to me much later on that it was no wonder she was drawn to that room in the eaves at Gatehouse Park full of macabre specimens; somewhere in her soul she must have known that she was one herself.

By mid-way through the autumn term, my mother had made one of those swift returns to health that the terminally ill sometimes make. One of those heart-breaking reprieves in which one allows oneself to think the unthinkable: that it must be all right, that everything could go on as it always had done. That miracles are possible. If all that probing machinery couldn't find a single damn cancerous cell in her whole body who were we to doubt?

She came back to Wickenden and even started doing a bit of teaching again: small groups of girls in her sitting-room. She tired terribly easily but these sessions with her pupils invigorated her (or so she said) and gave her hope, not only for their future but for her own. She was back on her own turf again. Her book, a biography of the women in the poet Shelley's circle, was almost finished. There were notes to be written, an index to be put together, a task she roped her first-year-sixth students into helping her with. She liked the life of the school ebbing and flowing around her. She was used to the sound of elephants galumphing overhead and up and down the stairs, voices chattering in the corridors, doors slamming. One had to have something to work against, she told me. Too much solitude and peace was one reason writers who went to beautiful tranquil places in order to work never got anything done. (I recalled that particular pearl of wisdom in later life and found it true.)

A month after the start of term, she had to go up to London for a consultation with Professor Tompkins. I went with her as a bag-carrier and companion. Once again, we were to stay in Aunt Dolly's flat which I had come by now to think of almost as another home. Ted greeted us like long-lost friends and insisted on coming up in the lift with us to make sure that everything was all right in the flat.

'Lord Gatehouse is in and out,' he said, 'but I just want to check that the new cleaning woman is doing everything she should. Nice girl, Concepcion, from the Philippines, she is. Got her through Father O'Callaghan at the cathedral.'

Ted was distressed to find a pile of sheets and towels on the kitchen floor. 'I had a feeling,' he said, shaking his head. 'A hunch. I'll have a word with that young lady when I see her next. If she thinks she can get away with this sort of thing she's very much mistaken.'

He put the sheets and towels in a black plastic rubbish bag and took them with him when he left, ignoring my mother's protests that they could just go in the machine in the utility room off the kitchen.

'That's letting her off the hook, madam,' he said. 'If I confront her with the evidence, then she can't wriggle out of it. I'll send them to the laundry when I'm done. Quite simple. I do an order every week with the White Thistle, very good they are too. Leave it to me, madam.'

The lift was jammed when I came in later on that day with the shopping and there was no one at Ted's desk as I went past, but as I walked up towards the first landing I heard the sound of loud voices, Ivar talking to Ted, coming from the passageway that led to Ted's sitting-room at the back.

'I told that half-wit of a girl just to leave everything,' said Ivar. 'I particularly didn't want Mrs Diamond to find a mess when she came in. I don't know why these bloody women just can't obey the simplest order.'

I wondered why he was so upset over such a trivial matter. His rage and tone of voice seemed completely disproportionate to the crime committed. Only later did I realize that of course the sheets and towels had been used during some dalliance with another girl, but it was the rage that puzzled me; it was such a little mistake. Why get so terribly angry? A Filipina girl who didn't speak much English had made a mistake, that was all. This was the angry, cruel Ivar I had heard in the library corridor at Gatehouse Park talking to his wife. The other Ivar.

The Ivar who made his daughter cry when she displeased him. I fled as fast as I could upstairs with the shopping banging against my legs.

Twenty minutes later Ivar rang from Ted's phone to say that he was here and could he come up for a moment or two. I mouthed to my mother, who was watching me through the open door from the sofa, that it was Ivar from downstairs and she made a face and rolled her eyes slightly. I put the intercom back on its hook.

'I couldn't tell him not to come, for God's sake. It is his flat.'

'I know,' she said, 'I know, I'm sorry.'

Later on in the diary she kept at that time (which I discovered after her death), she wrote:

*

IG came up to see us after L & I arrived here. He is one of those people I find I am physically allergic to. I wish I knew why. He makes the hairs on the backs of my arms stand up and I find myself almost unable to contemplate speaking to him. Why does he come so much? I am afraid, I know this is illogical but . . .

*

Once again, Ivar was dressed in one of Mr Boland's suits, a chalk-stripe with a cerise lining. He had a drink and chatted to my mother who did her best. After half an hour she said she thought she would go to bed.

'But you haven't had your supper!' I said.

'I'm not hungry. I'm afraid I find the travelling very tiring,' she said to Ivar. 'I seem to need to sleep and sleep.'

'Probably a good thing. The body knows what it needs. Perhaps Lucy could come and have supper with me.'

'Lucy has homework to do,' said my mother sharply. 'She needn't think an outing to London is an excuse to get off lightly on that score.'

'I've done my homework,' I said. 'I did it on the train, I told you.'

'Well then,' said Ivar, getting up. 'That's settled. I'll take you somewhere more exciting than the House of Lords this time.'

'I don't want you to be late,' said my mother.

'She won't be,' Ivar replied, 'I promise. Not a moment after eleven, hey Lucy?'

Ivar had a car outside, but not one that I had ever seen before. It was a pale blue Bristol, the sort of car Lady Penelope in *Thunderbirds* would have looked good in.

'I have to drop in at home for just a second, Lucy,' said Ivar, 'that all right with you?'

'Of course.'

When we pulled up outside the house in Eaton Terrace, I expected to stay in the car but Ivar came round to my side and opened the door for me, before going up the steps two at a time. I followed him down the Picasso-lined corridor and into the sitting-room which looked as if someone had just that moment walked out. A cigarette smouldered in an ashtray already full to overflowing, and a glass of red wine half drunk stood on a table next to an almost empty bottle. My eye fell on the wastepaper basket under the desk where another empty bottle had been disposed of. The dark red damask sofas were littered with newspapers and magazines and the cushions were dented as if the person so recently in this room had been asleep with their feet up. Ivar hadn't mentioned Claudia so I assumed the recent incumbent to be Davina who had probably gone upstairs to change before going out.

'Sit down a moment,' said Ivar distractedly as he went out, having thrown the smouldering cigarette end into the fireplace. I could hear him going up the stairs two at a time. Somewhere in the distance a door banged. I looked up at the Salvator Rosa landscape on its heavy chains over the fireplace and recalled how intimidated I had felt when I had first entered this room with Sarah only months before.

I picked up the new copy of *Vogue* that was lying open face-down on the sofa and found myself looking at a photograph of Claudia by Snowdon in another of those endless fawning features. This time it was 'Working Wives of Prominent Politicians'. The photograph had been taken in Claudia's Kensington studio and portrayed her at the easel in paint-splattered jeans and a white tee-shirt with her hair in a loose ponytail, her only piece of jewellery the Glacier mint on her left hand. Snowdon had contrived to make her look cool and businesslike. 'Lady Gatehouse,' I read, 'works under her maiden name of Claudia Baillie-Maclehose at her Kensington studio. Her great love is painting *al fresco* either in the Mediterranean or in India. She has recently spent time in North Africa working on an exhibition to be held at Spinks next year.'

While I was reading this piece and looking at the other photographs I was dimly aware of the sound of raised voices upstairs. A door opened and someone came running downstairs, hesitated a moment, and then burst into the sitting-room. It was Claudia, immaculate as ever from a distance in a suit even I knew was Chanel (early intimations of power dressing: short skirt, padded shoulders, tons of gilt buttons), but clearly drunk.

'Jesush Chrish,' she said, 'what the bloody hell are you doing here? You're s'pozed to be at school arntcha? Howareyoudarling?'

'Fine,' I said, nervously, as she navigated her way round the furniture towards her glass.

'Where's Sarah for Chrishsake?' she said. 'Hope you haven't losht her.'

'She's at school. I came up for the night so that I could go to the hospital with my mother tomorrow.'

'Poor blurry mother, I'd forgotten. Howareyoudarling?' she asked again. 'Itshbeenages.' She swayed slightly and put out a hand for balance on the great rolltop Boule desk that had been purchased for a song by an eighteenth-century Anwoth, amongst other things (including the Salvator Rosa) after the outbreak of the French Revolution.

'I . . .' I began and then saw Ivar in the doorway.

'Darling, please don't do this,' he said. 'Come back upstairs.'

'Oh shut up you nagging son of a bitch,' she replied, lighting a cigarette, and sinking into one of her sofas. 'I'm talking to Rosie here, aren't I, darling? So how is your mother, poor Mummy? Is she better?'

'Lucy,' said Ivar, 'I want you to do something for me. Call this number immediately.' He wrote something down on the back of one of his cards. 'Tell them her nurse had the day off and everything's gone wrong. Tell them to send an ambulance at once.'

'I'm not going,' said Claudia, 'I'm not going, not goingnot-goingnot going . . .' her voice rose to a scream.

There was a telephone on the desk. I called the number, which was the emergency line of a very expensive private clinic south of the river. A calm voice took details and the address and said an ambulance would be sent immediately 'for Lady Claudia'. By the time I finished making the call Claudia had subsided into one of the sofas and was lying propped up like a spindly doll on a mountain of tasselled cushions of all sizes and shapes with her eyes closed. The skirt of her Chanel suit had ridden up slightly showing her bony knees and tiny concave little girl's thighs. I found myself wondering how someone so fragile and tiny had managed to give birth to four children. There were tears still on her cheeks and she reminded me pathetically of Sarah at Katie's ball in the summer. Ivar was pacing up and down in front of the window that looked out on to the street.

The ambulance came within minutes with its light revolving but no siren to disturb the stuccoed hush of the quiet Belgravia streets. To my surprise Claudia tottered out quietly, holding on to Ivar for support. I watched from the window as she was helped into the back of the ambulance by a man in a green scrub suit. The doors were closed and the ambulance moved swiftly away. Ivar came back up the steps and into the house. I heard the front door shut with a muffled thud. I went out into the hallway.

'I'll get myself back,' I said, imagining he would be following the ambulance by car.

88

'Why?' he asked in a surprised voice. 'Don't you want to have dinner with me?'

'But aren't you going to follow . . . your wife?'

'No,' he said harshly. 'She won't know the difference. Does that shock you, little Lucy? You look as if it does.'

He put his arm round my shoulders as he came past and then turned me gently to face him. It seemed the most natural thing in the world to put my arms round his neck. He didn't kiss me, not then, not yet, but a door had opened and I had passed through it, never to return. I don't know how long we stood there with our arms round each other, melting into one another. After a while, Ivar pulled away and walked into the sitting-room. I followed him.

'I'm sorry you saw that,' he said.

'I'm sorry too.'

'She won't remember anything about it,' said Ivar. 'She never does. But I had to come back to see what was up. The nurse who was looking after her had a sick child of her own at home so I let her go. It was she who warned me that my wife was not in a good way. It's happened before, but you probably knew that. Everyone else seems to.'

He went to the drinks tray which had been placed on top of a grand piano that stood slightly to the left behind the door and poured a strong gin and tonic which he then handed to me in a Waterford tumbler as heavy as a cannon ball. Nothing but the best. I thought briefly of Norah's cut crystalware kept behind the closed doors of a glass-fronted cupboard in the dining area at Badger's Holt.

'Here you are,' he said, 'you probably need it after that. You were very cool, Lucy. You kept your head.'

'There wasn't much else I could do.'

'Did you know that my wife had a serious drink problem?'

'No,' I said cautiously.

'Sarah hasn't told you?'

'She doesn't say anything much about either of you.' I didn't tell him how often I had found her in inexplicable tears. Or what I knew of his marriage, a mosaic that I had put together with information gleaned from conversations overheard, hints dropped, Sarah's hesitations.

'Sarah knows when to keep her mouth shut,' he said. 'But I worry about her and the effect her mother's behaviour has on her. I know she's been damaged by it.'

'She's OK,' I said, 'Sarah's quite tough.'

Ivar looked at me and smiled. We clinked our dead-weight Waterford tumblers together. We were conspirators, I knew it, he knew it. My reply had, as I had intended it should, detached me from my role as Sarah's keeper. Sarah and her mother were problems that had become all of a sudden peripheral to what was really at hand. We sat in the leather-scented interior of the Bristol discussing where we would go for dinner. Ivar put his hand on my knee. I made no attempt to remove it. I was as high as a kite on a mixture of gin and euphoria and the sense that my life could go in any direction. I did not know what would happen next and found that I loved it.

What kind of man is it who is only sexually turned on by young dependent girls? Who can only get it up when he is in complete control of the situation? Who turns nasty when anything he says or does is threatened or challenged? Later on, I was told by psychiatrists that this type is characterized by an inability to control his impulses; he demands instant gratification; he is emotionally immature and he is very, very jealous. He is also at the same time cold with an ability to withdraw his feelings from a situation and compartmentalize them and, if necessary, to forget them all together by suppressing them so completely that he will deny ever having had them and believe what he says. When I look back at that first night with Ivar almost all of this makes sense. I was targeted early on, but he waited until the time was right. I suppose he had had plenty of practice. I also think he enjoyed the waiting period because it was so filled with fantasies of fulfilment as to seem not to tax his patience at all. In his mind's eye, I was already his.

The events of that night remain in my mind as if they

happened yesterday. We went to a restaurant just off Notting Hill Gate, an Italian place where Ivar was known but the waiters were discreet and the food exceptional. We had calves' liver and some very strong red wine. There was cold spinach in olive oil as a side dish and zabaglione, which I had never had in my life, for pudding which we shared. Then Strega and black coffee. So many smells: scent and leather, garlic and oil and coffee, the smell of Ivar's neck, and, later, the smell of sex.

We drove back to the house and for the first time I followed Ivar up that elegant stairway to a landing with a tall window which overlooked a floodlit sunken garden where, in niches behind trellis-work arches, busts of the late Roman emperors had been placed on plinths. Another flight of stairs; lights going on ahead of me, a door opening into a room papered in a dark stripe containing a bed and a chest of drawers but dominated by an enormous wardrobe. There was a painting that I knew for a fact to be a Fragonard hanging over the fireplace: a girl and her lover in a garden of rococo delights. I determined to have a better look at it later on. My passion for pictures had begun very early and was constantly gratified by the Gatehouse mania for collecting. I wondered if Ivar could imagine what it meant to lose your virginity in a room with a Fragonard in it; there seemed to me something exquisitely humorous in it, as if the painting were giving commands to the occupants of the room. The look on the lover's face was one of fiercest rapture as he gazed at the pretty girl with her highly coloured face amid the froth of ruffles.

'My dressing-room,' he said, turning round to face me and at the same time loosening his tie with one hand. 'Are you scared, my darling?'

'No. Should I be?'

He began to say something but stopped himself. Then he took me in his arms and began to kiss me. After a moment he stopped and looked at me. 'Shall I go on?'

I looked back at him. 'What do you think?'

'You haven't done this before, have you?'

'So let me start with an expert.'

'I'm not sure how to take that.'

'Does Claudia know that you do this with other people?'

'I don't make a habit of it, although I'd like to with you. You're lovely, you know.'

'I always think I'm too fat.'

'You have the most beautiful breasts,' he said.

It went well. I was new to it but my body seemed to know what it was doing. I suppose that by the age of sixteen in the steppes I would already have had a child or two. If racial memories are held in the body then I would have been a very hot little number indeed in the *shtetl*.

'Can I see you again?' he asked in the car on the way back to Evelyn Gardens.

'I'm going back to school tomorrow.'

I remember that I felt strangely detached, numb almost, on that homeward journey, as if I were floating slightly above myself. In the few short hours that had passed I appeared to have become someone else altogether.

'When can you get out again?'

'I don't know,' I said vaguely. 'Half-term maybe. It depends how Mum is, I suppose.'

'You'll come to Scotland then,' he said. It was not a question but a command.

'I can't if Mum needs me.'

'Perhaps your mother could come too.'

'She wouldn't like it. It's not her scene. She's too shy and retiring. Drop me here,' I said as the Bristol turned into Evelyn Gardens, not wanting to be eyeballed by the night porter in Aunt Dolly's block. Obediently, Ivar pulled over and stopped at the kerb. I decided that I liked telling the great Ivar Gatehouse what to do and then, rather to my surprise, watching him do it.

'I'll ring you,' he said.

'I don't think that's a very good idea.'

'I'll write then.'

'Sarah will recognize your handwriting. Our letters go into communal pigeon holes.'

'Lucy,' he said, 'I –'

'I hope Claudia gets better,' I said, slamming the door and walking off up the street. I just wanted to get away from him. I didn't want to talk or exchange these absurd banalities, I wanted to be alone. I needed time to think.

On the spur of the moment I decided to go to the corner shop and get some chocolate and some cigarettes. I could feel a fruit and nut craving coming on. As I rounded the corner, the Bristol drew alongside.

'Where are you going?' he asked through the passenger window.

'To get some fags and some choccie.'

'I want to be sure you get safely home.'

'I'm not a child, Ivar,' I heard myself saying. 'Go home before somebody sees you. This is your patch after all.'

It was my first taste of Ivar's recklessness. He enjoyed risk but at the same time he didn't really think there was one; that was one of the many paradoxes about him. As I stepped into the garishly-lit interior of the Paki corner store, out of the corner of my eye I saw the Bristol gliding away.

My mother was in her bedroom when I came in but the door was open and not closed as it usually was. It was exactly a quarter to eleven.

'Did you have a nice time?' She had obviously fallen asleep with the light on. Her left hand lay on the book she had been reading.

'Very nice.'

'Where did you go?'

'Just to a restaurant.'

'*Just* to a restaurant?'

'Yes.' I almost asked her why she had asked that question with such emphasis and then thought better of it. My mother's bloodhound capabilities appeared to have been refined by her illness, if such a thing was possible.

'What did you talk about?'

'Everything. Books, pictures, that sort of thing.' I yawned. 'I'm off to bed.'

'Just be careful,' said my mother faintly, sleep overcoming her police court instincts. 'Turn my light out, Lucy, would you?'

Professor Tompkins was pleased with my mother's progress.

'You're not off the hook yet,' he said, 'so you mustn't get too excited, but well done. Keep it up. Back in a month, please. And don't overdo it. I know your sort. How's the book?'

'Nearly done, thanks.'

'And you, young lady,' he turned to me. 'How are you these days? Done in by the looks of things.'

I had and have an allergy to people who address me as 'young lady', so I replied coldly, 'Fine, thanks.'

'Too many late nights at your age are not a good thing, young lady.'

I said nothing and could feel my mother glancing at me anxiously.

Afterwards, walking down the infinite length of gleaming hospital corridor, she said to me, 'I feel I'm beginning not to understand you any more, Lucy. You're becoming hard. He was only trying to be kind.'

'He's a patronizing old fool,' I said, 'and you know it, so why pretend? Anyway you're what matters, not me.'

'Manners maketh man,' said my mother crisply, 'or woman. And he's right. You do look shattered. I can't think why really. You weren't all that late.'

Things appeared to go quiet once we were back at Wickenden. I heard nothing from Ivar but then I had not expected to. I wasn't even sure I wanted to. The experience had detached me in a certain way from my peers and reinforced an instinct that I already had for secrecy. Every now and again I would take my secret out and look at it and then put it away again.

94

I found that days could go by when Ivar never crossed my mind. I think now that this was exceedingly unnatural and that my ability to compartmentalize things (usually a masculine trait) was some deeply submerged response to the death of my father and the now you see it/now you don't manner of his passing. It was almost as if I expected a serious involvement to include a savagely random and unpredictable element leading to the total annihilation of one or other partner. Now I know that the silence emanating from the grave eventually becomes something palpable but I had not reached this stage yet with my lost father.

Sarah was in a subdued mood but she was up to her old tricks in the cubicles and was keeping vodka in a Perrier water bottle on her shelf. I told her that our matron, Sister Smithey, would find out sooner or later and if not Sister then one of Sister's acolytes. There was a new one this term: a young, bossy Irish girl, Mary McNicholas, not much older than us, who had taken a dislike to Sarah and referred to her behind her back as 'The Posh One' or 'Her Ladyship', and was always on the lookout for misdemeanours in the rest of us which, as she was nearer our age, she was all the more likely to spot.

Two weeks or so after I had returned to school with my mother, Sarah cooked up a scheme to enable her to go over to Eton and see Tom. I was to go with her. We were allowed out on certain Saturdays but not for weekends (this was long before the palmy days that prevail in establishments like Wickenden now) and we had to be back in school by 8 p.m. Sarah had other ideas. There was a party in London given by one of Davina's friends that we had all been asked to, or so she said. All we had to do was to ring up the school and say that Tom's car had broken down in the middle of nowhere and that we would do our best to get back but don't bet on it.

'They'll say take the train.'

'We have no transport. Can't get to a station. Tom has no AA cover. He's gone to find a garage. It couldn't be simpler, Luce. It's foolproof.'

'Where will we stay?'

'Eaton Terrace. It's peasy. They're away, at least I think they are. She is anyway. I'm not so sure about him now I come to think about it.'

'Where is your mother?'

'Painting somewhere,' said Sarah vaguely. 'Sitting at the feet of the feet of her guru in Kathmandu.'

'Smelly, I bet.'

'But madly uplifting,' said Sarah in her mocking voice, raising her hands and closing her eyes, 'especially if you've just had a nice strong joint.'

I glanced at her as she took a swig from her Perrier bottle and then offered it to me. I took such a large mouthful my eyes watered.

'Leave some for the rest of us,' said Sarah, grabbing the bottle back. 'I've managed to corrupt you nicely since I arrived, wouldn't you say?'

I made a playful swipe at her with my towel. Somewhat to my relief I had discovered that I wasn't pregnant. He had used a condom but it had split and by then it was too late anyway.

'What's going on in here?' called Mary McNicholas's voice. 'It's after lights out.'

'Nothing,' said Sarah, screwing the lid back on her bottle. 'We're just coming.'

'What's that smell?' asked Mary McNicholas as Sarah drew level with her.

'What smell?' asked Sarah opening her mouth wide.

'There's no need to play the fool with me, your ladyship,' said Mary McNicholas, recoiling from the blast of Listerine.

'Am I?' asked Sarah innocently.

'The nuns would know what to do with you, madam.'

'As a matter of fact,' said Sarah, 'they didn't.'

'Don't let me catch you at this hour again.'

'Yes, Miss McNicholas,' Sarah replied demurely.

'Or your little slavey for that matter.'

'No, Miss McNicholas.'

We reached our dormitory in a storm of giggles. 'I feel sick,' said Sarah, 'I had to swallow the Listerine. Please, miss, will I need an operation?'

Tom was in Mr Hayden's house at Eton, known simply as Hayden's, the usual shabby Victorian establishment with warrens of dark corridors, battered paintwork and an inadequate number of bathrooms. A burly-looking man in a dark suit was standing outside when we arrived, pretending to read a newspaper.

'Katie's obviously here already,' said Sarah.

'How do you know?'

'That's her bodyguard. I recognize him.'

'But he looks too like a bodyguard to be one, surely?'

'Well, he is,' said Sarah. 'The great heiress needs protecting.'

'You're not going to start all that again, are you?' I asked wearily. 'You knew she was going to be here today. If you don't like it you shouldn't have come.'

'How dare you speak to me like that!' said Sarah angrily, stopping in her tracks.

'Somebody has to tell you how bloody impossible you are,' I replied, nettled by the way she turned on her grand manner when she was put out.

'I'm not impossible.'

'Yes, you are. You're a nightmare. If you don't like something you think it should be put right at once. It doesn't work that way, Sarah. You're just spoiled.'

'You don't understand,' she said coldly, walking on. 'It's too complicated to explain.'

'To a mere mortal, you mean?'

'Don't be childish.'

And thus we arrived at Tom's room not on speaking terms. Tom opened the door to us, took one look at his sister's face, and rolled his eyes at me over her shoulder. I winked back. We understood each other perfectly, even then, Tom and I.

All Etonians have their own rooms. Everyone knows that, together with the fact that they wear a ridiculous but rather elegant uniform of tail-coat and striped trousers which they have carried on wearing for some arcane reason since George III's funeral in 1820. We found Tom in his room wearing an extravagant version of this fancy dress. His white shirt had a stick-up collar with points so sharp that they could have had a dual function as toothpicks. As a member of Pop (the Eton Society to you and me) he was allowed to wear a *special waistcoat* of his own choosing, in this case of pink brocade, made for him by Mr Boland. His trousers were not striped but were of the houndstooth Mad Hatter variety. This, according to Sarah, was another special privilege conferred on members of Pop. He had grown again and his bony wrists stuck out of the tail-coat that had once belonged to his grandfather (it being exceedingly chic to have the shabbiest hand-me-downs) and would soon be put away wrapped in tissue paper and mothballs and laid in a zinc-lined airtight trunk in the attics at Gatehouse Park until it was time for a little Tomlet or Gawain or Sholto to wear it again some time in the next century. There was a fire in his grate and a three-bar fire on full blast, for Tom, like Sarah, was always cold. No posters defaced the walls of this boy's room which were adorned instead with Brangwyn etchings for which Tom had a passion.

Katie Gresham was sitting in an armchair by the fire with her feet up on the club fender wearing jeans and a shabby old sweater with a scarf wound round her throat. She was also wearing those striped hippy mittens that leave half your finger free. Her long fair hair in a ponytail hung over the back of her chair. She was beautiful and cool and I could feel Sarah hating her already.

'Hi,' she said, raising a mittened hand, 'escaped from prison, have you?' Never, before or since, have I seen anyone with such blue eyes.

'Yah,' said Sarah who never used words like that. 'You?'

'I'm at an open prison,' said Katie in her lazy way, 'we get any weekend off, so, yeah, I guess.'

Her accent tipped between Queen's English and the transatlantic drawl her father affected that had so upset Katie's grandmother before her death.

'Hi Lucy,' she said, 'good to see you. How's your mother?'

'Much better, thanks.' I was touched that she remembered.

'What's the plan, Tomo?' asked Sarah, pointedly ignoring Katie. 'We're not going to stay in this dump all day, are we?'

'What do you want to do?' Tom gazed at his sister as if he had never seen her before.

'I want to go to London and have some jolly fun, don't we, Luce?'

'Ah, Lucy, yes,' said Tom, peering at me now in his demented way. 'You look different.'

'She's lost weight,' said the armchair, 'that's why.'

'Is it really that noticeable?' I knew I was thinner but it annoyed me when people commented on it as if it was a matter for congratulation.

'*Ravissante*,' murmured Tom. 'Very Loretta Young.'

'Vivien Leigh,' said Katie who shared Tom's passion for Thirties Hollywood.

'Oh shut up, you two arseholes,' said Sarah. 'Leave her alone.'

Katie laughed. 'If someone told me I resembled Loretta Young I'd be pretty thrilled.'

'Well I hate being told who I look like,' said Sarah in her acid way, 'especially when it's that fucking Sargent set piece.'

'Tut, tut,' said Katie, 'I adore that picture. I worship it. And I only meant that Lucy is looking great and I thought it would nice to say so, that's all. OK?'

I liked Katie very much for saying that. She had clearly inherited all her mother's ability to charm people.

'A guided tour is about to commence,' announced Tom in his housemaster's voice, clasping his hands and closing his eyes as he spoke. He looked so ridiculous that we all began to laugh.

'Can we meet them?' said Sarah. 'I want Lucy to be able to sample the joys of Trevor and Teresa.'

'Trev sees parents on Saturday mornings,' said Tom, 'and as for Teresa . . .' He raised one shoulder provocatively, 'Well, who knows what *she's* doing?'

'Satin nightie off the shoulder, full make-up, reclining against a pink quilted headboard, her full breasts rising and falling . . .'

'Come on, infants,' said Katie getting to her feet, 'time to go.'

Sarah claimed to be bored by architecture and immune to paintings, but I wanted to see round. It was what Sarah called my 'tourist' leanings. Tom however, for all his posing, was both gripped and excited by the surroundings where he was supposed to have spent the happiest days of his life and eventually we found ourselves alone together in St George's Chapel while Sarah sat grumpily on a chair by the door, having refused Katie's offer to go shopping with her.

'My little sis is in a bad way,' said Tom apropos of nothing at all. 'The psychiatrist says she's on the verge of a breakdown.'

'What psychiatrist?'

'She doesn't tell you she goes to see someone in the hols?'

'No.'

'She's very screwed-up,' he continued, 'I mean I am, too, but the difference is that I know I am. Sarah doesn't.'

'She's always in tears,' I said, 'and won't tell me why.'

'Boyfriend trouble?'

'She hasn't got one, has she?'

'She hasn't told me if she has,' said Tom, 'but you can see for yourself what she's like with Katie. Nightmare, fucking nightmare.'

'What do you think's the matter with her?' I asked.

'Something to do with them,' said Tom. 'She takes them too seriously. She and he have always had problems. They fight. I think he picks on her. But our mother is no use. You probably know she's a serial lush. In and out of clinics, all hush-hush. Goes without it for a while and then it all starts again. Don't say I told you that.'

'I wouldn't dream of it,' I said. 'You'd never know it when you read about her.'

'That's just PR,' said Tom. 'All that stuff is organized by Dad and Lowell.'

'Why, though?'

'Because it makes our father look good. To him that's the most important thing in the world,' he added bitterly. 'Lowell has to clean up after him too of course.'

'What do you mean?'

'Oh forget it,' he said. We walked on past a statue of some long-dead grandee. 'I'm sorry,' he said, 'that was bloody rude. I shouldn't have brought the subject up in the first place, but there's something about you that invites confidences.' We walked on a little further. 'Don't let him get you too roped in with my sister Sarah, though. In some ways she's just a spoilt bitch.'

'She isn't really. I don't think she can help it. There's something incredibly sad about Sarah. If that sounds patronizing it's not meant to be.'

'It doesn't,' said Tom. 'Sarah *is* sad. She's never really had any friends. Just me, I suppose, and now you, Luce. She really needs you, you know. Don't abandon her, will you?'

'Why should I?'

'I dunno,' said Tom, 'there's something about Sarah that drives people away. Look at her on her chair, for God's sake: she's the picture of bloody misery.'

'She does rather bring it on herself though.'

'I know,' he said, squeezing my shoulders, 'you're right, she does, silly cow.'

'Do you have any idea what the problem is between your father and Sarah?'

'Not really,' said Tom, but I noticed how his tone of voice had lost its warmth and become evasive. He did know but he wasn't going to tell me. I could come so far but no further. 'But there's always one child who attracts the ire of the paterfamilias in larger families, or so I've heard, and with us it's Sarah.'

Tom retrieved the Morris Minor, known as Hope, from the car park at Windsor station. Katie's bodyguard insisted on following us in his souped-up Cavalier. When we stopped at a pub the London side of Kew Bridge for lunch, the bodyguard stopped too and sat on a wall outside whilst we loitered inside drinking the very strong beer that Tom recommended.

Once in London, Tom parked Hope round the back of Harrods. Tom and Katie went off tipsily together to the pet department where Tom said he intended to order an elephant. He kept saying he wanted to see the invoice with '1 Loxodonta africana' on it. The bodyguard followed them at a discreet distance.

'OK,' said Sarah, 'let's do Haberdashery first.'

By 'do' I soon realized she meant shoplift. I watched amazed as she pocketed things she would never have any use for in a million years: jewelled hair combs, cut-glass scent bottles, a notebook for recording guests who came to dinner and the menus they were served, the sort of thing the cook, Heather, at Gatehouse Park might just conceivably find some use for, but not Sarah. We moved on through the Perfumery into the famous food halls.

'What happens if you get caught?' I asked, as she pocketed some chocolates from a display with a sleight of hand any professional would have envied.

'I won't.'

'But you might,' I insisted. 'They've got cameras everywhere. Why do you do it, anyway?'

'It's fun,' said Sarah. 'Life's so boring otherwise.'

At half-past-five when it was getting dark we returned to find Hope had been given a parking ticket.

'I'll pay it,' said Katie, snatching it from underneath the windscreen wiper. 'My fault.'

'No, you won't,' said Tom, whisking it out of her hand. 'S'mine. My car. My ticket. Bugger off.'

They scuffled on the pavement for a moment, causing other pedestrians to make a detour round them.

'Well!' said a voice. 'Who should it be causing a public nuisance but my nephew!'

'Hello, Aunt Marian,' said Tom, letting go of Katie. 'What are you doing here?'

'And why shouldn't I be here? I only live round the corner, as you know. A more pertinent question would be "What are *you* doing here?" I thought you were all supposed to be at school working, or pretending to.'

'We're just up for the night,' said Tom, glancing at his watch. 'Ought to be getting a move on, in fact. Is our father around do you know?'

'He's gone to stay with Cosmo Nevele for the weekend, I believe.'

'Good, good.'

'Why "good, good", pray? Hello, Katie, hello, Sarah. Please introduce your friend.'

'You've already met, Aunt Marian,' said Sarah, 'this is Lucy. Lucy Diamond. You met in the summer.'

'Oh yes,' said Aunt Marian. 'You're Joe Diamond's daughter.'

'Actually, I'm not,' I said.

But Aunt Marian's interest had now settled on Katie. 'I had lunch with your mother last week,' she was saying, 'so she could tell me about the new house. Absolute heaven. Rosa's over the moon about it. Have you seen it yet?'

'Which new house? Paris or London?' asked Katie sounding slightly bored. 'She's always buying new houses. The only one that doesn't change is Balmachie, that's why I love it. It's always the same. Dad won't let her change it. He won't let Mrs Richardson anywhere near it.'

'That bloody woman,' muttered Sarah.

'Your language!' said Aunt Marian, who was tiring of us

103

rapidly with our rowdy behaviour and lack of serious interest in important subjects such as houses and the spending of money thereon.

The basement area of the house in Eaton Terrace had been turned into an enormous kitchen cum dining-room with French windows leading from the sitting area to the garden I had looked down upon from above the last time I was here. Davina was talking on the telephone in the drawing-room when we arrived and waved us away towards the nether regions whilst she finished her call.

'Must be the lover boy,' said Sarah.

'Who is he?' I asked.

'Waldy Harcourt.'

'*Waldy?*'

'Waldo. His father's Earl Harcourt. They live in Shropshire. Big bucks. He's a complete thicko. Perfect for Davy. It's his party we're supposed to be going to. There's a younger brother, Yvo, who's quite nice. He's going to be there. That's why we were recruited.'

We were lounging around in front of the television eating toast and bowls of cereal when Ivar came downstairs. None of us had heard him arrive. It was immediately clear that he was in a terrible temper.

'Just what the bloody hell is going on here?' he asked the room at large, before turning to Sarah. 'Who gave you permission to come up to London?'

'It's OK,' she began, 'it's not a —'

'It is not OK,' said Ivar. 'You have been expressly forbidden to leave that school until half-term. You knew that. Lucy knew that.'

'No, I didn't,' I said.

'Don't contradict me,' he said coldly. 'You're the one who is supposed to have some sense, for God's sake, and when I think what this family has done for you, I'm astonished at your lack of gratitude.'

I fell silent. However I had expected Ivar to behave when I met him again it was not like this. I couldn't understand what his game was. If it was a game.

'Hey, listen, Pa,' Tom began, but Ivar silenced him too.

'Don't you "hey, Pa" me,' he said. 'I don't like being taken advantage of. I consider that your sister and her friend have done exactly that. Sarah is very easily led astray it seems.'

'You can't blame Lucy for that,' said Tom indignantly. 'This whole thing was cooked up by Sarah and Davy. I just happened to get roped in as did Lucy and Katie.'

'You're to leave immediately,' said Ivar. 'Barry will drive you both to the station. I will ring Miss MacMaster to say that you're on your way.'

'Please, Pa, please can we stay?' said Sarah. 'Tom's already rung to say Hope's broken down and we can't get back tonight. It'll just make more trouble if you ring Mac.'

I could hear the tears in her voice. It crossed my mind fleetingly that there was some drama here between father and daughter that the rest of us had somehow become tangled in and that Ivar's aim was to use me to get at her – or was it the other way round? I was shocked and also confused, just as Ivar had intended.

Of all of us, only Katie appeared unfazed. I watched her glance at Sarah and me, then at Tom. Finally, her gaze rested on Ivar.

'Do you know something, Ivar?' she said, when he had finished ranting. 'You're just a horrible bully. I wouldn't let anyone talk to me that way,' she added, getting to her feet. 'You lot shouldn't stand for it.'

Ivar gave her a look that would have withered a mere mortal, but Katie appeared not to notice. Tom, Sarah and I sat and looked at our hands.

'Barry is outside,' Ivar said. 'You're to go upstairs and tell him that I said he was to drive you to Paddington. I'll be late for my next appointment, but I suppose that's just a cross I have to bear.'

'They can take a cab,' said Katie, 'you don't have to martyr yourself, Ivar. Jesus Christ,' she added under her breath.

'Please don't interfere,' said Ivar coldly. 'I should like you all out of here within ten minutes.'

'Willingly,' said Katie, making a face at us over her shoulder. I glanced at Tom and Sarah but they were still behaving as if they'd been turned to stone by the parental displeasure.

'Come on,' said Ivar, 'out. Now!'

There was a huge row when we got back to school about the lie Tom had told on our behalf. Mac was furious particularly with me. Sarah and I were summoned to see her separately in her room.

'If it were not for the fact that your mother has been so ill, Lucy,' she said, 'I would have expelled you. You simply cannot behave like this and expect to get away with it. I rue the day I was persuaded to take Sarah Anwoth on. She has caused nothing but trouble ever since she arrived in this school. Sister Anselm was accurate when she described her as having an authority problem. I'm disgusted with you, Lucy. It's as if you're mesmerized by her and can't see sense.'

'I'm sorry.' And I was. But not that sorry. I suppose I knew, even though I didn't want to admit it, that my mother was dying. At any rate, I didn't believe in miracles. There had to be something one could do, someone one could punish, even if it turned out to be oneself. And if there was punishment then there had to have been a crime somewhere along the way. I felt guilty about my mother. I was in the mood for a little masochistic self-mutilation, an ideal victim in fact. I felt it was right that I should hurt. Ivar's treatment of me chimed exactly with this mentality, as if he could somehow tune into a signal I was emitting that no one else could pick up, like one of those dog whistles that only dogs can hear. Later on of course I realized that it was all part of the way he operated: first the victim is made to feel 'special', then she is humiliated before being rehabilitated, a cycle designed to wear out resistance and to convince the victim that there is no other place, no safe harbour, only the unsafe place you know. You are scum, worm, worse than vomit, and at the same time an angel of joy, beloved, special, *secret*. Always secret. The secrecy is the cancer; as in a cancer where cells divide maniacally, secrecy is as viciously infectious, dividing the needy from the help, mother from child, isolating the keeper of a secret in a grim, lonely universe where your only companion is a terrible guilt.

'Sarah's not well,' I added, thinking of my conversation with Tom.

'What do you mean?' she said sharply, putting the pen she had been turning over and over in her hands down firmly on the desktop.

'She's anorexic. She's getting thinner and thinner.'

This piece of information halted Mac in her tracks somewhat.

'She's naturally a very thin girl anyway,' she said. 'Has Sister been informed?'

'I don't know.' I wanted to say, but didn't, that surely it was Sister's job to notice these things, not mine. And what did she do all day if she couldn't notice that a girl whose health was her job was practically fading away under her nose.

'Well,' she sighed, 'anorexia or not, this just can't go on. You two are gated until December. I'm also going to put you on bottle rota until the end of term.'

This meant the washing of the half-pint bottles of milk drunk by the Lower School at break, a disgusting and much-loathed task, as a result of which I have never been able to drink milk since.

'Does that include half-term?'

'Unfortunately not. Your mother tells me you're going to stay with the Gatehouses. Is that wise, Lucy? I'm surprised they still want you after what happened.'

It was the wrong question to ask. At sixteen one is not interested in whether something is 'wise' or not. I certainly wasn't. All I knew was that I wanted to go for reasons that

I didn't particularly wish to examine too closely myself, let alone reveal to Mac or my poor mother.

When she heard what I had been up to my mother was surprisingly unbothered; as a misdemeanour she regarded it as minor (although she did her best to conceal this) but I think now that her attitude was coloured by the fact that the 'sin' had been connected with Tom and Sarah rather than Ivar. Ivar's rage comforted her because she regarded it as an appropriate reaction from a senior member of the older generation; what had really bothered her was the fact that Ivar was paying too much attention to me. She preferred his displeasure.

Michael Gresham was on tour in Asia that half-term. 'The China Syndrome', his latest hit album, had just come out. He was on the news one night filling a stadium to capacity in Bangkok. Pauline, who would normally have been at Stanborough Farm at this time of year and Christmas shopping in New York, was at Balmachie because that was where Katie wanted to be.

Claudia was also absent.

The press had got hold of the fact that she was in The Priory. First 'Pandora' in the *Daily Mail* had made mention of Claudia in her column . . . 'Claudia Baillie-Maclehose, the painter (and wife of drop-dead-gorgeous agriculture minister Lord Ivar Gatehouse) is "resting" at present in The Priory. A Gatehouse family spokesman said that "Lady Gatehouse had picked up a virus when she was last in North Africa on a painting trip . . ." Oh yeah? What Pandora wants to know is since when did a nasty bug caught from drinking water in a third-world country mean a trip to The Priory, the top people's nut house?' The *News of the World* followed suit the next Sunday. Then the story vanished completely.

'Lowell,' said Sarah when we were discussing it after I told her that Tom had given the game away about her mother's whereabouts.

'But how does he manage it?'

'Bribes them to shut up,' she said matter-of-factly, 'or threatens them. One or the other.'

'Like a gangster would?'

'That sort of thing,' she admitted.

'I thought Lowell was meant to be respectable.'

'Some of him is. It's the same with everyone in public life, private life, whatever. Everyone has something to hide, even you.'

'What do you mean?'

'You've just proved my theory,' she said smiling. 'You shouldn't overreact.'

'I thought you were on to me,' I replied, trying to sound joky and detached. 'I thought you knew.'

'Did you guess about her?'

'Yes,' I lied, wondering with sudden terror whether Claudia would remember seeing me that night at Eaton Terrace when she had been so drunk, but then it occurred to me that I could just deny it. She was after all the one with a credibility problem.

'Tom says everyone knows. Is that true, do you think?'

'Does it matter what people think?' I asked. We were walking back from the games fields in a straggling group after a bracing game of lacrosse, a sport we both loathed. Our games uniform consisted of a short kilt, Aertex shirt and navy-blue crewneck jersey, an outfit which prominently displayed Sarah's Belsen-like legs.

The day before I had seen her in the nude sitting on her bed in the dorm rummaging under her pillow for her pyjamas. Her body looked starved and shorn, exactly like the bodies of the women in the queues for the showers in the death camps.

'Have you looked at yourself in the nude lately?' I asked her, closing the door so that we could be alone for a moment.

'It's something I avoid on principle,' she said. 'Why?'

'You're so thin.'

'You're the one who's lost weight,' she countered. 'At least a stone, I should say.'

'I know,' I said, 'but I needed to. You didn't.'

She made no reply to this but began to pull on her pyjamas. She had that closed look on her face that I had grown so familiar with during the time I had known her.

'Can't we talk about it, Sarah?'

'About what?'

'Why you're starving yourself to death.'

'Oh don't be so melodramatic . . . it's nothing. I never did eat all that much anyway. It runs in the family. Look at my mother.'

There were tears in her eyes, however. I watched as she blinked them away.

'Why do you make yourself so hard to reach?' I asked. 'Every time I try to get near you, you retreat.'

'There are things about me you wouldn't want to know.'

She meant Ivar, of course. And she was right, I wouldn't have wanted to know, but I wonder now, when I look back on it all, if I shouldn't have tried to force her to explain what she meant. If she had told me that her father was sexually abusing her then I myself would never have had the relationship with Ivar that I did; and there would have been no guilt.

'What things?'

She shook her head. 'Don't ask, please. Nobody would believe me anyway.'

In the absence of Claudia, Ivar had wanted Davina to be the hostess for his shooting party but she was on a fashion shoot with *Vogue* in New Mexico. Louise was at university working for her finals, so the task of helping her father fell to Sarah with me as her deputy.

Ivar behaved towards me as if the scene in the basement kitchen in Eaton Terrace had never taken place. The first night at Gatehouse Park after Tom and Sarah had gone to bed he came to my room, now known after even such a short time as 'Lucy's room'. I was one of the family it seemed, here to stay. The room, on the second floor looking out towards the estuary, was large and old-fashioned with twin beds and watercolours by long-dead Anwoth great-aunts on the faded walls. There was a fireplace with a paper fan in its black grate and pretty glass candelabra on the mantelpiece that tinkled gently when the door opened, and a dressing-table with pink-shaded lamps and cut-glass pots with silver lids containing cotton wool.

He turned out the lights on the dressing-table but opened the curtains; it had been a fine day followed by a cold night with a full moon.

Afterwards, we talked for a while in whispers although Tom and Sarah's rooms were miles away and Sarah, as I knew for a fact, slept like the dead.

'Not angry with me any more?' I said, stroking his cheek.

'I was never really angry with you,' he replied.

'I was scared of you that night.'

'No need to have been,' he said.

'You're frightening when you're like that, in a rage I mean. I felt like I didn't know you at all.'

'It was necessary,' he said rather coldly. 'Surely you could see that?'

'Yes, I . . .'

A game. Of course it was. A game that nobody else knew about; and yet, I remember that Katie's face came to mind once more and unbidden, as if her inscrutable expression held the key to something that bothered me, a deeper secret still in this labyrinth of guessing games and rages and absences, of people who appeared to be one thing and were in fact another.

'Katie has too much freedom,' he added abruptly. 'I think she's leading Tom astray; that was one of the reasons I had to break it up, quite apart from the fact that Sarah has got to be made to stick at something otherwise God alone knows what'll become of her.'

'And what about you?' I asked teasingly. 'Don't you think you're leading me astray?'

'Am I?'

'Yes, but I like it. It would kill my mother if she knew.'

'But you won't tell her, will you?'

'Why should I?'

The shoot was an important one in the annual scale of things. Ivar's grouse moor was famous; an invitation to the October shoot conferred a certain *je ne sais quoi* upon the invitee of whom there were to be several staying: Lowell for one, Cosmo Nevele who always came to stay but walked with the beaters and never shot, Father Cottrell and another priest who were doing some research in the muniments room about recusant families, Aunt Marian and her unspeakably pompous husband, Sir Oliver Beaton-Smith ('Just Smith really,' said Sarah. 'Beaton was chucked in to glam it up a bit'), a grand civil servant, recently knighted for unspecified services rendered, who was the permanent secretary in a Whitehall department, what is known by the popular press as a 'mandarin'. There was a marquess and his new wife, the old one having been ousted by a fresh, American version with long curling dark hair and a flat Irish face with huge blue eyes; Lady Castlehill's tweeds were made especially for her in New York and were beautiful but comically inappropriate for the purpose for which they had ostensibly been designed. The first morning she came down to breakfast wearing a cashmere sweater and a long tightly-fitting tweed skirt with a fishtail pleat at the back which made Sarah giggle uncontrollably, until Ivar sent her out of the room.

'She's a little old for that sort of thing, isn't she?' pronounced Sir Oliver. 'When I was her age I was expected to pull my weight. How old is she, eighteen?'

'Nearly sixteen,' said Ivar.

'When I was sixteen,' said Boo Castlehill, 'I was living on my own in New York and modelling.'

'The less said about that the better, my dear,' said her new husband, whose greying corkscrew curls and weatherbeaten face made him resemble some jovial caricature of a Trollopian country squire.

Cosmo Nevele told me later that morning when we were

clambering into the Land-Rovers that Boo Castlehill had made several pornographic films with titles such as *Dizzy Babes in the Wood*. 'She's a tart,' he said, 'poor old Planty Castlehill doesn't know what's hit him or his bank balance, not yet anyway.'

'He seemed to know what she was doing when she was sixteen,' I said.

'He doesn't really. It's a knee-jerk reaction to anything the female of the species says, just a kind of registering squawk. She'll fleece him, then she'll be off blood-sucking somewhere else.'

'You don't like her?'

'Don't like vampire bats much.' He settled himself on the ledge that passed for a seat and lit a cigarette. 'The lady of the house isn't well, I gather.'

'No.'

'You know what the problem is of course?'

'Yes. Everyone does.'

'It all leaves a larger and larger hole in Ivar's life, although I'm sure he's to blame for some of it. He can be a very cruel man, Ivar.' He glanced at me. 'Do I shock you,' he asked, 'talking about mine host in such frank terms?'

'No, not really.' It seemed that I was the kind of person people told things to, God knows why. I thought of Rosa Richardson's Cassandra-like predictions of doom about Ivar's family, the Fall of the House of Anwoth.

'Watch him,' Cosmo said, flicking his ash on to the floor, 'he's a predator. Likes young flesh; devours it and spits out the bones.'

'You really don't like him,' I said.

'My dear girl, it's not a question of liking or not liking when you've known someone as long as I've known Ivar. We were at Eton together. Our mothers were best friends. I've been coming to this house since I was a babe in arms. That's why I know what I'm talking about, but alas I gather from your tone that he must already have made inroads.'

'That's rubbish,' I said, 'I'm just a schoolfriend of Sarah's, that's all.'

'But you like it,' he said, 'I've been watching you. You like this life and who could blame you. It's heaven except there's a serpent loose in this Eden. You have been warned.'

He turned his attention to Lowell who was clambering into the front seat. 'Hello, Lowell. You're wearing a nice new Eddie suit I see.' Eddie, as I knew, was Mr Boland in Artillery Row and Lowell was wearing a very swanky pair of plus-twos with a matching jacket. 'You'll have to roll in a few cowpats for the right look, a little cowshit works wonders on that Harris tweed, must be something chemical. Hasn't Ivar told you?'

'I got this suit for a very good price,' said Lowell scratching his ear, unperturbed by Cosmo's teasing, 'and I've no intention of rolling in cowshit.'

'Grouseshit then,' said Cosmo. 'Lucy here's got the right idea, she's wearing the oldest clothes she could find.'

'They're Sarah's,' I said, looking down at my threadbare Levi's.

'What's the matter with Sarah?' asked Lowell. 'She's so thin.'

'All those Anwoths are skinny,' said Cosmo, 'they all look fashionably undernourished; but I agree. Sarah's too thin, it's not natural.'

'She's got anorexia,' I said.

'Can't eat, won't eat? That one?' asked Cosmo.

'Won't eat, can't eat,' I said, 'it's that way round. You stop eating first for whatever reason and then you find you can't start again.'

Ivar drove us what seemed like miles on empty single-track roads through bare hills to the meeting point where the other guns and beaters were assembling, with Jack McGaw, the keeper, organizing the men and giving instructions. As we arrived so did the party from Balmachie; a Senator and his wife, together with a Hungarian count and his son, cousins, or so she claimed, on Pauline's Milo side, plus my friendly sheep, Sandy Carsluith.

Katie was there too in a waxed jacket and a rakish dark green felt hat with a feather. She waved to us and as Tom went over to talk to her I saw her tilt her head at Ivar who was standing behind his son pretending to talk to the Senator. He gave her a look and turned his back.

Pauline was to walk up with the Senator whose wife had decided not to stay but would meet us instead for the lunch that Heather was even now organizing at a cottage further on into the hills which was kept in repair especially for these occasions, and then let in the earlier summer months before the start of the grouse season on August 12th. Tom, Sarah and I would walk together and I had assumed that Katie would join us, but as the guns moved off I saw to my astonishment that she was with Ivar and that they were engrossed in conversation. I was astonished at how jealous this made me feel. Why should she have the best pickings just because she was Katie Gresham? I could feel myself becoming like Sarah about Katie and I could see how unattractive a state it was, but there was nothing I could do about it.

Tom, who had seen the look on my face, said bitterly: 'He's one of those fathers who likes pinching his son's girl-friends.'

I stared at him, my brain refusing to take in what he had said. 'What do you mean?'

'What I say,' said Tom. 'Look at him. He's busy seducing Katie.'

'Katie! But . . . he's known her since she was a baby and, besides, she's your girlfriend, isn't she?' I heard myself say. It was as if none of the gossip I had heard about Ivar until this point made any sense and still didn't. Did I really believe I was the only one? Could I have been so unbelievably naive? And still I couldn't make the connection between what Tom was telling me and what was wrong with Sarah.

'She is my girlfriend,' Tom said, 'or she's meant to be. You know what I'd like to do? I'd like to put a bullet right through that bastard's brain.'

'But surely,' I persisted, 'you don't mean –'

'He fucks them,' said Tom furiously. 'Shocked? I hope you are because I was when I found out. He likes fucking young girls and he gets away with it. Never mind what it does to my mother or us. Never mind that Sarah's starving herself to death to attract his attention. It's "I'm all right, Jack" and that's all that matters. He'll sleep with her, then he'll get bored and chuck her away; she's just another scalp.'

I wasn't shocked by what he said so much as numbed by it. I hadn't exactly thought I was the only one; it was more that I hadn't thought at all. I certainly had no thought of competing with Katie, how could I? She was everything I wasn't: rich, beautiful, confident, the list was endless. Katie had power. I had none.

All morning I tried to think about this as we walked in the bare landscape with a light breeze in our faces but I couldn't make any more sense out of it. There were three of us, a fact both horrible and somehow compelling. I couldn't really take it on board. What would my mother say if she knew? It would kill her.

The birds were driven up out of the heather by a walking wall of beaters shouting imprecations and beating the heather with their sticks. Ivar, accompanied by Katie, was shooting beautifully, missing nothing, egged on no doubt by the admiration of the beautiful young girl by his side. As I looked at her I felt a wave of envy and resentment so strong I was almost sick into the heather.

'No tantrums this morning,' I heard Tom mutter as he watched his father get a right and a left, a bird out of each barrel, the shooting equivalent of the most elaborate balletic feat. I watched with admiring horror as the wind-driven scuttering birds were shot out of the heavens time after time to be retrieved by dogs reared on the smell of blood and clotted feathers. It was as if I had wandered all unwitting into the equivalent of the games in the arenas of ancient Rome and I as much as the grouse were prey, but at the same time there was something in me that wanted the opportunities this strange closed world had to offer, a predatoriness that in its own way was as pronounced as Ivar's.

The old shepherd's cottage was painted pink with black window surrounds, the standard Gatehouse livery, and sat charmingly on the edge of a rushing stream known in this part of the world as a 'burn'. The downstairs of the cottage was one large room incorporating sitting-room and kitchen, dominated by a long refectory table with places already laid by Heather, the Gatehouse Park cook, and her minions. The social divide was absolute and unquestioned: toffs indoors, beaters outside, although Sarah remained out there for a little talking to various old friends, laughing and joking and smoking a cigarette once she was sure her father was safely indoors.

Lady Castlehill, who had somehow managed to walk all morning in her skin-tight tweeds, was flirting with the Hungarian count as she perched on the edge of the table, causing Heather to scowl as she made her way round her. Katie, with Tom standing slightly out of the circle, was in a group with her mother and the Senator, a neighbour at Stanborough Farm, and Ivar who was recounting a conversation he had had with Mrs Thatcher about how to choose a new Archbishop of Canterbury.

'But you're Catholic, Ivar,' Pauline was saying, 'doesn't she know that?'

'She chooses not to understand,' said Ivar. 'She's an iconoclast.'

'What did you say to her?' asked the Senator, a white-haired, square-jawed, All-American specimen of successful manhood whose deep tan looked orange in the weaker northern light.

'I told her on no account to choose Bishop North. He's a revolutionary-minded evangelical who'll have women priests and bishops as soon as he possibly can.'

'But she's a woman,' exclaimed Katie, 'surely she would want to see women priests?'

'She's as much a woman as Queen Elizabeth I; she has the heart and stomach of a man,' said Ivar, 'and, quite apart from that, she rightly loathes the idea of women priests.'

'Maggie as Gloriana?' broke in Tom abruptly. 'I don't think so.'

'That's how she sees herself,' said Senator Fowler, 'your father's right. She has vision. We just love that vision.'

At that point, Sarah broke into the group by announcing that she'd heard outside from the men that another girl had vanished, this time from a village called Crossluke near Kirkcudbright.

'That's terrible,' said Pauline, 'how many is it now?'

'Three at least. Just vanished.'

'Must be a drifter,' said the Senator, 'some guy roaming round picking them off.'

'It could be me,' said Sarah, her blue eyes wide with horror, 'or you.' She addressed Katie. 'You're the right age like me. This girl was sixteen, the last one was too.'

'Or Lucy,' said Katie, looking at me and winking. 'It could have been any of us.'

'Don't,' said Pauline quietly, 'just let's change the subject, shall we?'

'They'll get him,' said Ivar authoritatively. 'He won't get away with it. The police are very good at catching these kind of people.'

'They can't be that good,' said Tom sarcastically, 'or they would have got him by now. How many more will there be, we ask ourselves?'

'Please,' said Pauline, 'I just can't stand this kind of talk. It always makes me think of the poor Lindbergh baby.'

'They haven't found any of them,' said Sarah in her tactless way. 'Derry says (Derry Paterson was the factor to the estate) that the trouble is in a landscape like this there are so many places you could hide a body if you wanted to; there's so much wild country and bog . . . places that people never go. Those girls may even be buried on our land. Think of that!'

Watching her, I couldn't decide whether she really believed what she was saying or she was enjoying winding Pauline up as I had seen her do before, and if the latter was the case she was succeeding. Pauline had gone very pale.

'Don't,' said Pauline, shuddering, 'just don't.'

'Sarah,' said Ivar warningly, 'that's enough.'

'Derry says they may never catch him,' Sarah persisted, apparently oblivious to her father's request. 'He'll just go on getting away with it. We'll be the next!'

'Get out!' said Ivar, raising his voice so that everyone turned to stare. 'Just get out and don't come back.'

'But I —'

'You heard.'

'No, Ivar, it's OK,' said Pauline, 'Sarah didn't mean any —'

'Don't undermine me,' said Ivar in the same savage voice. 'Get out, you little bitch.' He pushed her shoulder. 'Just do as you're told.'

'I hate you,' said Sarah in a low voice, 'I hate you, lying bastard, child molester.'

Ivar raised his hand and struck his daughter a blow across the mouth. It was more than a slap to an irritating child, much more; it was the kind of blow one man might inflict on another.

Shocked silence. Low rumble of voices from outside where the beaters were by now eating their lunch. Everyone staring in horror as Sarah, with her hand against her mouth, made her way slowly to the door. Tom followed her.

'Lunch,' announced Heather briskly into the silence, 'please take your places.'

A sudden din of voices followed her command. I seemed to hear snatches of several conversations at once: 'Idiot child . . .' I heard Aunt Marian say, '. . . always provoking her father over some . . .'

'In America we're not allowed . . .'

'She shouldn't have spoken to her father . . .'

Katie was talking to her mother and had her back to Ivar who was handing a plate to Lady Castlehill, his face expressionless as if nothing untoward had happened. I was amazed at his capacity for dissimulation. I had yet to learn how well-rehearsed he was as an actor and how extensive were his skills in self-deception. To Ivar a thought was a fact. Therefore if he said something had or had not happened in a certain way that is how he believed it was.

'Ivar?' said Pauline in her gentle voice. 'I'm afraid we'll have to go. Katie's not . . .' she hesitated for a moment, 'feeling very well, I'm afraid. I'm going to take her home. I'm sorry to break up your party.'

'What's the matter, Katie?' he called, as if she were one of his own children going off in a sulk.

'Do I really have to spell it out to you?' asked Katie. The room had fallen completely silent again. 'That was completely unnecessary, Ivar. You should do something about that temper of yours.'

I waited for the explosion but there was none; nevertheless, given Ivar's temper, it was a brave thing to do. I admired Katie's guts.

'Damn cheek,' said a male voice, possibly belonging to Sir Oliver, but Ivar did not respond other than to shrug slightly. The Greshams left; the room was suddenly full of voices again and the clatter of knives and forks.

'Some of us,' whispered Cosmo in my ear, 'don't terribly care for seeing young girls beaten about the chops. I'm rather in agreement with Miss Gresham myself. Brave girl to speak out like that. Just as well Michael wasn't here. He'd have challenged Ivar to a duel.'

'I think I'd better go and see if Sarah's all right,' I said.

'Do you want some advice?'

'What?'

'If you know what's good for you, don't. Ivar Gatehouse is a dangerous man when roused. He'll turn on you like a snake and you'll be banished. He's reverting to type and behaving like a feudal baron. This is his land and his party and he's damn well going to do it his way.'

'Sarah could press charges. That was an assault. He hit her really hard.'

'Puh*leeze*,' said Cosmo, rolling his eyes and sighing, 'you still don't understand, darling, do you. The rules are different for the Ivars of this world. You and I, ordinary mortals, have to do what we're told – we're the poor relations and charity cases that existed in all medieval households – Ivar doesn't. Sarah knows that. She's one of them, one of the privileged ones. She understands the game but she's being tiresome, a little adolescent crisis, trying to wind Daddy up, rather successfully as it happens. But there will be no charges pressed. Things simply don't work like that in this world. Imagine the vulgarity of it, the long arm of PC Plod interfering in a little family dispute. Social workers . . .' He spat out the last two words as if they were a curse.

In the afternoon Ivar asked me to accompany him as the guns walked the hill towards the loch. I thought it best not to refuse in view of what Cosmo had told me but Ivar, as if to make up for ignoring me earlier, was charm itself, just as he had been when I had seen him again up here after he lost his temper with us all in London. It was as if losing his temper with Sarah had never happened. And in spite of all my earlier reservations I went with it, thrilled to be back in his good books again.

The loch was the local reservoir and on that cold clear afternoon its smooth waters gleamed in the slanting light of the setting sun. There was a boathouse and a jetty. In the summer I had fished there with Tom far out in the watery silence, with only the occasional call of a curlew or a peewit to break the spell. I remember watching Ivar's dog plunging into that shimmering smoothness, crumpling its surface as if diving through tin foil; there was the sound of laughter and voices, a stern voice calling the swimming dog to heel and more laughter as the dog, Ivar's black Labrador bitch, Jeanie, returned to an element even more native to her than the moorland she had worked all day, not heeding the command but swimming further and further out, her head just breaking the surface like a seal's. It was beginning to grow dark as we turned for home. In the meantime, Tom had taken Ivar's Land-Rover and driven Sarah back to Gatehouse Park.

*

The blow her father had struck her had loosened her two front teeth; her top lip was split and the whole area around her mouth and chin was swollen and bruised. Tom had given her painkillers discovered in his mother's bathroom cupboard and bathed her face. Heather, returning mid-afternoon, had given her some arnica ointment for the bruising.

'She should see a doctor,' Heather said. 'Do you want me to call Dr McManus?'

'No,' said Tom.

They were talking in the upstairs kitchen next to the dining-room, Sarah having been deposited by Tom in the library where there was a television, a comfortable sofa to watch it from and a fire laid by one of the fleet of cleaning ladies from Anwoth village who came each morning to wash up, make beds, clean the silver and do the thousand other tasks associated with a large and well-run house.

'She ought to be X-rayed and those teeth are going to have to be sorted.'

'The teeth can wait. Sarah doesn't eat anyway and an X-ray is out of the question.'

Heather met his gaze. 'I'll take her,' she said. 'I'll say it was an accident.'

'How could something like that be an accident?' asked Tom. 'She's still got his fingermarks on her cheek.'

'What does Sarah want to do?'

'You could probably see for yourself that she's too drunk to care. The only way I could get her to stop crying was to fill her up with booze. It seems to run in the family.'

'I'm going to ring him anyway,' said Heather, 'her jaw may be broken. She has to see a doctor.'

'How will you say it happened?'

'I'm going to tell the truth,' said Heather. 'He can't do that sort of thing. It's unbelievable. You can't want him to get away with it.'

'Oh, don't be naive,' said Tom.

'I know he's your father —'

'You don't understand,' said Tom. 'He'll sack you if you ring Dr McManus and that's just for starters.'

'There were witnesses, Tom,' said Heather, 'people *saw*. I'm not just imagining. You were there, for heaven's sake, why don't you do something? Don't you care?'

'Do what you fucking-well like,' said Tom, who did care but was terrified of his father, 'but don't drag me into it and don't say I didn't warn you.' He turned on his heel and went out.

Dr McManus was waiting in the library when Ivar returned. He needed parental permission, he said, to take her to the cottage hospital in Kirkcudbright for an X-ray. Ivar, pouring himself a drink, had his back turned and did not reply for a moment.

'I don't think that's necessary,' he said eventually, turning round.

'She's suffered a severe blow to the mouth and jaw area, Lord Gatehouse. She needs immediate attention.'

'The answer is no. Would you like a drink?'

Dr McManus however was not a man who gave up easily. 'Miss Carson told me that you and Sarah had had an altercation and that you had struck Sarah. Is that correct?'

'Miss Carson is no longer employed by me. Probably the best person to ask is Sarah herself.'

'Sarah wouldn't tell me anything. That's why I waited to see you.'

'Well,' Ivar shrugged, 'there you are then. Sure you won't have a drink?'

'No, no, thank you.'

'If you'll forgive me,' said Ivar, 'I have to go and change. We've got some people coming to dinner.'

'He treated me very courteously,' said the doctor to his wife

123

that night as he buttoned up his pyjama jacket, 'but at the same time made it quite clear that he thought I was a piece of dirt.'

*

The shooting party was held on the Wednesday. He came to my room that night and the night after. On the second night he wanted to tie me up; vile but true. That was one of the ways he got his kicks; by this time, however, in spite of my sense of triumph, I was beginning to be frightened of him; I could sense the hatred behind the lust. He was a man who enjoyed subordinating and humiliating women, particularly when he was angry, and he was very angry that week. I heard later that Claudia had let it be known from The Priory that she wanted a divorce and there was trouble afoot with Ivar's seduction of Katie. After what had happened over Sarah she refused to see him or to have anything to do with him. He had to work hard to get back into her good books and he found that humiliating. Katie, used to feeling in control, enjoyed her power over Ivar. It may have been the first time he found himself in a situation with a woman where he was not in the driving seat. It was as if a fuse had been lit and was slowly burning its way towards the explosion that would wreck us all.

We had been twenty for the dinner after the shoot. Luckily for Ivar Heather was so organized that everything was ready. Because Sarah was in bed, Tom and I, together with Agnes and Mary to help, served the dinner. I was glad to be in the kitchen that night and not sitting silently as the grown-ups gossiped across me or engaged me in the laboured question and answer pattern thought suitable for conversing with adolescents. The guests were of the kind I had come to expect at Gatehouse Park: a marquess and his wife from the next-door county, a famous American painter, Virgil Smith, who had arrived to stay in the late afternoon, a scattering of gentry, the factor and his wife (definitely *not* gentry), plus another local, but rather minor lord, Lord Glengap and his new Polish wife.

Cosmo whispered to me as they were going in to dinner, 'Look at that hair, will you! I call that colour "Baltic Brass",

124

she's a home-dyed Pole, her name's Wanda, I mean I ask you. She's changed everything at Glengap House; pride of place in the drawing-room is a framed photograph of the Pope, *il Papa*; I mean it's all very well for the help, but hardly for people like us. Imagine if Ivar who's quite as Catholic as any damn Pole did that. Rumour has it that Billy Glengap met her in an airport after Caroline died. She was the girl who looks at your tickets at the check-in desk. Silly old fool.'

When we were loading the two dishwashers in the scullery, Ivar came in to thank us and to chat to Mary and Agnes and pay them for their time. I listened as he asked after Agnes's auntie who had Parkinson's and Mary's son who was with the Army in Cyprus, managing to flirt a little with them at the same time, the personification of charm and *noblesse oblige*.

'The caring, sharing laird act is quite something, is it not?' muttered Tom to me when he had gone. 'Look at the old dears preening themselves. They love him, you see. Think the sun shines out of his arse.'

I made no reply to this. I don't think Tom expected me to. It was one thing to listen to what he had to say about his family but quite another to agree with what he had said; that way I think he could pretend to himself that he had not said it, that he was not guilty of the sin of disloyalty. I was dimly beginning to realize that the Anwoths were a tribal family; members of the tribe might grumble to outsiders but if I was, as Cosmo so delicately put it, just one of the hangers-on in this neo-feudal household then I was there to listen and most definitely not to comment.

On Saturday morning, Ivar took Claudia's Mercedes estate and set off for Carlisle to meet her off the London train. Neither Tom nor Sarah appeared to show much interest in the fact that their mother was reappearing after a considerable absence. Much later I understood that this lack of public show concealed deep feelings of anger and loss. At the time I naively assumed it was because Claudia simply wasn't important to them.

Sarah had taken to doing jigsaws on a table in her bedroom;

that morning I remember she was engaged on reconstructing a 5000-piece jigsaw of St Mark's Square with no picture to help her. It was a way of being concentrated that meant she didn't have to make eye contact with anyone. The lower part of her face was still puffy although the arnica ointment had made more difference than I would ever have thought possible so that the bruising had faded extraordinarily fast. She merely looked as if she'd had a rather unpleasant time in the dentist's surgery. The dentist in Kirkcudbright, Mr Johnson (who rented his house from the Gatehouse estate), had patched up her front teeth and done something clever but temporary with the gap left by the missing incisor. Later on in the term Sarah would make several trips to the family dentist in Lower Sloane Street where the damage was completely repaired, so well that one would never have known.

'Has he gone?' she asked when I came up to see her after breakfast.

'Yes, just. He's got things to do in Dumfries on the way to Carlisle.'

'What are the rest of them up to?'

'Aunt Marian's going into Kirkcudbright with Boo Castlehill, Virgil Smith has gone up to your mother's studio, Tom's around somewhere, I think. He might go over to Balmachie though.'

'To see that bitch, Katie, I suppose.'

'Give over, do,' I said. 'Why don't you just leave it?' I thought of saying, but didn't, that Sarah ought to be grateful to Katie for standing up for her when no one else did, not even her precious Tom. I also found Sarah's dislike of Katie irritating because it roused my own jealousy of Katie, a state of mind I disliked and wished to avoid.

'Oh she's so superior, so keen on herself, so fucking holier-than-thou.'

'She stood up for you at that lunch when no one else did,' I said, unable to resist the temptation.

'It was none of her bloody business. She shouldn't have interfered.'

'You are the most impossible person I've ever met. Nobody can ever get anything right with you.'

'That's not true,' she said coldly.

'Shall I go?' It was clear to me that I was about to be dismissed anyway but Sarah, in one of those strange emotional U-turns, said, 'No, don't. Please stay. Sorry, Luce. I don't know what's the matter with me at the moment. I'm sorry. It can't have been much fun for you this week.'

'It doesn't matter, I'm fine.'

'You mustn't mind Pa,' she added inconsequentially as if she had been saying one thing and thinking another, 'he just gets like that sometimes.'

'Like what?'

'Like Wednesday.'

I gazed at my friend but there was nothing I could say to her. At that moment I realized that we were both entrapped by Ivar, both of us locked into a cycle of humiliation followed by forgiveness. Sometime in the intervening two days since Ivar had publicly shamed his daughter he had privately obtained her forgiveness. How cleverly he had arranged it all to exonerate himself. Nothing had happened. Official.

That afternoon there was nothing happening so I took myself for a walk through the grounds. I had my book with me in case I found some sunny corner in which to sit and read. The weather was strangely warm for October as it often was apparently in this part of the world. After wandering round the house and garden for a while, I decided to go down to the bathing hut where I could sit on the verandah and read my book and sun myself at the same time. The hut was unlocked and so I was able to go inside, get out one of the long loungers and sun myself on the verandah. The unexpected heat and the sea air made me drowsy and I fell asleep over my book for about an hour, waking with a start at about four-thirty when I had to hurry back up to the house for the sacred ritual of tea.

Claudia and Ivar appeared at five o'clock in time for tea. I had thought Claudia would be brisk and fit, somehow in charge, as she had been when I first came here, but she wasn't. She was wan and fragile-looking and subdued. She drank a cup of tea with the rest of us in the library and then went upstairs to rest. A few minutes later, Ivar followed her out of the room. There was a guarded expression on Tom's face as he watched his father leave; I glanced in Sarah's direction over by the fire and was aware that she too was registering her father's departure. It seemed to me then that they already knew something was wrong, the first gust of wind in the gathering storm.

Before dinner, when I had changed, I went along the endless corridors to Sarah's room. She was seated at the jigsaw table, still in her jeans and several sweaters, her head swathed in a pink fringed scarf.

'You look like something out of the mummy's tomb,' I joked, putting my hand on the top of her head.

'She wants a divorce,' said Sarah. 'I knew something was wrong.'

'Your mother?' I sat down next to her and watched her long chilled fingers as they picked over the pieces of the jigsaw. A part of the Doge's Palace had been assembled, but little else.

'She's asked him for a divorce. She told me when I went in to see her just now.'

'What will he do?'

She shrugged and shook her head slowly. 'He won't give her one. We don't divorce in this family. We never have, we never will.'

'Spoken with authority,' I said, trying to lighten the situation slightly. She had made her statement with a firmness of purpose I recognized as an inheritance from her father.

'You see,' Sarah said, trying a piece and then discarding it, 'she's a convert, poor old thing. She never really understood it properly. Pa always says real Catholics are like Hindus, born not made. She'd never get an annulment, he'd make sure of that.'

'Doesn't sound very democratic, your church.'

'It's not meant to be. It's all about authority, absolute power. We have a monopoly on truth,' she said without irony.

'What will you mother do then?'

'Stop being so bloody silly, I should think,' said Sarah. 'She knew when she married him that it was for keeps. She can't change the rules now just because she feels like it.'

'Is there someone else?' I asked.

'God knows,' Sarah said, 'don't ask me, I don't know and I don't bloody want to know either.' She banged her hand so hard on the surface of the table that the pieces of jigsaw bounced about and some fell on to the boards under the table.

'I'm sorry,' I said, getting down on my hands and knees. 'I shouldn't have asked. It was tactless of me.'

'Don't mention that I told you, will you?' Sarah asked, coming face to face with me on all fours under the table. 'Nobody's meant to know. He'd be furious if he knew I'd spilled the beans. Poor old Pa, he was pretty devastated as you can imagine.'

We were all in the salon drinking champagne when Claudia came in. I was enjoying the heady sensation of drinking champagne on top of the effects of the customary pre-dinner joints smoked with Tom and Sarah in that strange room at the top of the house.

The agency in London had sent a new cook, a girl called Camilla something, who had taken charge with astonishing rapidity, according to Agnes whom I had had a chat with briefly earlier on when she arrived on her bicycle from the village.

'I hear Lady G's back,' said Agnes tilting her head to one side. 'Sober as a judge, so Mary says.'

'So far, so good, but she's only just got here.'

'It's difficult to keep off the hootch,' said Agnes, 'I should know. My Jimmy's been through it, dragging me with him. He's OK now, but he doesn't go to the pub any more. Lady G's surrounded by it all the time and that's very difficult. I've seen her right away with the fairies in my time, I can tell you. Lord G doesn't like that. Lets the side down,' she said, in a mincing imitation of a Sassenach accent, 'and he's not a person I'd like to get on the wrong side of. He's got a terrible temper, a really terrible temper. He scares the living daylights out of me, I can tell you.'

'But you seemed on such good terms with him, Agnes,' I said, teasing slightly.

'I'm just staff,' she said, 'and it suits me to be on good terms with the boss. That's just plain common sense, Lucy. Now, let me away to see what bossy boots in the kitchen wants doing, otherwise I'll be out on my ear like Heather.'

Claudia was wearing a full, rather stiff taffeta skirt in hunting Anwoth tartan, a concoction of greens and soft blues, with a tightly-fitted black velvet jerkin on top; she looked both fragile and magnificent with her pale hair twisted up on the back of her head and a large pearl and diamond cross round her neck. As she came into the room, a waitress approached with her with a tray of glasses of champagne already poured and I watched as she took some champagne and sipped it. Ivar, talking to Virgil Smith on the other side of the room, glanced up as she did this, giving his wife an angry stare. He knew by this action that the gauntlet had been flung down in the way that things were done in this house: silently but unmistakably.

At that moment, Katie Gresham came into the room and my attention was distracted. She had never looked more beautiful. Her smooth fair hair was loose and hung down her back as it had done the first time I had ever seen her in the summer. She was a rich girl and it showed in her clothes; she was dressed as opulently as any pre-Raphaelite fantasy woman and was wearing an ankle-length dress in burnt orange taffeta shot with gold thread with a green and gold sash round her narrow waist. On top of this dress was a heavy dark green brocade coat embroidered with leaves and flowers and edged in dull gold braid. On her feet were long pointed slippers in pea-green satin. She looked ravishing and she knew it, but not everybody was admiring her. I heard Aunt Marian mutter that she looked as if she'd come wearing the contents of the dressing-up box, but to me she looked wonderful and magical, like a princess out of Grimm or my childhood edition of Hans Andersen and, in true fairytale contrast, I felt poor and plain, more than ever like the little match girl of legend with her nose pressed against the glass watching the rich folks at play on the other side.

'Going, going but not quite gone . . .' murmured Cosmo in my direction when we were just putting our spoons into our soup. 'How long do you give her? Half an hour, ten minutes?'

He was referring of course to Claudia who was talking very loudly at the other end of the table to Virgil Smith, the American landscape painter. Virgil was a taciturn sort of man who didn't say much at the best of times, but it was clear that even he was wondering what would happen when his hostess fell into her soup.

Ivar, with Katie on his left and Boo Castlehill on his right, was pretending not to notice, but Agnes told me that when she handed the vegetables that went with the pheasant, she noticed that he had his hand on Katie's knee, 'and not only that, if you get my meaning,' she said. I got the meaning all right. Later on, when I recalled what Agnes had said to me, I realized that Ivar had somehow managed to do with Katie what he had already done with Sarah and effect a reconciliation. How and where he had managed this I could not say, but it was obvious from their demeanour towards one another that they were plunged back into their own twisted little power game.

From where I was sitting, three-quarters of the way down the table between Cosmo and some stuffed-shirt merchant banker neighbour with ginger hair and a pink bow tie, it was apparent that Tom's anger was becoming as pronounced as his mother's drunkenness. He gave up pretending to talk to his neighbours and sat in stony silence, occasionally glancing up the table to where Katie sat apparently oblivious to what was going on around her. At length, when the puddings were being circulated, he pushed back his chair with a screech, causing the people round him to stop talking and glance up at him. The only people not looking in his direction were Ivar and Katie who were laughing together over some joke at the other end of the table.

'What is it, Tomikins?' called his mother tipsily. 'Sit down, why don't you . . . I can't bear people wandering around at my dinner parties,' she said to no one in particular.

'It's nothing, Ma,' said Tom.

'Sit down, Tom,' called his father. 'You're disrupting our dinner.'

Tom glanced at his father and for a moment I thought he would embark on a slanging match right there in front of everyone, but then he turned on his heel and walked out of the room. Ivar did not try to detain him but, knowing Ivar as I was beginning to, I could see that he was very angry indeed. He didn't like having his authority so publicly contested. Tom would pay for that humiliation later, one way or another.

'All boys have to kill their father at some time or other,' murmured Cosmo in my ear, 'I think Tom's just ritually slaughtered his lordship.'

'I don't think his lordship is very happy about it,' I whispered back.

'The Anwoths have a temper: it's their fatal family flaw; doesn't appear in every generation but when it does one knows all about it. Ivar's grandpa, Sholto, used to smash the furniture when he lost his rag; he broke up a whole set of priceless George II chairs that way. Ivar's the same. He's done for some very good Hepplewhite in his time.'

'He petrifies me,' I said, glancing at Ivar. 'They're all frightened of him too.'

'With reason,' said Cosmo. 'Steer well clear for at least a day, if you want my advice. Going too near him at the moment would be like sailing into a tornado.'

Shortly afterwards, the dinner party divided when the women

left the men to port and cigars. Even then, this was a habit I could not abide. There was something inherently demeaning in women trooping obediently out of the room so that the men could get on with the serious talk. I found the drawing-room gatherings of women gruesome and the conversation excruciating. Aunt Marian on houses and babies and how the Templeman girl married the Cavendish Dunckley boy; how so-and-so's boy was at Eton now 'doing so well, he's *frightfully* clever' and somebody else was selling a Rembrandt to do the roof and pay the school fees: the smug, claustrophobic in-house gossip of her kind, the white noise of the upper class, a perpetual drone of loaded detail, mostly meaningless to outsiders. That night, however, Aunt Marian was occupied in taking Claudia to her room and getting her to bed without further mishap and as we walked out into the hall from the dining-room, Sarah grabbed my wrist and dragged me to the foot of the stairs.

'Come on,' she said (in my memory I hear Katie's voice in conversation with Lady Castlehill as they stand in the doorway to the dining-room), 'let's not hang on with the wimmin. There's only La Gresham and she's off home any second now and that old slag Boo Castlehill, made for each other I should say. We'll go up and find poor Tom.'

But Tom was nowhere to be found and so we were in bed by ten-thirty with the lights out and asleep shortly afterwards.

I fell asleep easily but woke again just after one. My sleep in the afternoon had made me restless and I couldn't get off again. I also wondered where Ivar had got to. I had come to expect him to make an appearance in my room and when he didn't I felt absurdly rejected. I allowed my mind to dwell on Katie's astonishing appearance at dinner and how she was so much everything that I would never ever be. I was suddenly irrationally sure that he was with her somewhere; with her rather than with me. My insecurity about Ivar began to bleed into the ever-present worry about my mother. Thinking I would read to quell these thoughts which made me feel so wretched, I reached for my book but it wasn't there. When I thought back I realized that I must have left it at the bathing hut that afternoon. My restlessness and wretchedness increased. The only way I could ever get back to sleep, it seemed, would be to start reading again. I decided that I had to have the book. Good little schoolgirl that I was, I even had my torch with me.

In those days, Gatehouse Park had no alarm system that prevented guests from wandering about in the middle of the night. I knew the garden-room door had a key in it and I knew the way to the hut. There was also a very full moon that night which cast a strange cold blue light into my bedroom once I had drawn back the curtains that made me more determined than ever on my plan. I had to have my book.

I put a sweater over my pyjamas, pulled on my gym shoes and set off down the long corridor with its Turkish carpet and cabinets full of Chinese porcelain, loot brought back by an Anwoth after the Opium Wars, so Tom had told me. 'Accumulation is our middle name,' he had said jokingly, 'some people call it greed.'

Jeanie, Ivar's Labrador, was asleep in her basket by the fireplace in the hall. Jeanie was the nearest the house got to a burglar alarm in those days, but hearing footsteps approach from the stairs did not bother her. In her Labrador brain this meant 'guest/friend' not 'threat, bite it'. She merely thumped her tail as I crept past, allowing the library corridor door to close gently behind me.

There was a flower-room at the far end of that corridor, a charming place with a tiled floor, long shelves containing vases of all kinds and shapes and a huge Belfast sink; there was a smear of blood in the sink. Tom sometimes used this room to gut birds or rabbits he had shot so it wasn't unusual to see the grisly remains of guts and feathers in here during the shooting season. Rather to my surprise the garden door was unlocked. Either whoever locked up had forgotten this door or someone had gone out ahead of me.

Outside, the temperature had risen and a light wind had blown all but a few black rags of cloud away. There was a moon and stars and the reedy salty smell borne on the breeze from the estuary.

I had a tremendous sense of illicit freedom once I was outside in the night. I walked across the black velvet lawns and down the sloping grass pathway to the bathing hut; in this season the tall grasses of summer had collapsed; there was a brackeny smell of moss and frond. I could hear the swirl of the sea ahead. The tide, so far out earlier, was sweeping in now.

As I approached the hut, I became aware that there was some kind of flickering dim light inside as if someone had lit several candles. I also became aware that there were two people inside engaged in furious argument. Emboldened by my own daring in being there at all, I crept up the steps and peered through the glass. Katie, shouting, was standing up holding a glass in her right hand, wrapped only in a towel (of which there were invariably several in one of the cupboards for swimming parties); her gorgeous party clothes lay in a tumbled heap together with the pea-green satin shoes. There were candles burning inside hurricane lamps on the table, together with what looked like a bottle of whisky with the top off.

The person she was shouting at was Ivar. He stood facing her wearing some kind of a navy-blue towelling robe that I remembered seeing him in in the summer after swimming. They had obviously come here to drink and to make love but something had gone horribly wrong. Katie was clearly drunk, Ivar scarcely less so.

'You'd better watch it,' she was saying in a harsh voice, 'or I'll call your bloody bluff, Ivar. I'm not frightened of you, unlike your daughter Sarah and her friend. You're such a shit. The newspapers would go crazy if they knew. You're so arrogant, you think you can get away with anything, do anything, even down to screwing your schoolgirl daughter and all her friends and relations. Jesus Christ, when I think of it, I just can't believe it. Not to mention my mother too. She's the only person who ever had the guts to refuse you.'

Screwing your schoolgirl daughter. It was the first time I acknowledged to myself that Sarah was involved in the sexual tangle surrounding her father. Before this, I had tried not to know, but here it was, fair and square. I could no longer avoid it. Katie, more streetwise than I, had somehow cottoned on to this.

'You wouldn't dare,' said Ivar loudly. 'You should just keep your silly little schoolgirl mouth shut. No one would believe a teenage fantasist in any case.'

'Oh yes, they would,' replied Katie in an equally loud voice. 'They'd believe me all right. I don't need you, Ivar, I'm the only one who doesn't need you and your games. Christ, when I think of what you put poor Sarah through, I just can't believe it.'

At that point I ducked as Ivar lurched towards the table, presumably to fill his glass. The next thing I heard was a scream and the sound of breaking glass. I could hear some kind of tussle going on inside which gave me the opportunity I needed to run for my life. I suppose that I should have stayed to see if Katie was all right, but I was just too scared and I justified my cowardice by telling myself that Katie was a tough cookie who could protect herself from the Ivar Gatehouses of this world. The guilt I have felt that I did not have the courage to look one last time through the glass of the verandah window has stayed with me ever since.

The path in the starlight, the door ajar. The library corridor and then the great staircase, the corridors which led to my room: of these I remember the barest outline. The lustres on the glass candlesticks tinkled as I opened my bedroom door. I threw myself on my eiderdown. My heart hurt, I thought I would never get my breath back. If I could have left then and there like Sophia Bain I would have done. The ugly scene I had recently witnessed together with the appalling tensions in the household made me realize that my mother had been right, as usual, all along. I just wanted to go home.

*

The parents of teenage children don't expect to see their children at breakfast time, particularly if, like Pauline Gresham, they invariably have breakfast in bed. Like the Queen, Pauline had a dresser, Mrs Collins (always known as 'Collie'), a local woman who had worked for Sissy after Michael had started to keep his mother in some style. When Sissy died, Pauline kept Collie on, gradually transforming her into a cross between dresser, housekeeper and domestic tyrant.

When Collie brought Pauline's breakfast at nine-thirty on that fatal morning, it never occurred to Pauline to ask her if Katie was up. Katie usually slept until eleven or half-past after a late night, then she might get up, have a bath and then wander downstairs in search of coffee and something to eat in the kitchen where Dan, the chef, would be preparing lunch according to a set of menus discussed with Pauline at the beginning of each week.

Pauline was awake as she usually was when Collie came in with her tray and had just finished talking with Michael who had called her from a luxury hotel on one of the beautiful paradise islands situated in the Gulf of Thailand. At that time Michael's name had been linked with a beautiful Italian model and photographs of him embracing her on one of those beaches with white sand, palm trees and a limitless azure horizon had been taken by a paparazzo and sold to one of the tabloids. The photographs turned out to be of someone else, not Michael, but it was a low-life story that was enjoying a short, lucrative run until it was chased out by what happened later.

Thus it was that no one discovered that Katie was missing until lunchtime. Collie and the cleaning staff were forbidden to go into Katie's room until she was up and about and had given the go-ahead.

During the winter months Pauline always had champagne served before lunch in the white drawing-room. During the summer, if the weather was good enough, the champagne ritual moved to the folly by the loch where the party would dine *sur l'herbe* with food served from within by Dan and his minions, and admire the black swans from a safe distance.

When Katie did not appear by a quarter to one, Pauline sent Collie upstairs to get her out of bed.

'She must have been awfully late last night,' she said to Collie.

'I don't think so, madam,' said Collie. 'I heard Jimmy bring the car in about eleven or so.'

Jimmy was the Balmachie chauffeur and handy man, who looked after the cars and the fabric of the house when the Greshams were elsewhere. He and Collie had flats (Collie liked to refer to hers as 'an apartment') in the Georgian stable block, where Katie's beloved old horse, Gimlet, was kept when she was at home, next door to the Balmachie vehicles: Pauline's Range Rover and Michael's Land-Rover. Jimmy would have driven over to Gatehouse Park in the Range Rover, which he also used when the Greshams were away. Only Michael drove the precious Land-Rover that had once so famously adorned the cover of 'Desert Days', one of the best-known record covers of all time, almost on a par with 'Abbey Road'.

'I can't understand why she's slept for so long then,' said Pauline. 'Be a dear, Collie, and go get her up.'

'The young,' said the Hungarian count, 'have this extraordinary capacity for sleep. I don't think we slept as late when we were their age.'

'We weren't allowed to,' said Pauline. 'My mother would have had a fit if I'd still been in bed at lunchtime. But I used to like to get up to ride. I'd be off round the farm long before breakfast.'

'What was that horse called that you rode in those days?'

'Johnson,' said Pauline, smiling. 'My darling Johnson. He lived until he was thirty-five, you know. Even when he was old and mostly blind, he would always come at once if he heard my voice. I adored that horse. He's buried at Stanborough Farm. My mother started the cemetery for all the animals . . . what is it, Collie dear?' she broke off, as Collie came hurriedly back into the room.

'It's Katie,' said Collie, 'she's not in her room. Her bed's not been slept in and her clothes from last night aren't there. I've asked Jimmy what time he came home and he says he was back here by eleven. They were that tired at Gatehouse Park the party broke up early. Lady Gatehouse wasn't well. Katie telephoned Jimmy at ten-fifteen, he says. He picked her up and came back here, saw her into the house. He did all the things he usually does: saw her into the house, made sure the alarms were set when she'd gone up.'

'Oh, OK,' said Pauline, frowning slightly, 'don't worry, Collie. She's probably gone over to see Tom. I'll give them a ring at Gatehouse Park. They're bound to know where she is.'

*

I remember that telephone call very well. We were trooping through the hall about to go into lunch, just as they were at Balmachie. There was a bell for the telephone in the hall (because otherwise in a house that size no one would ever hear it ring) although the nearest extension was in the library.

'I'll answer that,' said Ivar, 'you lot go on in and start.'

Claudia did not appear that day until the evening, I remember, and probably would not have done so even then if the police had not wanted to talk to her.

'You're not eating your lunch,' said Cosmo, when we had all helped ourselves and were seated. 'You look ghastly, darling Lucy. Are you sickening for something, as my darling mama would have said, or did you sit up too late with naughty Tom and those illegal substances he's so fond of?'

'I'm just not hungry,' I said, gazing at my plate where slices of cold roast beef marbled with yellow fat lay amongst the baked potatoes and Camilla's ravishing herb salad.

'We were both in bed early last night, like good little girls,' said Sarah. 'Tom was in a foul mood and still is, so I can't vouch for him.' She shot her brother a dirty look which he ignored.

'Not what was it, "Won't eat, can't eat"? Have I got that the right way round?' asked Cosmo gently.

'Yes, you have,' I said, 'and, no, it's not that.'

'Something's put you off your stroke,' said Cosmo, picking up his wine glass. 'I wonder where Ivar's got to. He's been gone ages.'

I said nothing. I had woken feeling exhausted thanks to my broken night. Tom was in the depths of depression over Katie, and Sarah, in spite of her early night, seemed sombre and withdrawn.

When Ivar returned after some considerable time, he asked casually if anyone had seen Katie, looking particularly in the direction of his son.

'Nope,' said Tom, frowning. 'Why? Isn't she at Balmachie? I'm supposed to be taking her fishing this afternoon.'

'Apparently not,' said Ivar. 'That was Pauline on the phone wondering if she was here.'

'Why should she be here?' asked Tom. 'She went home last night with Jimmy as usual.'

I glanced at Ivar but he appeared not to notice.

'Perhaps she's gone off for a walk somewhere,' suggested someone else. 'It's a wonderful day.'

'That's more or less what I told Pauline,' said Ivar, 'but you know these American mothers, they're such worriers.'

'Katie would have told Pauline where she was,' said Tom. 'She knows how much she worries. I think it's strange too.'

'Well,' said Ivar shrugging, 'I'm sure she'll turn up.'

After lunch I decided to go to my room for a sleep. It was a beautiful day but I was too exhausted to enjoy it. As I was making my way along the first of the corridors that led to my room, I heard a door open and a voice, Claudia's, called out Sarah's name. When she saw me she said wearily, 'Darling Lucy, be an angel and find me Sarah. I've got Pauline on the phone making absolutely no sense at all. She can't find Katie anywhere. I said she's probably gone for a ride or something, but she's in a terrible state, talking about ringing the police, what for I can't think, the police are worse than useless. She thinks that Katie's been abducted like those other girls. She's practically hysterical.'

'She rang at lunchtime,' I said, trying not to stare. Claudia, who had clearly just woken up, looked terrible. 'She already knows Katie's not here.'

'I can't get her off the telephone,' said Claudia, 'she's in such a frightful stew. Just get me Sarah, there's a good girl.'

Sarah was sitting wrapped in an eiderdown at the jigsaw table.

'Your mother wants you,' I said. 'Katie's gone missing. Pauline's on the phone again in a panic.'

'I don't know what on earth it's got to do with me,' grumbled Sarah, 'I'm not Katie's bloody keeper. What's that fat sod of a bloody bodyguard for if he can't keep tabs on his charge?' She dragged out of the room, pulling the eiderdown behind her like a little girl in a sulk.

'She never came back last night,' said Sarah trailing back into the room. 'Her bed wasn't slept in, but Jimmy insists he saw her safe into the house as usual. But when Dan came down to start breakfast he says the alarm wasn't set.'

'Meaning?'

'Meaning, dim-bloody-wit, that she must have gone out again after she was supposed to be tucked up in her beddy-byes, that's what.'

'I see.'

'I think my naughty brother might be to blame for this particular débâcle. She's probably here somewhere sound asleep. We ought to look, search all the bedrooms. She probably just got stoned.'

'Don't be absurd,' I said, 'she isn't here. Anyway, you can look for her, I'm shattered. I've got to go and have a sleep. I didn't get a wink last night.'

'Why not?'

'Just didn't.' I shrugged, Ivar-fashion.

At about four-fifteen, Tom came back from Balmachie. When he had got there after lunch Pauline had been frantic, he said. The police had been called and arrived when he was still there. They would be coming to Gatehouse Park shortly.

'We thought you might know the answer,' said Sarah to her brother. 'You were the last one of us to see her.'

'I wish I did,' said Tom. 'Pauline's out of her mind. She's called Michael and he's flying back now.'

'Do you really think she has vanished?' asked Sarah, her eyes widening. 'I mean do you think it's serious . . . not a joke? Not just Katie wandering off and forgetting to tell anyone? I think she's been got by that man,' she added, her voice rising. 'That's what's happened.'

'It's weird that Jimmy saw her in but that the alarm was off this morning,' said Tom thoughtfully. 'Her bed wasn't slept in at all. She hadn't undressed or anything. She was still wearing what she wore to dinner. Hardly very practical gear to go shinning down a drainpipe in, if that's what she did.'

'What do you think, Luce?' Sarah turned to me.

I shrugged again. 'Search me. She's probably just playing games. I'm sure she'll turn up.'

Ivar and Lowell came back from wherever they'd been that afternoon. There was tea as usual in the library. Claudia appeared, rather to my surprise. She looked pale and exhausted but she was sober, carefully made-up and as immaculately dressed as ever. Ivar made a point of sitting next to her on the sofa, getting up and down to fill her cup and to tempt her without success to eat a piece of Camilla's delicious walnut cake. Watching him, I was aware that he had made one of those tactical behind-the-scenes rapprochements at which he was so adept. In the face of threat, the family was drawing together. Even Father Cottrell, who had never to my knowledge appeared at the tea ceremony, was present that day, happily accepting slices of cake brought to him by Sarah. I looked round and thought what a charming scene it made: the happy family at home with guests and pet priest, almost Victorian in that it seemed to uphold Mrs Thatcher's beloved 'Victorian values' so effortlessly.

At five-thirty the police arrived. A Detective Inspector Macmillan, whom I later gathered from Tom his father knew from their local Masonic lodge (Ivar was Provincial Grand Master of the district), and his sidekick, a pink-cheeked boy, Davy Carson, whom Sarah remembered from their time together at the village school, when he'd been one of the boys in the top class and she at the bottom.

'Hi Dave,' she said, as he followed his superior officer into the library.

'Hello, Sarah,' he replied, blushing deeply. I saw Boo Castlehill lean towards Cosmo and whisper something that made Cosmo's lips twitch although he never took his eyes off Ivar's face. I sensed that Cosmo was enjoying himself hugely at the sight of the police.

'Inspector,' Ivar said, getting to his feet. 'Do come in. Take a seat. You know my wife.' He introduced Inspector Macmillan to each person in the room, then offered him and Davy a cup of tea and a slice of cake.

'You've come about Katie Gresham, I take it,' Ivar continued, as the policemen sat down, awkwardly balancing their plates on their knees.

'Katie Gresham has temporarily – I hope it is temporarily – gone missing,' said Inspector Macmillan. 'She dined here last night her mother tells me, was driven home by the family chauffeur Jimmy Donald who saw her into the big house and then set the alarms before going to his own quarters, but her bed was never slept in. Mrs Gresham tells me that the clothes she was wearing, fancy ones, are not in her room either, which suggests that she may have gone out quite quickly after her return to Balmachie House. There are two factors which make this case more than just a lassie going AWOL and then being found in her boyfriend's house a few hours later or whatever. The first is that she's a big heiress who has been subject to kidnap attempts in the past; the second is that there has been a series of abductions in this part of the world, a fact I'm sure you're all aware of, and we're worried that Katie may be the latest. I'll need to talk to you all, one by one, so that I can start to get a clear picture of what her movements were last night. I hope that's all right with you, Lord Gatehouse.'

'Whatever you need, Inspector,' said Ivar, getting to his feet. 'Perhaps you'd like to use my study.'

Inspector Macmillan was very kind. (It was only much later that I learned that he had been told that I was recovering from a breakdown brought about by the stress induced by my mother's sudden, terminal illness.)

'So you're a friend of Sarah's?'

'Yes.'

'And this is your second visit?'

'Yes.'

'And you saw Katie at the dinner last night?'

'Yes.'

'Then you went upstairs with Sarah, is that right?'

'Yes.'

'And went to bed?'

'Yes.'

'And you've nothing else to tell me?'

'No,' I said. After all, what did I know? There had been a bit of a scene in the bathing hut but that was all. End of story, as Lowell would say. And in a strange way I felt I owed it to Ivar not to let on to this flunkey about our relationship. That was our secret.

'All right, Lucy, that'll do for now,' he said, making a note on his pad. 'If we need you again, which I doubt, we'll send for you. Let's hope we don't. Let's just pray that the lassie turns up safe and sound.'

'Yes, let's,' I said.

'You never know,' he said, trying but failing to conceal his yawn. I was the last interviewee and clearly the least important in his view. 'You just never know in this game. She's a wild girl, she may just be playing games. She's been hemmed in a lot and she likes to escape. Let's just hope this is all it is.'

The Gresham jet landed at Prestwick airport at midnight, by which time Katie had been missing for about twenty-four hours. Someone had alerted the press and they were out in force waiting for Michael. Being Michael, he gave a press conference although he was exhausted and it was the middle of the night. Even in moments of extremity Michael always knew what was expected of him and did his best to provide it.

The *Telegraph*'s northern edition which was printed in Manchester was held so that Michael could appear on the front

page: KATIE COME HOME: ROCK STAR MAKES IMPAS-
SIONED PLEA FOR RETURN OF LOST CHILD. There was
a photograph of Michael smoking, looking exhausted but as
glamorous as ever, and one of Katie, tanned and slender,
lounging on the verandah of the bathing hut the day before
her birthday ball.

By the next afternoon, the press were camped all over
the Balmachie estate as well as at Gatehouse Park. The old-
fashioned bell in its niche next to the great front door tolled
all morning with journalists wanting pictures and statements.
At midday Ivar went outside to talk to the assembled throng
and to offer food and drink and the use of a lavatory to those
who wanted it. He was always very professional in his dealings
with the press: polite, apparently eager to please, quick to laugh
and, on this occasion, suitably sombre. He was interviewed on
the six o'clock news, after Michael and the chief constable
(who I remembered had shot grouse on the Gatehouse moor
in August), to talk about the disappearance in his capacity as
great family friend.

If he came back to my room the next night, I wouldn't have
known. I had taken the precaution of bunking up with Sarah
as we had done when I first went to Gatehouse Park. What
I had seen frightened me sufficiently to break the spell. Ivar
scared me. I wanted out.

By the time we went back to school a day or so later,
the press interest in the story had changed direction and the
disappearance of Katie Gresham had begun to be linked to
the abductions of the other girls in that part of southern
Scotland. Pauline Gresham offered £100,000 to anyone who
knew anything about the fate of her daughter but nobody
came forward, although there were one or two sightings in
the usual places: a shopping mall on Merseyside, a bowling
alley in Wigan. Katie, it seemed, had vanished without trace.

Sarah, rather than I, was the focus of much interest at school.
I was only a hanger-on, after all, an extra: Sarah's house and
Sarah's parents and Sarah's family featured constantly that

season in the run-up to Christmas, particularly when Davina announced her engagement to Waldy Harcourt on December 15th. The brief friendship I had enjoyed with Sarah was waning. She withdrew from me and I from her. Once, when I asked her what she thought had happened to Katie she said she imagined that the abductor had got her. What else could have happened? Where the hell else could she have gone? She knew of her father's relationship with Katie but chose, like Tom, and like me, to say nothing. Tom, she said, had come to the same conclusion. I knew too much and she somehow knew that I knew about her sexual involvement with her father; besides which, I could hardly broach such a sensitive subject without mentioning exactly how I had come by my information. During the short time I spent in such close proximity to the Gatehouse family it seemed that I had become alarmingly like them. We were all of us joined together in a conspiracy of silence.

My mother died in hospital on St Stephen's Day, December 26th. On the second day of the New Year she was cremated and all that remained of her was a handful of dust. Earl and Countess Gatehouse sent a huge, tasteful wreath from some chic florist in Sloane Street. Mac and I scattered her ashes in the azalea grove at Wickenden.

When the man, who later became known as the Falkirk Abductor, Jock Kettle, was caught quite by chance in a vehicle check outside Ayr four months after Katie's disappearance, he confessed to the police that he had indeed abducted and murdered Katie Gresham in October 1979 and buried her body in moorland north of Newton Stewart. When the police looked in the indicated place they found the very badly decomposed remains of a girl's body, but what they did not say – even to Pauline and Michael Gresham – was that the body was not that of Katie Gresham. The public outcry was so great and the pressure to end the mystery so intense that a decision was taken at the highest level to agree with Kettle that the remains were those of Katie. I remember how relieved I felt when I heard this news during the spring term at Wickenden and how guilty I felt about my relief. But I was off the hook. Official. There was a funeral (which I did not attend), rows of Milos, Greshams and Anwoths in black and pearls (with Michael's dark glasses adding a Mafia note), a public laying to rest, a Katie Gresham Memorial Fund (an offshoot of the Milo Foundation) which made donations to various trendy touchy-feely causes.

It was all over, and with it that part of my life, or so it seemed.

PART TWO

May–June 1998

The headline caught Lucy's eye as she walked out of Lincoln's Inn Fields into Kingsway. FALKIRK ABDUCTOR RECANTS: KILLER DENIES GRESHAM MURDER ON DEATHBED.

Lucy looked away and then back again towards the *Evening Standard* booth with its diagonal stripes in orange and white, hoping that she had somehow imagined what she thought she had read. But it was still there when she looked again. For a second she thought she might pass out but she managed to pull herself together by doing a breathing exercise learned in the trendy ante-natal classes she had attended in Notting Hill Gate before she had given birth to Maud, who was now eight.

And there was a taxi. She raised an arm and the driver indicated left, pulling to a halt directly in front of her.

'Where to, love?'

'The Coburg, please,' said Lucy, sitting back in her seat and getting out her mobile phone in order to discourage conversation. She desperately needed time to think and therefore dialled her own voice-mail which would confuse Maggie, her assistant, but too bad.

She was going to have lunch with a potential client, a Polish count domiciled in Britain for work purposes, whose wife wanted to divorce him for big bucks. The count was mad keen to get her to represent him but Lucy wasn't sure she had the time which only made the count, who was used to getting what he wanted, all the more keen. He had taken her out to dinner at Le Caprice and now he wanted to lunch her at the grandest and most discreet of London's stuffier establishments. It wouldn't surprise her if the count made a pass at her, but she had decided that if he did she definitely would not find the time to deal with his tedious divorce with all its usual constituents of grasping ex-wives, spoilt-brat children, too many houses, too much money.

Divorce was Lucy's forte: she was one of an élite squad of divorce lawyers, a group numbering not more than a dozen who dealt with the high-profile divorces of pop stars, Eurotrash, minor royalty, not to mention members of the British aristocracy. She had heard and had managed to forget that she had heard last week that Tom Creetown was seeking a divorce from his Anglo-German wife Caroline, on what grounds she couldn't quite remember; some tedious tale of adultery and betrayal, no doubt, although she was slightly surprised to hear that Tom, of all people, should find himself in the divorce courts. She had known someone who had been up at Cambridge with Tom where he had become so devout that he had begun, or so the story went, to consider the priesthood for himself until his father had got wind of the fact and swiftly disabused him of the notion. The friend, with the humorous disbelief of the liberal atheist, had quoted Tom's sister Sarah: 'He has to breed: the priesthood is for spares.'

That note of realism had been authentic Sarah all right, Lucy remembered thinking. Sarah's face was liberally sprinkled throughout the fashionable press these days in much the same way as her mother's had once been; she was here, there and everywhere, known by some as 'the dancing duchess'; no opening, no display of pickled animals, no weird atelier party was truly complete without the attendance of Sarah who would arrive together with the sheep on a motorbike. The sheep's grandfather, the dribbling duke, had died several years ago and this was followed by the shock death of the sheep's father two years later in an avalanche at Gstaad; Sarah, to her obvious delight, had become a duchess at an unusually early age. The Annans were seriously rich grown-up, well-managed, very old money: there were houses everywhere from London to Mustique to Annan House, the enormous Glamis-like pile in Wigtownshire, where the Scottish country life that Sarah had once affected to loathe went on these days with a vengeance: houseparties, reeling parties, shooting parties, fancy dress parties: 'Tartan with Attitude' as *Vogue* had famously dubbed it in a sycophantic piece on the glamour of the Annans that Lucy had read only last week.

It all looked so wonderful: Tom married to the Anglo-German Caroline with a couple of boys, Louise parcelled off to Sir Peverel Jardine, an elderly Ayrshire landowner whose family had made a fortune a century before from shipping and cotton; they apparently had produced several children in quick succession. Davina was married to Waldy Harcourt (also a Catholic) with several children. Only Sarah was without, but she was still young. There was plenty of time. Or was that, Lucy wondered, the kind of thing that people with children invariably thought or said about those without, a remark that appeared comforting but was in fact rather callous.

Lucy would have liked another child herself but lately that had begun to look less and less likely because of Simon's absences in Brussels that were getting longer and longer. She remembered reading somewhere that about fifty per cent of so-called 'infertility' was due to the fact that the couple in question didn't make love enough, which was certainly true in her own case, she thought sadly. The chill in her own marriage, caused by overwork on both sides, made her reflect how solitary her life could so easily become without family. In some ways, her state of mind lately had been the same as it was when she was an undergraduate at Oxford: self-contained, rather lonely, papering over the cracks with hard work. If it weren't for Maud, Lucy thought, she might just freeze over altogether. Nothing in her life seemed to be 'fun' any more. Unlike Sarah, whose whole life appeared to consist only of 'fun'. Lucy, however, in her role as expert dissector of marriages, wondered how much was truly fun with Sarah and how much a frantic bid to overcome the gruesome wounds of her childhood. When Lucy allowed herself to think back to that period and what Ivar had done to her, she realized that she had had an exceptionally lucky escape. The emotional damage done had been minimal or had somehow become subsumed into the fallout surrounding her mother's death and the disappearance and death of Katie Gresham. That had been a truly terrible thing, so terrible that it towered over everything else: that someone so bold and beautiful could just vanish had seemed unbelievable; and until the Falkirk Abductor had confessed to the killing, Lucy had felt the most terrible guilt: should she have mentioned to the police the row she witnessed or not? Was Ivar in some way involved? Was Ivar capable of such an action? There was a huge difference between having a dreadful temper and actually killing someone. And she was not sure that she thought Ivar was capable of that; capable of hitting, perhaps, but not killing. Or was there a very thin line between the two, so that one could lead on to the other? Clearly there was – she saw it all the time in her own line of work. But then the disappearance of Katie had become a part of the dreadful reputation of that man Kettle. Until today, the death of Katie Gresham had long been relegated to a place in her mind similar to the manner in which nuclear waste is dumped in the ocean floor in sealed containers: out of sight and as much out of mind as she could manage. She had a horrible feeling all that was about to change.

During the intervening years Ivar's public reputation had, if anything, grown. There had been no divorce, although amongst their circle it was known that he and Claudia scarcely spoke. They had always kept separate rooms, now they kept separate lives. Claudia lived quietly at Gatehouse Park, spending most of her time painting and walking. Every now and again she vanished from sight altogether into The Priory but she lived such a quiet life that nobody really noticed. The parties of the old days at Gatehouse Park were a thing of the past; the Annans were now the big party givers and goers of the family, and although Ivar always attended any bash at Annan House Claudia was seen there in public only rarely. Ivar was also a good deal in London attending to his ministerial duties and seeing to his business affairs, not to mention the religious side of his life which included at least one trip a year to Lourdes; in the past year there had also been a journey to that famous shrine in Yugoslavia whose name she could never remember, as well as an audience with the Holy Father in Rome with Claudia accompanying him, a rare outing together. A picture of them, taken by a passing photographer, had appeared in *Hello!* magazine: Ivar wearing an Eddie suit of incomparable cut with his arm companionably round Claudia's shoulders and Claudia herself Vatican-chic in ankle-length Dior with her mother-in-law's mantilla draped becomingly over her head and shoulders. Looking at that photograph Lucy was struck for the umpteenth time by Ivar's apparently casual ability to get things just right, although of course she knew perfectly well that it was not as random as it seemed: the photographer would have been primed just as Claudia had been.

However, over the years, particularly since she had become so successful in her own field, it had come to Lucy's exceedingly unwilling attention that there had been other incidents involving Ivar and his treatment of young girls. One girl, the daughter of the chairman of a large public company, had consulted a lawyer friend of Lucy's (a girl she had known slightly at school but become friendly with when they were up at Oxford), but had then decided not to press charges.

'Much as it pains me to say so,' Dilly told Lucy, 'I told her not to go ahead. He's too powerful even for a girl who's the daughter of somebody pretty formidable, and as you know yourself the law is still biased in these cases; the judges all think the girl is a schemer who asked for it. God help us all, I say.'

'You couldn't have done anything else,' said Lucy, 'he's a formidable enemy. Had a lot of practice. He'd have made mincemeat of her or his lawyer would.'

'You were friendly with Sarah Anwoth at school, I seem to remember,' said Dilly. 'Do you ever see her nowadays?'

'Not really,' said Lucy. 'She lives on a different planet to the likes of us wage-slaves. She's a duchess now, you know, she made an arranged marriage. Although strangely enough she's come to live practically next-door to me in London, so I have seen her once or twice.'

'But didn't you keep in touch after school?'

'We went our different ways. I went to university, I had my living to earn, Sarah didn't; she went to parties, met a lot of people, married a duke.'

'Were you envious?'

'I was never a member of Sarah's world.'

'What do you mean? You stayed at their house, didn't you?'

'Yes, but very much as a pensioner, like some poor relation in a Russian novel.'

'Good heavens, Lucy,' exclaimed Dilly, 'you really sound as if you minded. I always think of you as such an independent person who wouldn't give a shit about all that class stuff.'

'I don't,' Lucy said. It was a lie of course. She knew perfectly well that one of the reasons she had chosen her particular line of work was its contact with the rich and famous. She enjoyed the power that sorting out the chaos in their lives bestowed upon her, although she would never have admitted it.

Sarah and Sandy Annan had recently bought a house in Clarendon Road, Notting Hill Gate, very near Lucy and Simon. Lucy, returning late from the office, would see Sarah on her way out for the night zooming off on the bike with Sandy or, if the occasion were grand rather than funky, being driven by her husband in his Aston Martin, Sandy sharing with Prince Charles a passion for these cars. Sarah had forced Sandy to pull over for a chat on their way out only a couple of days before in spite of the fact that they were already late for their party. Lucy, in theory unwilling to make contact, found herself absurdly glad to see Sarah again after so long. Why waste an old friendship, she asked herself? She was quite surprised to find how fond she was of Sarah, who appeared to have changed very little if at all.

'Bloody weird that we should be neighbours,' Sarah had said, 'but you'll just have to put up with us. I want you to come to supper. I'll ring you.'

'I'd love that,' said Lucy. 'Have you got my number?'

'No,' said Sarah, as the car pulled away, 'but I'll find it. *Ciao, bella!*'

'I see her mug staring at me almost every time I open a newspaper or a magazine,' Dilly was saying. 'Old Ivar Gatehouse used to be a publicity hog like that although you don't see so much of him these days. He obviously has a predilection for young flesh, wouldn't you say? Lara told me she was one of millions. Rather dangerous for a man in his position I should have thought, especially in our current climate of anti-sleaze.'

'The public face and the private one don't always match,' said Lucy. 'You of all people shouldn't find that fact particularly surprising.'

'You were there when the Gresham girl vanished, I remember now,' said Dilly thoughtfully. 'You were staying at Gatehouse Park, weren't you? That must have been awful.'

'I never think about it,' said Lucy, glancing at her watch. 'They caught him and that was the end of it.'

'Awful for the Greshams though. It never ends for the parents of the victims, you know. They go on suffering until they die themselves.'

'I must go,' said Lucy, signalling to the waiter that she wanted the bill. 'I have to be up very early in the morning. The nanny's sick and Simon's in Brussels, as usual, so no back-up.'

'How is Simon? We haven't talked about him at all.'

'He's fine,' said Lucy, 'except that I never see him.'

They had been married for eight years, together for ten, since

Lucy's twenty-fifth birthday, when her good friend, Andrew, whom she had also been at university with, had insisted on dragging her to a ball at Lincoln's Inn saying that he had to be seen to be there and that it would help if he had a pretty girl on his arm. Simon had been of their party and she had been attracted to him at once although she pretended not to be. He was five years older than her and tipped as one of the coming young men in his chambers. The next day he had called her at the office although she did not recall telling him which firm she worked for.

'Do you like theatre?' he had asked.

'Love it. Why?'

'I've got a couple of tickets for *Uncle Vanya* for tomorrow night. Can you come?'

'Let me check,' she said. 'I'll call you back. How did you know where I worked?'

'I asked Andrew.'

'I see.'

They had gone to *Uncle Vanya* and then out to dinner afterwards, at an Italian restaurant where Simon was known, near his flat in Tite Street, a nice unpretentious place where the waiters were civil but did not fawn and the food was simple and delicious. Simon was clever and funny but also grave. She liked his seriousness which made a good foil to his cynicism. They talked until the politeness of the waiters wore thin and chairs began to be stacked on tables around them. Simon found her a taxi and put her in it without jumping on her. She liked that too. These things had to be done properly. The next night he took her out again and they went to another Italian restaurant near Lucy's flat in Brook Green. This time Simon stayed the night.

At Christmas she went home with him to the Devon village where his mother lived. It was the end of her lonely Christmases – even the ones spent with Nigel and Norah and her Auntie Jenny and the kids had seemed lonely – it was family, real family at last, the kind she had dreamed of. There were two elder brothers with wives and children who farmed in the area and welcomed Lucy with open arms. At last she felt she belonged somewhere and fell in love with the deep countryside, the steep-sided coombes, the way the church towers appeared through the trees. A year and a half later they were married in Chelsea Register Office and stood on the same steps to have their photograph taken that Michael and Pauline Gresham had appeared on so long ago. Once, a year or so ago, at a party at the Ritz to which they had been asked by a corporate client of Simon's, Lucy saw Ivar coming towards them as they walked along the corridor into the party. There was nowhere to run to. She and Simon were holding hands and laughing about something. As they drew level Lucy found herself desperately trying to think of something to say but instead Ivar, ever master of the moment, glanced at her coldly as if she were scarcely worthy of his attention, and passed on.

'Remind me of who that person was,' said Simon when Ivar had gone.

'Ivar Gatehouse.'

'He knew you,' said Simon, 'and yet he didn't speak. Why was that?'

There were times when she cursed her husband's perspicacity although it was one of the things about him that she loved dearly.

'I don't know,' she said unwillingly.

'Yes you do. You weren't one of his many conquests, were you?'

'Why do you ask?'

'I know that look and, besides, I have a pupil, a very pretty girl called Clara Holland, who told me that old man Gatehouse made a pass at her not so long ago. Her father has some connection with him, I forget what. She sat next to him at dinner and he was all over her like a rash.'

'What did she do?'

'Removed his wandering hand as firmly as a Norland nanny, and moved herself at the first opportunity. How did you cope?'

'With what?'

'With Ivar Gatehouse.'

'Can we talk about it later?'

As Lucy was taking off her make-up in the bathroom off their bedroom later on that night Simon came up behind her in the mirror.

'I want to know about you and Ivar Gatehouse,' he said.

Lucy's eyes met his. 'There's nothing much to tell. I was at school with Sarah, his youngest daughter, the one who married the Duke of Annan, and I stayed at Gatehouse Park a few times. That's all there is to it.'

'But why doesn't he greet you like a long-lost friend of his daughter's? Why did he blank you?'

'Because he's a rude bastard, I suppose.'

'Or because you rejected him. Come on, Luce. I'm intrigued by your hesitation over this.'

Lucy turned to face him. 'It was a long time ago,' she said. 'I was very young and inexperienced and, yes, he did make a pass at me, and, yes, I did reject him. He didn't like it very much. That's why he blanked me tonight.'

'Why did you never tell me?'

'Because it was a long time ago. I'd forgotten myself.'

'How old were you?'

'About sixteen and not very confident. It was the first time I'd been there. The house intimidated me and so did the company. I wasn't used to that sort of life: top civil servants, grand aristocrats, Cosmo Nevele, the American ambassador, and me. Lucy from nowhere.'

The great secret of lying, she knew, was to mix in some truth along with the lies so that it sounded convincing without being completely over the top.

'What a bastard,' he said, 'what an abuse of hospitality. It's the sort of behaviour that makes one want to man the barricades, a true abuse of privilege; and there he is swanning about, leader of the House of Lords, Knight of Malta, OM, you name it. I'm amazed he hasn't been outed by some feminist group.'

'He's an operator,' said Lucy, 'he thinks he's got it all sewn up. I suppose he has really.'

'One day, sooner or later, he'll make a mistake,' said Simon. 'They always do in the end in my experience. But wasn't it about the time the Gresham girl vanished? They were neighbours of the Gatehouses, weren't they? I remember now. She went missing and then that serial killer, the Falkirk Abductor, owned up to having been responsible for her death too. Did you know her?'

'Very slightly,' said Lucy, reaching for another piece of cotton wool.

'And you never told me. We've been married for some years and I didn't even know you knew the Gatehouses, let alone that poor girl. You have a very secretive side to you, Luce, you know that, don't you? You can conceal things other women would have blabbed out years ago.'

'For a start you shouldn't have married a lawyer,' said Lucy. 'I'm not a "blabber" as you so gracefully put it and it was a very long time ago. My mother died shortly afterwards,' she added. 'That tended to obliterate what had gone before.'

'I suppose it would,' he said thoughtfully, 'but I'm still amazed you never told me about it. It's like not owning up to having known Profumo or something.'

'Don't exaggerate,' said Lucy, putting her head on his shoulder.

Lucy asked the cabbie to drop her in Berkeley Street as she was slightly early. Against her better judgement she bought a copy of the *Evening Standard*, feeling the need to know so strongly that her hand trembled as she handed over the money and took the newspaper from the vendor. She walked on into Berkeley Square gardens and sat down on a bench. The cover photograph to go with the headline was of Katie; it was the same picture of her at the bathing hut that had been used when she vanished; nearly twenty years later she was still stunningly beautiful; because she was only wearing a bikini there were no clothes to date and the photograph could have been taken yesterday. Lucy's heart lurched in sorrow and in apprehension as she began to read the piece.

Jock Kettle, the Falkirk Abductor, had confessed on his deathbed to the prison chaplain that he had not murdered Katie Gresham after all; the others, yes, the Gresham girl, no. She was a stain on someone else's conscience, not his. Why, asked the reporter, had he wanted to claim this death as his? The chaplain said that it had been part of Kettle's revenge to confuse and mislead the police into thinking that he had been responsible. So who was responsible, asked the reporter, what would happen now? Would the police start to look for the person who was responsible? Another manhunt in south-west Scotland?

'Without a body,' said the Procurator Fiscal for Dumfries and Galloway, a woman named Stella Atkins, 'there is very little we can do although we will naturally look into the affair. Questions will be asked about how the original investigation was conducted.'

'So the whole affair will be comprehensively re-investigated, is that what you're saying?'

'In essence, yes,' said Stella Atkins. 'I think we owe that to Michael and Pauline Gresham.'

Pauline Gresham, thought Lucy, poor, poor Pauline. After Katie had vanished, Lucy had written a letter of sympathy to Pauline and had received a prompt, grateful letter in response, offering condolences for Lucy's own loss. Lucy had never quite got over Pauline's emotional generosity. And now, she wondered, what must Pauline be feeling? What a horrible business. And if not the Falkirk Abductor, who was guilty? Was it, after all, Ivar Gatehouse? She had no wish, none at all, to have to disinter her guilt about what she had seen. *The only thing necessary*, said the motto in the school hall at Wickenden, *for the triumph of evil is for good men to do nothing*.

The count, whose name was Nicholas, had been brought up

in England. He had attended a Catholic public school and then Cambridge where he had achieved a first in history at Peterhouse. Intending to make money he had then gone into the City. He wanted to become a merchant prince as rapidly as possible and to a large extent he had succeeded in his aim. He had married well and (he thought) carefully: the girl, Isabella, was the daughter of an English Catholic earl (not a recusant family but the descendants of an Oxford Movement conversion in the nineteenth century) and like many Catholic girls of her kind had behaved quite badly here and there before she met Nicky and settled down into marriage and motherhood; as a couple they had an understated foreign kind of chic in their cashmere sweaters and tweeds; the children, two girls, wore loden coats with silver buttons sent by Nicky's mother who lived in Budapest and button-shoes in maroon leather made by Startrite which also came in sky-blue and palest pink for parties. They had a house in Kensington Square with a blue plaque on the outside and a country cottage near Fonthill in Wiltshire. There were also the Polish estates which were Nicky's next project, or had been before Isabella had begun an affair with her personal trainer.

This lackey, as Nicky thought of him (one of the advantages of being a foreigner in England was that one need pay no attention whatsoever to the Major/Blair crap about a 'classless' society. No one in their right minds wanted such a thing anyway) had entered Isabella's life on the recommendation of a friend and had begun to call each morning at some ungodly hour to take Isabella jogging in Kensington Gardens. Nicky, in a hurry to get to work, had paid little attention to the hulk at the gate wearing those ghastly clothes, whose name was Rod or Bod, until he was forced to by Isabella's demand for a divorce. Nicky had tried to laugh her out of it, then he had tried charm; neither had worked.

His next response was to try fear. He said that she would have to leave the house without the children if that's what she wanted. Let Bod support her. Isabella refused point-blank to leave. He suspected she had been taking advice from a lawyer. A colleague at his firm, Paderewski Asset Management (or PAM as it was more commonly known), suggested the firm of Lawrence Scanning & Co as being particularly good at managing difficult, potentially high-profile divorces. Two names were suggested: Charles Butcher and Lucy Diamond. Butcher was the titular head of the family department but Diamond was the crown princess. It was Diamond who had handled the recent scandalous divorce of a male member of the royal family with tact, good humour and great good sense, so much so that the other side had, or so the rumour went, sent flowers when matters were completed. She'd even managed to keep out of the newspapers the fact that the royal prince was a homosexual and a porphyriac. The wife, a Eurotrash 'princess' (descended on her mother's side from the upstart Bonaparte) had been a scandal-seeking whore who enjoyed taking her clothes off in public, but even she had been tamed and soothed by Diamond's ability to strike a deal that suited both sides.

Nicky fervently hoped she would help him do such a deal with Isabella. If it got out at work that his wife was fucking one of the servants he would look like a fool. People would talk. He could not abide the thought of being laughed at.

Lucy left her newspaper on the bench in the gardens of Berkeley Square. The report said that Jock Kettle had died last week, but not before he had signed a last confession retracting his guilt in the Gresham case. Quite how the report had reached the newspapers was not clear, but presumably someone in the prison or the police had leaked the story to the press. The police would have egg on their faces but would no doubt use the excuse that the case was nearly twenty years old and that all the officers involved were now either dead or long retired and therefore beyond reach. Briefly, Lucy allowed herself to remember Inspector Macmillan's perfunctory questioning of her so long ago in Ivar's study at Gatehouse Park. He had seemed so unconcerned by the whole thing, so calm. With this new revelation the case would be reopened, but without a body, as the Procurator Fiscal had said, the police had precious little to go on, especially after nearly twenty years. The trail had gone cold years ago.

'Count Paderewski is in the bar, Miss Diamond. Would you like me to show you where that is?' asked the flunkey who appeared as Lucy made her way into the hallway.

'No thanks,' said Lucy, 'I know the way.'

He too was reading a copy of the *Evening Standard* at his table when she came in, but he thrust it aside and strode across the room to greet her with a kiss on both cheeks.

'Lucy, my dear, how nice. Can I get you a drink?'

'No thanks,' said Lucy. 'Just some mineral water or orange juice, thank you.'

'Oh come on,' said Nicky, 'surely one glass of champagne won't hurt?'

'I don't drink at lunchtime, Nicky, it makes me fall asleep in the afternoon just when I'm supposed to be paying attention.'

'Orange juice it will have to be then.'

He sounded regretful, as if this meeting was to have been some kind of an assignation rather than a business meeting to discuss what was to be done about his deteriorating personal situation.

'I'm horrified to see that the Gresham case is to be reopened,' said Nicky as they sat down. 'That will be terrible for Pauline. Truly terrible.'

Lucy glanced at him in surprise. 'Do you know her?'

'She's a cousin on my mother's side, the Hungarian side. My mother was a Milo, a niece of Lewis Milo's. Sadly, the money wasn't distributed amongst the family. It's now a charitable trust, with an HQ in New York, and a large staff to distribute and protect it. Maddening really, we could have done with some of those millions ourselves.'

'I always heard that the Milo money was tainted, so maybe it's poetic justice.'

'There is nothing poetic, my dear Lucy, about having money

165

in your family which you know you will never get your hands on.'

'Quite,' said Lucy, trying not to smile. 'I didn't know the Milos had grand relations like you, Nicky.'

'I know. So much money always seems indecent to the English. So they make the family *nouveau*. Well, in this case it's not true. The family is old but the money is new. Not that the money has helped Pauline particularly. In a way it's been a bit of a curse. I almost think it would have been better if that dreadful man, Kettle, had kept his mouth shut. What good will it do now for Pauline to know that the case is still unsolved?'

'I couldn't agree more,' said Lucy, not meeting his glance. Somewhere inside she felt a pang, a faint tremor of hysteria, like the pre-shocks of an impending earthquake.

'But who else could have done it?' Nicky was saying.

'We don't know that she was actually murdered,' Lucy said. 'Vanishing isn't quite the same thing, you know.'

'That's the lawyer talking,' said Nicky. 'Of course she was murdered, but it's odd that there was never any kind of a ransom demand; you would have thought that would have been the first thing whoever took her would do.'

Lucy shook her head. 'These stories in the press are always misleading. That man Kettle, the abductor, was probably lying. He probably did kill her and he's just saying he didn't to cause trouble.'

'Why would he do that?'

Lucy shrugged. 'You tell me.'

A waiter handed them menus. They ordered and went into the dining-room which was half full. At a table by a pillar a man turned in his chair as Lucy followed Nicky in. It was Tom Creetown. Briefly their eyes met. He waved at Lucy who nodded formally as if she scarcely knew who he was. She made no effort to cross the room to his table. Tom turned away as the man sitting opposite him said something and also glanced with interest at Lucy and her companion.

'That's Nicky Paderewski,' said the man Tom was lunching

with. 'Who's that good-looking girl he's got with him? I'd heard his marriage had gone belly up but it's a bit soon to be lunching a stunner like that wouldn't you say?'

'She is a good-looking girl,' said Tom, 'but that's not why he's lunching her, I suspect. That's Lucy Diamond.'

'Ah! *The* Lucy Diamond, you mean? The one who did Prince John's divorce?'

'That's the one,' said Tom. 'She's very good at her job, so they say.'

'Must be if Paderewski's consulting her. He's a tight bastard, if you'll forgive my French. His wife's run off with her personal trainer, so Jenny tells me. They sit on a committee together to raise money for street children in Vietnam.'

'Caroline's involved with that too,' said Tom.

He wanted very much to turn round and look at Lucy but decided against it. She had looked so pretty but awfully severe when she came in with that shit Paderewski. He also registered the fact that she had barely acknowledged him, but that could be because she was working. It could also be, Tom admitted to himself, because she did not wish to revive their friendship, but he hoped it was not. Any acquaintance now would be a direct link with that appalling period when Katie had gone missing and the four-month wait that followed until her body had been exhumed from the Jardine-Thwaites' land north of Newton Stewart. He had been in his last year of school then; somehow, he never really knew how, he had passed his A-levels and got the grades he needed to stay on the extra half for the Oxbridge entrance examinations.

He knew that Lucy's mother had died at Christmas, two months after Katie had disappeared. To his shame he had never written. There had seemed no point in anything at that time with the horror of Katie hanging over them all. It had seemed impossible that someone you loved and had known all your life could just vanish. There had been that and so many other things to try to cope with. The way his father had nearly cracked up: the tears, the recriminations; to be a teenager and to have to not only forgive your father for trying to poach your girlfriend but also to listen to his guilt, his tears, his longing for forgiveness had made Tom feel physically sick. He had forgiven him or tried to, but it had made him go numb. For a while he hadn't wanted any feelings at all, he had just wanted to be left alone.

'Ghastly about the Gresham thing, isn't it?' his companion was saying. 'I suppose the police notified your family that the case has been reopened . . .'

'What?' said Tom. 'What did you say?'

'Oh Lord! Have I put my foot in it? But it's the headline in the early edition of the *Standard*. I imagined you knew all about it.'

'Have you got a copy?' Tom asked, unable to contain himself.

'No.'

'I'll be back in a minute.'

Lucy looked up as Tom dashed out of the dining-room. Again, she felt a pang of foreboding mingled with something else she couldn't quite identify. Her life and her work suddenly seemed dear-achieved and exceptionally precious. She thought of Maud, whom she had dropped at school that morning wearing her summer uniform of boater and blazer, and the way the little girl had run up the steps of the school without even saying goodbye, barely pausing to greet the teacher on duty at the door. It had been a moment of profound satisfaction to see her child so happy.

'Lucy, you have to help me,' Nicky Paderewski was saying. 'My wife won't leave our house, but she wants to divorce me to marry this astonishing person. I think she would like me to leave in order that she can move her lover into *my* house with *my* children.'

'I really have a lot on my plate at the moment,' said Lucy. 'You would have to deal with my next-in-command. I would oversee the case, but Maggie would do most of the basic work. Of course there's always Charles. He's winding down a bit these days, he may be able to take you on.'

'But I want you,' said Nicky pitifully. He didn't see why she would act for one of those Hanoverian upstarts and not for him. His ancestors had been ennobled by Charlemagne and in the nineteenth century genealogists had traced the family to the legendary priest-kings of Wodz who had emerged from the steppe centuries before Christ, whom the Paderewskis had always considered something of a johnny-come-lately.

'Do you really want a divorce?'

'No, of course not. I'm a Catholic for a start. It's my wife who wants a divorce.'

'She may just be trying to attract your attention.'

'Funny way of going about it.'

'Look, Nicky,' said Lucy earnestly, 'woo her back. She's probably just bored. You're busy, you keep long hours, you're often late home. She resents it. She doesn't work so she's bored and then distracted.'

'She has the children,' said Nicky.

'They're at school. She wants something for herself. Take her out to dinner somewhere wonderful. Pay her attention. Buy her things. Go on holiday together somewhere exotic, the Bahamas, Mauritius. Encourage her to do something intellectual. She's probably highly intelligent but bored.'

Having too much money was a trap, she had seen it so often: bored, empty-headed, spoilt women wasting their lives playing tennis, lunching in Daphne's or having an affair to while away the time.

'It'll cost a fortune,' said Nicky in a less petulant voice. It flattered him to think that Lucy thought Isabella highly intelligent, as if he had owned something precious for a long time but had only just noticed its value.

'Not as much as I'll cost you,' replied Lucy. 'I'm very expensive, so is Charlie.'

'Did you advise Prince John to try to win back Princess Ariane?'

'Certainly not. Short, sharp and to the point was what was required in their case. I told him to give her as large a settlement as possible with a fierce gagging clause, so that she would quickly attract a new suitor and vanish back into Euroland where she came from. The most important thing was to stop her giving those interviews to *Loaded* and *Men Only*. She was even contemplating the *Playboy* centrefold. The Family was having a fit. The worst thing is to leave a woman like that without enough money. Look at Fergie, for God's sake. Ariane was just a foreign version, but malicious with it. She knew exactly how much trouble she could make.'

Back in her office later that afternoon, Lucy found the conjunction of the day's events had unsettled her badly. The settled, solid surface of her life had shifted slightly; she had read somewhere that in China these days they advised people in earthquake zones to pay attention to the behaviour of their animals, as beasts were known to be able to sense the coming cataclysm. Was she in the same condition, she wondered, as domestic beasts in a remote province of China, sensing the thinness of the earth's crust, feeling the tremors of some terrible disaster yet to happen?

She was still in the office at 6 p.m. Simon was away and Maud was spending the night with a schoolfriend. The story was the second item on the news after some scandal to do with one of Blair's cabinet ministers. The BBC had a reporter outside the grim high-security jail where Kettle had spent the last twenty or so years. The reporter described how the Falkirk Abductor had confessed to the prison chaplain and then signed a typed statement before dying. Stella Atkins, the Procurator Fiscal, then made an appearance. The investigation would be by police under the general direction of the independent Procurator Fiscal. She was a formidable-looking Scotswoman in her mid-to-late forties, Lucy guessed. She said there was no point in not admitting that a terrible blunder had been made twenty years ago but she swore that the case would be reopened and prosecuted with dispatch. They were still trying to discover the identity of the body Kettle had claimed was that of Katie

Gresham. Lucy believed her, but at the same time wondered with a lawyer's cynicism what on earth they hoped to achieve without a body.

When Simon rang her much later from his hotel room in Brussels, she waited for him to mention it, assuming that he would have seen something about it in the news, but when he didn't she decided she wouldn't either. However, when she put the phone down she realized she had wanted to talk to Simon about it all, wanted his comfort, and that by not being frank with him she had added to the growing distance between them. She thought of calling him back but he was tired as was she and so she didn't.

Ten days later Lucy was once again working late in her office when her private line rang. Only her husband and her daughter's school had this number although she occasionally gave it out to important clients such as Prince John or the cabinet minister last year who had had such a messy divorce with the tabloid press camped out on her doorstep every morning.

'Lucy, it's Tom, Tom Creetown.'

'Tom,' she said flatly. 'How did you get this number? It's my private line.'

'Prince John gave it to me. We were at the same college at Cambridge and we've been friends ever since. He told me you were a wonder when it came to unravelling his marriage to the frightful Ariane. He said you were the only person who ever managed to tame her.'

'That's very kind of him, Tom, but you didn't ring me up to tell me how well I handled the latest divorce in our glorious royal family.'

'I need your help. My wife, Caroline, wants a divorce –'

'There are plenty of other good lawyers for your kind of divorce,' said Lucy. 'I can give you names. Have you got a pen?'

'Lucy, listen to me. It's you I want.'

'They all say that.'

'No, truly. Caroline is tricky; she's a drunk for a start, just like my mother. You see I can say these things to you because you know us. I can trust you.'

'Tom, you can trust any good lawyer. We're all brilliant in the confessional, we have to be, but I'm not the person you need.'

'No, listen, Lucy, there's more. In the early days of our marriage my father made a move on Caroline. At the time she took it as a joke, shrugged it off . . . we laughed about it together, but now she says she'll expose him if I don't give her exactly what she wants.'

'Can't Lowell see to her? I notice he's been booted upstairs to join your father in the Lords.'

'Dear old Lowell, I don't want to drag him into this. He's Pa's henchman, totally loyal and all that; what Caroline is saying would kill him. It can't be Lowell but I don't want to drag in an outsider. You're not an outsider, Lucy, you're one of us. You must understand what I'm saying.'

'I do understand what you're saying and I am declining,' said Lucy. 'It would be unprofessional. Sorry, Tom.'

'Please, Lucy. Please just meet me to discuss it.'

'What's happening with the Gresham thing?'

She hadn't meant to ask. She knew it was fatal to appear to be interested, but she couldn't help herself. And there had been no one she could discuss it all with. Simon had come back for the weekend and then gone again; this time he would be away for at least another week. Somehow he had missed the news about the Falkirk Abductor and after the initial flurry of interest newspaper coverage had gone dead for the time being.

'I'll tell you exactly what's going on, but only if you agree to meet me. What are you doing in an hour's time?'

'Tom, I have to go home to my child. The help leaves at eight o'clock.'

'What! Haven't got a nanny?' he said teasingly.

'Not at the moment. She walked out on me with no notice,'

said Lucy, trying not to let the tell-tale note of working-woman exasperation creep into her voice.

'No husband at home?'

'He's in Brussels on a case. He's a barrister, but I expect you knew that.'

'As a matter of fact, I did. Why do you sound so cross? Is it a secret?'

'Of course not.'

'What about lunch tomorrow?'

'I'm in court all day.'

'Dinner? Get the sitter to stay on?'

'All right,' she said reluctantly, 'I'll try. Give me your number and I'll ring you back.'

As soon as she put the telephone down she knew she had done the wrong thing.

Stella Atkins went to see Dan Macmillan, the detective who had done the leg work on the Gresham case twenty years before who was now in dozy retirement in a bungalow in Kirkcudbright growing outsize dahlias and huge vegetables; he was also a local bowls champion. He had bristled like a cactus when it was suggested that the whole thing had been bungled. He believed that Kettle was the perpetrator of the crime and nothing would disabuse him of that notion.

Dan's deputy, Davy Carson, wasn't much use either. He was still in the force, and still a humble constable, the sole policeman in the outlying village of Crossluke, policing an area of bog and hill and occasionally breathalysing tourists when they drove through in the summer months going at 32 mph instead of 30.

Both men were insistent that they had followed every lead, but that from early on it was clear that this case resembled the other abductions in south-west Scotland, all of which were eventually pinned on Kettle. An open and shut case. Simple.

That half-term the girl had been shuttling between her own house and that of the Lord Lieutenant, Earl Gatehouse. Stella

Atkins perused the guest lists of both houses for that period looking for clues: there had been a shoot on the moor at Gatehouse Park with guests staying in both houses, not to mention the assortment of local grandees. The Procurator Fiscal in those days had been invited but had had to decline on account of a conference at the Home Office. There had been a famous Republican Senator, Senator Fowler staying at Balmachie, together with a Hungarian count, a Mr and Mrs George Milo of New York City (relations), not to mention Viscount Carsluith, now the Duke of Annan and married to the third Gatehouse girl, Sarah Anwoth. No leads there. The Gatehouse Park party had been composed of similar types: a man called Cosmo Nevele who wrote a social column these days in the *Sunday Times* of the most repellent snobbishness, a couple called the Marquess and Marchioness of Castlehill (he was now dead and she had married for a fifth time, to Dieter Schlunk, the agri-chemicals baron). There had been Lord Gatehouse's brother-in-law, the Cabinet Chief Secretary, Sir Oliver Beaton-Smith and his wife, Lady Marian Beaton-Smith, the painter Virgil Smith (a particular friend of Lady Gatehouse's), and the rest: Gatehouse children and assorted hangers-on, including a girl called Lucy Diamond who was at school with Sarah Anwoth in those days.

Stella Atkins put the list down. Lucy Diamond. That name rang a bell but she couldn't think why. She called in her PA, Angie, and asked her. Angie read all the mags, she'd know.

'Lucy Diamond, Angie, who's she? Why do I know her name?'

'She's the lawyer who helped Prince John divorce Princess Ariane. She's famous. I saw her on *News at Ten*. She's the one who stopped Princess Ariane having her picture taken for *Playboy*. There was a picture of her in *Hello!* last week walking down the street with her wee girl. She's really lovely-looking. The *Sun* said Prince John had fallen for her.'

'You don't have to believe everything you read in the newspapers, Angie,' said Stella.

'I wish he'd fall in love with me, he's absolutely gorgeous,' replied Angie.

Stella Atkins had heard of Elizabeth Dunbar before she met her. Elizabeth and her colleagues, a select little bunch of detectives, all graduates, were the brainchildren of some *wunderkind* at the Yard who had had the brilliant idea of having an élite squad of police officers who could be sent anywhere at any time to help with intractable cases that had attracted too much undesirable publicity, examples exactly like the Gresham case where a wrong decision had been taken because a provincial force was being hassled by the press. She liked the sound of Elizabeth Dunbar for several reasons: she was a woman, she was clearly bright and also, invaluably for this case, she was a local girl. Incredibly she had even been at school with one of Kettle's victims, and so she was acquainted with the kind of fear a roving random murderer like Kettle could engender. She would remember the atmosphere of that time and know from first-hand experience the public pressure that had been brought to bear on the force to find the killer. She would also be a girl who could hold her own in a peculiar case such as this one where she would be dealing with formidably spoilt people who were used to getting their own way in everything, people like Michael and Pauline Gresham, although it was said locally of Pauline Gresham that she was a pussycat; no one had a bad word for her in spite of the stupendous wealth.

When the news had been broken to the Greshams that the remains in the mausoleum were probably not those of Katie (an assertion later backed up by forensic tests), Pauline had wept. It was Michael Gresham who was so angry.

Stella Atkins knew of the Greshams but had never met either of them. Michael she remembered from her own student days – there was still an old LP of 'Horseferry Road' somewhere in her attic that her son kept begging her to find so that he could flog it in the record exchange on his campus – he was as glamorous as ever, the sapphire eyes were still as blue in middle age, the rangy figure still intact (she had had to suppress the frisson she had felt when she had gone to meet him for the first time only recently, even on such tragic business); he still occasionally came to Balmachie and had been seen on the harbour at Kirkcudbright looking at the boats, (reminding people of 'Seashore Belle', another of those early albums of genius, written just after his marriage to Pauline Milo Saintsbury Gresham), or rambling along the shore at Carrick or Cardoness, but Pauline came less often, although she was known to be passionate about the garden at Balmachie that her mother-in-law, old Mrs Gresham, had saved from ruin.

After Kettle had been tried and sent down she had, not unnaturally, returned less frequently. Scotland was Michael's territory. The place where her daughter had died. Pauline withdrew to Stanborough Farm, her family estate in Connecticut, the place where she had grown up; pictures of it appeared now and then in *Architectural Digest* or in the American edition of *Country Life*: a dreamy Georgian rosy brick mansion with formal gardens and extensive grounds; there were sightings of her in New York waiting under an awning on Fifth Avenue for her chauffeur and occasionally walking in Paris where she liked to attend the couture. It was rumoured that she spent even more money than Mrs Kempner at the shows. But all the beautiful suits and all the exquisite facelifts that California had to offer couldn't make Michael Gresham a faithful husband. The rumours of his infidelity persisted: a Peruvian model here; a glamorous member of the British aristocracy there; Lady Livilla Johnson (the editor of the desperately trendy magazine *Flesh*) had her name linked with his on several different occasions. It was even rumoured that she was having his child. Indeed, a child was born to Lady Livilla, a boy, Poseidon, who was rumoured to be Michael's son and who became known as the *Flesh* baby. It was a shame that that poor woman Pauline Gresham had only been able to have the one child.

In recent weeks, however, Pauline had returned to Balmachie for a long stay, in contrast to the fleeting appearances of the last twenty years – a week here, ten days there every few months or so – since the remains of what she had believed to be her only child had been buried in a specially designed mausoleum on the far side of the loch (an edifice modelled in part on the Harpy tomb at Xanthos in Lycia), which the locals referred to as 'Katie's Kirk'. Collie, now in a retirement bungalow in Kirkcudbright, said that Mrs G only returned to pay her respects at the grave and tend to the garden; the rest of the place was unbearable to her.

Security at Balmachie was discreet but intense: there were cameras at the pistachio-green lodge with its gothic windows and doors (the double of the one at Gatehouse Park: one of the Earls Gatehouse had so liked his neighbour's design that he had had it copied for himself), one on either side of the posts beside the folded-back gates and more concealed among the branches of the grand old beeches that lined the long, winding drive. According to local rumour, security men patrolled the perimeter of the house and grounds night and day when Mr Gresham was in residence and rumour had it that Mrs G had insisted on whatever there was in force being doubled for her own visit. Much good it had done them first time round when they badly needed it, was the opinion in the public bar.

In the office they had allotted her at Kirkcudbright police station Elizabeth Dunbar had studied the Gresham files with care, including as many of the sycophantic profiles and fawning pieces on Pauline's so-called 'perfect' taste, Michael's passion for collecting the Scottish colourists and French furniture, Pauline's clothes, Pauline's houses, Pauline's lost child and so on as she could lay her hands on, but she was interested to find that she was still unprepared for the formal beauty of the house: the immaculately-kept grounds, the ancient trees, the beauty of the view, the way the servants appeared before she had even noticed them.

A butler in a white jacket and gloves opened the front door to her and led her through to the back of the house and settled her in a cosy sitting-room that she felt she might have already seen in a magazine, prettily furnished in slightly worn chintz with the requisite light dusting of dog hairs, adorable porcelain in painted glass-fronted, silk-lined cabinets adorned with cherubs, garlands and swags; serried ranks of small watercolours and oils in old-fashioned frames lining the walls. The whole impression was charming, the 'Completely Pauline' effect *House & Garden* had talked about, Elizabeth found herself thinking, very clever, very beguiling, if you happened to like that sort of thing. A room like this arranged with such evident knowledge of effect but masquerading as apparent insouciance could almost deceive one into thinking that all of life was like this: no pain, no horror, only the smell of flowers and polish, only pretty pictures and inviting sofas; death and sorrow, begone!

Pauline Gresham, wearing a grey sweater and grey flannel trousers, came swiftly into the room followed by a procession of dogs who proceeded to climb unchecked on to the sofas and chairs. She was tall and willow-thin, too thin, Elizabeth thought; her hair, once auburn, had lightened with age and was now a shade of ash-blonde; her skin was the porcelain complexion of cliché, eerily unlined around the eyes and mouth, but the expression in her eyes could not be ironed out or removed by a surgeon's scalpel. The eyes gave the game away, truly in this case the windows of the soul.

She was holding out a hand. 'Thank you for coming to see me,' she said. 'Would you like a cup of tea?'

'I'd like that very much.'

'I'll go order some for us. One moment.'

She turned back towards the door, causing consternation amongst the dog population who were just getting themselves settled.

'No, stay there, boys,' said Pauline, pulling a bell rope by the door. Seeing Elizabeth's expression she said, 'Quaint, isn't it, but I'm not allowed to change anything in this house. It's still my mother-in-law's domain really, not mine, and she's been dead for many years. Michael rearranges all the pictures from time to time and sometimes moves the furniture round when he's bored or he's bought a new piece, but it was always made clear to me that this place was off-limits as far as I was concerned in spite of what you read in the magazines.'

Elizabeth smiled politely and waited. She felt a mixture of curiosity, impatience and sympathy for this woman; she wanted to get through the ritual dance and out the other side to the real reason she was sitting here captive in this gilded cage listening to stories of how the super-rich spent their spare time, but she concealed her discontent. Pauline Gresham was like some nervous, highly-strung animal who needed to be coaxed from the safety of the bush. Very rich, very protected people were like another species compared to the ordinary mortal, used to looking at the world as it were from the other side of a glass screen; to them, unadulterated reality must seem very brutal, very crass. And I am that reality, Elizabeth thought. I represent exactly what she has shielded herself from all these years: the horror, the questions, the vulgar probing, the loss of the one human being she must have loved above all others; removing the scar tissue of twenty years from such a wound would have to be delicately done; she was in no doubt in her own mind that there were some wounds that could never heal. Her mind went back to Kirsty Carson's mother in the kitchen at Kilmuir Mains after Kirsty had disappeared, and she, Elizabeth, had gone with her mother to offer sympathy.

Morag Carson had been a quiet, dignified woman, a bit dour, but a good soul who taught the little ones in the Sunday school and did a half-day on the reception desk once a week for nothing in the local cottage hospital. Mrs Carson had looked the same outwardly, but Elizabeth remembered the way her mouth kept trembling when anyone spoke to her. A month afterwards, she had waited for her husband to go to the weekly livestock market before taking one of his guns and blasting herself into oblivion in a deserted pigsty.

Pauline came back and sat down again opposite Elizabeth. 'This is very painful for me,' she said. 'As you are probably aware, I haven't been back here very much in . . . twenty years. Since my daughter vanished. When that person confessed to her murder there was at least an end to that part of it. We knew or thought we knew who had done it. Believe it or not, there was a certain cold comfort in that. Time could start again. Life could go on. Now . . . I don't know. I don't know what to think. How do we even know that Kettle was telling the truth?'

'You already know that the body Kettle claimed was your daughter Katie's was not in fact hers. That was known at the time by the police but not disclosed.'

'Because they wanted a conviction, right?'

'Right,' said Elizabeth.

'So now, with this retraction, we have a crime without a body?'

'I'm afraid so. I'm so sorry, Mrs Gresham.'

Pauline was silent for a while. Then she said, 'The worst thing is hope. Do you understand what I'm saying? She can't be alive after all this time, but I can already feel a part of me hoping she is.'

'I understand,' said Elizabeth, who was awed by Pauline Gresham's dignity. Her suffering was palpable but she continued in the face of it.

'Do you think Kettle was telling the truth?'

'We'll never know the answer for sure. The prison chaplain is convinced that he was. His theory is that Kettle waited until the end because he knew he would not be believed otherwise. His timing is significant.'

'Was it a genuine conversion, do you think?' Pauline asked. 'Don't they just convert for show?'

'He was a dying man,' said Elizabeth. 'It seems he was thinking about judgement in the next world. He had nothing to gain from his confession in this one.'

'Yes, I see. That makes sense.'

There was a pause during which the tea tray arrived. 'Just

put it here between us, Roger,' said Pauline. 'We can look after ourselves then. Oh, and thank Mrs Crosbie for the cake, would you? Tell her she's a genius.' Jean Crosbie had taken over when Dan had retired some years earlier. 'You have to have some,' she said to Elizabeth when they were alone again, 'otherwise Mrs Crosbie, our cook, takes offence. I've tried to get her to stop baking but it's a part of the culture. She has a wonderfully light hand with the sponge.'

'I won't, thanks,' said Elizabeth. 'I never eat cake.'

'Not even Mrs Crosbie's?'

'Not even for Mrs Crosbie.'

Both women laughed.

'I've spent my whole life being tyrannized by servants,' said Pauline. 'My mother used to say, "Pauline is a pleaser," but I don't see anything wrong in it if it makes other people happy.' She poured a cup of tea and handed it to Elizabeth. 'Help yourself to milk, or there's lemon if you prefer. So what happens now?'

'We'll have to unpick the whole thing all over again,' replied Elizabeth, adding once again, 'I'm sorry, Mrs Gresham.'

'Pauline, please.'

She put her hand over her heart. She had beautiful hands with long, tapering fingers and well-shaped nails. The skin was freckled, with here and there a brown age spot. She was somewhere in her mid-to-late sixties but could have passed, at a distance, for forty-five. The tears in her eyes did not run down her cheeks but somehow dispersed. She did not blow her nose or sniff; perhaps, Elizabeth thought, she was too used to the tears to notice them. Against her will, and she was ashamed of herself for this, Elizabeth found she was almost unbearably moved.

'Twenty years is a long time to ask someone to think back in detail,' said Elizabeth gently. 'It might help if you sorted the people surrounding your daughter into groups: school, home, staff, boyfriends, that sort of thing.'

'But that was all done in the beginning,' said Pauline flatly.

'I can't see how it would help now. The police already have those notes in their reports.'

'Very often, in the beginning, things are overlooked owing to shock. You were in shock that first week or so, probably even longer. I know a long time has passed but something might come back to you, something vital that was missed at the time. Just think back calmly. Don't force anything; a good time to do this is when you're almost asleep. Keep a notebook by your bed. There may be something she said or did that would provide us with a lead, something you remember as her mother. Your husband was away at that time, wasn't he?'

'He was touring in Asia,' said Pauline, 'he'd been away since the beginning of September. Katie wanted to come to Scotland that half-term, although I would rather have been in New York. She was dating Tom Anwoth at the time. I don't think it was serious on her part. He was keener on Katie than she was on him, but, you know, she was a teenager; it was often hard to read the printout.'

'But she still wanted to come to Balmachie enough that you changed your own plans to suit?'

'Yes, she did.'

'Do you think there was some other reason for that? Someone she was seeing whom you didn't know about maybe?'

'There wasn't anyone else, not from round here.'

'You're sure of that?'

'I think so.'

'The night she vanished Katie was having dinner at Gatehouse Park. Why weren't you there?'

'I had friends staying and a dinner party of my own. The kids were friends and they arranged things themselves. Katie just said she was going over for dinner.'

'Where was her bodyguard?'

'She dismissed him. She was always doing that without telling me. He told the police that she had threatened to get him sacked if he told me she had given him the evening off. She got Jimmy, Michael's chauffeur, to drive her over to Gatehouse Park and she called him to fetch her home again. Jimmy assumed that I knew Katie was alone. He would have driven them anyway, you see, so it didn't seem strange to me that Jimmy had got the car out. I've been over all this so many times in my mind and I still can't make any sense out of it.'

'And she came back in good time, Jimmy said? Were you up when she returned?'

'I didn't hear her come back although we may have been up. The young don't always announce themselves. I didn't think anything of it.'

'So, she came back to satisfy Jimmy and then went out again to meet someone?'

'Yes. That's how it must have been.'

'But it was never established who that person was?'

'No. Tom always denied any plan for a further rendezvous that night. But Katie was wild and independent. She wanted to do things her way. It would have been her idea of a joke to go back to Gatehouse Park without telling Tom.'

'How would she have got there? It's too far to walk.'

'We don't know how. Jimmy heard nothing. She may have started to walk, we don't know, but in the end we assumed that that's what she did. Then she got picked up by Kettle. That was the way he operated and that's what we thought had happened to her.'

'It all made perfect sense in retrospect,' said Elizabeth thoughtfully, 'Kettle's activities blinded everyone to the truth, but they should have searched for her harder at the time.'

'We did search,' said Pauline. 'Everyone joined in. The police were short of men. We combed our land and the Gatehouses' land; all the estate workers helped. We never found a thing. But you must know all this, surely? It's all in the file.'

'I want you to think of it as like unpicking a tapestry,' said Elizabeth. 'What we have on file is a picture. It looks solid . . . all the detail is there, or so it seems, but the solidity of it is an illusion. We need to look at all the facts again but in a different way. Somewhere in your memories of that night or of the day or days preceding it is a clue to what happened to your daughter.'

Elizabeth sat on the steps of Pauline's folly and gazed across the loch at the slender, graceful columns of the memorial which had housed the remains once supposed to be those of Katie Gresham. A path led there through woods that began at the bottom of the slope by the south wall of the famous garden. Four miles to the west of this place lay Gatehouse Park perched on the edge of the estuary that eventually swept into Kirkcudbright with its famous ruined castle and tolbooth, and the Georgian streets where a colony of artists had lived and worked at the turn of the century. And somewhere else within the four-mile radius between this house and the other great house of the neighbourhood might lie the body of Katie Gresham, or what remained of her. It was always possible of course that she could have been moved that night or the next day; Kettle had pounced on girls unexpectedly and moved them around in his van, but by the time Katie had disappeared the police were setting up the occasional roadblock; whoever killed her would not have risked moving the body too far. This lowland landscape was water-bound, bog-ridden with treacherous quicksands at the shore where the strange currents and freak tides swept at least one tourist a year to a watery death; the good land where the cattle grazed was on the low ground by rivers which often flooded in winter; last year the tides of the spring solstice had shifted the mud and sand downstream a little from the harbour at Kirkcudbright to reveal a Celtic harbour with its timbers uncannily preserved by nearly two millennia of salt and mud.

That night, in the house she had rented in Kirkcudbright from the local architect, Archie Jamieson, Elizabeth unfurled an ordnance survey map of the region on her kitchen table. Balmachie House was marked, as was Gatehouse Park: the two estates marched with one another for a considerable distance, but the Gatehouse Park estate was very much larger than Balmachie, ten thousand acres to two thousand, with better land, less marsh and loch, more pasture and arable; she noted that a large area bordering the estuary, a hundred acres or so, was known as the Coulter Moss, and was marked as a site of special scientific interest. She looked at the date of her map and noted that it was 1997, presumably the most recent edition. In Scotland and the north of England, 'moss' was a word for a bog, usually a peat bog; the Coulter Moss extended a long way to the east of the house: a vast area of undisturbed peat bog submerged in what looked from the map to be dense woodland; some of it had been cut for peat earlier this century and in the last; presumably it was approachable by boat from Gatehouse Park, but so much would depend on the radical tides of this treacherous coast and on detailed knowledge of the terrain. If the peat had been cut in the past some of the Moss might be accessible, given the tides and amount of rain, but most of it would still be primeval swamp.

She had known such a place as a child at Bole on the farm where her father still worked: the trees that flourished in a moss were alder, willow, aspen and birch and in the springtime the yellow of broom would blaze, but to her it was always a sinister place with its deep, hidden pools, some of which, her father told her, were thirty or forty feet in depth, fringed by reeds and the fossilizing remains of trees; she would never forget one of her father's cows straying into Kilmuir Moss and vanishing as if it had never existed, eaten alive by the bog. Iron Age man believed that eternity lay down through the waters of the moss, that those dense, impenetrable places were gateways to the next world. She remembered her father weeping for the fate of that poor cow who had been a favourite of his known as Bridie. If the body of Katie Gresham had been hidden in the Coulter Moss then they would never find her, not a hope in hell. Nevertheless, she wasn't going to allow that possibility to deflect her. Tomorrow, she would begin to interview people on the list she had made of those still alive who had taken part in that original search.

* * *

'They're reopening the Gresham case,' said Claudia to Ivar, at the beginning of June, 'but I suppose you already know that. Pauline rang me today. She said there's a new detective dealing with it, a woman. She said this woman had been to see you. I said I didn't know anything about it.'

It was the first time she had spoken to her husband in private for a week, possibly slightly longer. They were in the drawing-room of the house in Eaton Terrace, waiting to be collected by the Annans. Claudia, together with Sarah and Sandy, was accompanying her husband to a dinner at the House of Lords in honour of the master of his college at Cambridge who had recently been awarded a Nobel Prize for literature. She would attend the odd cultural occasion when she was up to it but refused most other invitations on principle.

'You didn't have to know about it,' replied Ivar, glancing at his watch. 'I don't know why they're bothering at this late date. It's a waste of public money.'

He had met and instinctively disliked Stella Atkins at several local functions. She was one of those women who talked in clichés about 'glass ceilings' and women's 'issues'; in a largely agricultural area she was all for tightening up regulations on shotguns and having more police on the roads to deal with drunk drivers, both measures deeply inimical to the locals. He remembered with affection the days when old Dougie Fraser had been Procurator Fiscal. Dougie had liked a dram and loved a day blasting pheasant or grouse. He could hardly ask Stella Atkins for a day's shooting or to a dinner where half his guests would be over the limit after their first drinks.

'Is that all you have to say?'

'What do you expect me to say?'

'Oh, there are several things you might have said, Ivar, but I ought to know you well enough by now to know that none of them would have occurred to you.'

Ivar looked briefly in the direction of his wife. 'Ghastly for

Pauline and Michael,' he said. 'Here's Sarah now. I'll go and let her in.'

'Hello, Poppy darling,' said Sarah, bounding up the steps in a sugar-pink Versace dress, clutching her embroidered pashmina shawl round her shoulders with one hand. 'Hurry, or we'll be late. Is Ma ready?'

'Yes, she's here. Come on, darling,' he said to Claudia, who was picking up her handbag from the hall table.

Ivar was a great believer in appearances. In public, he and his wife behaved like an affectionate and long-married couple. They were grandparents, Gammer and Grandgam, to innumerable little Harcourts, Jardines and Anwoths, but not yet, alas, to any baby Annans. Not for the first time, Ivar found himself examining his daughter's pin-thinness for a sign of pregnancy, the faintest outline of a breast larger than a bee-sting or a suggestion of roundedness over the hips, but sign came there none. Of course she was terribly like her mother had been at that age, stick-thin, the other two were the same but, rather like their mother, it hadn't stopped them breeding. Sarah was his favourite daughter, always had been, although he only mentioned this to a few people, and Sandy was a wonderful fellow, one of the richest landowners in Scotland but with, thank God, huge holdings in Canada and Australia too; good to hedge your bets these days with the rise of the SNP; he himself, advised by his trustees (of whom his son Tom, the financial wizard, was one), had seen all this neo-Communist talk of giving land back to the people coming years ago. He was well-protected. It was one of his boasts that he had a genius for reading the auguries.

Of course he had known that the Gresham case would be reopened once the Falkirk Abductor had had an attack of religion before he died of an appropriately painful form of cancer, but it was of no account. People were so credulous. They believed anything they read in the newspaper was gospel truth. There was no body and without a body there was no case.

The policewoman Claudia mentioned had come to see him last week when he had been on a flying visit to Gatehouse Park to see to some estate business. Derry Paterson was an excellent factor but Ivar was aware that it was politically expedient at present to be the reverse of an absentee landlord. Unlike Michael Gresham, however, he did not believe in helicoptering in. That sort of thing was vulgar, pop star behaviour and not suitable for the Lord Lieutenant – it also alienated the local gentry most of whom, as working farmers or hard-pressed landowners dealing with the mountain of EC paperwork, found Michael and Pauline slightly preposterous – but Michael had long ago adopted the mannerisms of his repulsive trade and made a virtue of them: helicopters, private jets, islands in the Bahamas, all the classic showy behaviour of new money: but even if the money was new the family was old and Michael, as poor old Sissy had been fond of saying, really ought to have known better.

Ivar made a point of travelling north by train (first class, on House of Lords expenses, of course) because one was seen on a train not only by people one knew but by ordinary people. He liked to have the same steward, made a point of tipping lavishly and was invariably excessively civil to any member of the lower orders who helped him on his way, from the porter at Euston to Davy in the ticket office at Dumfries who, if he saw Ivar, always came out of his glass box to shake hands. Davy's daughter was married to the dairyman at Gatehouse Mains and had just had a third baby. Ivar retained the family trees of numerous of his employees and tenant farmers in his head as a matter of course. It required no effort and was something he had always known the value of. The policewoman, Detective Inspector Dunbar, was also a dairyman's daughter. Lowell had run a check on her through a contact at Scotland Yard: humble beginnings but bright at school (and clever enough to have Latin teaching out of school), classics at Edinburgh where she had gained a first-class degree. It wasn't Oxbridge, of course, but it was still an impressive feat.

She was an attractive girl in a rather healthy sort of way; there was something crisp and fresh about her appearance. According to Lowell she was thirty, but she could have passed for twenty-five or even less, but Ivar had quickly realized that she was either immune to or had been warned about his legendary charm and had changed tack. She was the kind of girl, the career-woman type, who wanted to be treated as an equal. No wonder Ms Atkins had chosen her for the task. She had *don't patronize me* written all over her face and was hilariously prickly about being offered a drink in the library instead of a cup of tea or whatever proletarian beverage, decaffeinated coffee or herbal tea, was in vogue at that moment.

All she had wanted to do, all she could do, was to go over old ground. What time Katie had arrived and what time she had left. Who had been staying. All the old stuff on the file. There was nothing new. She had asked questions about the search: who had been involved, where had they looked; she had asked him how he *felt* when he heard Katie was missing, the vocabulary of emotion, of the touchy-feely revolution brought about everywhere in public life by the death of that silly girl the Princess of Wales.

'Not particularly worried to start with,' he told her. 'The young round here all roam about the place on their own. It's an essential part of a country childhood. When I was a boy nobody knew where I was a lot of the time.'

'But Katie was hardly your ordinary young girl.'

'One of the reasons Katie liked coming here was that it was a place she could be free in. At Balmachie she could dodge her mother, play the truant a little bit.'

'Mrs Gresham told me that Katie dismissed her bodyguard against her wishes.'

'Mrs Gresham was the kind of mother who always worried about such things.'

'With reason, so it seems.'

'Yes, with reason. But Galloway was not then and is not today, America.'

'So you're saying it was just bad luck that Katie vanished.'

'That's exactly what I am saying, yes. Do you not think Kettle was just playing a last game with your chaplain?'

'The chaplain doesn't think so. He's convinced that Kettle was in earnest.'

'But we only have Kettle's word for it and the chaplain's – shall we say – credulousness. I know how these clerics like to notch up a scalp or two in the interests of productivity, the bottom line that is so popular these days.'

'That's quite a reductionist view of the chaplain's role, Lord Gatehouse. You're a religious man. I would have thought you would attach more value to a prison chaplain's work.'

'That particular prison chaplain is an evangelical, what they call a happy-clappy, in other words a scalp-hunter. They need souls for their balance sheet, Miss Dunbar.'

'So you say. Would it be possible to have a word with your wife, Lord Gatehouse?'

'I'm afraid she's not feeling very well today. Another time, perhaps? It can hardly be classified as urgent after twenty years, surely?'

'It would only take a minute or two of her time.'

'I'm afraid it's impossible today.'

Ivar rose to signal that the interview was at an end. Claudia was on the downward curve of one of her cycles of depression. She began drinking at about 10 a.m. and was in no fit state to encounter anyone, let alone a policewoman, at tea-time.

'Would you mind very much if I walked your grounds?'

'Of course not,' Ivar said, 'I'd be delighted. There are some pheasant pens in the woods beyond the walled garden that Martin, the keeper, would be obliged if you would not disturb, but otherwise help yourself. The locals all use the park whenever they feel like it. In summer they can swim from the hut if they so wish. I take a traditional view of these things, Miss Dunbar. I regard my tenants and estate workers as my family.'

She had given him a look then that he had not cared for at all, a commissar's glance: the girl was a classic revolutionary type disguised as a pillar of society; being in the police force evidently gave her an inflated sense of her own power and the chip on the shoulder deriving from her humble origins provided the fervour: she would have him in a tumbril in a second, given the chance. He had seen the way her eyes registered his library and his paintings – devoured would perhaps have been a better word. But he didn't fear her. After all, what was there to fear? She was just a local girl throwing her weight around. He would allow her a month or two then he would make a complaint through his contact on the police board. Resources were after all scarce these days.

And nobody would talk. Derry had made it clear in his own way to the folk on the estate, the tenants, the staff, indoor and out, and the tenant farmers that police enquiries were to be barely tolerated but no more. Since the advent of Ms Atkins, the police were not particularly popular in the vicinity, and there was a general feeling locally that it was better to let sleeping dogs lie. As Derry had said: 'What Jock Kettle did will scar people's memories in southern Scotland for generations. Why delve into the Gresham case again now on the say-so of a convicted murderer?'

People felt sorry for Pauline and Michael of course, but they had become more and more remote figures during the last twenty years; their great wealth and Michael's enduring stardom made them seem somehow not quite real, not in the way that Ivar and Claudia were real and Tom and Caroline and the two little Anwoth boys, Sholto, aged four, and Miles, aged two. The tragedy that had befallen the Greshams twenty years ago had long faded from the forefront of people's minds. Life had to go on and there was a feeling in the village and in Kirkcudbright that if you were very rich as the Greshams were you needed or deserved less sympathy.

As he took Claudia's arm to descend the steps to where Sandy's car was waiting at the kerb, Ivar was aware of a nagging worry to do with Tom and the state of his marriage. Caroline had rung him at the end of the previous week to announce that she was seeking a divorce from Tom. As usual, she had been drunk and he hadn't paid much attention to what she said until the end of their conversation.

'If you think you can go on getting away with your little antics,' she said, enunciating carefully, 'then you can think again. I'm sure the world would be interested to know you wanted to shag your daughter-in-law, Ivar. I'm thinking of selling my story. After all, it gave Ariane a wonderful hold over that poisonous little creep, Prince John.'

'It's your word against mine,' Ivar replied, recoiling slightly from his daughter-in-law's phraseology. 'If you do anything of the sort, I'll sue you,' he added, trying to make it sound as if he might just have thought she had been joking. His instinct was to treat Caroline as a naughty child. One of the problems was that she had received no discipline when growing up; her father had been a prominent SS officer who had shot himself when Caroline was two after a journalist had revealed his true role in the Second World War.

'Wouldn't look good, Ivar,' said Caroline, 'be very embarrassing for you.'

'Listen, Caroline,' said Ivar, 'stop being such a silly girl. Go and see Father Harry.'

'Why? He's just one of your pocket priests, Ivar. I don't want to be spun the party line. I want out.'

'Why? Tom is an exemplary husband.'

'Your precious Tom's a prig. He thinks more of the look of things than of things themselves, just like you do.'

'That's no reason for divorce,' said Ivar. 'You need marriage counselling.'

'What! From Father Harry? Give me a break, Ivar.'

'You should stop drinking. That's your first priority.'

But Caroline had put the telephone down as she so often did when told things she didn't want to hear. It was a shame, really. She had seemed so ideal when Tom met her at Cambridge: clever, glamorous, Catholic, fantastically well-connected. To Ivar it had been a marvellously fortuitous meeting. Tom had just come out of his excessively ascetic phase during which he had kept threatening that he was going to become a Carthusian monk. Carthusians were contemplatives whose lives were spent in prayer and silence. Too much Thomas Merton, combined with the unfortunate events of the previous year, had clearly gone to his head. Strings had had to be pulled at the highest level to prevent such a calamity. In a family such as theirs with only one son there was no question of the heir becoming a monk, it simply wouldn't do. Then mercifully along had come Caroline and all had been well until she had had Sholto. The drinking started then, according to Tom. Post-natal depression apparently, a condition Ivar secretly thought simply gave women yet another excuse to behave badly. Caroline had been sent against her wishes to a clinic in Surrey and the newspapers had somehow got hold of the story. Lowell had told him that it was Caroline herself who had tipped off the gossip columnist who had run the piece. In the article she likened the Gatehouses to a Mafia clan, with Ivar as the Don, and her husband as his subordinate. 'They demand total loyalty,' she said to the journalist who got the scoop. 'If you don't toe the party line you're in trouble. It's all about appearances. You have to look the part, never mind what's really going on. Show any weakness and they're after you like sharks after blood. That's why I was shoved away in here and not allowed to see my children. I'm like some Victorian wife stowed away in the attic going bonkers, the Mrs Rochester of re-hab, that's me.'

'Perhaps her marbles are going, Ivar,' Lowell had said. 'It's not a very loyal thing to do, wouldn't you say?'

Caroline had then been sent to a very famous clinic in America on the basis that it was further away and that she would be of less interest to journalists in a clinic full of film stars. By this time she was in full-scale rebellion and the *National Enquirer* had run a piece about an affair she was supposed to have had there with some former but now rather clapped-out Hollywood icon, but Lowell had advised

Ivar to ignore it. 'It's not for people like us, Ivar,' he had said, 'it's for the bum scrapings, trailer trash; believe me, I know these things, but I think you should know just for the record that it was Caroline herself who contacted them. You should watch her, Ivar, she's unsound. Her values are upside-down. Loyalty's the thing, I know you would agree, Ivar.'

'Tom says she's threatening to divorce him. She wants custody of the children. Altogether it's a rather ugly situation. She's discovered what a good weapon publicity is, after all she had Ariane as an example. They're cousins, of course.'

'Well, you have to hand it to little Lucy,' said Lowell, 'she did a fine job there.'

'Who?' asked Ivar.

'Lucy. You remember, Lucy, Ivar. Lucy Diamond. Sarah's friend.'

Ivar looked blank. 'Can't put a face to the name. There've been so many of them over the years. When you have four children you can't remember all their friends.'

'Poppy, you're in a dream,' said Sarah, as they went through the revolving doors of the peers' entrance. 'What were you thinking of?'

The first night Tom had taken Lucy to a smart new bar in Soho, followed by a state of the art Indian restaurant in a street off Westbourne Grove where the food was as fashionably minimalistic as the interior. 'Food as sculpture, perhaps,' Lucy had said, examining the prawns she had ordered. 'It almost makes me yearn for the return of flock wallpaper.'

Rather to her surprise, she was enjoying herself. It made her aware of two things: one was that she hadn't enjoyed herself very much lately, there had been a distinct lack of fun in her life; the second was that she had forgotten how kind Tom was and how amusing. Simon was amusing too; she had always liked men who made her laugh but then she hadn't seen much of him lately.

'Sarah tells me flock wallpaper is the coming thing,' replied

Tom. 'She's my style informant on these matters. She says she saw you the other day and that you looked radiant or ravishing, I can't remember which, but she was right, you do.'

'What else does she say?'

'That she envies you your useful life. She dashes around all the time and her life is full of entertainment, but I don't think she enjoys herself very much somehow.'

'And she thinks I do? Do you know something, Tom, I'm a bit sick of very lucky people like your sister Sarah telling me – or rather you – that she envies my "useful" life. You can't have everything. I might rather like being a duchess, but I wouldn't expect also to be "useful".'

'Ouch,' said Tom. 'Have I struck a nerve?'

'Yes,' said Lucy. After a few seconds both burst out laughing.

'Sarah always was a bit of a spoilt cow,' said Tom, 'a bit of a mad one too, poor old thing. A pity she hasn't had you to keep her on the rails all these years. You rather lost touch, didn't you?'

'We did rather, yes.'

'Why?'

'We chose different paths,' said Lucy, trying to sound vague. How much did Tom know about the relationship between his father and sister, or between Ivar and Katie? It was difficult to remember from this distance, easier just to let the whole stinking mess subside.

'Why won't you answer my question?'

'It was all a long time ago,' said Lucy reluctantly, knowing perfectly well that her evasiveness was only making Tom keener. His eagerness to probe dismayed her. He was too upfront, too confrontational; and he was also too attractive. She found it difficult to look at him normally because he made her want to stare; he was just the same but different – same old mad black curls (dark where all his sisters were blonde), same old humorous glint in the eye – but of course he wasn't the same strange boy of seventeen that she had once been a little in love with; it was twenty years on and enormous changes had overtaken them both: careers, marriage, children, all the usual junk . . . but she had been with Simon, she liked her life, she wanted everything to go on the same, or told herself she did, but just as at the beginning of *Buddenbrooks* the teacups on the dresser are rattling with the faint vibrations of war and upheaval so her own life had lately acquired a feeling of unsettledness, almost of unreality that was connected to everything she wished to forget.

'Lucy,' said Tom, 'you're not listening to me, are you?'

'I think I'd better go,' she said, rising. 'I knew I shouldn't have come. I knew it as soon as I'd agreed to it.'

'No, don't go,' said Tom, 'I mean you can't just leave. I haven't seen you for nearly twenty years and you want to go already.'

'You know why, Tom,' she said, sitting down again.

'I don't think I do. Explain to me why we can't have supper like old friends.'

'That wasn't the original reason you asked to meet me,' said Lucy.

'You're so cagey,' he said. 'Look, I know the Katie thing was awful but it wasn't any fault of ours; there was nothing we could have done, and I know your mother dying must have blended with that. Sarah said you were very cut up, very withdrawn; she said you didn't want to be friends any more. She was very hurt by you, very baffled. And I understand that but I don't see why we shouldn't be friends again now. Please, Lucy.'

'All right,' she said after a moment. He had a point; she should stop being so silly. They were bound to meet again somehow or another, it was practically inevitable, particularly since Sarah had come to live next-door. This was what she told herself at any rate. And she had to know what was happening about the Gresham case.

'Tell me about Katie first. Then we can talk about Caroline and you.'

'The murderer, Kettle, said he didn't do it, OK? You know that?'

'Yes.'

'The resulting hoo-ha means that the case has had to be officially reopened. There's some new detective dealing with it. A woman. Pa said she came to see him. He said it was like having a member of the Red Guard in the house. The New Scotland, he called it.'

'Doesn't sound as if their meeting was a great success.'

'It wasn't. He also thinks the whole exercise is a waste of public money. I mean what on earth can they hope to gain after all this time?'

'No doubt the Greshams feel it has to be taken seriously just as much as the press do. You can't blame them for that.'

'Hardly,' said Tom. 'One can't blame them for anything, but the truth of the matter is they're not viewed with particular sympathy locally. She's an outsider and too rich and he's just too rich and famous altogether, even though he is one of us.'

'One of us,' repeated Lucy. 'Does that still apply in Mr Blair's New Britain?'

'You know what I mean,' said Tom unapologetically.

I suppose I do, Lucy thought. The same old tribal-speak.

'Pauline's offered a reward. A hundred thousand for information.'

'She did that last time, didn't she?'

'She says somebody knows something. Or so Pa tells me. He tried to talk her out of it, but she wouldn't have it. They had quite a set-to about it. He said she shouldn't waste her own money as well as the public purse. He said it would just encourage loonies to come out of the woodwork.'

'They can come out all they like, but until they actually find the body of Katie Gresham then there's not much of a case.'

When they had ordered pudding, Tom said, 'So how's your life, Lucy? You've heard about my fuck-ups and I watch you nodding coolly and making mental notes. What's happened to you between the time you left GP and the moment I see you walking across the dining-room of the Coburg looking so ravishing? The man I was lunching with thought you were Nicky Paderewski's new squeeze.'

'What a horrible thought,' said Lucy, pouring herself some more wine. 'My husband is not the Paderewski type, thank God. He's a hell of a lot nicer, for a start.'

'Are you happy?'

'We have been very happy,' said Lucy.

'What a cagey reply! Aren't you happy any more?'

'We hardly see each other,' said Lucy, allowing the wine to talk. 'He's in Brussels all the time – EU law is his speciality – I'm here. I miss him. Or I did miss him. I don't so much any more, I find. There are so many things I meant to say to him but haven't had the opportunity and now I've forgotten what they were. There's some coolness between us on the subject of jobs. He wants me to go to Brussels, but I won't. My life is here. My daughter's life is here. I don't earn as much as he does, but I make good money. Why should I give up my career?'

'Did you meet him up at Oxford?'

'No, later. The law's quite a little club, you know.'

'Pa always said that. I told him I was seeing you. I had lunch with him today.'

'How is he?' asked Lucy, trying but failing to sound enthusiastic.

'Why are you so hostile to him?' asked Tom. 'Come on, admit it, you are.'

'Can I really be frank? You might not like what I have to say.'

'He jumped you, that's it, isn't it?' said Tom. 'Sarah thought that was what had happened.'

'Yes, he did. I was one of a number, I suspect, including poor Caroline.'

Their eyes met.

'He was always very sorry about it afterwards,' said Tom, putting his hand over hers.

'Sorry! Sorry's not much use to a teenage girl, Tom, for God's sake!'

'No, I know,' said Tom humbly. 'He's a blighter. Imagine how it feels for me to hear these things.'

'Are you about to do the same?'

'Would you like me to?'

'It's extremely unethical,' said Lucy. 'This is supposed to be a business meeting, isn't it?'

'That was just an excuse,' said Tom.

They took a taxi to the Pimlico square where Tom was renting a flat at the top of a tall white house with a view of the tops of the trees in the gardens.

'What happened to Aunt Dolly's flat?'

'I'd forgotten you knew that place. It's Sarah's. She lets it, I think.'

'Are you still as close to Sarah as you used to be? Two against the world?'

'There have been problems. Caroline resented it. She says Sarah always has to be first and that sometimes it was as if I were married to Sarah and not to her.'

'And what did you say to that?'

'I told her to stop being so bloody silly.'

'Did you put Caroline through an initiation test like you did with me?'

'We'd put away childish things by then,' Tom replied, putting his hands on Lucy's shoulders and turning her to face him.

'And now you've found them again.'

'Will you tell Sarah about us?' she asked, after he had kissed her and then drawn back to look into her face.

'Why should I?'

'Caroline might have had a point.'

'Come to bed,' said Tom.

'Answer the question.'

'No, I won't. May I kiss you again?'

'I can't think quite how this has happened,' said Lucy, allowing Tom to lead her from the sitting-room down a corridor and into a bedroom with the same view of the square.

'I wanted to sleep with you as soon as I saw you crossing the dining-room that day at the Coburg.'

'Whatever happened to Jip?' asked Lucy sleepily, putting her hand on Tom's shoulder.

'How funny that you should remember her.' Tom turned round to face Lucy. 'The next year, in the summer, she sickened and died. Poor old girl. The vet thought she might have been bitten by a snake. In a way I suppose it was a good thing. I wasn't at home much for the next few years and nobody else liked her much, not even Sarah.'

'You were at Cambridge. Sarah left Wickenden the following summer after exams. What happened to her after that? She didn't go to university, did she?'

'She's a girl,' joked Tom, 'what do you expect? Actually, she refused to go to university. Pa wanted her to try for Oxford. He sent her to Westminster Tutors and she got a place but then wouldn't take it up. I think she did it to annoy him, really.'

'And did it?'

'Of course. The response was incredibly gratifying to Sarah. She was rebelling with a vengeance by then. Sex, drugs, rock'n'roll, you name it.'

'But then she married Sandy and conformed with a vengeance. That must have pleased your father.'

'What father wouldn't be pleased, especially Pa who's always been keen on dynastic links. We hadn't married into the Annans for a long time and, besides, Sandy's a hell of a nice bloke. Everyone likes him.'

'You Anwoths always did hunt in packs.'

'It's family,' said Tom, 'family matters. It does to me anyway.'

'Except when you want a divorce.'

'That's a bit below the belt. I don't want a divorce. It's Caroline who wants it. We'll have to get an annulment. That's what they're for, when things go irretrievably wrong.'

'But you wouldn't have divorced if she hadn't wanted it.'

'No, I wouldn't.'

'And gone without sex?'

'I'd rather not have to answer that,' he said, touching her. 'You have the most beautiful breasts, you know. I always thought so since I saw you in that amazing dress the night of the dance at Balmachie.'

'The night Sarah got so drunk.'

'I think we all did.'

'And Aunt Marian kept asking me if I was Joe Diamond's daughter? How is Aunt Marian?'

'Much the same. Uncle Olly's retired now and they live in Wiltshire all the time. Gardening, grandchildren, bridge, you know the sort of thing.'

'I don't think I do, really. I don't play bridge. I don't see myself gardening and grandchildren seem a long way off.'

'Maud is how old? Eight, ten?'

'Eight. How do you know that?'

'Lowell told me.'

'*Lowell!*' Lucy sat up in bed. 'What the hell has Lowell got to do with my life?'

'He keeps an eye on you from afar. He's full of admiration, as a matter of fact.'

'I suppose he knows how much I earn as well. Does he know I'm here with you tonight?'

'Of course not. I wouldn't have told you if I'd known you'd react like that. He's just interested in you, that's all, in a benevolent, avuncular sort of way.'

'OK,' said Lucy, 'I'm sorry. It's guilt, I suppose. I know I shouldn't be here.'

'But you're glad you are,' said Tom.

'Yes, I'm glad I am.'

They met again as often as they both could manage over the next few weeks, given their work and their family commitments. Tom liked to read to his two little boys at night if he could make it in time; Lucy felt guilty about leaving Maud so often with Magdalena. They also couldn't risk being seen anywhere too public and so more often than not they ended up at Tom's flat cooking themselves supper, listening to music and then going to bed. Lucy felt as if she'd been reborn.

One night when they were lying in bed, Lucy said, 'Who was your next girlfriend after Katie?'

'There wasn't one. Not for years. I gave up sex. I was going to become a monk. Caroline was really my next serious love.'

'What did you really think had happened to Katie – in the beginning, I mean?'

'To start with I just thought she was hiding. It was quite like her to do something like that. She liked playing games; she didn't always care much about how people felt.'

'She was brave though, I remember her standing up to your father.'

'She was brave,' said Tom, 'but she was also quite foolhardy. I think she truly thought she could get away with anything.'

'Was it because she was the Milo heiress or was she like that anyway?'

'That's what she was like,' said Tom, 'I don't think it was possible to distinguish which bit was which, if you see what I mean. She was just Katie.'

'So when did you start thinking that she hadn't just vanished?'

'I can't remember. Maybe when Kettle confessed. There seemed to be no hope then that she might just reappear. What about you?'

'I followed it all from a distance. I didn't really know what to think. And then when Kettle confessed, like you I thought that was it.'

'But for years I dreamed of her,' said Tom. 'A part of me went on thinking she might just reappear, back from the dead or the unknown or wherever she'd been. I was much more disturbed by it all than I allowed myself to admit.'

'Me too,' said Lucy.

＊　　＊　　＊

'There's somebody called Detective Inspector Dunbar on the phone for you,' said Cass, Lucy's secretary.

'What does she want?'

'She won't tell me, but says it's important. She's calling from Scotland.'

'All right,' said Lucy, 'put her through.'

It was three weeks since she had first gone back to Tom's flat but it seemed longer. She was frightened by the strength of her feeling for Tom; if she had been asked four weeks ago if it was possible to go from being moderately happily married to being madly in love in such a short space of time she would have said with her customary dryness, 'Don't be absurd.' Simon, during the short space of time that he had been back to the house in Coventry Terrace, had commented on the fact that she seemed, for her, unusually vague, but as he himself had been astoundingly distracted by the fascinating complexities of beer duties and the EU she hadn't rated his opinion very highly. Maud, on the other hand, had shouted, 'You never listen!' before slamming the door behind her this morning as the mother whose turn it was to do the school run drew up outside their front door, and that had made Lucy feel much more guilty than Simon's half-teasing remark.

'You'll know what I'm calling about, of course,' said the prim little Scottish voice in Lucy's ear.

'Yes. Of course.'

Tom had told Lucy that she would probably be contacted but hadn't asked her what she intended to say.

'I'd like to come and see you.'

'I don't think there's very much point,' said Lucy.

'I'm interviewing all the people who were at Gatehouse Park at the time of Miss Gresham's disappearance,' the voice went on.

'Is there really any point?'

'I think so, yes.'

'But if –'

'Miss Diamond, I surely don't have to point out to you the seriousness of hindering a police investigation.'

'No, you don't.'

'Well then, I would be grateful if you could make time to see me next week. I'll be in London then.'

'It may have to be in the evening,' said Lucy, glancing at her diary. 'I'm in court all next week.'

'What about Wednesday evening?'

'That's fine. Where shall I meet you?'

'There's a bar in Westbourne Grove called Leila's, I could meet you there at six-forty-five. Do you know it?'

'It's round the corner from where I live,' said Lucy, 'so yes. Fine. See you then.' She tried not to sound too surprised. The woman had probably done her homework and knew that Leila's was her local. She had just put the telephone down when Charles, her senior partner, put his head round the door.

'Got a mo?' he asked, perching on the edge of her desk without waiting for her answer in his usual maddening Charles-like way.

'Not really. Is it urgent?'

'You sound rattled, my dear.'

'Not rattled, Charles, just desperately busy.'

'A little bird tells me Tom Creetown is a friend of yours.'

'I've known him since I was sixteen, why?'

'I also gather he's in the market for a divorce.'

'Go on, Charles.'

'The little bird tells me there are certain complications where you two are concerned.'

'Which little bird?'

'I don't think you need to know that. I know that Lord Creetown is a friend of Prince John's but I do hope you won't be allowing him to instruct you.'

'I'm not quite sure what you're getting at, Charles.'

'Just a friendly nudge' said Charles, glancing at his watch and standing up straight. 'How's Simon? Still frightfully busy, I gather.'

'Yes,' replied Lucy, 'we both are at the moment.'

'It's a dog's life,' said Charles, sliding round the door.

Or a bitch's, thought Lucy. Someone somewhere is making mischief. Three nights ago the phone had rung at some God-forsaken hour well past midnight; she had picked it up instantly from the depths of sleep half expecting it to be Simon and a male voice she did not recognize had said, 'Parasite . . . whore . . .' at which point Lucy had slammed the receiver back and lain there in her bed with her heart banging in her chest and her palms sweating. She told herself it was a random call, a lunatic in the night, that these things happened, that there was nothing to it. She picked up the phone and dialled 1471, knowing perfectly well whoever had rung would have covered his tracks.

She had received threats before and had always prided herself on the fact that she was not easily rattled. A divorce lawyer was not always a popular figure and many of her clients were powerful people with powerful opponents, but she felt this was different although she could not say why it should be and it alarmed her that she felt so easily persecuted. She got out of bed and went barefoot upstairs to the next floor to see if Maud was all right. There was no reason why Maud shouldn't be but the call coming as it had straight into the intimate middle of her dream had caught her on the raw; she felt scared and vulnerable. She found herself thinking, what if something should happen to her child? But why should it? Maud lay adrift in the innocent sleep of the very young, the curve of her cheek accentuated against the pillow, safe in the cocoon of her ordered cheerful world. The book she had been reading when she fell asleep had fallen face-down on the floor. Lucy picked it up, smoothed the duvet and found herself wondering how often her own rather unmotherly mother had performed such actions.

She went back downstairs to her own room and got into bed. Somewhere, perhaps a street away, a car alarm was going. She thought of ringing Tom but what could she say? I had a crank call and I'm scared. Tom would laugh at her and tell her to go back to sleep. He couldn't come here and hold her in his arms just as she couldn't go there, alone as she was in the house with her child. Someone knew that she was sleeping with Tom Creetown and that someone minded.

Elizabeth looked up from the copy of that day's *Guardian* that she was reading without much enthusiasm in Leila's. It was seven or so in the evening and the bar was quiet; a few couples, women having a post-work drink, the odd lone male, a couple of girls who looked scarcely old enough to be drinking. She recognized the woman approaching her table as Lucy Diamond from the one or two photographs she had seen of her: slim but curvaceous, dark curly hair restrained by a velvet scrunchy, wearing one of those ruinously expensive suits that make a working woman look both sexy and severe, exquisite legs and skin, expensive briefcase, an air of contained energy.

'I'm sorry I'm late,' said Lucy, putting down her briefcase and holding out her hand, 'but there was a last-minute crisis, as usual, in the office. I'm in court all this week and when I am in the office the phone never stops and it's always urgent. Can I get you a drink?'

'How did you know who I was?' asked Elizabeth.

'It wasn't very difficult.'

'I'll have a Diet Coke, please.'

'So,' said Lucy, when they were seated with their drinks, 'you'd better tell me what brings you to London that we couldn't discuss on the telephone.'

'You were very close to the two families during the period before Katie vanished. It was your first time in the area, I need to know if there's anything, however little, that you can remember that might be a pointer in the direction of the person responsible for Katie's disappearance. We know that she went out again once she had got home that night. Now, we do know she was having a walkout with Tom . . . Lord Creetown, but he swears he didn't see Katie again after she had left Gatehouse Park that night.'

'If that's what he says, then it's true. Tom is a very truthful person, but I need hardly remind you that it is also a very long time ago. Is there really any point in reopening an investigation when there isn't a body?'

'We think so,' said Elizabeth Dunbar. 'Ms Atkins is of the opinion that the evidence should be re-examined, which includes re-interviewing the people who were there at that time.'

'It still seems a bit pointless without a body,' said Lucy. 'Sorry, but I'm not convinced.'

'Let me explain it to you. If Kettle says he did not kill Katie Gresham and we accept his word on that, then what we are looking at is a small group of people who were on the spot at the moment that Katie vanished: I am convinced that her murderer was staying either at Balmachie or Gatehouse Park on the night she disappeared. The more I look into this case, the more I see wheels within wheels: I'm sure your little girl has one of those Russian dolls, Miss Diamond, you know the ones I mean where you find a doll within a doll within a doll. That's what I'm dealing with here.'

'That's what you would be dealing with in any murder investigation, I imagine,' said Lucy, sipping her drink.

'Now, you were at school with Sarah. What kind of girl was she in those days?'

The former headmistress of Wickenden, Miss MacMaster, presently in genteel retirement in Hove with her 'friend', had been devastatingly frank on the subject of the present Duchess of Annan. 'Sarah Anwoth, as she was in those days, was one of those tragic cases of what I always call "upper-class neglect", and, as a result, was in a state of perpetual rebellion against all forms of authority, primarily (as is usual in these cases) her father and all he stood for. She had been expelled from several convents before she came to us at Wickenden; she was clever but self-destructive; by the time we got her she was anorexic; the psychiatrist she was seeing said to me that she was displaying classic symptoms of sexual abuse, but you know these people make everything up as they go along. I never cared for Lord Gatehouse, but to make that kind of suggestion was utterly preposterous; she dragged poor Lucy into her net, although fortunately, after that awful Gresham case, they drifted apart. Lucy's mother had just died and I remember thinking she was on the verge of a nervous breakdown. Sarah left the following summer, thank goodness, but Lucy stayed on and began to flourish again. Her fees were paid by her grandfather in Golders Green; the good soul helped her at university too. Poor Jane, her mother, had nothing and we were a school short of bursaries for girls in Lucy's position. I think she conquered her misery through hard work: she won an exhibition to St Hilda's, you know, just like her mother before her, and of course she's gone on to do very well for herself. I'm very proud of Lucy, not that I ever see her these days. She's too grand for me now. Ruth saw a picture of her in *Hello!* magazine with her little girl. She handled Prince John's divorce, you know. The Queen was very grateful.'

'Sarah was great fun,' said Lucy. 'I'd never met anyone quite like her. She had a wonderfully anarchic sense of humour. She was always in trouble.'

'How would you say she got on with her father?'

Damn, thought Lucy. 'OK,' she said, 'although they had their differences like any father and daughter.'

'Was she an attention-seeker, would you say?'

'Sarah? Yes, I would, but I still can't see what this has to do with the Gresham case.'

'It has a great deal to do with it, in my view. You may not be aware of the fact that the police investigation twenty years ago was hardly what would pass for such a thing nowadays. Kettle made a very convenient excuse for the local police to do very little. There he was on their doorstep, a ready-made killer: the Greshams for all their money and power were completely unnerved, as anyone in their situation would be; they accepted what they were told. Now they intend to move heaven and earth to find out who could have done such a thing.'

'Assuming she's dead of course. You don't really even know that.'

'You surprise me, Miss Diamond. I would have expected a greater zeal, a more pronounced thirst for justice from someone in your position.'

'It was all an awfully long time ago,' said Lucy. 'I'm afraid I think you're barking up the wrong tree. Without a body, you'll have enough material for a press story no doubt, but not for a court case.'

'Lord Gatehouse is already making it quite clear at a senior level that he thinks this investigation is a waste of money.'

'Oh?' said Lucy.

'You don't seem surprised when I tell you that, Miss Diamond.'

'What do you expect me to say? I deal with people like Lord Gatehouse all the time. I know what they're like when they're crossed.'

'He didn't like me,' said Elizabeth.

'He wouldn't. As far as he's concerned you're a member of the lower orders. You don't count. You're not One of Us.'

'And are you?'

'I'm Jewish. Not a grand Baghdad Jew like the Sassoons or a French banking Jew like the Rothschilds, I'm just a Polish Jew from the steppes; unimportant scum.'

'Is that how you see yourself?'

'No. That's how people like Lord Gatehouse see me and you.'

The advertisement in the *Galloway Messenger* read as follows:

GRESHAM CASE

Large Reward for information. My daughter
vanished nearly twenty years ago. If you have
a child or children you will know what this
means. Please, if you know anything about

209

the above case, contact Pauline Gresham at Balmachie House, or DI Elizabeth Dunbar at Kirkcudbright police station.

Heather Paterson read this before handing the paper to the woman behind the counter in the paper shop, although she did not mention that she had done so. 'And twenty Silk Cut, Jessie. I've still not managed to quit. I really thought I was going to do it this time.'

'Never mind, Heather. Try, try and try again. That's my motto.'

Heather, once the cook at Gatehouse Park, now ran a tea room in Kirkcudbright with her husband Robbie, who was a potter when he wasn't serving teas or cups of coffee to the local ladies with whom Heather's standing as a baker was exceedingly high. Jean Crosbie, the cook at Balmachie, swore that Heather's Dundee cake was the best by far that she had ever eaten, and she should know.

By early June things were beginning to get busier again what with the tourists and the odd twitcher in the bedrooms she and Robbie let upstairs, so maybe it wasn't the best time to give up smoking, particularly with that letter from the bank this morning wanting to see them both as soon as possible to discuss the overdraft. The last two years had been pretty dire for a business such as Heather and Robbie's. The weather, always unstable in their part of the world, had become positively psychotic: you only had to see what had happened in the harbour with the uncovering of those Celtic remains to understand that, Heather thought, as she made her way down the High Street towards the Harbour Tea Room where Robbie was holding the fort until she got back. They'd had to give up having a waitress last year and since then they'd shared all the chores, which meant that Robbie had hardly managed to produce any decent pots, which was not helping their marriage. He grumbled that he hadn't envisaged being a tea-room skivvy as his life's work and you couldn't blame him. When she got in there was a party of men and women she recognized as archaeologists just leaving.

'Fantastic cake,' said one of the men.

'Haven't had such a good cup of coffee since I was in Italy last month,' said another.

When they'd gone, Robbie said excitedly: 'One of those guys thinks he can help me have a show in Edinburgh. He knows someone who owns a gallery with some space for ceramics. He says he'll put the person in touch.'

'That's good,' said Heather warmly, 'that's really good, Robbie.'

She unfolded the newspaper, trying as she did so to decide whether this was a good moment to broach the subject of Pauline's announcement with her husband. She had been at this point with Robbie before over his work: he was still naive enough to imagine that his big break was coming; she knew that unless he was astoundingly lucky it wouldn't. The pots might sell, but how much would they bring in? And how could one rely on something so random to make a living? The bank manager wouldn't be impressed. He wanted hard facts not excitement, not Robbie's pie-in-the-sky.

'Have you seen this?' she said, spreading the paper out on a table.

'What?' asked Robbie, not looking. He was still revelling in the thought of a show, head in the clouds as usual.

'This advertisement, announcement, whatever you call it.'

Robbie scanned the few lines at speed. 'You can't,' he said. 'Don't even think about it. You know what Derry said when we got married.'

'That was then,' said Heather. 'Kettle had been put away, the whole thing was sorted. But you know what I thought about it all at the time.'

'Yes, I do,' said Robbie, 'of course I do, but Derry warned you that if you ever talked about why you left he'd lose his job and we'd have this place closed down.'

Derry, Robbie's elder brother, was the factor to the Gate-house estate and lived handsomely, as befitted the steward of such a property, in a large and comfortable farmhouse at Mains of Gatehouse, at the top of the back drive to Gatehouse Park, with his wife Kirsty and three sons who ranged in age from twelve to six. Only last year, Lord Gatehouse had himself paid for the Patersons to install a tennis court so their boys could learn to play. Kirsty, who had ambitions centring on such things, had been beside herself with joy at the social cachet this bestowed.

'How will anyone know?' asked Heather. 'And the money would come in handy.'

'He'll know. He always does. He finds out everything.' *He* was Ivar Gatehouse.

'No, he won't. You shouldn't make him out to be so powerful. OK, he's rich and posh but he isn't God Almighty, Robbie.'

'He's very powerful and very dangerous when he's crossed. He hasn't forgotten what you did reporting him to the social services like that.'

'And a fat lot of good it did too!' exclaimed Heather. 'They thought I was making it all up, especially when Sarah wouldn't cooperate.'

'Just forget it,' said Robbie, 'put it right out of your mind. It's all circumstantial stuff anyway. OK, so he gave his daughter a knuckle sandwich but that was twenty years ago, for God's sake, woman. And Lady Muck, her Grace, the Duchess of Annan, would never back you up. She really loves her Daddyo. I saw a picture of her with him in the newspaper last week, all lovey-dovey and Daddy's girl. They were outside the House of Lords or somewhere fancy.'

'OK,' said Heather, folding up the newspaper. 'I get the message.'

'You won't, will you?' Robbie entreated, as she went behind the counter to take off her jacket and put her apron back on.

'We'll have to go and see the bank,' she replied, 'you saw the letter. Maybe you'd like to ring for an appointment while I start on the lunches.'

A week later, the desk sergeant held out the telephone to Elizabeth as she came in from her lunch in the Harbour Tea Room. 'Boss on the phone for you,' he said, 'she already called once but I told her you were in the pub.'

'Thanks a bunch, Billy, put it through,' said Elizabeth, 'and I'll take it in my office.'

'I'm being put under pressure to stop wasting money by having you idling your life away at Kirkcudbright. You were out to lunch when I rang first. Did Billy tell you?' Stella Atkins sounded amused.

'I have to eat,' said Elizabeth. 'Let me guess: Lord Gatehouse is bringing the famous Gatehouse pressure to bear. This place is riddled with his influence. I'm even beginning to think I'm being watched.'

'Oh, you are,' said Stella, 'of course. What do you expect? How's it going?'

'Why is he so keen to get me off the case?' asked Elizabeth. 'I think his interest in me is significant.'

'You mean has he something to hide? The answer is undoubtedly,' said Stella, 'people like that always do; he wants to get rid of you because you're an unauthorized presence in his fiefdom; he doesn't like it and because he's who he is he thinks he doesn't have to put up with it. He's the most monstrously arrogant man I've ever met. Thinks he can walk on water. I'm rather enjoying baiting him. How was the solicitor, Lucy Diamond?'

'Cagey, but she is a lawyer. Says she sees Lord Creetown "occasionally" and is still in touch with the duchess.'

'I see. What about Lord Creetown himself?'

'A pussycat compared to his dad. Nice, uncomplicated, but cagey too, although not for the same reasons as La Diamond. Tribal loyalty in his case.'

'What is it in Diamond's case then if it isn't tribal?'

'She's a lawyer so she's naturally cagey but she knows something. I can smell it on her. When I asked her about Sarah's relationship with her dad she flinched. This is a case founded on sex, I know that for a fact. Sarah's old headmistress mentioned in passing when I went to see her that Sarah displayed all the classic signs of sexual abuse when she was at that fancy school in England. I think Ivar Gatehouse is a teen-fucker, but I can't prove it.'

'Your language!' exclaimed Stella Atkins. 'So you're suggesting that Lucy Diamond may have fallen within his remit at one point.'

'Lucy and possibly Katie Gresham, even his own kid.'

'Oh dear,' said Stella, 'oh dear, oh dear. This is shaping up explosively except that you haven't a shred of evidence. And just because he likes teenage girls doesn't mean he's another Kettle figure.'

'I know. I'm off to see the duchess tomorrow in Wigtownshire, then I'll go to Mum and Dad for the night. Maybe we'll talk when I get back.'

Annan House was a Victorian pile set on a slight rise in the middle of parkland dotted with magnificent trees. The house was surrounded by a balustrade above which loomed enormous windows with the blinds pulled down. At one end was a square tower with a belvedere on top and at the other end of the vast building, a previous duke had built an enormous conservatory which contained a very famous vine, a rival to the one at Kew or so it was said. Like the vine at Kew the Annan Vine also had a keeper all to itself. Of course, thought Elizabeth, it would have. These people probably thought a vine, an historic object, was more important than a human being.

The drive, after meandering to and fro to give as good as possible a view of the front of the house, snaked away behind some trees and Elizabeth found herself turning into a large courtyard, two walls of which were made by the house and outbuildings, the third being part of the wall around a large garden of which it was possible to catch an intriguing glimpse through a gateway. There were several cars parked in the courtyard one of which, a sky-blue Aston Martin, had the boot open. A tall man with very curly fair hair, wearing a shirt and jeans, possibly the duke himself, turned round when he heard Elizabeth's car and watched as she parked, before turning back to whatever it was he was doing.

'I have an appointment with the duchess,' Elizabeth said, closing her car door as he looked across at her once more. 'My name is Elizabeth Dunbar.'

'Oh yes,' said Sandy, 'you must be the policewoman. Sarah said you'd rung. I'm not quite sure where she is – we've got a few people staying – but she won't be far, I'm sure. I'm Sandy Annan, by the way,' he added, holding out his hand, 'how do you do. I gather you're here to talk about poor Katie Gresham. I hope some sense can be made of all this, it seems an awful mess. Terrible for Pauline and Michael to have the whole thing exhumed again, if you'll pardon the expression.'

'It is terrible,' said Elizabeth, thinking that he was the first person she had talked to who seemed genuinely sorry for the Greshams. He was clearly a decent man but in a way it was odd that this should surprise her. Just because he was a duke didn't mean he couldn't be decent, but she had definitely been expecting someone more snooty and ogreish, not this pleasant self-effacing man. Classism, she thought to herself, just keep an open mind for God's sake.

'This way,' said Sandy, holding the door open, allowing Elizabeth to pass in front of him into a long dark corridor lined with oils and watercolours of what looked like early nineteenth-century views of Rome and other famous Italian cities.

'The tenth Duke went on the Grand Tour after Napoleon had finally been banished to St Helena,' said Sandy, noticing

Elizabeth's interest. 'He got the bug and went back frequently; these are some of his trophies.'

'They're wonderful,' said Elizabeth, examining a small oil of the Forum in a heavy gold frame. 'That's by James Dawson. I've always loved his stuff.'

'There are many more by him,' said Sandy, 'I just don't have room to display them all. I've got some in my study. Perhaps you'd like to come and have a look when you've seen Sarah.'

The duchess was in the kitchen sitting on the kitchen table swinging her legs and smoking a cigarette. Apart from the enormous scrubbed oak table, so large that it must have had to have been made in situ, there were two dressers displaying an assortment of china, soup tureens, stuffed animals under glass, and old sporting trophies: a large two-handled cup bore the inscription, 'The Simla Polo Cup – 1919', and one other item in particular caught Elizabeth's attention: a glass specimen jar with a tiny human hand suspended in it.

The duchess, who had had her back to the door when Elizabeth came in, jumped off the table as her husband spoke to her. She was wearing a cerise cardigan edged with lilac velvet ribbon, and velvet jeans; on her feet, Elizabeth noticed, she wore mules in a black-and-white zebra stripe; her pale hair was scraped back off her face and secured with what looked like a piece of gold wire and she wore no jewellery other than her wedding ring and, on the same finger, a diamond the size of a small ice cube, the famous Annan diamond. The people she had been talking to, a man and two women, were lounging on a huge sofa with scrolled gilt arms and legs upholstered in pink towelling, which was positioned under a window with a view of the park and to their immediate left the conservatory.

'This is the policewoman you were expecting,' said Sandy.

'Doesn't look much like a policewoman to me, darling,' murmured the man on the sofa, staring at Elizabeth.

'Oh yes,' said Sarah, 'I hope you aren't going to arrest me, Pa said you were terribly savage. How long will we be?' She looked at her husband. 'I wanted to show Hamish and the girls

Annan Craig; we were going to have a picnic tea; Mary's made cakes especially.'

'I won't arrest you on this occasion,' said Elizabeth, deadpan, 'but we shouldn't be too long. Is there somewhere we can talk in private?'

'About a hundred rooms actually,' said Sarah, putting out her cigarette in a saucer.

'Use my study, Sarah,' said Sandy. 'Miss Dunbar was interested in the Dawsons. It means she has the chance to have a look.'

'The Dawsons!' exclaimed Sarah. 'God alive. If I had my way we'd give them all to the BM on permanent loan. Hamish, go and play with the girls while I'm being cross-examined.'

'I long to see you carted off in a Black Maria, darling,' said Hamish. 'I'd make sure they lined it with tartan for you.'

'Hamish did the upstairs loos in tartan,' said Sarah, as Elizabeth followed her down one long passageway and then another, all lined several deep with pictures. 'He said it was so unpleasant having to pee in something colder than Antartica and that they should be made as cosy as possible. Now you almost have to book one when the house is full. Kevin Took fell asleep in one. Marisha woke up and thought he'd overdosed. Hamish is Rosa Richardson's sidekick and much more inventive and interesting than poor, darling old Rosa who's still chintzing and swagging and ghastly-good-tasting her way round all Mummy and Aunt Marian's dreary old fogey friends. They love her in New York; all Pauline's friends in Bedford have had Rosa in. Hamish is too scary for them but I adore him. We're going to do the dining-room next. Hamish wanted to upholster the William Kent chairs, all forty-eight of them, in pink towelling – pink is his signature colour – but Sandy wouldn't let him, the spoilsport. I told him we could do what we liked, we don't have to please tourists thank God, and that every generation should do something radical and interesting but he said you didn't have to be radical to be interesting.'

'Really?' said Elizabeth, who hadn't a clue what Sarah was talking about, and cared less.

'Here we are,' Sarah said, leading Elizabeth across a domed hall with a double staircase lined with statues in niches and row upon row of portraits almost to the height of the dome; it was a dizzying and imposing place awash with afternoon light, an astonishing setting in which to lead your life, but the duchess, Elizabeth noted, stalked across the hall apparently oblivious to the classical grandeur of her surroundings; she might have been in Harrods or Harvey Nichols for all she appeared to care.

The duke's study was in another warren of rooms through a door behind the grand staircase where Hamish hadn't yet run riot although no doubt he had plans to gild the statues and line the stairs with industrial rubber.

'So,' said Sarah, closing the door by giving it a shove with her foot, 'sit anywhere. Is this an interrogation or just a chat? I haven't a thing to tell you about poor Katie that you don't already know.'

'You and everyone else,' said Elizabeth, sitting herself on a sofa at right angles to the enormous desk, behind which hung a full-length portrait of a man with a sombre expression dressed in First World War uniform. She did not dare glance in the direction of the Dawsons for fear of distracting herself.

'Not getting anywhere?' asked Sarah, lighting a cigarette and leaning out from her armchair for an ashtray which she put in her lap. 'Can't say I'm surprised. What do you expect to find at this late date? Katie vanished and Kettle, I bet you it was Kettle, disposed of her remains, then he says I didn't, all a hoax, but awfully sorry I've got to go now and everyone gets excited about it; it's beyond me, I'm afraid.'

'If Katie Gresham was murdered, then the person who murdered her is walking free. I'm sure you would agree that there is something wrong in that, Duchess.'

'If it's true, yes I do agree, but until she's found, *if* she ever is, I can't see the point of all this agony, especially for Pauline and Michael.'

'What would you say your father's relationship with Katie Gresham was, Duchess?'

'Poppy's? I dunno. We were just kids. Different generation, all that stuff.'

'But he likes young girls.'

'I'm not sure what you're getting at.'

But you do, thought Elizabeth, you know very well. From being all insouciance and careless dressed-down grandeur Sarah's tone of voice had suddenly changed, as had her body language.

'At that time were you yourself not going through a difficult time?'

'I don't see that that's any of your business.'

'We're treating this as a murder enquiry, Duchess; I am trying to establish the basic facts about what was going on in your parents' household at that time; it is, after all, where Katie Gresham spent the evening before she disappeared.'

'That doesn't mean we were to blame, Miss Dunbar.' Sarah got to her feet abruptly, forgetting the ashtray in her lap, which fell to the floor scattering ash but did not break. 'I think you'd better leave. I don't see why I should have to answer these sort of questions.'

'You can either answer them here or come back to the station in Kirkcudbright.'

'You can't force me,' said Sarah haughtily.

'I'm afraid I can, Duchess. No one is above the law.'

'My father was right about you,' said Sarah. 'He said you'd have him in a tumbril in a second. It's the politics of envy, it makes me sick, people like you, jumped-up little people who –'

At that point, much to Elizabeth's relief, the door opened and the duke came in.

'What's going on?' he said, going up to his wife and putting his hand on her arm. It was a gesture designed to calm and to restrain. He looked, Elizabeth thought, both wary and weary as if he were used to having to rescue and to soothe his wife.

'I want our lawyer,' said Sarah. 'She's asking me the most vile questions about Poppy, which I don't see why I should have to answer.'

'We are conducting a murder investigation,' said Elizabeth quietly, 'which means that I have to ask awkward and unpleasant questions. By all means contact your lawyer. I'll be glad to see you at Kirkcudbright police station at your convenience.'

She turned as if to leave.

'I'll see you out,' said Sandy, closing the door.

As they walked across the great hall, past the statues and the rows of pop-eyed, bewigged grandees, he said apologetically, 'I'm afraid she's very easily upset. She's a very volatile person. Sarah would be the first person to want to help. She just got a fright, that's all; after all, it's not every day the police come to interview you about a murder. I'm afraid she just lost her cool.'

'Of course,' said Elizabeth, 'nevertheless, I will need to continue our interview. Perhaps I could arrange a time with you now.'

'By all means,' said Sandy. 'We're here for the next five days, then we're off south again. Ascot and all that. My in-laws are staying at Windsor this year so Sarah and I are keeping the family end up; we're going every day so there's rather a lot to arrange. Do you go to the races, Miss Dunbar?'

'No,' said Elizabeth. 'My dad thinks gambling is a deadly sin, so I've never even been to Ayr races.'

'It's not really my scene either,' said Sandy, 'but the Gatehouses have always been keen racegoers, so I do it for Sarah really. She likes seeing everyone she knows.'

Some days later, the telephone on Elizabeth's desk in her office rang. It was Pauline Gresham.

'I've been contacted by someone who says they have some information that may have a bearing on Katie's case. A woman. She's called Heather Paterson. She says she knows you.'

'She runs the Harbour Tea Room. Her husband's the potter.'

Archie Jamieson had told Elizabeth about the Patersons

earlier. 'He makes that wholemeal pottery that every third-rate craft shop in rural Britain stocks. His brother's the factor to Himself. She was once the cook at Gatehouse Park but got the sack for reason or reasons not divulged.'

'How old was she?'

'About twenty then, I should think. She's my age, Heather is. We were at the Academy together.'

'The right age for his Lordship to exercise *droit de seigneur?*'

'A little bit old for Himself,' Archie had replied, 'and a damn sight too feisty. It's a mystery to me why she married Robbie Paterson.'

'Most marriages are,' said Elizabeth. 'Love is OK as an initial impetus but the longest-lasting marriages are the arranged ones where each side has too much to lose to dissolve the union. Look at the Gatehouses: dynastic alliance. She does her thing, he does his, but they stay together and are loyal to one another.'

'In public,' said Archie. 'Lady Gatehouse used to sit in the cocktail bar of the Anwoth Arms when she was full-time in that studio on the harbour. The barman, old Billy, was fantastically discreet, but once she was in her cups, there was no telling what she wouldn't come out with. It's no secret to the locals that it's a marriage of convenience. They don't speak in private apparently.'

'What did she say exactly?' Elizabeth asked Pauline gently, dismissing Archie from her mind.

'She said that she knew something that had a bearing on the case; that she told the social services what she knew twenty years ago but nobody would listen to her.'

'Did she tell the police?'

'No.'

'But why not?'

'She said that the police wouldn't have listened; that what she had to say didn't fit their case scenario for what had happened to Katie. She said the police were in Lord Gatehouse's pocket. And when they eventually caught Kettle she knew there was no point in pressing the matter. She let it go.'

'OK,' said Elizabeth. 'We should definitely see her. Do you want it to be at Balmachie or here at the police station? Maybe Balmachie would be better as it's more private. If she's seen going into the police station everyone will know about it.'

'She can come tomorrow. It's early closing.'

The next day in the back sitting-room at Balmachie House in the company of Pauline and Michael Gresham, Elizabeth listened to Heather Paterson telling her story.

'The Wednesday before Katie Gresham vanished all those years ago, I witnessed a very distressing incident between Lord Gatehouse and his daughter, Sarah. You were there too, Mrs Gresham, so you'll know to what I am referring.'

'I remember it very well,' said Pauline.

'You never mentioned it to me,' said Michael.

'You were away, Michael. And then she vanished. It went out of my mind.'

The great rock star himself, dressed in jeans and a shirt which looked a size too large, listened impassively while Heather spoke.

'Sarah and her father had a row at the lunch after the morning's shoot during the course of which he punched her in the face. I didn't hear all of it, but she was talking about the abductions, winding herself – and as it happens her dad – up, saying that there might be bodies hidden on his land, stuff like that.'

'And I was very upset,' said Pauline, 'which made Ivar all the angrier. No mother can listen to stories about children being kidnapped and murdered even in jest.'

'Why did he hit her, do you think?' Elizabeth asked. 'It seems a very violent reaction to teenage nonsense.'

'He just kind of snapped,' said Heather, 'but I couldn't hear all of what was said beforehand. Some people are like that. They can get so far and then they just lose it. It was unbelievable.'

'Had you seen it before, Heather?'

'I'd seen symptoms. He was a domestic tyrant. Sometimes a nice one, if you can have a nice tyrant, but sometimes not. A lot of the time he was very pleasant, certainly to the staff anyway. It was another matter with the family.'

'He hit her because she called him a child molester,' said Pauline suddenly. 'I remember it now. It didn't seem important at the time because he was already so angry. I tried to stop him, but I couldn't. I just put it down to more of Sarah's challenging behaviour. She was going through a difficult period. She was rude and tiresome a lot of the time. I remember Rosa Richardson being furious with her, but I felt it necessary to make allowances. Her mother was in and out of the clinic the whole time in those days. Sarah was a very screwed-up girl. I remember Katie saying so.'

'So the row between Sarah and her father could have had causes other than the immediately visible?' asked Elizabeth.

'Possibly, yes.'

'Did he ever make a pass at you, Heather?'

'He looked as if he might try but I gave him the evil eye.'

'Ivar tries it out on everyone,' said Michael suddenly. 'He was always like that. He had a go at Pauline years ago. Any woman was fair game to him.'

Pauline nodded at this.

'Would Katie have been "fair game"?'

'What are you saying?'

'He likes young girls. It's even been suggested that he was abusing his own daughter, Sarah. Maybe that's why he was so angry with her that day. She may have refused his advances the night before or something.'

'Ivar was always a spoilt shit who had a disgustingly bad temper,' Michael said into the stunned silence that followed what Elizabeth said. 'I've known him all my life. His mum, Gina, let him get away with anything, but I still don't see that this means he was a goddam child molester; that's putting the cart before the horse, isn't it?'

'He has a long history as an abuser of young girls,' said Heather. 'I saw it myself and I've heard things, other things, over the years.'

'Yeah, yeah,' said Michael, 'we all know Ivar likes the ladies but that doesn't make him a murderer.'

'"Like" isn't the word I would have used,' Heather replied. 'You don't hit women in the face in public if you "like" them, do you? Sarah was lucky that blow didn't kill her. If you strike someone in the wrong place on the head it's very easy to kill them outright. The punch he inflicted on Sarah was the kind of blow you would deal another man, not a fragile reed like Sarah.'

'I think you're exaggerating,' said Michael.

'There was violence in the air before Katie vanished,' Heather said. 'A flame had been lit. That's what I wanted you to know.'

'So where do we go from here?' asked Pauline calmly. 'What can we do now?'

'Nothing,' answered Michael, 'that's obvious. Look, don't get me wrong,' he continued, looking at Elizabeth, 'if Ivar's our man then I'd have the greatest pleasure in seeing him locked up for life, but there's no way we can make hearsay and rumour into a charge that will stick. You don't need to be a lawyer to work that out. There's no body, for a start. The girl who was in the temple out there,' he jerked one shoulder in the direction of the loch, 'is probably some tart from the Gorbals. The whole thing is an almighty cock-up, a complete frigging pig's breakfast.'

'Michael!' said Pauline.

'Well, it's true,' he said savagely, 'why deny it?' He turned to Elizabeth. 'If you can find my daughter's body, then I'll cooperate, I'll go to the ends of the earth, but otherwise you can forget it. I don't want to even think about it any more. And you'll never find the body. Whoever did it, wherever Katie is, *if* she still is, which I doubt, you'll never find her, not here. I know this land and you'll never find her. I don't know how you can ever hope to. It's a farce, and a fucking painful one too.'

'I understand how you feel, Mr Gresham,' Elizabeth began, but he stopped her.

'How can you understand how I feel? What do you know about losing a child? She was Pauline's only child. There are no words for that.' He wiped his eyes with the back of his hand and sniffed.

'Nevertheless,' Elizabeth persisted, 'I am going to search the grounds both here and at Gatehouse Park again.'

'What's the point? It was thoroughly done at the time,' said Michael, when he had lit a new cigarette.

'I believe Katie's body is somewhere in the vicinity of either this house or Gatehouse Park and I therefore intend to have both places searched again with a fine-tooth comb. The policies, the woods, the lochs, the surrounding fields, as much of the Coulter Moss as we can manage.'

'Has Ivar agreed to it?' asked Michael, shaking his head wearily.

'He can hardly refuse,' replied Elizabeth.

'When?'

'Next week.'

'And if you don't find anything?'

'We'll cross that bridge when we come to it.'

Stella Atkins had agreed to broach the subject with Ivar Gatehouse but she had made it clear she thought the exercise risky in terms of public relations. 'The vultures will be in there following your every move,' she said. 'I'm having enough of a struggle keeping them at bay as it is. If you have a massive police search and find nothing, then what?'

'I know,' said Elizabeth. 'You'll look a fool and so will I. Ivar Gatehouse will have his way and all will be lost.'

'How many men will you need?'

'Forty or so.'

'For how many days?'

'About a week.'

Stella Atkins considered this. 'OK,' she said, 'but you'd better find something.'

During Ascot Week there was a photograph of the Duchess of Annan in the newspapers every day: she wore Copperwheat Blundell and Philip Treacy hats, tottering through acres of newsprint in Jimmy Choo's shoes; on other days she was head to foot in Starweski and Gina couture or Versace with witty accessories; she was photographed talking to Sophie Rhys Jones and the Schlunks, drinking champagne with the oafish and much-sought-after members of the band Scurf, laughing at a private joke with Cosmo Nevele. Ivar was also photographed in the royal procession sitting in a carriage with a po-faced minor royal while Claudia chatted brightly to the American ambassador. She was dressed in Chanel from head to foot and looked as bird-like and fragile as her daughter, Sarah. There was even a feature in the *Daily Telegraph* about those famous mother and daughter clothes-horses Lady Gatehouse and her three daughters, with a portrait by Snowdon of Claudia seated among her girls: the Duchess of Annan, the Countess Harcourt, Lady Jardine: 'the equivalent' wittered the piece of 'those incredible Miller sisters in the States: these are our home-grown beauties the Anwoth sisters . . . what a wonderful subject they would have made for Sargent who painted the famous portrait of Lady Creetown that still hangs at Gatehouse Park . . .' and so on and so forth, complete with a reproduction of Sargent's great painting.

On the evening of Ladies' Day, Sarah and Sandy were having their annual drinks party in their house in Clarendon Road.

'I want you to come with me,' Tom said to Lucy, some days before when they were having supper in a restaurant in Pimlico that Tom often went to on his own and where he never saw anyone he knew.

'How can I?' she asked. 'Everyone will talk.'

'No they won't. No one will know if we arrive separately. You're an old friend of Sarah's after all and she's longing to see you again. You live round the corner, for God's sake. It would seem as natural as . . . falling in love with you.'

Their eyes met. 'Don't fall in love with me, Tom,' said Lucy. 'I'm not free. I see trouble ahead.'

'Damn trouble,' said Tom, taking her hand and kissing it.

'What kind of a party is it?' Lucy asked, removing her hand and finding that she had to resist the temptation to look over her shoulder to see if anyone had noticed. Either she was run down and particularly tired at the moment or the two further late-night calls she had received had unnerved her: the voice had simply repeated the two words the second time, but the third call had contained a new threat: 'Lay off, Jewish slut.' Twice the voice had been male with a regional accent that she thought was Scouse, but the last time it had been a woman with a foreign voice, impossible to identify exactly, possibly Polish.

'Just drinks,' said Tom, 'but stay to supper; Sarah always keeps a few people back; there'll be a tent in the garden I expect. Lulu says Sarah keeps people around her because she can't bear to be alone.'

Lulu was his sister Louise, now married to an elderly land-owner and living in Ayrshire.

'With the poor old sheep, you mean?'

'Sandy's very good to Sarah,' Tom said quickly, 'I just wish Sarah would respond. She's vile to him most of the time and he doesn't deserve that.'

'She used to find him the most boring man alive if my memory serves,' said Lucy, who found Tom's habit of defending his tribe from any slight made her want to attempt to provoke him into disloyalty just to see if it was possible. Dear, kind Tom: too dear, too kind, they didn't really deserve him.

'That was then. He always adored her, right from the word go. Fortunately, Sarah had the sense to see it.'

'Perhaps it's not enough. Being adored can be incredibly tedious.'

'Can it?' said Tom. 'Please don't look away or brush off what I'm saying. I mean it. I adore you.'

'Tom, we mustn't let this get too complex; it's all been so quick.'

'Are you backing off?'

'No, I'm not. I wish I could.'

'No, you don't.'

'You're right,' she said, 'I don't. But I'm afraid, Tom. Afraid of what's happening to me, where all this is going.'

'I want to marry you.'

'I'm married to Simon, you're married to Caroline. You of all people can't say that, Tom. You're committing adultery already; that's one mortal sin for starters.'

'I'll get an annulment.'

'And that'll make it all right? I'm Jewish, Tom. You can't marry a Jew.'

'You could convert.'

'I don't want to. That's what I mean. You're being unrealistic.'

'I love to be with you,' said Tom, 'I love to sleep with you. Is that unrealistic?'

'No, but what you said before was. Maybe going to Sarah's party also falls into that category.'

'It's a huge affair,' said Tom. 'No one will connect that you're there so I can look across the marquee and see your beautiful face.'

'If you do that they'll know at once. Sarah will guess.'

'No, she won't. She'll be too busy. She'd love to see you. Say you'll come, please.'

'Will your father be there?'

'Of course. He'll be thrilled to see you too.'

'I don't think so,' said Lucy. 'Last time he saw me he cut me dead.'

'He can't have seen you properly,' said Tom. 'He'd never do that. He doesn't wear his glasses sometimes because he's vain; he dreads having his photograph taken wearing them.'

'Will Caroline be there?'

'No, I told you. Sarah can't stand Caroline, never could. She put up with her while she had to.'

'She is the mother of your children though. It seems rather a short-sighted way of looking at things.'

'That's what Sarah's like; she makes up her mind about something and nothing will sway her.'

The Annans' London house in Clarendon Road, Notting Hill Gate (Annan House in St James's Square was now the head-quarters of a well-known brewing conglomerate) was a big square white stucco villa with a black front door which stood open to reveal a broad hallway with a black-and-white tile floor and yellow walls. The road was crowded with cars dropping off passengers. As Lucy walked round the corner from Coventry Terrace she saw Ivar alighting from an old-fashioned Bentley accompanied by Lowell. Claudia was evidently worn out from the vicissitudes of a carriage ride down the racecourse at Ascot with the American ambassador and was not present. Lucy went up the steps and into the hall where a maid stood holding a tray of glasses of champagne or Buck's Fizz. The walls were bare except for a large white canvas on the wall to her right with a woman's suspender belt pinned askew in the middle, adorned in one corner with a tiny little clump of what looked suspiciously like pubic hair.

'Lucy?' said a voice from the staircase to her left. 'Sarah said you were coming.' Louise Jardine came down the stairs holding by the hand a little girl with fair curly hair and enormous brown eyes who couldn't have been more than three. 'You remember me, don't you?'

'Of course I remember you,' said Lucy, 'you look exactly the same; besides, didn't I read an article about you the other day in the *Telegraph*?'

Louise laughed. 'That piece of nonsense. But I asked if I could keep the dress and they said yes to my amazement.' She was wearing a black dress with spaghetti straps and floaty panels and a great collar of pearls that wouldn't have disgraced Queen Alexandra in her heyday. 'And this is Georgia, my third,' added Louise, looking down at her child.

'How many do you have?' asked Lucy curiously, smiling at the little girl in her smocked dress and big pink sash.

'Four,' said Louise. 'The baby, Augustus, is upstairs. Gus we call him. How many do you have?'

'Oh, only one,' said Lucy. 'I thought that was enough to be going on with. You don't look as if you've had four children.'

'I'm like Mummy. Scrawny. It runs in the family. Davy's the same and so's Sarah although she hasn't had any infants yet,' she added, dropping her voice, 'we're all terribly worried. Sandy needs an heir and they can't adopt. It's jolly hard on Sarah as the rest of us are as fertile as rabbits. Davy's got five, can you imagine, all frightfully spoiled, three boys and two girls; little Waldy is the sweetest thing you can imagine.'

'Is she here?'

'No. She's just had number five; they were worried about her having a prolapse. Sorry,' she giggled, 'it's all we talk about at the moment. We're obsessed with our wombs. I read about you, Lucy,' she said, 'you did awfully well with the ghastly Ariane. We were so impressed. I boasted about you to all my friends. Tom's wife, Caroline, is Ariane's cousin, you see, and between you and me just as much of a nightmare. She wants to divorce poor Tomo who hasn't done a thing to deserve it. She said in the press we were like a Mafia family, I mean can you beat it? Poor Pa was dreadfully upset. She drinks unfortunately, won't go to AA. We all think Tom would be better off without her but he doesn't want a divorce. Poor old Tomo, he's so loyal. But look, I mustn't keep you pinned here, we should be circulating. Have you seen Sarah yet? Let me take you to find her. The marquee's a scrum but Georgie wanted to come down and see the party, didn't you, darling? I promised her she could stay up and wear her best dress.'

Sarah, in a magnolia satin sheath by Armani, her hair

scraped off her face to show to best advantage the magnificent Annan ruby earrings and matching necklace, was talking to a young man with heavy sideburns wearing a velvet frockcoat.

'That's Pinky Kilgowan,' said Louise in her ear, 'fresh out of the Scrubs. He says he's kicked drugs, but all those Kilgowans are addicts. He inherited millions when he was twenty-one, such a bad idea.'

'Tell me about it,' said Lucy, 'I did his divorce from the Vegas hooker. He wanted me to be one of his trustees, but I had the sense to refuse, thank God. Charles accepted but says he's always having to refuse him money. Pinky doesn't like that; he throws tantrums or sits on Charles's doorstep crying. Can you imagine?'

'Look who's here,' said Louise, tapping her sister on the shoulder.

'Lucy, what a treat!' exclaimed Sarah, kissing the air on either side of Lucy's face. 'Do you know Pinky Kilgowan?'

'Oh yes,' said Lucy, 'Pinky and I are well-acquainted. How's Scheherazade?'

'Don't ask,' grinned Pinky, holding out his glass to the waitress who was hovering. 'I might have to come and see you again shortly.'

'I didn't know you were *such* friends,' said Sarah crossly, 'stop hogging her, Pinky, she's mine but I haven't seen her for about a hundred years.'

'Don't let her bully you,' said Louise. 'She's still happiest when she's cheeking people. Some things never change, do they, brat?'

'Look, I can't talk now,' said Sarah, 'for obvious reasons, but I want you to enjoy yourself. You probably know everyone here. Tomo's somewhere in the herd, so's Poppy. But you must promise to come and stay in Scotland. What about next weekend?'

'I'd have to look at my schedule,' said Lucy, 'I've got an awful lot on my plate at the moment.'

'Oh, stop being so grand,' said Sarah. 'You can't have anything more important than us, surely?'

'Some of us have to work,' said Lucy, 'although you wouldn't know anything about that.'

'What cheek! I work all the time. Having people to stay is exhausting. Bring your husband if you want to, I long to meet him.'

'He's away a lot of the time right now.'

'I can't remember what he does.'

'He's a barrister, working most of the time in Brussels for reasons I won't you bore you with.'

'No, don't,' said Sarah, 'but come by yourself. I want to talk to you. We've got a lot of catching up to do. Say you'll come. I'll ring you, darling. Kiss, kiss.' She turned away into the crowd.

'Hello, Lucy,' said a voice. 'It's been far too long.'

Lucy turned. It was Ivar.

'Hello, Ivar.' She glanced to her left looking for a space to exit through but the crush of people seemed thicker than ever in this part of the marquee.

'That colour suits you,' he said, looking her up and down as if pricing her dress and shoes, and giving marks out of ten for hair and make-up; the old raking glance of yesteryear, Lucy found herself thinking. 'How many years is it?'

'You tell me,' she said.

'Lowell tells me you've done very well for yourself.'

'How very kind of him to notice.'

'You certainly look very well, Lucy.'

'Thank you.'

'Was that man I saw you with last year or whenever it was your husband?'

'Why?'

'I just wondered.'

'You know the answer, Ivar, so why do you ask?'

'Leave Tom alone.'

'I'm afraid that's absolutely none of your business.'

232

'Oh, but it is. Tom's business is my business. A divorce for Tom is going to be a very expensive affair.'

'I agree with you there,' said Lucy. 'If what I've heard is true she's going to cause you a barrel of trouble. I gather you jumped on her too even though she is your son's wife.'

'You shouldn't believe everything you hear,' said Ivar, 'as a top lawyer I should have thought you would have known that.'

'As a top lawyer, I know what to believe and what to discard,' said Lucy. 'You have a reputation, Ivar. People are talking.'

'*People*,' he said contemptuously, 'what do I care for people? They've always talked about us. Tom and Caroline must reconcile their differences and get on with their marriage.'

'If you say so, Ivar.'

'I do, yes.'

'You have that on good authority, I take it,' said Lucy, nettled in spite of her determination to stay cool.

'Indeed,' Ivar replied, 'the very best. Here's Tom now. Let him tell you himself.'

Lucy saw Tom making his way towards them through the crowd with some difficulty. He winked at her when he saw she was looking in his direction.

'Hello, Pa, hello, Lucy. What am I supposed to be telling you?'

'I was just saying to Lucy how wonderful it was that you and Caroline have managed to reconcile your differences.'

Tom looked at his father. 'It's the first I've heard of it.'

'I must go,' said Lucy. 'Goodbye, Ivar.'

'What already? We'd only just begun to catch up,' said Ivar jovially. 'Don't see her for twenty years and then she runs away.'

On the steps, Tom caught up with Lucy. 'It's not true, you know. The old rascal just says the first thing that comes into his head. He thinks if he says it it might become true. He feels very badly about it all; it's a matter of pride. Anwoths don't divorce, you see.'

'I seem to have heard that somewhere before,' said Lucy coldly. 'It's part of your family double-speak: say one thing, do another. Don't do as I do, do as I say.'

'Why are you so angry?' said Tom staring at her. 'I've just explained it to you. It's Pa's form of wishful thinking.'

'I have to go,' said Lucy turning away and beginning to walk down the steps. Tears came into her eyes. I love him, she thought, it's already too late. What a fool I am. And he knows, Ivar knows that. I've walked straight into the trap.

Cars and taxis were still coming and going, bringing people to the party. Lucy walked as quickly as she could in her beautiful but deeply uncomfortable very high heels round the corner to her own house before she could run into someone she knew. Maud was in the basement kitchen with Magdalena, Lucy's Portuguese cleaning lady. Maud, in her nightie and slippers, was winning at snap, but when she heard her mother on the stairs she leapt up.

'Mummy!'

'Hello, Mrs Lucy,' said Magdalena. 'You back early than I expected.'

'I have a lot of work to do,' said Lucy, kissing Maud.

'You're always working,' said Maud. 'We could play racing demon. Please! Please let's play cards.'

'Let me pay Magdalena and see her out, then I'll have a game with you, but only one, then it's bed.'

'Can't we have best of three?'

'No.'

'Best of two then,' said Maud, not for nothing the child of two lawyers.

Lucy had just shut the front door when the bell rang, startling her. Thinking Magdalena had forgotten something she opened it again, only to find Tom standing there. He had taken off his black tie and his exuberant hair looked as if he had been running his hands through it until it stood on end defying gravity.

'Can I come in?' he said.

'Maud's still up,' Lucy replied, dismayed by the shock of pleasure she felt at just the sight of him.

'Can't I just say hello? I am a friend of yours after all, aren't I.'

'Who is it, Mum?' Maud came bounding up the stairs from the basement. 'Are you the duke?' she asked Tom.

'No, I'm exceedingly sorry to say I'm not,' said Tom, making her a deep bow from the waist.

Maud laughed. 'Who are you then? You're not my daddy, anyway.'

'Unfortunately not,' said Tom, bowing again.

'You may kiss my hand,' said Maud grandly.

'Your Highness is very kind,' murmured Tom, going down on one knee to the accompaniment of peals of laughter from Maud.

Much later, when she had finally managed to get Maud into bed and extracted with dire threats a promise that she wouldn't come down again, Lucy returned to her basement kitchen where she had left Tom with the newspaper and a large glass of wine. He stood up when he heard her on the stairs and opened his arms wide.

'We've just had our first row,' he said.

'Tom,' Lucy said, 'you must listen to me. You have to go. You shouldn't have come here in the first place. Maud was terribly taken with you. No, listen,' she said, trying not to laugh as he made a face, 'I'll never hear the end of it.'

'She's adorable,' said Tom, taking Lucy in his arms, 'just like her mother. She looks exactly like you.'

'Tom, listen to me.' Lucy tried without success to push him away. 'You must go. Sarah will be wondering where you are for a start. She'll be expecting you for dinner.'

'WGF,' said Tom.

'What?'

'It was one of Sarah's pet jokes, don't you remember? Who gives a fuck?'

'Someone does.'

'What do you mean?'

'Someone knows I'm seeing you.' She told him about the calls that always came late at night.

'It's just a random thing,' he said, 'what else could it be? It's no one else's business but ours. You mustn't let these things rattle you. Report it to BT if it goes on. It's just classic abusive rubbish.'

For a moment she was tempted to confide in Tom but what good would it do? Tom would never believe her, nor would anyone else. She had no evidence. It was her word against Ivar's. And how could she say to her lover that once, when she had first known him, she had been his father's mistress, albeit one among a number and only for a short time? Tom knew his father had made a pass at her and she had deliberately let him think that Ivar's advances had been rejected; what she didn't want him ever to find out was that she had been a willing victim. After hearing that row between Ivar and Katie, Lucy had taken good care to avoid Ivar coming to her room again by moving back in with Sarah until they had gone south.

The visit of the policewoman, Elizabeth Dunbar, had rattled her more than she realized at the time. It made her think about the scene she had witnessed so long ago that maybe now had a new and horrible significance. Ivar must have been the last person to see Katie alive. Previously, she had allowed herself to think – on the rare occasions she did think about it – that Katie must have fled from Ivar and been caught by someone even worse, but now she wondered about it and she didn't want to wonder, she just wanted to be left in peace to love Tom a little longer.

'You over-complicate everything,' said Tom, walking her to the sofa and sitting her down with his arm round her. 'Just let Uncle Tom take charge,' he went on, stroking her hair.

'I wish I could,' she said.

'Why the tears?'

'Just tired,' she said, turning her face away.

'I'll make us some supper.'

'I didn't know you could cook.'

'Caroline couldn't and in the end wouldn't, so I had to learn or eat out every night. I enjoy it. I'll make us a risotto.'

'Why did you marry her?'

'Because she was sexy and well-connected and clever.'

'In what order?'

'Any order you like.'

'Did you love her?'

'I suppose so.'

'*Suppose?*' said Lucy.

'She seemed right,' said Tom. 'Pa adored her. He said it was time we married out of Scotland. My mother is Scottish, as you know, and my grandmother was as well. Pa thought a bit of foreign blood would be a good thing.'

'Hell's teeth, Tom, you make it sound as if you're breeding racehorses.'

'That's the whole point, we are.'

'And do you always do what your father tells you to?'

'Of course not,' he said, opening and shutting cupboard doors. 'Do you have any of those dried porcini? They're always delicious. Besides,' he added, 'when I met Caroline I had been thinking of becoming a monk, I told you. She sort of burst upon me like a firework.'

'A monk,' Lucy repeated incredulously, 'you? What a waste.'

'As you can see I didn't,' said Tom, 'but waste is the wrong word. I think praying continuously for the salvation of the world is a wonderful and necessary thing, but I was trying to escape the world and that wasn't right. Luckily, I found out in time.'

'What were you trying to escape?'

'Everything, I think. After Katie vanished, Sarah had a breakdown. Did you know that?'

'I could have guessed at it, I suppose,' said Lucy, 'she was working up for it before it happened. She was very weird in those days. There were lots of things about her that I couldn't figure out. Then she left and that was that. Why do you ask?'

'Because it meant I couldn't have one. It would have been a bit much to have two children in one family falling to pieces. I had to find some other way of dealing with the agony of it all. Katie was the first girl I was ever really in love with, I think.'

'She was very lovely,' said Lucy carefully. 'Your father certainly thought so.'

'Pa loves youth and beauty. Always has. He adored Katie. It nearly killed him when she vanished. He took it very hard.' Tom turned away to fill a saucepan at the sink.

'Why do you always defend him, Tom?'

'I don't.'

'You do, you know. I remember you telling me in quite strong language how your father felt about Katie. At the shoot the day before, don't you remember?'

Tom shook his head. 'I don't actually,' he said calmly, 'but I know there are things missing from my memories of that time. After she vanished, I kept having flashbacks of her as she had been the last time I saw her on the night of the dinner, crossing the bit in front of the house to where Jimmy, the chauffeur, was waiting for her in the Balmachie car. I was standing in the window and she turned round to wave. She was wearing that amazing dress, do you remember?'

'Yes, I remember.'

'What is it?' said Tom, coming over to the sofa. 'Are you all right? You look so stricken.'

'You can catch a plane from City Airport,' said Sarah, 'a tiny little airline called Scotair will fly you to Stranraer where Sandy will come and meet you. Tomo's going to be here – don't worry, I know that's why you're coming – and Davy and Waldo; they're leaving all but the youngest of the babies, or at least I pray that they are, and there'll be one or two other people. Cosmo Nevele's coming. Do you remember Cosmo? He certainly remembers you; got that column now even though he's the age he is, quite amazing really. Bring something warm even though it is June. You can never be sure in bloody Scotland what it'll do.'

Stranraer airport was little more than a Nissen hut with a runway attached. The arrivals lounge had the look and feel of a village hall with its makeshift café and a stand selling *The Scotsman* and the *Glasgow Herald*, a copy of which Sandy Annan was reading as he waited for Lucy.

'Hello, Lucy,' he said, kissing her warmly. 'Long time no see. I don't count the scrum Sarah told me you attended the other night. Too many people, so you never see the ones you really want to. Let me take this.' He picked up her case and they walked out to the car park together.

'Quite fun, this little place, and useful now the railways have almost completely ceased to function. I've got shares in Scotair. Tom told me they were going to thrive and he always seems to know what he's talking about when it comes to investments.'

He put her case in the boot of his pale blue Aston Martin (which reminded Lucy of Ivar's pale blue Bristol of yesteryear – what was it about men and baby blue?) and held open the passenger door for her in his formal old-fashioned way.

'You look just the same, Lucy,' he said, as they drove off rather fast. 'As pretty as ever.'

'You haven't changed much either,' said Lucy, examining Sandy's profile; his hair was still the mass of blond curls that had reminded her so much of a rare breed of sheep when she had first met him and he was as bony and as pale as ever, a thin, fair man with light blue eyes and long narrow hands and feet. So much breeding and yet a man who couldn't breed, she thought, thinking of her conversation with Tom on the subject of bloodlines.

'I never learned to do Scottish country dancing,' said Lucy. 'Will I have to make a fool of myself this weekend?'

'Not if you don't want to,' replied Sandy. 'We're having a dinner party tonight and we usually dance a bit after that, but it's not compulsory. Sarah's friends think it's hilarious; they join in and muck about a bit. That makes the locals cross of course. Rather a problem really. Do you know Hamish Blundell?'

'The one whose perfect taste launched a thousand magazine articles, do you mean?'

'That's the one,' said Sandy with a sigh. 'I was at Eton with Hamish and I'm very fond of him but his ideas are so tawdry and drearily trendy. Sarah, needless to say, thinks he's heaven. "Cutting edge" is the expression, I believe.'

'Magazines always refer to people like Hamish as "eclectic", said Lucy. 'How I hate that word.'

'Hamish studied fashion design at Central St Martin's; unfortunately his fashion career didn't take off, so he turned to decorating instead. All our upstairs loos are now kitsch little havens covered floor to ceiling in hunting Annan.'

'You don't sound very pleased about it, Sandy,' said Lucy smiling.

'I'm not, as a matter of fact. *Vogue* did a piece about us.'

'I read it,' said Lucy. '"Tartan with attitude".'

'Yes,' said Sandy gloomily. 'My poor old mother was outraged. She felt she was being mocked.'

'Times change,' said Lucy. 'But I sympathize with your mother. What about the new Scottish parliament?'

'I wish I could feel enthusiastic,' said Sandy, 'but I fear it may turn out to be a second-rate affair. Various people I know are suggesting their spare sons as members, very much in the way they sent them off to the colonies in the past or lobbed them into the church. London is still going to be the centre for a long time to come.'

'What about tax-raising and all the other nasties? Giving the land back to the native Scottish?'

'We'll have to wait and see,' said Sandy, 'but I can't say I'm optimistic. It's the politics of envy, a kind of neo-Marxism cut to fit the prejudices of the Scots Nats. The only comforting thing about it all is that the Labour Party will suffer.'

'Not a fan of New Labour?' enquired Lucy.

'New what? It's the same old power-broking fraternity

wearing a different suit and calling itself Mister Clean. Fresh Hypocrisy would be a better name.'

'I think you should go into politics, Sandy. You're just the sort of person they need.'

'I would have done if my father hadn't died when he did. I was expecting a longer period of probation, but my father was the duke for only two years before he was killed.'

'Big responsibility?'

'Feels big. Sarah says I take myself far too seriously. That's why she likes Hamish. Hamish thinks it would make me feel better if he covered my William Kent chairs in pink towelling.'

'Are you going to let him?'

'Of course not, but he'll think of something else, no doubt.'

'Hamish wants to replace these bits of old tapestry with some fabulous wall-hangings by a friend of his,' said Sarah, flinging open the door of the Green Drawing Room. 'The man from Christie's said all this was a fake, a piece of Victorian kitsch in other words, but Sandy, who has no sense of humour whatsoever, says that they must stay because they've always been there. I ask you!'

'Show me the loos,' said Lucy quickly, hoping Sarah would not ask for her opinion on the Green Drawing Room, 'I read about them in *Vogue*.'

Upstairs, Sarah said, 'What's going on with you and Tom?'

'Why?'

'Something's going on,' said Sarah, 'I always know. This is your room in here, as far away from Tomo as I can manage. I don't approve.'

'Of what? You still haven't said.'

'That you're having an affair. You're both married.'

'I don't think it's any of your business,' said Lucy, closing the door.

'He is my brother,' said Sarah. 'I think I'm allowed to have an opinion on the subject.'

'You can have an opinion,' said Lucy, 'but you should probably keep it to yourself. Stop playing the duchess, Sarah.'

Sarah glared at her, opened her mouth to say something and then closed it again. Rather to Lucy's surprise she sat down on the chaise-longue at the end of the impossibly grand four-poster bed and began to cry.

'I'm just jealous,' she said, 'pathetic, isn't it? You've probably noticed we have no children.'

Lucy waited.

'We have no children because we never have sex. Sandy's tried but he can't do it, or not with me anyway.'

'Is he gay?' asked Lucy, sitting down beside her friend and putting her arm round Sarah's bony shoulders.

'No, I don't think so. I used to look out for signs, but then I realized Sandy was too prim to be gay even if he wanted to be. I mean gay sex is pretty heavy-duty stuff; I just couldn't see Sandy doing it. I think he's a neuter, a nothing.'

'Have you tried to get some help? What about sex therapy?'

'Very funny,' said Sarah, wiping her nose with the back of her hand. 'My husband is not the type to go into sex therapy. He's so fucking prim.'

'So what are you going to do?'

'Christ knows. Fertility treatment. Sandy wanking into a paper cup: me with feet in stirrups waiting for a woman in a white coat with a turkey baster. Sounds fun, doesn't it? Davy and Lulu keep popping out babies like bloody guinea pigs and putting me to shame. I'm sure they do it deliberately.'

'Didn't you know all this when you married him?' Lucy asked. 'Didn't you . . . ?'

'Sleep together? No, actually. I'm a good Catholic girl, at least that's what Sandy thought, so he never tried. I was quite happy to leave it.'

'Why?' What Sarah was saying wasn't so much a succession of lies exactly, more a procession of half-truths. The Sandy-wouldn't-sleep-with-her bit was probably Sarah's way of saying she was frigid.

'Why not?' Sarah shrugged. 'I'm sorry. I don't know why

I've dumped all this on you. I hardly know you any more.'

'Yes you do.'

'I want to tell you something,' said Sarah, looking away. 'Did you know my father was fucking me when we were girls? "Abusing" is the euphemism they use these days.'

'I sort of knew, yes,' said Lucy.

'Did he do it to you too?'

'Tom asked me the same thing.'

'Did he?'

'Yes, he tried.'

'And Katie was part of it too, wasn't she? One of Poppy's little numbers, like that girl Sophia Bain. There were so many of us, we were legion.' She shook her head. 'Jesus Christ, Luce, when I think of it I just can't believe it. How he did it. For ages, I sort of believed I was making it up, then I cracked up but I never exactly admitted to any white-coated shrink what was happening.'

'Why not?'

'Because he would have been put in prison.'

'Don't you think he deserves to be?'

'No.'

'Why not?'

'Because he's my father and I've forgiven him.'

'The damage is done, eh?'

'Sort of, yes. We don't have children because I can't screw. Does that shock you? I can't bring myself to do it, not even with Sandy. He's desperate for an heir.'

'Oh Sarah!' said Lucy, putting her arms round her old friend. 'What an awful story.'

'I'm just a bloody mess,' said Sarah, 'I always have been, but you're not, you're the very successful Lucy. Very, very pretty Lucy. But maybe not so happily-married either Lucy?'

'I wasn't screwed by my father,' said Lucy. 'But my life isn't perfect either, no one's ever is, whatever it looks like on the surface. Things aren't working out at the moment. My husband's in Brussels most of the time, and I'm here. I'm not the type to give up my job and follow him loyally. I worked as hard as he did to get where I am. I wouldn't ask him to do it for me.'

'By golly, but you're formidable, aren't you?' said Sarah. 'I feel rather sorry for . . . what's his name?'

'Simon.'

'For poor old Simon.'

'Well maybe I feel sorry for Sandy too.'

'Well, you would say that wouldn't you?' said Sarah and they both suddenly laughed.

'That foul policewoman, Detective Inspector Dunbar. She came here and asked me all kinds of questions about Poppy. I threw her out,' she added grandly, choosing not to add that it was Sandy who had had to see her to the door.

'She came to see me in London. Don't underestimate her. She's as sharp as blades.'

'Poppy says the whole thing is a travesty. He's made a complaint. The file should be closed. There's no point in prolonging the agony. They'll never find her now.'

'It would be better if they didn't,' said Lucy.

'The whole thing's ridiculous. I don't know why they took what Kettle had to say so seriously. The man was a pathological liar. Who the hell else could have done it? It's not as if men like Kettle are two a penny in remote rural districts.'

'Quite,' said Lucy, looking away.

'There's tea in the kitchen if you want,' said Sarah, 'or you can sleep until dinner. Take your pick.'

'Sleep, I think,' said Lucy, looking longingly at the four-poster.

She was woken by the door opening and then closing softly. A late shaft of sunlight fell across the polished floor illuminating the rich colours of the brocade hangings but leaving the rest of the room in deep shadow.

'Who is it?' asked Lucy, sitting up in alarm.

'I thought I'd find you here,' said Tom. 'I had to stop

Cosmo following me upstairs. He's dying to grill you about your clients. Poisonous occupation being a gossip columnist, but Cosmo was made for it.'

'Does he know about us?' asked Lucy, putting her arms round Tom. 'I hope not.'

'Why would he?'

'Sarah does.'

'Does she?'

'We had a long talk when I arrived. Where've you been?' she asked, changing the subject.

'Playing tennis with Pa. We drove over together from GP. Ma's here too, for once.'

'So, almost all the family?'

'Lulu's coming for dinner tonight; Davy and Waldo might show, I'm not sure.'

'A full house, then.'

'Who's looking after the adorable Maud?'

'My mother-in-law. Do you miss your little boys, Tom?'

'Yes, of course. But what can I do? You must see it all the time with your clients.'

'I do. It doesn't make it any less depressing, however.'

'Can I get into bed with you?'

'Is it wise? This room seems as busy as Grand Central Station.'

'I'll lock the door. We've got an hour before we need to appear anywhere.'

At about the moment Tom was getting into bed with Lucy in the Green Bedroom at Annan House, a young American student by the name of Connor Cruickshank was climbing over the dyke that ran alongside that part of the Coulter Moss accessible from the Kirkcudbright road. His landlady, a farmer's wife on one of the smaller of the tenanted farms on the Gatehouse estate, had told him the Moss was out of bounds to everyone as it was a site of special scientific interest but Connor found himself irresistibly drawn onwards by the overgrown romance of the place where no one ever went, the thick vegetation sloping downwards over quite a distance towards the glint of water amongst the birch and alder, the buckthorn, the willow and the aspen. There was a sign saying 'No Entry – Protected Site' but the birch had grown up thickly in this part of the bog since the last time the peat had been cut here, which would be, Connor reckoned, some while after the end of the Second World War when the old world, Britain included, was suffering incredible privations and there was a demand for the peat which burned so slowly and so well.

It was a strange sensation he thought, as he walked over the squashy ground, to know that you were walking on what amounted to a pillar of water, several fathoms deep; it was a little bit like walking on a water bed; he could feel small ripples fanning out from under his feet and smell the pungent scent of crushed moss; somewhere a snipe made its harsh call of love. To his left he could see through the trees the tall chimney pots and gables of what his landlady called in her cute way the 'big hoos' where the local lord lived in secluded splendour. If he went in a straight line from this place at the bottom of the slope amongst a labyrinth of ancient drainage ditches and peat cuttings (much earlier in date, Connor reckoned, than the first stuff he had encountered), Connor knew that he would eventually end up in the estuary with its tall rushes and the grey mud of low tide.

He walked on towards the bog intrigued by the quality of the silence and the strange atmosphere of antiquity that seemed to hang over the place; the stillness was so powerful that he began to imagine that he could have slipped unawares through layers of time into another era. Looking round him at the vegetation, cinquefoil and cranberry, he realized that in a way he had: that what he was looking at was a snapshot of two thousand years ago when this place would have been much the same. He began to pick his way in the direction of the house through one of the ancient channels dug a hundred or two hundred years ago, now fantastically overgrown; he stumbled over a root hanging from the peat wall and fell on his knees in the bog. Glancing to his right as he got up he saw what appeared to be a human hand protruding from the peat, rather as the hand of the soldier protruded from the side of the trench in the famous story his granddad had told him about the First World War, about a foot above the ground surface. Intrigued, and unable to believe that he was seeing what he thought he was seeing, Connor bent down to touch the hand, which appeared to lie between the layers of soft peat, and tugged at it. Nothing happened. He then began to scrabble at the turf which came away in slices to reveal to his astonished gaze the naked body of a young girl lying on her back as if she had just lain down to sleep, her flesh the colour of milkless tea. She was so fresh-looking that Connor was certain she had recently been placed there – sleeping beauty in the peat – and that if he bent and kissed the smooth cheek nearest him she would open her eyes and stretch out her hands to him. Her hair covered the part of her face and shoulder furthest from Connor. The expression on her face was one of despairing agony.

What had happened of course was that the water level in the bog had shifted between the time the body had been hidden here, however long ago that was, and now; the weather in this part of the world (like everywhere else) had been truly weird of late: what might have remained hidden had been revealed, rather as the Celtic harbour at Kirkcudbright he had been looking at only yesterday had been revealed after thousands of years.

Connor made a note of where the body was, but even as he stumbled back up towards the dyke and the road he had a strange feeling that when he returned she might not be there or he might not be able to find her again.

Elizabeth was in the walled garden at the back of the house in St Mary's Street when the telephone rang. It was a fine clear day, a rarity in Scotland, and she wanted to make the most of it by being outside until dusk came. The ordnance survey map was spread over Archie's teak garden table and she was quartering the areas to be searched and trying to suppress the sinking feeling in her heart at the enormous task in front of her.

The desk sergeant from the police station, Billy Cormack, was his usual deadpan self: 'There's a body been found in the Moss, the Coulter Moss, ma'am, a young lassie. She was discovered by an American tourist, a Mr Connor Cruickshank, who's staying at Jessie McGaw's place. I think you'll be wanting to go down there yourself.'

'Is he there, the American?'

'Aye.'

'Let me speak to him.'

She questioned the boy who was remarkably calm and matter-of-fact for one who had made such a discovery. He had made a detailed note of the position of the body and was sure he would be able to lead her to it without trouble.

'Do what has to be done,' Elizabeth said to Billy when the American passed him the receiver, 'get me a photographer, call the doctor and the pathologist. I'll collect Mr Cruickshank now and get on down there immediately. Oh, and Billy?'

'Yes, ma'am?'

'Don't tell anyone. Do you understand? I don't want any trouble.'

'Of course, ma'am,' said Billy.

By the time they reached the dyke by the Moss on the Kirkcudbright road the shadows were lengthening. For all it was summer, Elizabeth shivered as they made their way into the bog.

'I lived by one of these places when I was a girl,' she said, picking her way carefully through the ancient weed-choked drainage channel, 'they give me the creeps. They were places of sacrifice during the Iron Age and the Bronze Age and you can feel it; the atmosphere is bizarre.'

'They still are places of sacrifice,' said Connor, 'if what I saw is anything to go by. Do you have any idea who she might be?'

'Yes,' said Elizabeth, and told him about Kettle and his activities and the deathbed confession.

'Wow!' said Connor. 'That is truly weird. If I hadn't fallen like that I'd never have seen her. She was incredibly well-hidden; no one would ever have found her. It's pure serendipity. Here she is,' he said, indicating the body.

The other guests were in what was known as the Music Room, a spare, pale room containing a copy of a classical frieze, a harpsichord in a painted case and, in one corner, a harp played by 'the singing duchess' over a century before.

'Well,' exclaimed Cosmo when Lucy appeared in the doorway, 'at last! Not before time, Lucy dear. We're all two drinks ahead, but it was worth waiting for. Is that dress by Tomasz?' he asked in a whisper that could be heard round the room.

'No,' said Lucy, catching Tom's eye and looking quickly away.

'Let me get you a drink,' said Cosmo, taking her arm and steering her towards the harpsichord where Hamish was presiding over a tray containing a cocktail shaker and various other bits of paraphernalia necessary for the making of knock-out cocktails before dinner.

'Don't give her one of your Torpedoes, Hamish,' said Sarah, 'you need stamina and plenty of practice to drink those.'

'I'm sure Lucy's had plenty of practice,' said Cosmo. 'Now tell, darling Lucy, about Nicky Paderewski and the divorce. I want to know everything.'

'She wouldn't be so foolish,' interjected Lowell, handing Lucy a glass. 'Her professional integrity would prevent her from saying a word, wouldn't it, Lucy my dear?'

'Naturally,' replied Lucy, taking her glass without the least intention of drinking any of it.

Lowell, wearing what had all the hallmarks of an Eddie dinner jacket with diamond studs in his shirt and shiny pumps with grosgrain bows, looked more and more like the Jewish industrialists and panjandrums of old who had amused kings and grandees with their passion for all things expensively English and their ability to always look wrong whatever they wore.

'That's a wonderful frock, Lucy my dear,' said Claudia, swaying over to her side clutching her glass, 'I very nearly bought it myself, but I'd already got most of my summer wardrobe. Do you know the Hergstroms? They've just bought the MacAllisters' estate at Upmannoch. Ettie, Raoul, this is Lucy Diamond, the famous solicitor; an old friend of Sarah's.'

'How do you do?' said Raoul, looking down the front of her dress with his pale piggy eyes. He was a Norwegian industrialist with the kind of glance that priced everything and valued nothing. The number plate of his new Bentley in the courtyard was RAO 1. He liked shooting stags and Ettie liked tweed: Upmannoch, a Victorian shooting-box with endemic dry rot, was their latest toy.

'Do you do only divorce? I am needing a new solicitor for my affairs.'

'Only divorce,' said Lucy, looking for somewhere to put her glass down.

'You must come to see our wonderful Upmannoch House,' said Ettie. 'Hamish is making me a drawing-room with sofas in a fabulous tweed that is being woven especially on Rhoig.'

'I won't have time,' said Lucy, 'I'm returning to London tomorrow.'

'Oh, but you are lunching with us tomorrow,' said Ettie, 'so you will be able to see the marvellous things that Hamish is doing.'

'Mrs Hergstrom,' whispered Cosmo, 'has bought Hamish's nonsense hook, line and sinker, something our beloved duke has had the sense to avoid, although it's wonderful to see Hamish doing something constructive with his life and at such prices! His fee is positively eye-watering. He used to be such a terribly bad boy when he was living in New York and running about after Andy like a lackey, not to mention the drugs. You should see his arms, Lucy, covered in scars like fretwork, darling. Now there was a little something I wanted to ask you about that only you would know.'

'No, Cosmo,' said Lucy.

'But you don't know what it is yet.'

'I can guess.'

'Oh, no, you can't. A little bird tells me that Nicky Paderewski –'

'Which little bird was that?' enquired Lucy sharply.

'Ooh, you're so fierce these days,' said Cosmo. 'I remember you as rather a lot more mousey and quiet. Little Lucy meek and mild. "Demure" is the word I would have used if anyone had asked me.'

'Which they haven't, thank God,' said Lucy. 'It was nearly twenty years ago, Cosmo. Things change, you know. I've grown up since then.'

'Something not everyone does, you know. Our dear hostess, for instance, appears to me to be in a state of arrested development. She's like a child playing sandcastles on the beach.'

'This is the Cosmo I remember,' said Lucy, amused in spite of herself, 'you were always astute. Tell me more.'

'Off the record?'

'What do you take me for?' said Lucy. 'Discretion is my middle name.'

'If only . . .' said Cosmo, gazing at Lucy appreciatively, 'if only . . .'

'If only I were twenty-five years older or you were twenty-five years younger. It's OK, I understand.'

'Did you talk to Prince John in that way?' asked Cosmo. 'No wonder he loved you so.'

'He didn't love me,' said Lucy, 'I merely undertook to do the job properly. We were frank with one another. I got him what he wanted.'

'Not even the tiniest indiscretion? I never reveal my sources.'

'You wouldn't have to,' said Lucy, 'he'd know immediately it was me. You're simply not worth it, Cosmo.'

'So cruel.'

'What's she doing here?' said Davina Harcourt to Sarah, inclining her head in the direction of Lucy. 'I didn't know you two had kept up. Cosmo told me she's Tom's mistress; it's the 'sort of disgusting detail Cosmo makes it his business to know, so I have to believe him.'

'Don't be such a ghastly prig,' said Sarah, 'just because you haven't got a lover.'

'I wouldn't want a lover,' said Davina indignantly, 'I'm very happily married.'

'I'm sure Waldy would be pleased to hear you say it,' said Sarah, 'perhaps you should remember to tell him some time.'

'At least we have some tangible proof that our marriage works,' said Davina in her inimitable way. She always knew and rarely refrained from telling the truth. 'Unlike some people. I'm going upstairs to check on the baby. I don't think this monthly nurse is much cop. I'll be back in a minute.'

'I don't know why you couldn't leave it at home,' said Sarah.

'I wouldn't expect you to know,' said Davina, 'as you haven't had any children yet.'

'You're such a cow,' said Sarah, 'you always have been.'

'Not very appropriate language for a duchess,' retorted Davina. 'You really ought to have some regard for your position.'

'Oh, go fuck yourself,' muttered Sarah, taking a swig of her drink.

'Sarah,' said Sandy, taking his wife's arm. 'You must stop Hamish making such strong drinks. Everyone's getting drunk.'

'You stop him,' said Sarah, 'it's your house.'

Sandy sighed. 'At this rate your mother will have to go to bed before dinner.'

'Oh, Ma's all right,' Sarah said, draining her own glass, 'she's used to it. Pa can take her up, I'll go and ask him to. Dinner should be ready soon.'

'How soon?'

'Very soon, pretty soon, soon. That's why we have a chef, so that decisions like that are taken out of our hands.'

'All right,' said Sandy, carefully, 'please control yourself.'

'I wish everyone would stop telling me what I should and

shouldn't do,' said Sarah in a loud voice, causing heads to turn.

'Oh dear,' said Hamish, replenishing his own glass, 'we're just getting ready for a little tantrum. Take cover, everyone. Flak jackets at the ready.'

'My daughter has trouble controlling herself,' said Ivar to Lucy, whom he had managed to separate from the plump and cold-eyed Mr Hergstrom. 'It seems to run in my family.'

'Really,' said Lucy.

'Don't try to tell me you have no idea to what I am referring,' said Ivar.

'I have no idea to what you are referring.'

'You're still shagging my son,' he said, lowering his voice.

'Who tells you these things, Ivar? Is it the same person who rings my number late at night to try to frighten me off?'

'Dear me!' exclaimed Ivar. 'So cool, so calm, so bright little Lucy. Who would have thought you too have your paranoid side?'

'He's very good in bed,' said Lucy, 'much better than you, Ivar, did you know that too?'

'Don't be vulgar,' said Ivar, 'but I suppose you can't help it.'

'He doesn't have to get his kicks by inflicting pain, Ivar. My arms aren't covered in bruises.'

He gave her a look. 'I've no idea what you're talking about.'

'Oh, I think you have. Sophia Bain. Does that name ring a bell? I found her in tears in the bathroom on my first visit to Gatehouse Park. You had carefully not touched her face. I was so naive then it never occurred to me what had happened.'

'A tissue of lies,' said Ivar, 'I have no recollection of this whatsoever.'

'Why do you do it? What makes you so angry? What makes you hate women so much, Ivar?'

'What rubbish,' he said dismissively, 'pure fantasy. I adore women. Women adore me. I've been married to my wife for forty years.'

'And just look at her,' said Lucy pityingly, 'just look at her. A monument to your loving attention.'

'How dare you.'

'Listen,' said Lucy, 'listen well, Ivar. I was just sixteen when you started fucking me. That's not very old. I'm not one of your lackeys, jumping to attention every time you make a pronouncement, Mafia-style, not any more. I know what you are. I know what you did.'

'And I know what you are too,' said Ivar, riled. 'A trollop from below stairs who mistook friendship for a bribe. You used us to become what you are today.'

'I worked very hard to get where I am today,' said Lucy. 'If I hadn't been so strong I might have ended up on the emotional scrapheap like Sarah. I know what you did to her, Ivar. She told me herself.'

'I shouldn't be too eager to denounce me, Lucy my dear, you have an awful lot to lose yourself, these days, in your position. Lawyer to the stars, friend of the rich and famous, it makes me laugh every time I think about it. Just a social climber, that's all you are, like so many of your kind.'

'Well, we all have to start somewhere, Ivar. Even your esteemed family were social climbers once.'

'My family achieved their position with honour,' said Ivar pompously, 'not by –'

'What are you two arguing about?' asked Sarah, taking her father's arm. 'Come on, Poppy, it's dinner. I want you to take Mrs Hergstrom in. Cosmo's going to take Lucy.'

On the other side of the great hall beyond the double staircase and the statues was the dining-room containing the William Kent chairs that Hamish was so set on, not to mention several Guardis, a Canaletto and a double portrait by van Dyck of the first duke and his wife seated side by side, their laps strewn with flowers, the duchess's hair looped with fat pearls.

As she entered the room, Lucy looked back over her shoulder and saw Sandy helping Claudia up the stairs; she was leaning heavily on her son-in-law and dragging her feet.

'Time for Lady Gatehouse to proceed to summer quarters, wouldn't you say?' murmured Cosmo in her ear. 'The Priory, darling Lucy, such a restful place. Claudia has her own room. Now Caroline's at it too. What is it about these Gatehouse men?' He gave her a look from under his eyelids.

'What's Caroline like?' asked Lucy, in order to deflect Cosmo's attention, knowing that nothing pleased him more than to be able to give an accurately cruel portrait of someone he knew quite well.

'Good-looking, dark, mad as a snake, sexy, huge trouble: excellent background but blood wearing a little thin; her father was in the SS, a real bugger, if you know what I mean, a swine, not a nice Nazi; mad keen on quarterings. Caroline went to Cambridge where she met Tom. Now everything's gone sour; it does rather seem to run in the family, you must admit.'

'Things do tend to, I agree,' said Lucy, allowing Cosmo to pull out her chair for her. Somewhere a telephone rang; as usual in a house this size there were bells stationed in corridors and passageways so that the telephone could be heard.

'And of course Tom is nice but weak; I doubt he has the strength to deal with Caroline. There's no iron in his soul as there is with Ivar.'

'No, thank God.'

'You didn't heed my warning, Lucy.'

'What warning?'

'Stay away from the Gatehouses. They're like an ammunition dump: the whole family is about to explode: between you and me, our friend Waldy is in serious financial trouble, Sarah is, as you see, on the verge of a nervous breakdown, Claudia may yet decide not to go on with her marriage; there are plenty of people to tell her that enough's enough and now there is Tom. And you. Stay away.'

'What happens if I can't?'

'Then you'll go up with them, I imagine.'

After dinner, a group of people who were staying in a nearby house came over to dance in what had once been the servants' hall which, at one end, led off the conservatory where non-dancers could sit out or gossip in peace.

'Just an eightsome,' said Tom pleadingly, taking Lucy's arm and pulling her to his side. 'It's as easy as falling off a log.'

'She won't dance,' said Waldy Harcourt in his jovial way, 'I've already tried.'

'I can't do it,' said Lucy, 'I never could. And I'm too old to learn.'

'What nonsense!' cried Waldy, to whom joining in was a kind of religion, whether it be The Game or a handful of reels. 'Course you can do it. Poor show, poor show.'

'Where's Davy?' asked Tom.

'Upstairs feeding the baby. That's all she ever does these days.'

'How many children do you have?' asked Lucy.

'Far too many,' said Waldy gloomily. 'The school fees bill is going to come to something like a million quid according to my accountants.'

'You could always send them to state schools,' said Lucy, 'and save yourself all that money.'

'Oh great God no!' exclaimed Waldy, shocked by such a suggestion. 'You must be a member of the Labour Party.'

'As a matter of fact, I'm not,' said Lucy, 'I'm not a member of any party. It was an altruistic remark made purely in the spirit of economy.'

'Better see if I can find someone to dance with me,' said Waldy who was baffled by Lucy on several counts but thought she was bloody sexy, 'or I'll be in trouble with our hostess. Have to do your stuff you know.'

'Doing his stuff is Waldy's mantra,' said Tom, 'especially when it involves lunching in White's, but you shouldn't bait him; he's incapable of knowing when he's being teased.'

'Look, you two,' said Sarah crossly, 'break it up. People are talking. Tom's got to dance. Come on, Tom. Make yourself useful.'

Watching Tom being marched off to do his stuff, Lucy

was suddenly overcome by a feeling of enormous weariness, coupled with a lonely sensation of being far from home. She decided that she would go into the conservatory to look at the famous vine before anyone else came to ask if she would dance one of their ridiculous dances. As she walked swiftly away in the other direction, she could hear the thump of the tribal music starting up on the state of the art sound system installed by Hamish behind the panelling. 'But you'll never need to hire a band again,' he had said, when Sandy demurred at the price. 'You can dance any time you want and the sound will always be superb.' When Sandy had mentioned that his grandparents had managed quite well with a wind-up gramophone bought in the nineteen-twenties, Hamish had caught Sarah's eye and smirked.

The vine, a monster with a woody central stem the size of a small oak, was at the far end of the conservatory, obscured a little from where Lucy stood by the leaves of the other trees and plants; the hot heady atmosphere combined with the strain of the evening made Lucy feel almost like a heroine in a Victorian novel escaping the importunities of some unwanted suitor. She found a wrought-iron bench set under a raised bed of some no doubt rare orchid with fleshy leaves and obscene petals and sat down to think.

'Derry says the boy was in there without permission,' said Lowell's voice suddenly, startling her.

'Permission or no permission, it makes no difference at this stage,' replied Ivar. 'It's a bit late for permission. It would look bad if we contested his right to be there. Do we know who he is?'

'An American student by name of Connor Cruickshank in search of an adventure. His family come from this part of the world. He'd come back to research his roots and was staying with one of your families called McGaw.'

'Jessie McGaw, that'll be right,' said Ivar. 'She does bed and breakfast during the summer.'

'The body's at the mortuary, then it will have to be taken

away for tests. Derry doesn't know where; he thought either Edinburgh or Glasgow. The Greshams have been notified. Elizabeth Dunbar was on the site before anyone else. Derry thinks she's seeing Archie Jamieson, the architect.'

'I see,' said Ivar. 'I know Jamieson. Father's a nice chap, well-to-do, although the boy's more suspect. He went to St Andrew's, I believe, and is of a more radical persuasion than his father.'

In the far distance, the dance music stopped. There was a sound of whoops and cheers and clapping, then it began again.

'Derry couldn't get anywhere near, he said,' Lowell continued. 'The police had roped off the site and there was a constable from Dumfries on duty, not one of yours, Ivar. There was nothing he could do.'

'What will happen now?'

'It depends on what the forensic pathologist comes up with.'

A silence ensued during which Lucy heard one or other of the two men get to his feet and pace about a bit. In the distance more whoops and yells as the music came yet again to a close.

'We'd better go back,' said Ivar, 'Sarah wants me to dance the Duke of Annan with her.'

Lucy closed her eyes and took deep breaths to calm herself. Someone – some boy – had found Katie's body in the vicinity of Gatehouse Park, probably in that sinister bog that none of them had ever gone anywhere near: the perfect hiding-place: and who would have known that better than anyone but Ivar Gatehouse himself? And when had he found out? Even as she asked herself that question the answer came to her. At the beginning of dinner the phone had rung, not long after she had had that unpleasant conversation with Ivar; that would have been when the news filtered through. It had been a mistake to come here, a mistake even to speak to Tom all those weeks ago: a huge error: she had known it at the time but it had not prevented her from falling into the trap.

In the distance, the music began again. Lucy slipped out of the conservatory and into the hall hoping not to be noticed.

'Ah Lucy,' said Lowell, rising from the sofa where he had been watching the dancing, occasionally tapping his foot to the beat. 'Could we have a word?'

'Not now, Lowell, I'm exhausted. I'm going to bed.'

'My dear, the night is young.'

How slick he was, thought Lucy, how serpentine; she was not deceived by his apparent composure, the relaxed way the foot went on beating time as if all he had on his mind was the dance or the chance to exchange a friendly word with her.

'I'm sorry, Lowell.'

She stepped past his foot: Ivar, in the centre of the dancefloor, was dancing a *pas de deux* with Mrs Hergstrom: a look was exchanged between the two men and Lowell was suddenly on his feet behind Lucy.

'It wouldn't take a moment,' he said, putting his hand on the back of her arm.

Lucy glanced in the direction of Tom, but Tom was immersed in the pleasure of the dance, twirling a girl in a spangly skirt and a tight tee-shirt, and didn't notice her imploring gaze.

Lowell put his arm through Lucy's and led her out of the servants' hall into a dark passage lined with antlers and photographs of previous Annans at play: bearded men with muttonchop whiskers and tweeds that would stand up by themselves stood in front of game carts laden with dead animals or looked on in sombre fashion at the corpses of a thousand pheasant or grouse, the fruit of a morning's work on the moor.

'What do you want to say to me, Lowell?' Lucy removed her arm from his grip and took a step backwards.

'Ivar tells me that you currently have Tom in your toils.'

'My *toils*?' replied Lucy incredulously. 'What kind of language is this?'

'You have become a very attractive woman, Lucy, very seductive. Does your charming husband know that you are seeing Tom who is, after all, also a married man?'

259

'What goes on between me and my husband is none of your business as you very well know. Now, if that's all you wanted to say, I'm going to go to bed.'

'I admire your spirit, Lucy, I do truly,' Lowell continued unperturbed, 'I like a bit of fight in a woman; it adds zest to an encounter particularly with someone as formidable as you. I just wondered if Tom was acquainted with all the facts about your background. Does he know, for instance, that you once seduced his father, that your career as a temptress started so early?'

'You tell me,' said Lucy, 'you're clearly going to anyway.'

'It's quite a thing, wouldn't you say,' said Lowell, 'when a woman moves from father to son. It would make quite a story in one of the tabloids, don't you think?'

Lucy waited, saying nothing.

'Let me get to the point,' Lowell said, lowering his voice and blocking Lucy's exit. 'A body has been found in the Coulter Moss. We are informed that it is probably the body of Katie Gresham. There will be publicity, the whole case will be raked over. The Marxist policewoman has got what she wants but I want you to be perfectly clear that if you have any intention of making any accusations about Ivar Gatehouse then your career will be ruined, as will your marriage and your adulterous love affair with Lord Creetown; there are pieces of evidence that we have gathered to support the contention that you are a dangerous meddler, the kind of sad, unbalanced person who gets kicks from dealing with the rich and famous, a fantasist who loves to bask in reflected glory.'

'I wonder how many times in your role as Ivar's flunkey you've been forced to confront the trail of devastation he leaves behind him,' said Lucy. 'I'm not interested in your threats, Lowell, you disgust me. Now get out of my way.'

'Brave words, Lucy,' said Lowell in his silken voice, 'I only hope you don't live to regret them.'

'Where have you been?' asked Tom, coming out of the

servants' hall into the passage where Lucy and Lowell were standing. 'What's going on?'

'Ask him,' said Lucy, pushing past.

'Lowell? What have you said to her? Why were you out here with her in the first place?'

'My dear Tom,' said Lowell, 'I merely strolled out after Lucy to have a chat. She seems to have taken umbrage at something I said. It's been a long day, we're tired, we've all had a lot to drink. I think she was upset at the news about the body they've found.'

'What body?'

'Perhaps your father hasn't had a chance to tell you.'

'Bloody right, he hasn't,' said Tom angrily. 'What body?'

'The body of a young girl was found in the Coulter Moss earlier this evening.'

'Who is it?' asked Tom, already knowing the answer.

'Until she has been formally identified, they're not sure.'

'Who is she, Lowell?'

'It is thought that it is the body of Katie Gresham.'

'And who found her?'

'A boy, an American student, who had no business to be there.'

'Business or no business . . .' muttered Tom, 'how did he find her?'

'History does not yet relate.'

'I suppose Derry telephoned Pa?'

'Indeed.'

'Why did you tell Lucy before you told me and Sarah? I think we had the right to know this news before anyone else.'

'I assumed that your father would have found a moment to tell you. I'm sorry, Tom,' Lowell said, diminishing his apology by fumbling for his handkerchief.

In the hall the music stopped with a flourish. Sarah, her arm through her father's, was talking to Hamish and the girl in the spangly skirt Tom had been dancing with, a very pretty blonde girl with a curvaceous figure and hair piled loosely on top of her head held in place with something resembling a small knitting needle.

'Pa,' said Tom, 'I want to talk to you. Sarah, you too.'

'But we're just about to strip the willow,' said Sarah. 'It's Hamish's favourite. Do you know Xanthe MacDougall? She's staying with the Ogilvie Smiths.'

'We have to talk,' said Tom ignoring his sister but giving his father a hard look, 'it's over to you, Pa.'

'Can't it wait?' said Sarah impatiently. 'We're having a party, for God's sake. What's all this about, Pa?'

'Come in here for a moment,' said Ivar, leading his children into the conservatory. 'Get Lulu and Davina as well, then close the door behind you.'

When they were clustered round an enormous terracotta pot containing a well-grown lemon tree, he told them what had happened.

'Derry rang through tonight to say that a body has been discovered in the Coulter Moss. They think it's Katie . . .' and here he paused for full theatrical effect and sniffed, 'but until she has been identified they can't say for certain. Pauline and Michael already know.'

'To think,' said Sarah, glancing nervously at her father, 'that she's been there all that time. Kettle must have . . .'

'Kettle had nothing to do with it, Sarah,' said Tom sharply. 'This is a different killing by person or persons unknown. So what next?' he said to his father, but without waiting for an answer he went on: 'The dancers should be sent home. I don't think we should be kicking up our heels here while Katie –'

'They don't know for sure that it is Katie yet,' said Davina. 'I can't see why we should stop having fun just because they've found a body in the Moss. She's been there all this time so what difference will it make? They're always dragging things out of mouldy old peat bogs anyway, aren't they, Pa? I saw a programme about it. It's probably not Katie at all but some Stone Age peasant. Apparently, there's something in the chemical make-up of the bog that keeps them fresh.'

'Davina is right,' said Ivar, 'until we know for certain, I think we should continue as normal.'

'Do we tell the husbands or not, Pa?' asked Davina, fishing out a tiny compact from her minute beaded handbag and proceeding to apply lipstick.

'Tell them when everyone has gone,' said Ivar, 'no point in spoiling people's fun. I'll have a word with Mummy when I go up just to reassure her.'

The children glanced at each other but no one spoke. They all knew that their mother would be sleeping the sleep of the deeply alcoholic and would not wake until morning.

'You lot can do what you like,' said Tom, 'but I'm going to bed.'

'Oh, don't be such an old spoilsport,' said Sarah. 'Poppy's right: until we know for sure it should be business as usual.'

'Who else could it be?' said Tom grimly. 'I'm astonished at you all.'

'Come on, little bro,' said Lulu, 'don't be so lumpen. Sarah needs you, she's short of men.'

When Tom had gone, Davy said, 'He was in love with her then, it brings it all back, that's all.'

'Come on, Poppy darling,' said Sarah brightly, taking her father's arm, 'you dance with Xanthe. I was saving her for Tom but you'll do.'

'I was going to dance with Lulu,' said Ivar, putting his arm round his middle daughter's shoulders, 'as she's looking so gorgeous tonight.'

'Thanks, Pa,' said Lulu, 'flattery will get you everywhere, particularly as my husband never seems to notice. He just wants to talk shooting with Sandy or business with that rather ghastly man Hergstrom that Sarah's so keen on.'

'Raoul?' exclaimed Sarah, looking amused. 'Yes, isn't he frightful, but that's rather why I like him. He's so easily impressed. I like feeding him bits of false info: for instance, I told him that Poppy always patronized Crosbie, the tailor in Kirkcudbright, and lo and behold old Raouly baby has ordered six sets of tweed somethings from him. Isn't it heaven! And I told Ettie that Queen Victoria was very keen on tweed and that it's deeply chic to have your sofas covered in it and that I'd do it here but Sandy won't let me and she fell for it hook, line and sinker.'

'Beast,' said Davy as they went back into the hall. 'I'd kill you if you did that to me.'

'I couldn't do it to you, darling Davy,' said Sarah, 'you're one of us, you'd know. Poor old Ettie's just a tragic fashion victim.'

'Lucy!' said Tom, knocking as hard as he dared on her bedroom door. 'It's me, open up.'

'Go away, please,' came Lucy's voice faintly. 'I just want to go to sleep.'

'I must talk to you,' said Tom, 'please open the door.'

'There's nothing to say.'

'I can't stand out here having a conversation with you,' said Tom, 'someone will hear me sooner or later.'

When she opened the door, she did not immediately stand aside to let him in. 'What?' she said. 'What do you want to say?'

'Let me in,' insisted Tom, 'what's the matter with you?'

'OK.' Lucy stood back to let him in then closed the door and locked it.

'Why the paranoia?' said Tom, looking round. 'What are you doing?'

'Packing my things. I'm not staying.'

'Lucy, what madness is this?'

'I'm not staying here. I want you to take me to Stranraer.'

'But there are no planes until tomorrow. And it's miles away.'

'I don't care. I'd rather sit up all night in that Nissen hut than stay a moment longer here.'

'Why? Because of Katie?'

'I'm frightened, Tom.'

'But why, my darling? There's nothing to be frightened of. If it is Katie's body – and even that has yet to be established – then the police will find the killer. They have a very high success rate in solving murders. That policewoman, DI Dunbar, she'll find whoever it was. She had all the instincts of a bloodhound in full cry. There's nothing to worry about. You're such a funny little thing: so poised and cool and yet so easily rattled. Trust me, darling; everything is going to be all right.'

Pauline Gresham was walking to and fro in her bedroom at Balmachie House in a white lawn nightdress and matching dressing-gown, her bare feet crossing and recrossing the scattered rugs and highly polished floorboards of her bedroom. It was one of those June nights when it was scarcely dark even at such a late hour as this and, looking out of the window at the end of her long room, she could see in the light of the almost full moon the shimmering surface of the loch and the subdued gleam of the temple in the unearthly light.

When the call had come from the police she had been in the walled garden situated at the bottom of the sloping lawns that fell away from the house towards the lower ground. Sissy, Michael's mother, had made the walled garden her life's work and it was open to the public every Sunday in June and July as part of Scotland's Gardens Scheme. The garden itself was a kind of paradise: south-facing with climbing fruit trees on sunny walls, it contained many joys including a laburnum tunnel, a fountain, rare old roses, hedges of box in geometric shapes containing herbs of all kinds, and there were glass-houses too against a wall where grapes were grown and rare flowers coaxed. The whole place had always been a refuge to Pauline: it was here, after Katie's disappearance, that she had found herself able to think of nothing but the job in hand, a kind of healing, during the most painful period of her entire life.

Fitting then, that it should be here that she heard the news from Elizabeth Dunbar that a body had at last been found. Peculiar timing in that it should be on the Saturday before the search was due to be renewed. A relief, that, in a way. She touched the head of one of her favourite pink peonies, a part of her still absorbed in the perfections of this garden, deciding on the spur of the moment to cut the perfect bloom and take it with her to the body of her daughter and place it in her hand as a memento of love.

As she walked across the lawn towards the house in her wide-brimmed hat, carrying her trug with the peony laid in it, and her gardening gloves, Michael came out of the front door and hurried towards her. He put his arms round her and held her so tight she could hardly breathe.

'Jimmy's bringing the car round,' was all he said. 'I don't think I could drive.'

The mortuary on the outskirts of Kirkcudbright was one of those jelly-mould buildings thrown up in the seventies constructed out of the ugliest possible red bricks and might equally well have been a health centre, an unemployment office or a school or even a church of the Basil Spence dispensation. Elizabeth took Michael and Pauline into a room containing some plastic chairs clustered round a table; dark blue velvet curtains were pulled across an interior glass wall.

'It will be a shock,' she said, sitting down on one of the ugly, uncomfortable chairs. 'Whoever we have in there,' she jerked her head in the direction of the wall of glass, beyond which lay the body on a high, wheeled mortuary table, 'is very well-preserved although it is impossible to tell at this stage how long the body has been in the Moss; the hair is discoloured and is a light red, but we think it was originally blonde. There are some external signs of violence to the right-hand side of the face and to the neck. It would appear that she struggled with her attacker,' she continued, 'but we'll know more about that once we have the pathologist's report.'

Pauline, clutching Michael's hand, hardly heard what came next. She could only think of the tiny baby who had been handed to her all those years ago, the fourteen-month-old tot who had climbed out of her cot and appeared at the top of the stairs at Balmachie in her little sprigged nightie just as they were all going in to dinner. In those days, Pauline remembered, Katie had had the most amazing fat, golden ringlets. Later on, when her hair grew longer and heavier the ringlets vanished, to Pauline's regret. She still had one, tied with ribbon, in a silver box that lived on her dressing-table wherever she was.

So many images of her daughter jostled in her head: the schoolgirl at prep-school in England with her long plaits and solemn pride in her new uniform, the older schoolgirl translated to Fox, an adventurous, American golden girl, almost as tall as her father that summer, so full of life with everything ahead of her to look forward to . . . but her thoughts were interrupted by Michael who had risen to his feet and put his hand under her elbow to suggest that she follow. She felt faint and weak, but Michael's arm was steady. She leaned against him as they followed Elizabeth Dunbar into the viewing-room. The lighting was discreet, good enough to see clearly, but not too bright. The searing brightness would come later when the pathologist did his job.

Pauline walked to the head of the table, drew back the cloth and looked, for the first time in nearly twenty years, upon the face of her daughter, the child who had vanished from sight longer ago now than the length of her entire life.

'This is our daughter,' she said quietly, 'this is Katie.'

Michael, crying silently, stood beside his wife gazing down at his daughter's face. 'I never thought I'd see her again,' he said to Pauline. 'I never thought I'd see my girl again.'

'I know,' said Pauline, 'neither did I. My baby. Can I touch her?' she asked, looking at Elizabeth who was standing by the door with her arms folded.

'Of course.'

Pauline stroked Katie's cheek and touched her cold lips. 'Who could do this?' she said to herself. 'Who could do such a thing?'

She rearranged Katie's hair. To Elizabeth's relief she made no effort to lift the sheet concealing Katie's body, but instead placed the flower she had been holding on the undamaged side of her daughter's face. It was as if, Elizabeth thought, some sixth sense warned her not to look at the rest of the body.

She stood with her eyes closed praying for her daughter's soul. Michael, holding her hand, did the same.

'Could Mr Kilbride be fetched?' she asked. Kilbride was the minister of the local kirk. 'I want there to be candles. I want prayers for her.'

'I'll go and ring him now,' said Elizabeth. She had checked earlier with him that he would be available without saying why, but when he asked her on the phone this time who the dead girl was she told him.

'So, she's been found at last,' he said. 'Poor Mrs Gresham, that'll be hard on her.'

'And on him.'

'Aye, and on him.'

Shortly after, Mrs Kilbride left the baby with her sister at the manse in Atholl Street and popped out to Presto for a couple of pints of milk, meeting her friend Heather Paterson in the High Street on the way.

'Colin's been called to the mortuary,' she confided, 'the police wanted him. They've found the body of Katie Gresham.'

'But they haven't started the search yet,' said Heather, puzzled, 'that was going to start on Monday. I know that for a fact. Elizabeth Dunbar's become quite a good friend of mine.'

'She's the one that Archie likes, is she not?'

'I've never known him so keen, our very own laid-back Archie. He's used to the ladies chasing him and that's a fact.'

'Well, they've found her, so Colin says. He's just had a call from the mortuary.'

'Where did they find her?'

'Elizabeth wouldn't tell Colin that.'

When Heather went back to the Harbour Tea Room, Robbie was just turning the sign on the door to SHUT, before locking up.

'They've found the body of Katie Gresham,' she said.

'Don't be stupid, they can't have done.'

'Well, they have.'

'Where?'

'Nobody knows. I heard it from Sheila Kilbride. She says Colin's been called to the mortuary and that it's definitely Katie Gresham.'

'You go upstairs,' said Robbie, 'I'll be along in a minute. I'm just going to finish cleaning up down here.'

When he could hear Heather walking about in the flat upstairs, he took the cordless phone and went down the path out the back a little way to the shed that he called his studio. The bloke's name was Mick, Mick Smiley, and he was the newly-appointed Edinburgh correspondent for one or other of those Sassenach broadsheets. Robbie had met Mick in Edinburgh when he went up to see the gallery that he was hoping to exhibit in and Mick had told him then that any titbits from the Galloway scene would be gratefully received and, this was where he had really caught Robbie's attention, handsomely remunerated. The scoop on the finding of the Gresham body should surely bring in a few hundred quid. And the beauty of it was that no one would ever know it was him who broke the story, not even Heather.

The telephone next to Elizabeth's bed in the big front bedroom of the house in St Mary's Street rang at exactly seven-twenty-two the next morning.

'Have you seen the papers yet?' said Stella Atkins' voice. 'If not, I suggest you arise and do so.'

'Why?'

'The Gresham story is on the front page of the northern edition of the *Sunday Telegraph*. I'd love to know how it got there.'

'So would I,' said Elizabeth, sitting up straight. From her bed she had a view through a tall window of the street; a dog, some kind of collie cross, made a crab-like progress across the empty road before pottering off round the corner. Otherwise, it was completely silent, but the silence in a place like this was deceptive. There were eyes everywhere. Someone had rung a national newspaper, which in itself implied a certain amount of organizational knowhow, and that newspaper had considered the news important enough to print on its front page. It was going to be tough.

'This shocking pace is the kind of thing you're going to have to expect. Are you up to it?'

She was aware there was an edge to the question, that it contained a challenge to her. 'Oh yes, I'm up to it all right. At least it's saved you some money.'

'There is that. I was worried you wouldn't find anything.'

'So was I. But I couldn't see any other way. We still might have missed finding her; the random element in these things is always scary, but it was a risk that would have to have been taken.'

'I agree. Now, I'm sending you Mike Farmer. He's one of my best. Make good use of him. What happens next?'

'I'll have to wait for the reports. Then interview, interview, interview. Ad nauseam, till I can crack it.'

'It won't be easy.'

'I never said it would.'

'It may even be dangerous. A trapped snake is always vicious.'

'Well, I'll have Mike and the team here. When's he coming?'

'Today. I'll get him to call you when he gets there.'

'What do I say to the press?'

'Nothing, other than the bare facts: the body, where it was found, etc. Everything you say will be twisted, be careful.'

'I'm taking Lucy to the airport,' said Tom, moving two paperback novels, a pile of newspapers and Sarah's whippet Bob, so that he could sit on the end of her bed.

'But she's not going until tonight,' exclaimed Sarah, 'don't be ridiculous.'

'She wants to go now,' said Tom, 'and I can't persuade her out of it.'

'But why? How rude! Doesn't she like our hospitality? Bloody hell, just because she doesn't like Scottish country dancing, that's no reason to leave a party. She could have just gone to bed and read her book instead of moping about making everyone feel guilty that she wasn't having a good time. Don't you agree? Or I suppose you won't because you fancy her,' she added sulkily.

'She was upset by the news about Katie,' said Tom, 'that's pretty understandable.'

'We're all upset by that,' said Sarah, 'why should she have a monopoly on "upset"? I don't like this diva stuff; it's bloody bad manners apart from anything else. I was thrilled to see her. I thought we were all going to be friends again, didn't I, Bobkin,' she said in a baby voice to her dog, stroking his long quivering nose. 'You liked Loocy, didn't you, babykins, angel-mine, clever poppet? Well take her,' Sarah continued to Tom, 'she can bugger off as far as I'm concerned. Don't bring her in to say goodbye, I don't want to see her. Tell her I'm asleep or something, I'll only be rude otherwise.'

Lucy, bag packed, went as quietly as she could down the passage outside her room. It was eight a.m. Tom had gone to tell Sarah she was leaving. Where the other members of the party were sleeping she knew not and cared less, all she wanted to do was to get away from this house, these people, the sense of unreality now turned to fear that had descended upon her when she arrived as if, like a latter-day Alice, she had passed into a looking-glass world and nothing was what it seemed. When a bedroom door opened behind her she jumped.

'Scuttling off, I see,' said Ivar, closing the door behind him.

Lucy walked on without replying; at the end of the passage she thought she should go left, and then down a flight of steps that would bring her out on to the landing where the huge double staircase was. She hoped that was the right way. She had a sudden irrational fear that Ivar would lock her into one of the innumerable rooms in this mausoleum and that, like the beast supposed to be incarcerated in the hidden room at Glamis, she would never escape.

'Cat got your tongue?' asked Ivar, putting his hand on her shoulder from behind. 'We know where to find you, you know; you're hardly living life incognito. Charles Butcher's a great friend of mine, did I tell you that? We were at Cambridge together. I'm awfully fond of old Charlie. I've given him some good tips in my time too; he bought his house in Arezzo from the last lot of advice I gave him and you know how fond he is of Tuscany, even talks about retiring there although I think he would be insane.'

'What are you so frightened of, Ivar?' asked Lucy. 'It's an open secret that you were fucking Katie before she vanished, and not just Katie either. There was me, there was your daughter, Sarah, there was Sophia Bain and God only knows who else.' She knew she was being reckless but couldn't stop herself. 'And some of us know that you, yes, you, were the last person to see her alive.'

'You're insane,' said Ivar, but his eyes flickered for a moment. 'I never saw her again after she went home that night. I can prove it too.'

'Quite sure?'

'Ivar,' came Claudia's voice through the closed door, 'who are you talking to?'

'Go and soothe her,' said Lucy, 'she needs you, Ivar. She's probably still seeing double or needs a few handfuls of Alka-Seltzer, maybe even the hair of the dog. I'll bet that comes into the equation somewhere.'

'Get out,' he said, keeping his voice low, 'you're not wanted here, you never were. Just go.'

It was a hot morning towards the end of June. The good weather had arrived days before and, as usual, had taken the city by storm; scantily-clad men and women lounged in any green space, optimistically displaying parsnip-coloured flesh to the devouring glare of the English sun. Cafés and restaurants tumbled out on to pavements with chairs, tables, awnings: the city seethed night and day: noise levels in Notting Hill Gate had risen to Neapolitan proportions.

The tube, even at the early hour that Lucy travelled to Holborn, was packed: she dreaded this journey pressed against people's armpits, the backs of their necks, awash with the smell of styling products and cheap scent, the suits that had been sweated into but not dry-cleaned.

The train crawled through the blackness towards Oxford Circus, slowed, speeded up, then stopped altogether. In the ensuing silence not one of the hundred or so people in the stifling carriage said a word. Someone's Walkman emitted a rhythmic scratching sound. A mobile phone playing the Marseillaise was rapidly silenced as if this carriage was a church and some sacred ritual was taking place outside in the dark of the tunnel. At last, the train juddered forward towards Oxford Circus.

As the doors drew back and the hedge of people waiting to fall into the carriage looked in, Lucy felt a sudden sharp punch under her left shoulderblade; a crescent of white light spun through her mind and then vanished. She felt herself falling into the person in front of her, but the press of bodies was such that nobody noticed; in this way she was carried on to the platform with people trampling round her as if she were no more important than a piece of paper, a mere scrap of humanity, a peeling, a fragment of something. The last thing she remembered seeing was the scrolled foot of one of the iron benches dotted at intervals up the long platform.

She dreamed that she was taking Maud to tea at Number 10 Downing Street: the house, as befits the residence of such an important person, had a huge complicated garden with a river in it and a maze; somewhere amongst the fountains was a zebra; Cherie Blair was very pleased to see her and Lucy remembered thinking that, close to, that mouth wasn't the strange hinged-looking object that it always appeared to be in photographs. The garden swung tipsily up and over; the croissant of sharp light lodged in her mind insistently, but still she dreamed.

Aeons later, a voice said: 'You are very lucky to be alive, Mrs Johnson.'

She heard that clearly and yet it was difficult to open her eyes.

Later still, someone else said: 'Your husband is on his way from Brussels.'

Husband. She thought of Tom yearningly, then remembered Simon.

'He's on his way,' said a woman, with a slight Devon burr, that conjured to Lucy's mind the fresh streams and steep-sided coombes of Simon's home. There was a place he had taken her the first time she had gone there: a sunken lane bordered by an avenue of the most majestic, fantastic beech trees she had ever seen: the leaves beneath their feet were the copper-gold of late autumn; the air had been frosty; Simon's dog, a grey lurcher, was already on the moor above, as swiftly moving as the shadow of a cloud on a windy day.

'We're all here for you, Lucy,' said her mother-in-law's voice. 'Maud is fine, so don't worry about her. We sent her to school today as she seemed to want to go. They feel routine is important.'

'Keep talking,' said another voice, 'it makes all the difference, even though they don't look as if they hear. They do. It pulls them back.'

But the dog had gone on up to the higher ground and they were following it with the wind blowing into their eyes.

'She was stabbed,' said the pin-striped surgeon, a Mr Mallett, to Simon, outside the door of Lucy's room at the Chelsea & Westminster Hospital.

'The knife narrowly missed her heart, but only just. Someone tried to kill her. Have you any idea why this should be so?'

'Of course not,' said Simon, who was incensed, but trained not to show it, by the surgeon's air of Olympian condescension. 'She's a lawyer – a divorce lawyer – hardly the same thing as representing contentious civil rights cases or the IRA, for goodness sake. It must have been some random thing, some madman.'

'She was on the Underground. It was very crowded. She was carried off the train at Oxford Circus by sheer crowd pressure. Luckily, someone called an ambulance, otherwise she would have bled to death on the platform. She's in a state of what we call semi-coma which I'm fairly certain she will come out of quite soon. The nurses who have been looking after her say she shows all the signs of surfacing. When she does and she's a bit stronger, the police will want to talk to her. I've managed to keep them out for the time being, but you know what these people are like. There have also been journalists sniffing around. I think your wife acted for Prince John, did she not?'

'Yes,' said Simon, 'she did. Can I see her?'

'Of course. Your mother's been in and out. She wanted to know what to do about your little girl. I said keep her away today. Children can find hospitals very frightening, particularly if they see their mother all trussed up.'

'Lucy,' said Simon leaning over her, 'can you hear me? Wake up, sweetheart. I need to talk to you. Don't leave me,' he went on, 'I need you. Please come back.'

The dog was dissolving but it had bitten her very hard in her shoulder and side; the white light had lodged behind her eyes where it burned and chafed. Her head hurt. She was thirsty, so thirsty she wanted to scream.

She opened her eyes and looked into her husband's familiar face.

PART THREE

From the moment I was stabbed in that rush-hour crowd everything changed. You'll say, 'Of course it did – you were in hospital. You nearly died,' but it was more than that. That knife was like a sword piercing the flimsy screen between past and present. The passage of time combined with my treacherous imagination had somehow convinced me that what I had seen so long ago was partly a figment of my imagination. It was all so long ago, so very far away, twenty years is a long time, more than half your life, you can't remember . . . this is the refrain I sang myself until I forgot about it for most of the time; it was sidelined in my life, an irrelevance, compartmentalized as a place never to be returned to . . . until I met Tom that is.

That first glimpse of him in the dining-room of the Coburg should have warned me. I knew it was dangerous. I knew he was vulnerable – as I was – but did that stop me? Did it hell. What happened after that seemed in retrospect to have all the horrible inevitability of an avalanche seen in a dream: the top comes off the mountain and rolls towards you in slow motion and you stand there waiting to be engulfed.

The stabbing changed all that. I had no doubt who was behind it but I would never be able to prove it. The police took the line that it could have been anyone and was probably something random, but do you have any enemies we should know about? I chose not to answer that question then and there with a drip up one nostril and the constant glow of pain in my left side, kept just below agonizing levels by morphine to start with and handfuls of huge hospital painkillers after that.

I would tell what I knew, I knew that from the first return to consciousness; there had to be a point to my being alive, there had to be some purpose to it: I soon decided that that purpose was justice, but I had to think it through, I had to plan my disclosure carefully. And I was scared too, scared to death.

You probably remember the furore that the discovery of Katie's body unleashed. The press were entranced by the macabre circumstances of the finding of the body and indeed one could see why: she was as perfectly preserved as if she had been deep-frozen rather than murdered: like Diana's, her death seemed unreal: she was Sleeping Beauty waiting for the prince's kiss, the lovely maiden of the marsh imprisoned by a ruthless ogre: the newspapers had a printfest, running endless articles about other bodies found in the marshes of North Jutland including the story of the Norse Queen Gunhild, a beautiful but ruthless queen who for her pains was beaten up by King Harald and then drowned and sunk in a deep bog. Some local hack discovered that Katie's wasn't the first body to have been discovered in the Coulter Moss: in the mid-nineteenth century the bog had yielded up as it periodically did one of its secrets: a body of a man had been found, so well-preserved that it appeared, as it did with Katie, that the death was recent. The locals who had found this body did not want to report their discovery and so reburied the body in a box, leaving its rediscovery to be made some time in the thirties. And of course there was the long-running story of Pauline and Michael Gresham for the press vultures to feast on: the meeting, the marriage, the numerous infidelities (on Michael's part), the love children that he produced here and there, the fact that Katie was Pauline's only child and the heiress to the Milo fortune.

This was the window-dressing, the frothy stuff that the

punters loved: the police investigation was anything but frothy: the fact that the body had been found so close to Gatehouse Park was highly significant; I heard on the news that they were looking for a murder weapon; there were police frogmen in the Coulter Moss searching the deepest pools and the peace of the dense reeds along the edge of estuary, haunt of water rail and duck, was disturbed by other policemen in waders going over every available inch; the bathing hut was cordoned off with white tape and the wicker chairs and all the other objects, old bathing towels, hats, waders, fishing nets were all taken away for forensic investigation.

As I lay in my hospital bed with a policeman on the door and a nurse in constant attendance, I wondered if Ivar was handling the publicity as well as he had when there had last been massive press intrusion at the time of Katie's disappearance, or did he feel the net was closing on him. I suspected the latter and it was part of my calculation: if I were to tell what I knew, I would have to do it before I left the hospital otherwise I might not escape the next attempt, for next attempt there would surely be, but first of all I would have to tell Tom.

It would be the end of us of course, I knew that and I regretted it terribly; in spite of all my resolutions not to, I loved Tom. How not? He was kind and intelligent and good-hearted and he needed me dreadfully and loved me back much more than I deserved.

It would also be the end of my marriage and very probably my job too; I was under no illusion – I would be taking on the Establishment: Ivar was tough and exceedingly powerful in his own way; he had tentacles into everything: politics, money, society; he knew everyone who was anyone; he could probably bribe the judge if he wanted to and might even succeed. So why do it then? Why put everything on the line when it looked certain that I would be crushed mercilessly?

For some reason when I asked myself this question I remembered my Golders Green grandfather, Simon, my educational benefactor. Once, as a young girl, when I had asked some thoughtless childish question about why he was bothering to record the lives of the long-dead whose village had vanished beneath the pillar of fire inflicted by the Nazis, he had said that it was important for the dead to know that he remembered them. This idea, novel to me then, returned to me as a revelation during those restless agonizing nights in hospital when time appeared to have played one of its little tricks and stopped altogether. I had a duty to the dead, to my parents and grandparents as well as to Katie: I had to bear witness to what I had seen no matter what it cost. I didn't want to be jolted out of my safe little cocoon, the present that I had so satisfactorily constructed for myself: my marriage, my job, my child: the good things I had achieved for myself. I didn't want to remember the past, or to re-find in myself the insecure little Jew-girl, the classic outsider who had been drawn to these people like a moth to a flame, seeking extinction; I didn't want to remember the sexual initiation at the hands of the expert and then the humiliation followed by an ever-greater eagerness on my part; I didn't want to remember that I had betrayed everything my mother had brought me up to believe in and so easily too, so carelessly, just chucked it away as if it meant nothing; I had played the game by other people's rules, not my own, and the memory of it all tormented me. All this added up to the fact that I had to speak out now. I had seen, unwittingly and unwillingly, the last act of a drama that had ended in Katie's death.

My mother knew that Ivar was a corrupter and I think she saw that he had sullied me but there was nothing she could do and, thank God, she never understood to what depths I had plunged. I was adolescent, she was dying; we had had to accept each other's limitations that last autumn of her life.

But first, even before Tom, I had to tell Simon. His mother, Diana, remained in London while I was in hospital and I was very grateful to her because it meant that I could see Simon alone without Maud in tow. He would look in each day early

282

in the morning and then again on his return journey on his way to the Temple. He knew something was wrong between us but he was waiting for me to tell him what it was. His training allowed him to be patient in that way; he knew how to wait.

I told him the day they took the tube out of my nostril. He had left work unusually early and was sitting on a chair by my bed at 6 p.m., drinking a glass of champagne from a bottle he had brought with him.

'We have to talk,' I said. 'Shut the door and put up the sign saying "No Visitors".'

'Sure,' said Simon matter-of-factly, putting his glass down and getting up. He had this steadiness in him that I loved, a kind of ability to absorb shock without falling to pieces; he would be good in an emotional earthquake, my Simon. He would have to be.

'OK,' he said, sitting down again and refilling his glass, 'fire away. What's going on?'

I told him the whole story, beginning with my first visit to Gatehouse Park and ending with my affair with Tom, the recent visit to Annan House and what came afterwards. He listened with professional attentiveness, nodding encouragingly at the points where I looked like wavering and occasionally questioning me carefully over certain aspects of the story.

'I knew you had some connection with Ivar Gatehouse,' he said, when I had finished. 'I should have persisted more in that direction. I'm sorry. I owe you an apology, I've been neglecting you.' He met my glance. 'You don't have to do this, you know. You don't have to make a sacrificial victim of yourself in order to achieve forgiveness from the world or from me.'

There was a silence.

'I can't live with it,' I said, 'not any longer. Kettle's confession let me off the hook, but I have to do something now. And I was a part of it but I chose to forget what I'd seen, I wanted to forget.'

'You were a young girl whose mother had just died, leaving you orphaned. Why should you be any wiser than a policeman, than a court? Kettle confessed. You had every reason to jettison your memories of the Anwoths.'

Another silence.

'Are you in love with him?'

'Yes.'

I looked at my left hand with its wedding ring and the pretty square-cut diamond we had chosen together from a shop in the Burlington Arcade, remembering how happy I had felt that day and the salesman's discreet amusement at the obvious pleasure we took in one another.

'I'm sorry, Simon.'

'I'm sorry too.' He thought for a moment, then he said: 'If you are determined on this course of action, you'll lose him. You do realize that, don't you?'

'You should be encouraging me to go forward,' I said, 'not playing devil's advocate.'

'You're my wife,' he said. 'I care about what happens to you.'

'Where's the anger?' I asked. 'Why aren't you more angry?'

'It seems a cowardly response to something that I am as much to blame for as you are,' he said. 'I've neglected you, I know I have, but the work seemed to take up all the space in my mind . . . I kept telling myself to make more of an effort. And I knew that your work was equally absorbing to you, and you had all the nanny problems to juggle with too. What a mess we've made of it,' he said, 'what an awful mess.'

He put his face in his hands for a moment. I looked at his hands and his hair, thick fair hair now laced with grey, hands I knew as well as I knew my own. He had the long, solid body of the farmers whose descendant he was; perhaps that was where his stoicism came from too: farming is all about defeat at the hands of the weather and disease; somewhere in him he had the courage to deal with failure, to pick himself up and go on, or at least that was what I had to hope for.

After a while he said, looking up, his eyes watery, 'If you are determined to do this, then I will do everything in my power to help you. I owe you that. Ivar Gatehouse will try to destroy you. He's completely ruthless and he has a great deal more to lose even than you. I don't have to point out that you may end up with a prison sentence yourself. The fact that you never said anything about seeing them together in the bathing hut will look bad, as will the fact that you slept with him before and then after.'

'I didn't sleep with him again afterwards. I went to Sarah's room so that I wouldn't have to.'

'Whatever,' said Simon. 'The fact that you were having a sexual relationship with him will tell against you. You should think about it for a few days. Don't do anything rash.' He bent to kiss me. 'I love you very much,' he said, 'I want you to remember that. I won't patronize you by saying what a wonderful woman you are, because you already know that or you should. I hope our daughter turns out to be just like you.'

'You know why I'm doing it, don't you?'

'Of course I do,' he said bravely, 'and I think you're quite right too.'

He knew as well as I did that what I was about to do might ruin his own exceedingly promising career, but he believed in justice and, as he said, if you believed in something you had to see it through. Simon's decency made me feel very humble and an altogether unworthy recipient of his love. I knew I didn't deserve to be loved by someone as good as he was, but when I asked myself why not (long hospital nights make you introspective even if you aren't in the habit of examining your conscience or your soul) reasons came there none; there was just one of those internal silences which, if one can be bothered to sit them out, are occasionally very productive.

There were things about myself that I had chosen to forget or to jettison deliberately: my adolescence was one such area; everything about it had seemed tainted with disaster. I could date the onset of the blight from the time I met Sarah Anwoth: if my mother's death was unfortunate, Ivar's appearance at that

point in my life was very nearly fatal. Ivar had put me in the
position of Bluebeard's wife: I had seen the bodies swinging
and dripping in the hidden chamber and I had had to forget
what I had seen if I wanted to survive. And so I had cut my
adolescence out of my memory with surgical precision, or
allowed it to drop out of sight as if it had never existed;
feelings of guilt surfaced occasionally like bubbles from a
wreck far beneath, but I ignored them. I had only myself in
the world, other than my Tenterden grandparents, and we
were never close. My Golders Green grandfather died suddenly
eighteen months after Katie's disappearance, leaving his estate
to me. In my trance-like condition I scarcely logged his death;
it was just one more vanishing, one more loss.

I made a decision to work and stuck to it. Law school
followed university. Eventually, I met Simon and got married.
We were dinkies for some years before Maud came along,
which had enabled us to buy our expensive house and live
in the rather luxurious and princely way that people like the
Anwoths take for granted.

And all the time, without realizing quite what was happening, I was once more drawing nearer and nearer to their world.
To start with, as one of Charles's assistants, I did the endless
donkey work that all legal practice entails; I would attend
conferences with barristers and take notes; I would make sure
the files, barrowloads of them, made their way from our offices
to whichever part of the Inns of Court required sight of them.
I would spend hours going over statements of income and
expenditure looking for mistakes or evasions, I would write
letters telling clients what time and where to arrive in court.

The clients of a firm like ours were almost invariably rich
(they had to be to afford our fees) and quite often desperate;
the family department bore the brunt of what we called 'the
hangover calls': the late-night rows, threats and occasional
woundings that occurred when clients met to discuss their
situation over dinner and drank too much. (Drink and divorce
go hand-in-hand.) For some reason, I had the knack of soothing

the savage breasts of these extremely spoilt people: wild-eyed wives would call me from the car phone in the Mercedes on their way to the gym or, occasionally, on the school run; against a background recitative of rioting small children I would listen to and attempt to decipher the litany of grievances against and cruelties inflicted by Charles or Piers or Sebastian, what shits they were, how they had stopped the money or the weekend or the skiing holiday or weren't paying the school fees. The complaints were remarkably similar and I was very good at dealing with them.

People began to ask for me by name and told Charles afterwards what an asset I was. My rise was swift, meteoric even. Family law appeared to be my forte. So much for a first in English, but the job had its compensations: grateful clients, moments of drama in court or out, the occasional sumptuous present: a fur coat, a car, a skiing holiday in Aspen or Gstaad. Eventually, through the word of mouth recommendation, HRH Prince John came to see me. He didn't want Charles to deal with his case with Ariane, he wanted me. Several people had recommended me he said and, besides, he found Charles pompous and hide-bound and far too easily shockable; indeed, their case would have shocked the rather pedestrian Charles hugely.

Ariane was a German princess from the obscure house of Groningen-Hassel. After her parents' divorce Ariane and her younger sister were brought up in London by their mother, whose persistent shamelessness in seeking favours from anyone and everyone (including a rather far-fetched claim that they were cousins of the House of Windsor) eventually bore fruit when Prince John met her at the opening dinner of the Scratch Bar in Soho. John Waldemar Alfred Christian Louis was the thirty-seven-year-old youngest child and by far the most problematic. Like Edward VII's son, Prince Eddy, there were many (mostly unpleasant) rumours about him: he was supposed to be a drug-user (true), gay (also true), wildly in debt (bigger overdraft than Fergie's) and so on. He was desperate to get married so that his mother would buy him a house and pay off his debts. His eye fell upon available Ariane whose enormous number of sexual liaisons (male and female) seemed to matter less the further away from the succession a person was. John was number ten or twelve, not really important enough to worry about. They were married in December 1996. By the end of the second month neither could bear the sight of the other; they had also more or less run out of options when it came to making money. Prince John had no allowance from the much-reduced Civil List, Ariane's column in the *Sunday Javelin* magazine had been scrapped (too tacky) and *Hello!*, *See Ya* and *OK!* magazines had all been allowed to photograph every inch down to the inside of the fridge of their lovely home at Otter Court in Weybridge, in return for a fat fee, all spent.

Their divorce had to be sensitively handled. My first task was to stop Ariane giving details of her husband's homosexual liaisons before and after their marriage, then I had to prevent her from posing naked for one of those laddish magazines – they were proposing a centrefold pop-up. I also had to put paid to any mention of Prince John's porphyria reaching the press. All this suppression of information meant that the press vultures were looking for a substitute and I became a much more prominent part of their story than I intended to, but the divorce went through thanks to the Queen's generosity and the dust settled.

In the meantime, almost without my noticing it, my marriage was falling apart from distance-related apathy. As so often when it comes to adultery, the time was ripe. I was ready, Tom was there. What I didn't bargain on was falling in love with him. I had been in hospital for several days before he came to see me. He discovered what had happened by ringing me at work and had wanted to come at once, but the hospital wouldn't allow me any visitors other than my immediate family to start with. No mention of the stabbing had, as yet, appeared in the press.

He came one morning quite early (missing Simon by a whisker, thank God) to see me before he went to work in the City, charming his way past the rather fierce sister at the nurse's station who told him he had no business to be there but let him see me anyway as I was still in a room by myself, courtesy of the NHS.

'I can't believe this,' he said, putting down an enormous bunch of flowers in all shades of white and cream before stooping over the bed to kiss me. He wanted to kiss my mouth but I turned my head so that the kiss landed on my cheek instead. I did not think that I would have the courage to tell him what I was going to tell him if I once felt his lips on mine.

'What does that mean?' he asked, touching my cheek with his hand before sitting down on the chair by the bed.

'There's something I have to tell you,' I said, ignoring his question, 'something appalling.'

'You're going back to him,' he said quietly, 'is it that?'

'No. It's much worse than that.'

'What then?'

'It's to do with Katie,' I began. 'I have to tell you before I go to the police. I saw her with your father in the bathing hut after the dinner. They'd obviously arranged to meet there. I went back ostensibly to get my book but also because I had a hunch he was somewhere around the place with her and I was jealous. I'd been waiting for him in my room. He was my lover too, Tom. It was more than just a routine grope by an older man towards a younger girl. Did you never guess?'

Tom did not reply.

I plunged on: 'I was angry but there was no one I could confide in. And then it seemed I didn't have to. Kettle's confession exonerated me. I was free. What I'd seen meant nothing – until recently. After the dinner that night at Gatehouse Park the Balmachie chauffeur came to fetch her. She was taken home by him. You saw her leave. They must have had an arrangement to meet after the dinner. Ivar took her to the bathing hut. They had an argument. My guess is she fled into the Moss and he followed her. There was a fight which he won. Katie was killed. Whether he meant to or not is anyone's guess. He hid her in the Moss; it was a brilliant choice. No one ever went there or had any need to. His crime would never be discovered.'

'It can't be true,' said Tom; his voice sounded monotonous, heavy as lead. His face had gone very white; there were dark circles under his eyes; for the first time I noticed the grey in his glossy dark curls. My poor Tom.

'It is true, Tom. Now the body's been found the whole thing's been torn open. Someone tried to kill me, that's why I'm here. I'm lucky to have survived. The knife was aimed directly at my heart. I have to tell the truth. I can't go on any longer. I had to tell you before it becomes public. That's why I wanted to leave Sarah's. I had a row with your father. I said more than I meant to. I had to get away.'

'Don't!' cried poor Tom. 'Please don't. It won't do any good. It'll ruin everything. We'll be torn to pieces. It will kill my poor mother. Please, Lucy.'

'I have to, Tom,' I said.

'You have no proof,' he said. 'You saw a row but not a murder.'

'I nearly died a few days ago. Someone tried to kill me.'

'You don't know that,' said Tom. 'It may just have been an unfortunate incident, one of those things; some madman on the tube.'

I shook my head. 'No, Tom, it wasn't.'

'Think what it will do to my mother and my sisters,' said Tom, 'and me.'

'I have thought,' I said, 'I'm sorry, Tom.'

He got to his feet and went to the door. He turned back towards the bed as if to say something but changed his mind. He went out leaving the door open. I could hear him walking away very quickly down the corridor.

'Who's handsome then?' asked the bossy sister, coming into

the room. 'Some people have all the luck. Why did he leave the door open?'

I shook my head but could not prevent the tears which welled up and ran down my cheeks.

'You all right, love?' she asked, staring. 'I wouldn't have let him in if I'd known he'd upset you. It's always the handsome ones that cause all the trouble.'

'It's all right,' I said, blowing my nose. 'Could you possibly get me the telephone?' I had to ring Elizabeth Dunbar before my nerve failed.

'It's Lucy Diamond,' I said, when I was put through. It didn't occur to me to give my married name, it never did: it was one working woman to another. She was tough and at the same time cool. She had alarmed me when she came to see me, as I think was her intention; it was her way of shaking the bough, I suppose, to get the fruit to fall. Now here I was, waiting to plummet straight into her lap.

'What can I do for you?' She had a measured, rounded Scots accent that made everything sound alarmingly precise.

'I have to tell you that . . .' but here I stopped, surprised by the tears in my throat.

'Take your time' she said, 'there's no rush.'

'. . . that I have an idea who was responsible for Katie Gresham's death.'

'I thought you did,' she said calmly, 'go on.'

I told her what I had seen and why I had kept my secret for so long.

'I'd better come down,' she said, 'we need to sort this out face to face. I'll be there this afternoon.'

'They must think you're ever so important,' said the bossy sister a little later, when she came in to perform one of the innumerable tasks that my wound required, 'there's yet another policeman on duty now. What have you done?'

Elizabeth Dunbar arrived in the late afternoon with a male detective whom she introduced to me as Mike Farmer.

'We'll have to go through everything carefully,' said Elizabeth, looking round the room, at the flowers. I could imagine a bubble coming out of her head saying, in her precise way, 'Spoilt bitch.' 'Get one of those lads out there to prevent anyone bothering us, will you, Mike?'

'Except my husband,' I said, 'he's coming when he's finished work.'

'What time will that be?'

'I don't know. I never know.'

She nodded. 'You lawyers, you're all the same.'

I exchanged an eloquent glance with Mike Farmer. She's hard work, he seemed to be saying, but hang in there, she's good.

When they were settled we went over the story I had told Elizabeth Dunbar on the phone.

'So, you're saying that what happened to you and to Katie is part of a pattern,' she said, looking up from her notebook. 'Where are all the others?'

'Out there,' I replied, 'like me, in hiding. I can give you names. He only picks women of a certain class, or a certain class of vulnerability in my case. I've heard things about him since I began to practise as a solicitor, so has my husband.'

'No one wants to go all the way against such a man,' Elizabeth said, 'that's understandable. He's formidable. Mrs Paterson, Heather the cook, seems to think something was going on with the duchess when she was a schoolgirl, that there was a strong possibility she was being sexually abused by her father. So did your old headmistress, Miss MacMaster.'

'Sarah was being sexually abused by her father,' I said, 'I know it for a fact. I remember watching her get thinner and thinner. She looked like someone from Belsen that summer; bones like blades. I don't know how long it had been going on for – maybe some time – but the realization that there were others – particularly Katie whom she felt in competition with – must have made her want to regain some kind of control, and what better way to do that in the modern world than to get thinner and thinner?'

'She's not much different now,' said Elizabeth. 'I thought

she might just break up in a cloud of dust. She seemed extraordinarily friable; she was practically jibbering by the time I left.'

'Is what I've told you enough for you to go on?' I asked.

'It'll have to be,' said Elizabeth Dunbar.

'One thing puzzles me,' said Mike. 'How did he get her there on his own? She was a very tall girl, very slim, but quite an awkward burden. He couldn't have done it on his own.'

'She may have run into the Moss, I don't know. But there was a boat, he could easily have ferried the body round and dumped it in one of the drainage channels. Ivar would know exactly how to go about something like that,' I continued. 'He was man and boy at Gatehouse Park; he was a brilliant shot and he knew every inch of his land, every hiding-place. He'd know that bog like the back of his hand. Even the few times I stayed at the house we were warned never to go anywhere near it.'

'It was a brilliant hiding-place,' Elizabeth agreed, 'because it was protected by superstition and rumour long before it got its special scientific status; the wood along the Kirkcudbright road is known as Gala Wood, a mispronunciation, so I'm told, of "gallows". Local justice was administered in that wood for centuries. He knew what he was doing all right.'

'So, what now?' I asked nervously.

'He'll be arrested and charged with the murder of Katie Gresham.'

'Will he be bailed?'

'Probably, given who he is.'

'Then what?'

'A trial, Lucy.'

'Trial by fire,' I said.

'There's more,' she said. 'Are you feeling strong enough? It's one of the worst things I've ever encountered.'

'You'd better tell me,' I said, feeling my heart sink.

I was still in hospital when the story broke. It was the lead item on the new 'soft' news bulletin. I watched it from bed with Simon holding my hand.

Together we watched Ivar accompanied by two burly police-man being hustled into Dumfries Sheriff Court to be formally charged with the murder of Katherine Consuelo Milo Gresham on October 27th 1979.

The trial would be at Dumfries Sheriff Court; bail had been granted and set at £500,000 (guaranteed by the Duke of Annan), as Elizabeth Dunbar had predicted it would be. He left the Sheriff Court in a dark blue Mercedes estate car driven by Claudia who looked as thin as a rail but who was as immaculately turned out as ever in a restrained Chanel suit and very dark glasses. No jewellery except the old familiar Glacier mint on her left hand glinting in the cameras' flash. Claudia always did have style. A procession of Land-Rovers containing the whole family (minus the large gang of children who were up at the big house with their keepers) and police cars followed them as far as the pink gothic lodge at Gatehouse Park where there were more photographers busily staking out their patch. Later, Ivar let it be known that he wanted all photographers and journalists to be given tea and access to lavatories where necessary. At tea-time (also included in this extraordinarily long news feature) he came down to the gates especially with Claudia in one of their oldest Land-Rovers with a tea urn in the back and cakes and biscuits baked by the latest cook whose name I did not know. Sarah followed on foot with Sandy. Tom appeared hand-in-hand with Caroline in silk scarf and dark glasses. They waved and smiled to the cameras and did the rounds with journalists as professionally as if they were royalty at a Buckingham Palace or Holyrood garden party.

'Lord Gatehouse,' said the BBC's court correspondent ('Court correspondent!' exclaimed Simon in disgust), 'is not only a close personal friend of the Queen, but is also her representative in Galloway, standing in for her on official occasions, a role Lord Gatehouse has performed for many years, as his father, the previous earl, did before him. Indeed it is something of a tradition for this family who have lived in this part of the world for hundreds of years.'

She asked Ivar if he would be standing aside now that he was on bail.

'Of course I'll have to,' he said sadly, gazing into the camera at exactly the right angle, so that he looked both handsome and run ragged, 'but I'm hoping my son, Tom, or my son-in-law, Sandy Annan, will take on the role, so that it can stay in the family while we fight this preposterous case.'

'I know you can't comment,' said the court correspondent (despite the fact that he just had), 'but what is your reaction to all this?'

'Justice will be seen to be done,' said Ivar. 'I intend to fight this disgusting allegation with the sword of truth and the shield of my innocence. I'm afraid I can't say any more now, but thank you, thank you all very much.'

He walked away, linking arms with Claudia, now in her working clothes of jeans and white shirt, but still with the protective dark glasses in place. They both waved to the crowd that had gathered by the gates and the photographers on the little stone bridge behind who were begging for one last pose.

'You'd think he'd just been elected the new King of Scotland,' said Simon quietly. 'He's doing it Blair-style with convincing poses and sorrowful foreshortened little soundbites.'

'Hush,' I said, as the picture switched to another group of photographers and press three or four miles away outside another, identical, gothic lodge, only this time painted pistachio green, at Balmachie House, where Pauline and Michael Gresham, also arm-in-arm were facing a battery of cameras and reporters.

Michael, unlike many other pop stars, had never believed in using a 'spokesman' to make public announcements on his behalf. He believed firmly in the value of doing his own dirty work, in fact I think he enjoyed it; even on painful occasions Michael *liked* publicity; you could tell from the way he looked into the camera and spoke with such simple ease. He was dressed in his usual louche fashion: baggy shirt, misbuttoned, jeans, a pair of espadrilles with the backs trodden down. Pauline was in black: black tee-shirt, black jeans, a pair of J.P. Tods, hair scraped back, no jewellery apart from discreet gold earrings.

A reporter had just asked Michael how he felt about the fact that the man accused of murdering his daughter was someone he had known all his life.

'Terrible, man, terrible. How would you feel?' was the response.

Michael put his arm protectively round Pauline's shoulder and she nodded in agreement with what he had just said but did not add anything. She was wearing wrap-around dark glasses but Michael wasn't. He knew better than to look into a camera with shades on; it alienated the fans, right? Made you look like some stuck-up prick who doesn't need an audience any longer.

'And you, Mrs Gresham? How do you feel?'

'I can't really talk about it,' said Pauline in her soft voice, glancing up at Michael.

'Will you stay here until the trial or will you go abroad?'

'We're gonna go to the Bahamas,' said Michael wearily, 'we don't really wanna be here until we have to. It's a very painful time, as I'm sure you'll understand.'

'Michael,' shouted another reporter, 'are you surprised that the lawyer, Lucy Diamond, has come forward?'

'Hey man,' he said, 'I ain't allowed to answer those kinda questions; it's called sub judice. Sorry, man, we gotta go now.' He waved a hand at the crowd and then the BBC man on the spot cut in and we were returned to the news desk for the next item in the bulletin.

'Perhaps his next album will be called "Sub Judice",' mocked Simon, reaching for the remote control. 'This playing to the crowd is pure America. It's appalling. We'll have to talk to your lawyer about it. It will have to be stopped pronto.'

'How do you think Ivar came across?' I asked.

'Brilliantly,' he said, 'that's what worries me.'

'What about Pauline and Michael?'

'Michael didn't looked bereaved enough. And I don't think bringing the Bahamas in like that would help their profile either. The piece on the Gatehouses stressed their relationship to the locality, their roots. Pauline and Michael have that absentee look, that rich absentee look. It won't go down well. People always think the rich feel things less because of their money.'

'Is it true, do you think?' I asked.

'It may or may not be true,' he said sharply, 'but it's not the point.'

He gave me a look and I read in his eyes although he did not say so that he was surprised that I of all people should ask such an asinine question.

Scots law and English law are different. The senior figure for the Crown vs Earl Gatehouse, known as the 'Advocate-Depute', was to be a woman named Verona Lord, a native of Edinburgh. Verona, about forty and the mother of three children, was married to the keeper of printed documents at the Scottish War Museum. When she heard the news, my old friend Dilly came to see me. She sat down by my bed and pulled up a chair.

'First,' she said, 'I must tell you that I think you're very brave, if not insane. That's off the record. Secondly, I can understand why you feel you have to do it. No doubt you know that you yourself may end up in prison for withholding evidence although no doubt there are mitigating circumstances.'

'There are, yes. There are also plenty of other facts that the defence will twist to make me look like a predator.' I proceeded to give Dilly chapter and verse.

'Listen,' she said, 'the predator in this case is Ivar Gatehouse. You know what he is, I've heard things over the years. So here we have a man with a pretty unbridled sexual appetite who likes young totty, eighteen is his limit or thereabouts, but he prefers sixteen-year-olds. He sexually abuses his daughter and his daughter's friend, and he goes for his friend's daughter, Katie: a nasty little triangle. His wife mutters divorce and

297

that means hassle and the haemorrhaging of a lot of that Gatehouse cash that he likes so much, so our friend Ivar's in a pretty filthy mood that weekend. He whacks his daughter one in the kisser just for starters, but there's worse to come. The really smashing totty, the ultimate arm candy is Katie G: she's beautiful of course, and very very rich and very spoiled albeit in a nice kind of way. She doesn't care what he thinks; she's too brash to realize that she ought to be frightened of him. You at least had the sense to be scared. Katie ain't scared. She ticks off his nibs in front of a crowd of people whose opinion he cares for; she spurns his advances, she thinks she's in control. It's a mind game really. But Ivar's one step ahead: he makes it up with her and raises the stakes. She must do something really foolhardy which appeals to her: go home and then go back again to the bathing hut at Gatehouse Park in her evening clothes; neither of them is sober at the start and the sex games raise their adrenalin levels even further. Then he wants her to do something, perform some little trick, that she doesn't want to do. She refuses. Ivar's anger is bubbling just beneath the surface and he can't control it. He taunts her; maybe he says you or Sarah will do such and such, he's quite drunk, don't forget, and she rounds on him like a snake; that's the moment where you, Lucy, look through the window and then, sensibly, having a sense of self-preservation, flee. He attacks her, she runs for it; when he gets to her he's so furious he begins to beat her. It wouldn't be difficult for a big strong man to kill a girl like Katie, although she puts up a struggle. He puts her body in the boat – there's a favourable tide that will carry him towards the part of the Moss where he knows he can hide her in an old peat cutting so that she'll never be found. And then, hey presto! the police blame the whole bloody thing on Kettle who, to cap it all, then confesses to the crime. OK, there's a bit of a time lag, but who cares? They've got him. That's all the public cares about.'

'You sound very confident,' I said.

*   *   *

Ivar instructed Geoffrey Graham QC, known as 'Gigi', to defend him. Gigi was probably the most famous defending advocate in Scotland, known for his deceptively mild manner and ability to charm juries into, as one Scottish newspaper wrote, 'believing the unbelievable'. He had trained as an architect but decided instead to become a lawyer. People who knew him said that the law was stronger in the family than the architectural streak which the family had been best-known for: Gigi's ancestor had been Adam's rival in his day, forgotten now; he was also descended from countless Writers to the Signet (an anciently-established society of solicitors in Scotland who still have the sole right of preparing crown writs) and the law ran in his veins quite as strongly as the urge to design beautiful buildings for rich clients.

Gigi was captured on film driving himself in a black Rover down the back drive at Gatehouse Park, past the handsome farmhouse at Gatehouse Mains which he slowed to admire: a crenellated building with the ruins of a more ancient structure picturesquely attached; the tennis court was mercifully disguised behind a line of young copper beeches. As a purist, Gigi disapproved of tennis courts and had been known to feel faint at the merest glimpse of swimming pool blue in the landscape.

Sarah Annan, whom Gigi already knew, was waiting for him outside the house. She was wearing jeans, a tee-shirt and a pair of tennis shoes with no laces in. Gigi was wearing an immaculate dark suit and tie. His shoes gleamed as did his car and his heavy old briefcase.

*

'Sarah, my dear,' he said, shutting his car door, 'how nice to see you here.' His tone of voice was mild and untroubled. He could have been coming to stay for the weekend, instead of to take preliminary notes from a client accused of a particularly brutal murder. He put down his briefcase. 'Perhaps we could walk a little before I see your father?'

'We can go to the walled garden,' said Sarah, putting her arm through his. 'This is all too awful,' she said, 'Poppy's very upset although he doesn't show it.'

'I saw him on TV the other day,' said Gigi, 'and I thought he came across very well, although I don't think television is necessarily the way forward.'

'Neither does he!' exclaimed Sarah. 'But because he's who he is, we're besieged. You saw for yourself. The press are everywhere. Poppy's keen on hospitality; it's practically an article of faith with him, so he thinks they should be looked after. He offers tea and biscuits and the opportunity to use the loo, nothing more than that. Pretty basic stuff really.'

'Of course I understand,' said Gigi soothingly. 'How is your mother taking it all?'

'Badly. She's in bed most of the time, but keep that to yourself. She totters out for photo opportunities but that's about it. That's why we're here. Davy is staying, plus Lulu with all their ghastly brats; just as well it's such a big house.'

They walked on in silence until they reached the door in the wall beyond which lay the garden. Sarah opened it and stepped inside followed by Gigi.

'As I remember,' he said, 'there's a nice bench in the far corner where we can see people before they can see us. Let's sit there, shall we.'

When they were seated he said: 'This is a terrible blow for your father, Sarah. Bad enough to have a body dragged out of the bog but then this on top. We're none of us as young as we were. Tell me about this woman Lucy Diamond.'

'She was a schoolfriend,' said Sarah, 'whom Poppy was kind to. He's always kind to the young. And now, all these years later, she's turned on him . . . or on us, I should say. She says he seduced her when she was under-age. It's all vindictive lies, of course. She's been having a fling with Tom as well. None of us liked that much . . . Tom and Caroline were separated, you see, but we like it even less now we know what she's saying about Poppy. It's disgusting.'

'There's no truth in what she says?' enquired Gigi in his mild way.

'How can you even ask?'

'Sarah,' said Gigi, 'you have to tell the truth. Was he having a sexual relationship with your friend?'

'That's what she says so it must be true.'

Gigi nodded slightly. 'And what about you, my dear?'

'What do you mean?'

'Was he not also sleeping with you, Sarah dear?'

'Never,' said Sarah ferociously.

'I'm afraid you don't understand, Sarah. You have to be truthful. This is not a game.'

'He didn't mean it,' Sarah burst out, 'he couldn't help himself.'

'And what about Katie Gresham?' Gigi's expression was grim.

'Oh yes,' said Sarah, 'he was fucking her too. Why not just throw in Uncle Tom Cobleigh and all.'

'He's going to need all the help he can get,' said Gigi sighing. This is an appalling case, you know. There's going to be an awful lot of dirty linen on display.'

'He didn't do it,' said Sarah vehemently.

'Who do you think did do it?' asked Gigi gently. 'Lucy Diamond's testimony is very damning as far as your father is concerned. If she's right he was the last person to see Katie alive.'

The forensic details were horrifying too, absolutely frightful, but he wasn't going to mention any of that to this poor girl who, it was perfectly clear, was nearly at breaking point herself. He could hardly bring himself to look at her legs which reminded him of spillikins.

'I don't know,' Sarah said in a savage voice, 'but it wasn't Poppy.'

'My dear Sarah, you mustn't allow yourself to get upset, you really mustn't.' Gingerly, he patted her knee. 'However, the public's appetite for scandal is very great and this is, unfortunately, a case which promises many titbits. The prosecution will delve into your father's past, they will no doubt try to prove a pattern of behaviour culminating in the murder of young Katherine. Press attention will be ferocious.'

'Poppy's past is exemplary,' said Sarah, 'he's always believed in *noblesse oblige*; look at all his committees, his public work. He and Ma have been married for nearly forty years, for God's sake.'

'I know, my dear, I know,' said Gigi in his soothing voice, 'but it will be hard on you all. Since the death of the Princess there has been a vacuum; a scandal in high society is what everyone has been waiting for, I'm afraid. You must brace yourselves. Each one of you will be under the spotlight.'

*

'Who's that man getting out of a black Rover out front?' asked Caroline Creetown of Tom as they crossed the hall.

'That's Geoffrey Graham,' said Tom. 'He's Pa's barrister. The best money can buy.'

'He'll need it,' said Caroline.

'Please, Caroline,' began Tom, 'don't start that again.'

'Start what? You know what I'm talking about, but like everything in this family it's not allowed to be spoken. No wonder you're in such trouble. Serves you bloody well right. You know your precious "Pa" is a crim.'

'I know no such thing,' said Tom savagely, 'and if you don't shut up, I'll send you back to your bloody room. You're still tight from lunch.'

'Have to be,' said Caroline, stumbling slightly, 'in this family. Need an anaesthetic to deal with all the undercurrents. No wonder two of your sisters are airheads and the third has had a frontal lobotomy; there's no other way of remaining sane.'

*

I came out of hospital after two weeks and returned to Coventry Terrace, London W11, my lovely home in achingly trendy Notting Hill Gate.

Actually, it was anything but lovely. There had been reporters outside my house since the news of my involvement in the affair broke, a fact which had not pleased my neighbours: a junior cabinet minister whose nanny had to fight her way through a cordon of reporters every morning to get the children to school, and a well-known novelist who felt all the attention should be focused on him not on me.

In order to reach my front door, two policeman had to barge a passage through; there were flashes and shouted questions from 'Are you going to be the next Countess Gatehouse, Lucy?' to the asinine 'How are you feeling now that you've confessed?' Mercifully, Simon had had the sense to provide me with a new pair of dark glasses. I did not want them to see the fear in my eyes or the fact that I was in tears by the time the front door had been slammed behind me. For the first time I felt some sympathy for the People's Princess. I could not imagine having to endure such torment every single day. Maud was at school when I came home, but Simon had taken the day off work. Magdalena was washing the kitchen floor when I went down the basement stairs.

'You allri, Mrs Lucy?' she asked, taking my hands in hers. 'I say praya for you.'

'Thank you, Magdalena.' I kissed her and then let Simon lead me away to the other end of the room where the long table was and the easy chairs. We could have gone upstairs to the sitting-room on the ground floor with the windows at either end, but I found the commotion in the street too disturbing. Simon told me that they had to keep all the blinds down because the reporters had ladders with them, ready to peer into any bedroom or bathroom on the street front at a moment's notice. While Magdalena made the coffee we talked in low voices.

'I'll have to go somewhere else,' I said, 'until the trial, whenever that is. There's no date yet, although Elizabeth thinks we could get a date some time in September if we're lucky, or possibly October at the latest.' In Scotland cases must come to trial within 110 days of committal.

'It's going to be even less fair on Maud if you move out,' said Simon. 'She'll think you've left because of something she's done. You know what kids are like.'

'My going, for a short while, is the least disruptive way of dealing with this crisis. It'll be less hard on you too if I'm not around.'

'Don't be ridiculous,' he said, 'you know what I –'

'Look,' I said firmly, having already thought all this through during the long hospital nights, 'it will be better this way. I don't see why you should have to go through agony on my account.'

'I am your husband,' he said quietly, 'I always thought that was a part of the deal.' Poor Simon, his forbearance made me want to scream. I truly didn't deserve him.

'This is something I have to do myself,' I said stubbornly, 'don't try to stop me. I'll explain it to Maud.'

'All of it?' He gave me the dirty look I deserved.

'No, not all of it, but the bits I think she'll understand.'

'She's already getting flak at school,' said Simon. 'She came back yesterday afternoon saying that one girl in her class had told her that her mummy was going to go to prison.'

'Then the school will have to try harder,' I said. 'I'm hardly the only notorious parent there. Look at Tony Schumann.'

Tony Schumann was a parent at Maud's school, Claridge Hall, who was doing time at one of those toffs' jails for perpetrating some huge fraud in the City that the experts were still trying to unravel.

'OK,' said Simon, 'if that's what you want. But we ought to talk to the school together.'

'Fine by me.'

'Where will you go?'

'I dunno. London's awash with flats to rent. I'll ring one of the agents and tell them to find me something prontissimo.'

'What about your work?'

'What about it?'

'Charles won't like it.'

'Fuck Charles,' I said. 'If Charles doesn't like it, then I'll find another job.' I caught his eye as I blustered. 'He's said something to you already, hasn't he? Own up.'

'He called me three days ago,' he said.

'The day he sent me those flowers.' The flowers were from Cosima, *the* florist, used by the Hamish Blundells and Rosa Richardsons of the decorating world. Cosima could do anything, they said. 'The bastard. So, what did he say?'

'He faffed around for a while and then he came out with it. "No partner of Lawrence Scanning & Co has ever been involved in any scandal whatsoever." So I said to him,' Simon caught my eye, it was an old joke, 'I said to him, I said, that it was hardly your fault.

'"But my dear Simon, I can't agree. Lucy knew. And yet she did nothing. I can't help feeling that that is thoroughly reprehensible."

'She was a young girl, Charles. Young and frightened. I think you ought to make allowances, at least until the trial.

'"My dear fellow, if it were up to me there wouldn't be a problem, but the fact is that Sir Lionel has put his foot down. In the interests of client base and all that, she has to be suspended. On full pay of course. Until the trial is over."'

'Well,' I said, 'at least they're going to pay me. I can spend my days shopping and going to galleries. The life I've never had.'

'You shouldn't be facetious about it,' Simon said crossly, 'it's important that you think it's important and show it. I think you should go and see Sir Lionel.'

'And say what? Hello, Sir L, sorry I didn't tell you I'd witnessed what amounted to the preliminaries to a murder. Come on, Simon. Sir Lionel will be scandalized not so much by my involvement as by what I have to say about Ivar. He won't believe a word of it. Everyone in this bloody country still loves a lord. He's bound to have been at Cambridge with Ivar. Charles was, so Ivar told me. And Charles is indebted to him for some hot stock market tips. Which doesn't give me much leeway, you must admit.'

'No, it doesn't,' said Simon, looking depressed. 'Damn this bloody cosy insular little world we seem to live in; everyone knowing everyone. Sometimes I've thought it was good but it's bad too, rotten through, corrupt.'

'You sound as if you've only just noticed.'

'I haven't "only just noticed", but I hate seeing you pinned down and at the mercy of those bastards.'

'It's all right, Simon,' I said, 'I'm resigned to it. *Que sera sera* and all that rubbish.'

'You might be,' he said, 'but I'm not.'

'That's because you're a bloke; it's a bloke's world still, just like it's a rich man's world still. Nothing ever changes, or not at the speed people would have you believe. Money and the power conferred by money will never change, not in a million years. The Anwoths are so entrenched, it's hard to realize how deep their tentacles go and their self-confidence.'

'It worries me that you sound so defeated already,' said Simon, 'before you've even begun.'

'I'm just tired,' I said, 'tired and shocked. I'll get over it.'

I went to get Maud from school at three-thirty. Simon didn't want me to, and insisted on driving me. The photographers were still there but didn't seem as interested in me as they had been that morning. Simon pointed out that they were waiting for a better shot: in other words, me with Maud: *Murder Trial Solicitor Fetches Daughter From School.* Big Deal. After his mother left, he had been sending Magdalena to fetch Maud. It was the kind of school where there were a lot of nannies and maids collecting, sometimes it was impossible to tell if a mother was a mother or just the help. Because of working, I'd hardly ever performed this ritual of city motherhood; the pavement outside the school was jammed with nannies and mothers with small children at their feet; along the kerb, the four-wheel-drive vehicles were lined up cow-catcher to cow-catcher; within, through tinted glass, it was possible to glimpse skinny women with blonde streaks talking on their mobile telephones, whilst in the back small boys in grey blazers fought each other or sat strapped in their specialist car seats in lonely immobility like animals, in the far back sections of their parents' plutocratic motors.

These were the women who telephoned me in my office when their four-wheel-drive marriages broke down. It was the first time I had experienced them in their natural habitat without the protection of my office, my staff, my status. Now, because of what I'd done, I was among them but not of them. I wished I hadn't come; I felt as if I'd strayed into the rituals of some alien tribe who would shortly tear me to pieces; indeed, as people glanced at me and realized who I was, they either froze and pretended they hadn't recognized me or moved away as if I had some communicable disease. Maud's class was the third or fourth wave of small girls to come out. The whole business was managed with military precision. I saw her come to the front of the queue, stand in front of the dispatching teacher to make her curtsy and then stand at the top of the steps scanning the crowd. When she saw my face her own lit up in response and she tumbled down the steps so fast, bag flapping, boater tipped forward into her eyes, that I was afraid she would fall.

Maud, with her dark curls and olive skin, her brown-black eyes, her own smell that was somewhere between the smell of hay and the freshness of new ironing, what would I have done without her? How could I have managed without her courage and her faith in me? Maud was one of the lucky few who was born with almost perfect self-confidence. She must have got it from Simon's side, not from mine.

'Careful,' I said, as she threw herself at me, 'I'm not quite mended yet.'

'Daddy said you were coming home.' She hesitated for a moment. 'Alice Whittaker said you were going to go to prison so I bit her and it bled. Miss Camilla told me that I shouldn't've, and that I should say sorry but I said if she said it again I'd bite her even harder, I would. I'd bite her bloody head off,' she added as an afterthought.

'You mustn't swear, Maud,' I said, trying to suppress my giggles. 'You're only eight.

'You swear,' she said.

'I know I do, but I'm older. I'm allowed to.'

'Will you go to prison?' she asked suddenly, just as we reached the car.

'Look,' I said, 'I hope not. I don't think I will, but I can't say for sure. I know that's difficult for you to understand, but I don't want to lie to you.'

'It's all right, Mummy,' she replied coolly, 'I know I can trust you.'

As the weeks went by, the furore died down a little. One morning Simon went out to take Maud to school and found there were no photographers at all; they had all vanished when it had dawned on them that I was no longer living there. I had found a flat in a group of blocks in Pimlico belonging to the Grosvenor estate, of the same hideous vintage as Dolphin Square. Once built as council flats (overlooking a central area of grass and parking spaces with a few sparse flowerbeds) these blocks had, for reason or reasons unknown, been returned to private use. There was a porter in a cap and uniform and car parking and signs that said 'Don't Walk on the Grass' and 'No Dogs Allowed'. I would have quite liked a little dog to keep me company during that lonely time when I felt as if I had lost everything that mattered in my life.

The residents of these blocks were on the whole elderly and well-to-do. There were a number of peers and MPs together with the widows of judges and country landowners who liked to come up to town once a fortnight to go to Peter Jones or the theatre; these people were the types who read newspapers avidly and gossiped amongst themselves around the bridge table. They knew who I was and why I was there (and even if they hadn't they soon began to protest about the photographers who stalked me everywhere I went) and their response was to ignore me, to pretend that I was invisible.

I was the class traitor, the snake in the grass, who had caused a high-ranking member of their caste to be thrown to the wolves. Photographers and journalists continued to pester the Gatehouses, remaining camped out at the lodge; one of the more ruthless paparazzi-types had taken and sold to the *Sun* intrusive photographs of Lady Gatehouse being helped from her car to the house by what looked like one of the legion of cleaning ladies. The *Sun* speculated that the strain was overcoming Lady Gatehouse, who was, it stated (unusually tactfully), 'an habituée' of The Priory.

The Greshams had escaped to the Bahamas which was paradoxically disapproved of: the feeling being that they should have stayed to face the music (never mind the fact that their child had been murdered and then her body discovered in the most gruesome and distressing circumstances) – but Ivar continued to behave in public with commendable restraint. After the débâcle of the drunken photographs Claudia graciously allowed herself to be interviewed in the *Daily Telegraph* on the subject of the vicissitudes of being the wife of a man of Ivar's standing faced with such a terrible accusation and she cleverly used the interview to promote Ivar as a model of wounded innocence who was behaving with the fortitude expected of an Anwoth faced with appalling circumstances.

'My father-in-law, Gawain Gatehouse, the sixteenth earl, came through a similarly difficult situation in Burma during the last war,' she was quoted as saying, 'and eventually brought his men to victory. I know Ivar is inspired by his example.' Never mind that it was an outrageously invalid comparison coupled with the fact that Gawain's valour was a fiction recently exposed by a new and radical Oxford don who revealed that Gawain had bungled his task and lost a great many lives unnecessarily.

But there were one or two decent people who didn't turn their back when I appeared or pretend that I was as invisible as a sheet of glass through which they simply stared: there was the mistress of a cabinet minister who smiled at me sympathetically and invited me into her flat for coffee, and a woman who I think was a whore, but a very high-class one, who turned out to have the flat next-door to mine. Her name was Milly Warner and she was the most beautiful girl I had ever seen, although I heard her long before I set eyes on her. Lying in bed at night I would hear Milly tip-tapping her way out of the lift in what sounded like very expensive high heels and letting herself into her flat. It was always late, almost invariably after 2 a.m., when she came in and because of our different timetables it took some time for us to meet. One evening when I had been living in Gunnery Mansions (the blocks were hilariously named Gunnery, Ordnance, Arsenal and Cannonry) for three weeks, a girl of about twenty-eight stopped me in the fruit and veg section of our local Hart's supermarket.

'Hello,' she said, as we were both reaching for the clementines, 'how do you do. I'm your next-door neighbour, Milly Warner.'

I had already noticed her and was staring (although trying not to show it) at her expensive but subdued clothes. Her restrained elegance reminded me of Pauline Gresham.

'Lucy Diamond,' I said. 'How did you know I'm your neighbour?'

'Oh, I just worked it out by magic,' she said smiling. 'No, in fact one of the photographers outside our block knows me. When I asked him who he was waiting for he told me and gave the number of your apartment. I've read about you. I think you're very brave to do what you've done.'

'Most people seem to think I'm some sort of class traitor. The old ladies all look straight through me. I've betrayed their hero, the glamorous Ivar Gatehouse.'

'He's not glamorous,' said Milly, 'he's dangerous, dead dangerous. That's why I think you're brave.'

She had the faintest trace of a regional accent beneath the smooth transatlantic drawl.

'Do you know him?' I asked.

'Oh yeah, I know him all right,' she said, adding, 'what are you doing next?'

'Next?' I looked blank. 'Nothing. Why?'

'Come in and have a drink with me. Maybe we should talk. I'm not out tonight, it's my night off.'

From what? I nearly asked, and then thought better of it.

Her flat was identical in layout to mine but was decorated in the same way that Milly herself was in expensive neutral colours, with a designer's hand apparent in the positioning of certain objects: an off-centre urn on a mantelpiece, a picture leaning nonchalantly against a wall, a beautiful statue of the Buddha on a low table. The sitting-room was dominated by a huge abstract painting in several shades of white and by a very large matching off-white leather sofa which gave out the faint comforting smell of horses when I sat down upon it.

'Bill Amberg,' said Milly, handing me a glass of wine.

'What?'

'My sofa. It's by Bill Amberg.'

I raised my eyebrows at this. A handbag by Bill Amberg was expensive enough; God alone knows what a sofa made by him would cost.

'How do you know Ivar Gatehouse?'

'I've met him round and about,' she said, looking at me over the top of her glass of wine. 'I'll cut to the chase: he likes inflicting pain. There's no doubt in my mind that he killed that girl. She would have said something he didn't like and he would've gone for her. He's like that when he's roused; maybe the sex went wrong or something. He was like that with me. I was one of the lucky ones. I got away with a few bruises. But I knew my place, you see. I knew not to argue with a man like that. Katie was his own class and she was bound to be worth more, the Milos are worth billions, and maybe she just wasn't frightened enough so she got killed. Simple as that, poor kid.'

'So what other gossip do you hear about Ivar Gatehouse?' I asked.

'That his wife's a lush, that he, pardon me, screwed his own daughter, the skinny duchess. He has a track record of cruelty and violence towards women. I guess your problem will be to get them to come forward to testify. Those people are all very loyal to one another, they don't like breaking ranks.' She met my glance and read it instantly: 'Sorry,' she said, shaking her head, 'but the answer's no. I'd like to help but seriously I couldn't. I'd never work again.'

What Milly said was true. I had already discussed the subject with Elizabeth Dunbar in depth the last time she had been to London to see me. She had asked me for a list of women who had suffered at the hands of Ivar Gatehouse and I had provided one, beginning with the young fashion journalist, Sophia Bain. She was now married to a Gloucestershire landowner; every now and again a photograph of her at a dance or a drinks party would appear in *The Tatler* or *Jennifer's Diary*; she looked as glossy and as prosperous as one might expect. When I telephoned her to try to persuade her to testify against Ivar she told me she had no idea what I was talking about; yes, of course she remembered staying at Gatehouse Park – 'such a wonderful place' – she still saw Davina and Louise because their children were the same age, but no, the bruises were a figment of my imagination and she was terribly sorry but she had to dash. In the background, I could hear a baby crying.

Heather Paterson was willing to come forward, according to Verona, but her husband was very much against it on account of his own connection with the Anwoth family through his brother, Derry, the factor to the Gatehouse estate. And there were others too but the response was always the same. Sorry, but (for whatever reason) we can't help.

One day, when I was walking up Pimlico Road on my way home staring into the windows of the glamorous shops that sold fabulous furniture and artefacts, I met Rosa Richardson who was just stepping out of Linley Furniture.

'My God!' she exclaimed. 'Lucy Diamond! How are you, Lucy?' She took my arm, turned me round and began to march me in the other direction. 'A little lunch, I think,' she said. 'I'd heard you were in Gunnery Mansions and I'd been meaning to call you up and ask you to supper or lunch. How are you, my dear?'

'Bearing up,' I said. 'How are you? Busy as ever, I suppose.'

'I'm as you see me,' Rosa said, 'older, fatter, not much wiser.'

She looked as imposing as always, her trademark bobbed hair a trifle shorter and lighter, but the well-upholstered figure was as formidable and as smartly dressed as I remembered from my youth. Her eyes were the same icy blue, the gimlet stare unchanged.

'I met your protégé, Hamish Blundell, when I was in Scotland with Sandy and Sarah. I'm not sure he's safe to let out in places like Annan House. Poor Sandy was having a hell of a time keeping Hamish from covering his William Kent chairs in pink towelling.'

'The young, especially the madly trendy young like Sarah with buckets of money to throw around, adore him; an old bird like me needs someone like Hamish to keep up with the youf. He's my partner now: we're Richardson & Blundell. But never mind me, what's going on in your life is much more interesting. I have to tell you, Lucy, that there are a lot of people who admire what you've done. A great many people would not have had the courage.'

'All the old dowagers in Gunnery Mansions avoid me,' I said. 'I'm a class traitor. I've let the side down.'

'There are quite a lot of people who think it's Ivar who's let the side down,' Rosa countered, 'not you. Now, come along, I'm going to take you out to lunch at Comelario. The head waiter's a great friend of mine.'

As we walked into the restaurant, I saw Cosmo Nevele at a table under the window, lunching with a young man in a green corduroy suit and a very starched pink shirt. He waved and I waved back. My heart sank.

When we were seated he appeared at our table. 'Well, well,' he said, kissing my hand, 'if it isn't our enfant terrible, Lucy Diamond. How are things, my dear? Are you better?' He rattled on, not waiting for an answer: 'More than a little tricky, I understand. The family is outraged, Lucy dear, but of course you know that. Even Caroline's been dragooned back into line. Rumour has it there's another baby on the way and it's happy families once more. What did I tell you? That family is like high-explosive, you were warned by Uncle Cosmo, but naughty, naughty girl, you paid no attention. Well, you aren't the first not to heed my words.'

'I know, Cosmo,' I said, hoping vainly that he wouldn't go on to say what I knew he was going to.

'I suppose this has put paid to you and Tom,' he continued, 'but it would never have done you know. He's a Knight of Malta, just like his dear Papa.'

'For God's sake stop maundering on, Cosmo,' said Rosa crossly, 'she's got enough on her plate without you butting in like the Ancient Mariner whispering prophecies of doom left, right and centre. You're neglecting Sebastian, he's looking wounded. Go away.'

'Word has it, he's pining for you,' Cosmo whispered, ignoring Rosa, 'that's the inside track – the baby thing is just to make the family look good, but don't worry, my dear, I won't say anything in the column. The Gatehouses have always been very good at managing their own publicity, so I won't be helping by writing cuchy-cuchy stuff about Tom's lovely home, you don't have to worry.'

Cosmo's column was entitled 'Moonraker' but was known by all and sundry appropriately enough as 'Muckraker'.

'Secretly, we're all rooting for you,' Cosmo said over his shoulder. 'We wish you well.'

'Cosmo,' said Rosa, 'kindly bugger off and let me talk to Lucy on my own.'

'Ooh,' said Cosmo, 'matron has spoken. Toodle-oo, darlings. I know when I'm not wanted.'

'The trouble is he doesn't,' said Rosa, 'he's staggeringly insensitive; that's why he's so damn good at being a gossip columnist. You have to be inquisitive and heartless to boot. Meddling old queen, there are times when I want to wring his blasted faggot's neck. I do think coming out, or whatever the disgusting procedure is called, has been bad for Cosmo.

I preferred him when he had a little more delicacy. I'd heard about you and Tom too,' she continued, 'my God, the gossip in this town; it must all be the most awful blow for you, Lucy, not to mention the stabbing. That's why I admire you even more.'

'I'm frightened, Rosa,' I said. 'I'm beginning to feel like a Christian who's been thrown to the lions. Everyone knows what Ivar is but nobody will come out in public and say it or back me up. Even the doughty Heather has been silenced. She's married to the brother of the factor to the Gatehouse estate and it's more than her life's worth to testify.'

'Courage, Lucy,' said Rosa, 'all will yet be well, I'm convinced of it. We're all behind you, we all admire you so much. Doing what you've done, not to mention giving up Tom . . .' She reached over and squeezed my hand.

'I remember you predicting the fall of the House of Gatehouse all those years ago,' I said, unwilling to discuss the subject of Tom in public as I was afraid I would cry. I found Cosmo's talk of a new baby almost more than I could bear. 'You obviously knew something we didn't, even in those days. You said they were very grand and rich but that they weren't invincible, that it could all come crashing down in months. You saw something no one else did. I couldn't understand what you meant. I think I thought you were jealous or something.'

'Hubris,' said Rosa, 'has a habit of attending on families like Ivar's, although unless you can find people to back you I suppose it looks as if he might get away with it. People like Ivar almost always do.'

'I know they do. That's what depresses me.'

'I remember you being besotted with that family,' she continued, 'almost as if you were under a spell.'

'I was mesmerized by them when I was young. I'd never met anyone like the Gatehouses: they seemed so exotic and glamorous that they almost seemed to inhabit a different planet from the mundane world where I dwelled. Then, after what happened, I had to forget them: forgetting them was crucial to my survival and for a long time it worked. I believed I'd got away, then I met Tom again the very day the papers were writing about Kettle's recantation, almost as if it were all meant in some strange way.'

'Or you could just say it was unfinished business,' said Rosa, 'with rather strange timing.'

'Very strange.'

'Good luck, my dear,' she said, patting my hand. 'You're going to need it.' I glanced at the large menu in my hand in order to stop Rosa going on. I remember that lunch in Comelario as my lowest moment. If I could have stopped the juggernaut I would have done, but by then it was too late.

*

A trial date was set: October 12th 1998 in Dumfries. Ivar continued to go quietly about his business in Scotland. There were no trips to London on the night train; he attended no parties, he did no shooting. The annual grouse shoot was cancelled as were all the other landmark shooting parties on both Ivar's land and Sandy Annan's. Likewise, Lulu Anwoth's husband, Sir Peverel Jardine, cancelled all his shooting engagements. Earl Harcourt, Waldy, had already sold the rights on his shooting for that year. He was careful to make this clear when some jackanapes from Dempster's page rang to enquire if he was joining the male members of the family in supporting his father-in-law.

'Of course I support him,' said Waldy in the sort of voice in which he addressed his dogs when they had committed some misdemeanour, 'he's family and one always does one's duty by one's family. I should have thought that went without saying. I don't know why you have to ring me up and waste my time asking these asinine questions.' There was a pause in the conversation and then Waldy shouted, 'How dare you!' and slammed the telephone down.

'What is it, darling?' asked Davina, coming into his study with a baby on one hip. 'I heard you shouting as I came downstairs. Guinevere's got a tooth, look! Show Daddy, darling. Show him your toothy-woothy.'

But Waldy couldn't attend to women's claptrap at the best of times. Liked kids, but didn't want them shoved in his face so to speak. Bad enough waiting for one's wife to get over having the blighters. A chap deserved his oats, for God's sake!

'Damned reporter said your father was sleeping with that Diamond girl, the one we met with Sandy and Sarah. And what did we think about that? I soon told him where to put his filthy questions; never heard such codswallop in all my life.'

'It's all rubbish,' said Davina stonily, shifting the baby, who was heavy, on to her other hip. 'But you shouldn't rise to it, darling. They'll only say you overreacted and that therefore it must be true.'

'What? Sorry. Don't get it. Your father's insulted and you tell me I'm overreacting. Well, I'll tell you something, at least I have a sense of honour. I know what's what. If the chap had been in front of me instead of on the other end of a telephone I would have punched him. How did he get this number anyway?'

'People give out numbers. He'd have rung someone we know. There, there, darling,' she said to the baby who had begun to cry, 'Daddy's just a bit cwoss about something, not cwoss with you, angel. You're making Gwynny cry,' she said. 'We're going to go for a walk in the park, aren't we, angel and leave cross-patch old Daddy to get happy again.'

Davina went out, pulling the door to. Waldy listened to her crossing the hall and then heard the muffled thwunk of the green baize door closing behind her as she made her way down the dark passage that led to the kitchen quarters, where Nanny would by now (judging by the reassuring smells of roast meat) be cooking lunch. Darling old Nan, there were times when he just wanted to go and lay his head on her darling old landslide of a bosom and be made to feel better in the same way she had done when he was a little boy.

What he hadn't told his wife was that another journalist had spoken to him only yesterday and had offered what Waldy regarded as an eye-poppingly large sum of money for the inside story of the family during this critical juncture. Waldy had been about to tell him to get lost when a certain sum of money was mentioned. He was disconcertingly aware that the chink of coin made him as eager as a hungry dog for its supper. He was so bloody broke, the trustees were being perfect shits, saying that their job was to protect little Waldy's inheritance, not to pay his bills. Davy's money was dispensed to her not to him; when, originally, he had objected to this, Mr Wilde of Wilde & Co had fixed him with a very cold eye indeed, pointing out in his poncy voice that it was Lord Gatehouse's express wish that the money should be paid to Lady Davina (as she was then) as a way for her to maintain her independence within the marriage; what sort of a way was that for Ivar to carry on . . . *maintain her independence* indeed . . . the whole point of marriage Waldy had felt like telling Mr Wilde was not to maintain independence but to join forces: barter was the whole bloody point of the old bride price: bird got title and house, chap got income stream or whatever lawyers call money these days when they need it to do the roof or pay their tailors, for God's sake. He had never quite forgiven Ivar for that early insult.

Seventy-five grand, the bloke had said, for two articles . . . no one would know where the info came from . . . his integrity would be protected and so on and so forth . . . they just wanted to know if there was any truth in the allegations about Ivar's behaviour in the past . . . rumours were flying round about girls who claimed to have been beaten up by Ivar . . . and did he happen to be able to corroborate any of their stories? Well, yes, as a matter of fact he could. He knew things, unsavoury things, about his father-in-law; stories were told in certain clubs and so on and so forth; and of course there was the business of Claudia and Ivar; like the Londonderrys years ago they never spoke in private unless they had to; the atmosphere on formal occasions in bonny Scotland could be absolutely poisonous because however hard you try to disguise that sort of thing it seeps through like bog water. At the thought of bogs, Waldy put his head in his hands and groaned aloud, so loud that his Labrador Ella got to her feet and came wagging to comfort him with her cold nose and her absolutely and utterly unsullied, uncritical love.

*

318

I hadn't seen Tom in person since he left my room at the Chelsea and Westminster all those weeks ago, but I'd seen him on television outside the lodge at Gatehouse Park with Caroline when I was still in hospital. Cosmo's gossip about a new baby was surely just pure malice; she would hardly have had time even to find out she was pregnant but it exacerbated my sense of loss, even if it wasn't true. The thought of him sleeping with his wife again made me absurdly jealous. I was still in love with Tom; anything to do with him lacerated me. I would have given anything to see him again. Simon was terribly patient and good about it all, but in the end all he could do was withdraw and leave me to my fate. He had his work and he had Maud who spent her weekends with me in Gunnery Mansions.

We quickly established a routine: breakfast in the same café on Sloane Square where I had first breakfasted with Sarah in London, then we would go shopping in Peter Jones or take a bus up Oxford Street. Sometimes we would go to the V&A, sometimes to the National Gallery. We would have lunch out too and then take a taxi home, stopping at the video shop on the way to rent some videos with which we whiled the evenings away. Sometimes we would go for a walk in Hyde Park if the weather was good.

During August, Simon took Maud to his mother in Devon. She would stay with Diana and spend time with his brothers' families. He worried that she was too much of a city child. He wanted her to know the life he had known when he was a boy on the farm. I liked the thought of my little girl having that kind of childhood. She loved her grandmother and the farm; there was an ancient pony for her to ride that had once belonged to Simon and his brothers. The beach wasn't far away; there were woods and dim high-sided lanes where the over-arching trees blocked the light. She slept in her father's old bedroom and Diana read his books to her after supper, *Treasure Island*, *The Children of the New Forest*, *The Princess and Curdie*. I loved the thought of her entering by such means that world of books that had sustained me throughout my childhood. A large ginger cat called Eigg slept on her feet each night purring like a dynamo.

One Saturday morning in late August, I was sitting in the Café Oriel reading the *Times* when a figure stepped into my light and stood looking down at me. It was Tom.

'Hello,' he said, 'I thought it was you behind those Jackie Onassis glasses.'

'Yes, it is,' I said stupidly, taking them off and then putting them on again. The light was very bright and I felt ridiculously vulnerable without a means of hiding my expression.

'Can I sit down?'

'Do you want to?'

'Of course I want to.'

'I really meant do you think you should?'

'Probably not, but I shall anyway.'

When he sat down he said, 'I've missed you. Where have you been?'

'You know the answer to that.'

'Yes.'

'Cosmo tells me Caroline is pregnant.'

'It's not true. We hardly speak. It's for show.'

'I don't think you should be telling me this.'

'Are you better?'

'Physically yes, mentally you can probably guess. I feel like I'm in hell. Is that what you wanted to hear?'

'Won't you . . .' he began, 'can't you withdraw, Lucy? My family is falling to pieces under the strain. My own marriage is a joke, my parents' likewise; Sandy says Sarah is worse than he's ever known her, like a cat on hot bricks the whole time. Gigi, my father's barrister, tells me that there are going to be the most lurid allegations of sexual abuse between my father and Sarah, and you. Everyone is whispering about the case. Couldn't you just say you'd made a mistake?'

'The whole thing's too far down the line for that, Tom. There's a body, for God's sake. It's a murder trial. Nothing I can say will prevent it from going through. Katie died.'

He was silent for a moment. 'I know she did,' he said, 'I know. Poor Katie, poor, poor Katie. Hardly a moment goes by when I do not think of that.'

'But you knew,' I said, as gently as I could, 'you always knew what he was. He was sleeping with Katie while she was sleeping with you, you admitted as much. You told me yourself at the shoot shortly before she vanished. You knew he was torturing Sarah by slow degrees, and me. Why do you pretend, Tom?'

'I love you, you know,' he said. 'My time with you made me happier than anything.'

'I can't, Tom. I've told you. It won't make any difference. It's going to happen. You must prepare yourself.'

'I'd better go,' said Tom, getting up.

'What are you doing here anyway in August?'

'I was spending the night at Eaton Terrace. Ma's in The Priory again, I had to bring her down. Caroline's in France with the boys. Her sister has a house there. I'm going back up to Scotland tonight to be with Pa. Poor Pa, he's very low indeed.'

I said nothing. I watched him go round the corner heading towards Eaton Terrace and that tall white house with its fantastic pictures and furniture and its air of total desolation.

PART FOUR

OCTOBER 1998

Simon's Journal – October 11th 1998

The Greshams have lent Lucy a cottage in the tiny village of Balmachie for the duration of the trial. It's the old schoolmaster's house where the dominie used to live with his family. It's extraordinary to think that well within living memory a local schoolmaster would still be called by a name derived from his Latin title. The cottage sits at the top of the sloping village street and is set back slightly behind a thick hedge with a gate in it. Opposite the gate is another gate leading to the churchyard. From the bedroom window there is a view of the old graveyard, long ago filled up with the Calvinist dead. The new cemetery lies just outside the boundaries of the village. At the bottom of the sloping street there is a river with an old stone bridge arching over it and a handful of cottages. There is a pub, the Gresham Arms, and a Spar that is also a post office but which stays open until ten at night.

Lucy is staying there alone. I am staying at Balmachie with the Greshams. Maud is being looked after by my long-suffering mother in Devon. She is missing school but we thought it best that she should be away from London during the trial.

Tomorrow is the first day of the trial. Elizabeth Dunbar will drive Lucy to Dumfries. I will go with Pauline and Michael although I have our car here with me.

Lucy has just rung me to say that there are photographers in the cemetery. They were there when she came back from the Co-op in Castle Douglas with the shopping. There will be pictures of her tomorrow carrying in those same Co-op bags in the schlock press and in the gossip-obsessed broadsheets. The *Telegraph* even had a feature on what Lucy might wear in court with accompanying illustrations. They seemed to think Jean Muir and Catherine Walker would be good for a murder trial; Vivienne Westwood was out apparently. *What to Wear for a Date with Destiny* it was entitled.

I dined alone in my room tonight – Pauline asked me if I minded and I said no. I don't think I could talk to anyone tonight. I need to think of Lucy and what she went through as a young girl, as if I need to prepare myself mentally to support her in her ordeal. I also think of Katie's agony. What happened to her in the end was so appalling that I can still hardly bear to contemplate it. What will Ivar be thinking tonight I wonder? Will he be at prayer like some penitent king in an old woodcut or will he be dining with his family and playing a few rubbers of bridge afterwards just to show phlegm?

Simon's Journal – October 12th 1998

Nothing can prepare you for the awesomeness of the law when you are caught in its toils. I am a lawyer. I have spent all my working life in and out of court; the law has provided my livelihood. I am married to a lawyer. But I have never been in a court without my protective professional covering. Lucy told me later that she felt like a mollusc without its shell or some grain of wheat waiting to be ground down into dust. She told me that she felt humiliated and frightened by the TV trucks with their masts and satellite dishes, the reporters and photographers, the mounted police and that it was all she could do not to cry when she arrived blinking in the dazzle from the flash of a hundred cameras.

As the prosecution's star witness she is not allowed to attend the trial until she's called to the bar. She cannot enter the courtroom.

We arrive an hour before proceedings are due to begin but the crowds are huge. The police have erected barriers to keep the hoi polloi back. The trial is a spectacle for the locals, a day out at the freak show especially now the electronics factory that caused the boom is about to close; the '*sans culottes*' need bread and circuses. And this is a circus with knobs on, literally.

Dumfries Sheriff Court is the equivalent of those *hôtels de ville* you see all over France where the mayor does whatever it is that mayors do, apart from marrying people and celebrating the storming of the Bastille. It is a nineteenth-century structure built out of the red sandstone that is quarried locally; Lucy finds it unbearably ugly and I have to agree. The Sheriff Court has a portico with a row of windows above and a flagpole with a rather tatty Union Jack attached.

Scots law is completely different to its English counterpart; as an English brief I know very little about it. Where in England there would be a judge there is instead a Lord (or in this case apparently a Lady) Justice Clerk. The trial will be prosecuted by an Advocate-Depute, again a woman called Verona Lord, assisted by counsel. Counsel for the defence, known as the defending advocate, is a QC called Geoffrey Graham who will be assisted by a junior. The accused, Ivar Gatehouse, is called 'the panel' and the jury consists of fifteen people not twelve. Unlike an English court, there will be no opening speeches. A précis of the case is read, the accused, Ivar Gatehouse, will plead (presumably) not guilty, the jury will then be empanelled after Ivar has pled. The prosecution will then lead with the evidence.

Geoffrey Graham QC is acting for Ivar, but everyone refers to him as Gigi. Gigi, apparently, is a bit of a holy terror: his quiet manner masks extraordinary charm: women love him because he doesn't bully witnesses but has a way of getting results all the same. Don't be deceived by his mildness, Pauline has told me; he disarms his victims and then quietly demolishes what they have to say.

Scottish courts do not accept hearsay evidence. Every crucial fact must be established by evidence from more than one source. They have a verdict, unique to the Scots, of not proven which is the equivalent of an acquittal and would mean Ivar walking free. This is what everyone is afraid of.

The crowd falls silent as we pass by. Michael is wearing a dark suit but no tie. On his feet he is wearing his trademark boots. He waves and smiles and looks haggard but glamorous. He grinds his cigarette end out under his boot before he enters the building and the crowd gives a ragged cheer. 'Go, Michael,' someone shouts. Pauline looks like a wraith, pale, ethereal, wounded. She is also in black. She does not look at anyone, she does not smile. If people still wore hats then they would remove them as she passes. Her dignity is incomparable. My heart goes out to her. I think how I would feel if it were Maud.

Then, behind us, the Gatehouses arrive. Claudia, sober for once, drives. The Scots have a strange attitude to toffs: they like the old ones like Robert the Bruce and James IV but are ambivalent about the living, particularly when they are accused of murder. There is the odd shout but most people seem transfixed by Ivar rather than openly hostile towards him. It still counts for a great deal up here that he is Lord Gatehouse.

Claudia walks with Ivar; Caroline, Tom and the Gatehouse daughters follow them, with the husbands behind like a royal funeral. Sandy Annan, whom Lucy always refers to as 'the sheep', even has his hands clasped behind his back *à la* Prince Philip. Poor Sandy. This must be agony for him although he doesn't show it. His expression is carefully neutral. Sarah looks numb. She's probably taken something to dull the effect of it all. Claudia is wearing a black Chanel suit. Her legs look like matchsticks. She totters a little, but her head is held high. On the left hand the familiar Glacier mint catches the light. Sarah, I notice, has not abandoned her ice cube in the interests of democracy. She looks pinched and anorexically thin. Her long black coat has real fur at the collar and cuffs. She never did care what people thought, according to Lucy. And in this part of the world animal rights activists are thin on the ground if not non-existent.

And Tom, my so-called rival. Tom, so like his father to look at but so unlike him apparently in character, looks grim and distant. It is the first time I have seen Caroline Creetown in the flesh. She's a looker all right: glossy dark shoulder-length hair, large dark eyes, pale skin. Like Sarah she is wearing a black coat but hers has a wide mock-leopard collar that makes her look almost like a film star. I can hear the noise from the camera shutters. CNN are here, as are teams from all the European countries. Because of the social standing and the money of the protagonists, this is a scandal for the global village.

Ivar is amazing: he walks with great dignity between the crush barriers like a king going to the scaffold. I happen to know he is a descendant of Charles I on the distaff side; how strong those genes must be: the air of martyrdom gene the strongest of all. The Lady Justice Clerk is a grey-haired, middle-aged Edinburgh woman. She has a severe expression about the mouth and her manner is icy. Her husband is a professor at Edinburgh University. Neither of them shoots or fishes and they are friends of the present Lord Chancellor, i.e. prosperous Edinburgh bourgeoisie with a social conscience. According to Elizabeth Dunbar, Lucy couldn't have done better, but I wonder. The Lady Justice Clerk speaks with a refined Morningside accent which somehow makes me think she might be susceptible to Ivar's world and Ivar's charm. I fear for Lucy.

Proceedings start at ten sharp. Ivar pleads in the dock and when he has pled the jury are empanelled. The jury consists of eight women and seven men. One of the women is Asian, the rest are white. The men are also all white. Ivar has taken his seat next to Gigi who doesn't quite pat his hand but looks as if he might like to. Heather Paterson is requested and called by the usher. Heather has refused her husband's request not to testify and, as a result, her marriage is in crisis, just one more casualty of this affair.

Verona Lord in wig and gown seems to be both efficient and relaxed. I feel I can trust her. I hope I can trust her.

'Nearly twenty years ago,' she is saying, 'you were the cook to Earl and Countess Gatehouse at Gatehouse Park. Is that correct?'

'Yes.'

'What were your duties?'

'I cooked three meals a day and teas for a varying number of people, depending on how many there were staying.'

'The household fluctuated?'

'Yes. Sometimes there was no one at all, sometimes the whole family and guests would be present.'

'But when the family was in residence they liked to give parties?'

'Yes.'

'So, the presence of the family meant quite a lot of people staying in the actual house? Friends of the parents and friends of the children and so forth.'

'Usually, yes. There was always quite a wide range of ages present. Teenagers upwards.'

'Earl and Countess Gatehouse were not often alone together?'

'No.'

'Why was that, do you think?'

'I object, my Lady,' called Gigi, rising to his feet.

'Please explain what it is that you object to, Mr Graham.'

'The prosecution is attempting to lead the witness into speculating about Lord and Lady Gatehouse's relationship. I do not consider such speculation relevant.'

'Very well,' the Lady Justice Clerk nods at the prosecution. 'You will have to find another way round, Miss Lord.'

'Do you remember the first occasion upon which Miss Lucy Diamond came to stay?' Verona continues calmly.

'Yes, I remember Lucy because she was the first friend that Sarah had brought home during my employment at Gatehouse Park.'

'Did the other children bring people back?'

'Yes they did.'

'But Sarah did not?'

'No.'

'Would you describe Sarah in those days as a loner, Mrs Paterson?'

'I would have said she was lonely, yes. A solitary type, although she was close to her elder brother Tom.'

'And what did you make of Lucy Diamond?'

'She seemed a nice girl, quiet and polite. She offered to help me in the kitchen.'

'And did you accept?'

'No.'

'Why not?'

'Because she wasn't staff. There were strong demarcation lines in that household between staff and guests.'

I glance at Ivar's face. He is listening carefully and to all intents and purposes dispassionately. He resembles a colonial official taking on board the tiresome and convoluted testimony of one of the natives under his aegis.

'Did you mind that?'

'Of course not. It was to be expected.'

'Would you say, Mrs Paterson, that Lucy Diamond was overwhelmed by her surroundings?'

'Yes, I would.'

'She appeared ill at ease, intimidated?'

'Somewhat, yes. She was only sixteen. She wasn't used to the kind of people who came to the house.'

'What kind of people were they?'

'Very rich people, aristocracy, ambassadors, those kind of folk.'

'In your view, she was out of her depth?'

'Yes.'

'Turning now to the Wednesday before the Saturday on which Katie disappeared. You had cooked a shooting lunch up the hill for the guns, is that correct?'

'Yes. There were the guns and then the ladies and the beaters.'

'And Lucy Diamond was there as a beater?'

'Yes. Lucy and Sarah and Tom were walking up with the beaters. It was a family tradition that the younger ones undertook every year. The ladies walked with the guns.'

'And who did Katie walk with?'

'With Lord Gatehouse, or so I was told. I was indoors cooking the lunch.'

'Describe what happened just before the luncheon commenced, would you please, Mrs Paterson.'

'Sarah and her father were talking in a group including Mrs Gresham and Katie. They had a disagreement. Lord Gatehouse told Sarah to desist. She refused. He hit her in the face very hard. I thought he might have broken her jaw. There was blood pouring out of her mouth. Her front teeth were loosened. Everyone saw.'

There is a stir in the courtroom as Heather says this. Gigi whispers something to Ivar who nods impassively. What was the secret of his composure I wonder.

'My Lady,' says Gigi, rising, 'I fail to see what this line of questioning is intended to demonstrate. Miss Lord is attempting to lead the witness.'

'You'd better explain yourself, Miss Lord,' says the Lady Justice Clerk sternly.

'I am attempting to paint a picture of an event that happened during the last week of Katie Gresham's life, an event I believe has a bearing on her ultimate fate.'

'I object,' says Gigi. 'This is pure speculation.'

'On balance,' says the Lady Justice Clerk, 'I am inclined to agree with Miss Lord. Continue please, Miss Lord. Silence,'

332

she says firmly as a murmur of astonishment swells through the courtroom.

'Please tell us what happened after the incident, Mrs Paterson.'

'There was a terrible silence. Everyone was very shocked. Sarah ran out of the cottage followed by Tom who drove her back to the big house. Katie Gresham was particularly shocked by what had happened. She and her mother left right after Tom, but not before she had told Lord Gatehouse what she thought of him.'

'And how did he respond?'

'He didn't really. He just let it go.'

'What did Tom do when he got back to the house?'

'He gave Sarah some drinks and made her rest on the library sofa. When I got back I told Tom to call Dr McManus, the local GP who was the doctor the family used when they were in Scotland.'

'And did he do that?'

'No. He refused.'

'Why?'

'Because he was afraid of what his father would say if he did.'

'So, it was left to you to call the doctor, is that right?'

'Yes.'

'And then what happened?'

'The doctor came. Lord Gatehouse was not yet back from the moor. Dr McManus waited. When Lord Gatehouse returned Tom told him what had happened. He came straight into my sitting-room next to the upstairs kitchen and gave me the sack.'

'Thank you, Mrs Paterson. No further questions.'

Now it is Gigi's turn. 'It must have been a great shock to get the sack like that,' he murmurs, almost as if he were talking to himself, 'but was it really necessary to go to such lengths to rile your employer by calling the doctor?'

'In my view, yes.'

'Did Lord Creetown, Tom, did he encourage you to ring the doctor?'

'No, he didn't.'

'Did he try to stop you?'

'Yes.'

'And you felt that you knew better than Sarah's brother what was good for her?'

'Yes I did.'

'Thank you, Mrs Paterson. No further questions.'

The press, not allowed to comment on the way the trial is going, is amusing itself by filling column inches with photographs and descriptions of the celebrities and society figures who are attending the trial, one of whom is Mrs Dieter Schlunk, the former Marchioness of Castlehill, who, in another incarnation altogether, had been known as Peek-a-Boo Babe. Boo, in baby blue Chanel, with a mane of dark curls and a flirtatious manner, is a comic sketch writer's dream in the witness box.

Verona Lord: 'Mrs Schlunk, you were present on the day of the shoot described by Mrs Paterson, as well as being present at the dinner after which Katie Gresham disappeared. Please tell us what happened.'

'Oh yeah, well . . . I had these new cute tweeds that Brian had gotten made for me as a part of my honeymoon trousseau and, uh . . . oh yeah, I guess I thought I'd wear them to the grouse hunt . . . and Ivar kept teasing me about how I wouldn't be able to walk in them, but I told him –'

'Please stick to the point, Mrs Schlunk,' says the Lady Justice Clerk. 'A description of what you were wearing is not necessary.'

'Oh sure,' says Boo. 'Well, there was a lunch party in this adorable little hut on the mountain and I guess Sarah said something that irritated her daddy and he got a little, uh . . . angry, but Brian just said that's how the aristocracy had always dealt with their kids and Sarah seemed fine about it all later on.'

'By "later on" you mean the same day, I take it?'

'Oh no. I didn't see Sarah again until the next day. She was

OK I guess although she did look a little swollen around the mouth, but nothing a good cosmetic dentist couldn't have sorted out for her.'

'Is it normal for fathers to give their daughters cause to go to "a good cosmetic dentist", do you think?' asks Verona Lord.

'No, I guess not.'

Titters.

The press adore it. Elizabeth Dunbar does not. 'It distracts from the seriousness of the case,' she says, 'all this focusing on trivia. This is a murder not a fashion story. I don't want all these people having their photographs taken outside either. I'm going to ask the Lady Justice Clerk to stop it.'

But there is nothing the Lady Justice Clerk can do either. 'Short of clearing my courtroom of the public, which I have no reason or inclination to do – this is not a trial that should be conducted in camera – I'm afraid I cannot control what the ladies and gentlemen of the press decide to write about or whom they decide to photograph.'

Slipping in almost unnoticed on the first day and on successive days is a tall, balding man in a three-piece suit. *Hello!*, however, pick up on him and include his photograph in their round-up of the first week of the trial.

'Famous heart surgeon attends the decade's most gripping trial,' the caption reads. 'Harvey Balniel, one of the most eminent heart surgeons in the world, attends the trial of Earl Gatehouse for murder at Dumfries Sheriff Court.'

'Moonraker' in the *Sunday Times* wonders if this is a get-out clause for Ivar. 'The spectre of Harvey Balniel at Ivar Gatehouse's trial begs the question, "Is he ill?"'

'*Is* he ill?' I ask Lucy on the telephone. 'He doesn't look it.'

'It's the first I've heard of it,' she says. 'Those Gatehouses have the constitutions of several oxen. They all live until they're a hundred and twenty. Gawain was ninety-eight when he died. Sholto Gatehouse was a hundred and one. *His* father had lost an arm at Waterloo.'

'*He's* not ill,' says Michael Gresham scornfully. 'He's just playing Houdini.'

'He's going to try to get out of it,' Pauline says to me during lunch the following Sunday. 'Harvey Balniel's a barometer of how well we're doing. The more he attends the more we'll know Ivar's panicking.'

'How are we doing?' I ask Pauline.

'It's too early to tell,' she says, 'but you'd better brace yourself, Simon. The other side are going to try to prove that Katie's killer was Jock Kettle after all.'

'But they know that he lied about that.'

'Just because the body they found at Newton Stewart wasn't Katie's doesn't mean Kettle didn't do it. Kettle was a notorious trickster. And they'll lead from Kettle's lies to Lucy's lies and evasions. I know about Gigi. It's inevitable he'd play it that way. He'll try to lump Lucy with Kettle in the public's mind, in the jury's mind.'

Pauline is so strong and so calm. I wish I knew where her strength came from. I'm worried about Lucy, I don't think she's coping well. I never realized how heartless lawyers are. I know they have to be; I know now that only laymen equate the law with truth and justice, but when you're a crucial witness in a murder trial you want to believe it and believing laicizes you if that's the right word. Because of Lucy I'm on the other side now; it's both very interesting and very painful. I wonder if she'll be able to cross back into her old world when this is over. I wonder if she'll want to.

Lucy's Journal – October 14th

Mac is staying here for a night or two. She's come up to take charge of me or at least that's how she puts it. I find myself glad to see her. I think I need some mothering. She is horrified by the scrum outside the court; she feels, like Elizabeth, that it devalues the law, but at least she has had the tact not to tell me that my mother would be turning in her grave by now. My Tenterden grandparents, both dead, must be spinning at a rate. As for Jenny and Roger, my mother's sister and brother-in-law, I have no idea. I lost touch with them years ago. Diana, Simon's mother, rang me last night just to see how I was.

'We're all rooting for you, darling,' she said. 'Right will triumph, mark my words. Ivar Gatehouse is a disgrace to his class. If he knew how to behave he'd fall on his sword.'

If only.

Lowell is with the royal party this morning wearing a beautiful Eddie tweed suit no doubt woven from the wool of those poor sheep on Rhoig that Ettie Hergstrom was plundering for her drawing-room at Upmannoch. He poses amiably enough for the press; I get the impression he is rather enjoying the attention. They love the fact that he is smoking a huge cigar and wearing a Homburg hat which he raises jovially in their direction as if he were on his way to a race meeting or to take the waters at Baden-Baden.

'They're all doing it,' says Mac who, in spite of her reservations about press attention, is glued to the window of our room looking out over the entrance to the Sheriff Court: 'Look, Lucy, that's Lord Stein waving his cigar about. And look at that woman in the pink suit! Where does she think she is! Her skirt is far too short. And what are all those chains for round her waist? She looks like a high-class courtesan.'

'Exactly what she is,' I say, 'although courtesan is not the word that springs immediately to mind.'

'But who is she?' asks Mac.

'She's called Mrs Schlunk.'

'And who's that behind her?'

'The Dowager Duchess of Annan.'

Sandy's mother, tall and distinguished in a good suit which displays her long, angular figure to full advantage, stalks along behind Boo Schlunk ignoring the crowd of journalists and the proles behind the barriers. On her head she wears one of those multi-purpose black velvet cowpats – with a copy of her husband's regimental cap badge in diamonds pinned into it – that are only available at certain very select retail outlets (such as Peter Jones in Sloane Square) which women of a certain class invariably wear to weddings and funerals or any other state occasion. They're probably buried in them too.

'She looks smart,' says Mac admiringly. 'I wish I had her figure.'

'It takes a thousand years of in-breeding to obtain a figure like that,' I say. 'Her son, the present duke, looks like a sheep, admittedly a rare breed, but still a sheep.'

'You always were too sharp for your own good,' Mac says reprovingly, glancing over her shoulder. 'I hope you won't give those sort of answers in court, dear.'

Simon's Journal – October 16th

'All rise.'

Today it is Ivar's turn. The courtroom is quite silent. Somewhere in the distance a bell tolls. How appropriate, I think. I wonder if Ivar has arranged that for his road to Calvary. Ivar is in a beautiful Eddie, blue shirt, yellow tie. He is handsome and unutterably distinguished. He has exactly the right amount of deference in his expression as he takes the oath, the look he wears on his face when he travels by carriage with the royal family at Ascot, the same expression with which he will attempt no doubt to confuse St Peter when his time comes.

'Lord Gatehouse,' Gigi is saying, 'would you tell us how well you knew Lucy Diamond.'

'She was a schoolfriend of my daughter, Sarah. I first met her at a speech day at Wickenden Abbey where my daughter Sarah then was. The headmistress, Miss MacMaster, had asked me to deliver the annual address to the parents.'

'But you'd heard about her before that?'

'Yes. She was very kind to Sarah when she first arrived and

was feeling lonely and a bit homesick, I suspect. My wife and I were very grateful to her.'

'So you were already predisposed to like Lucy long before you met her.'

'Very much so,' says Ivar nodding.

'After that speech day, I believe she came to stay with you at Gatehouse Park for the first time.'

'Yes, that's right. Her mother was a teacher at Wickenden but also a gifted writer in her spare time. She needed time to herself to work. Sarah wanted Lucy to come north with her and I and my wife were only too glad to be able to help.'

'Did Lucy enjoy her time with you or did you think she was nervous? After all, it would have been quite daunting for any young person to plunge suddenly into the rather grown-up and sophisticated world that your own children were used to.'

'From early childhood we always impressed upon our children that they had a duty to others. My wife and I agreed that Tom and Sarah did everything they could to make Lucy feel a part of the family.'

'And did she?'

'To a certain extent, yes, I believe she did. But I was very aware from early on in our acquaintance that Lucy was a very needy person.'

'Why was this?'

'I think the answer is straightforward. Her own father was dead, her mother was in failing health – so we discovered – and not at all well-off and she was an only child.'

'How soon were you aware that Lucy was becoming over-attached to you?'

'By late August of that year.'

'So, not long after you'd first met.'

'That is correct. I was strongly aware of it when I came south to help move Lucy's mother to St Thomas's where I happened to know the expert in Jane Diamond's particular condition.'

'Would you tell the court please, Lord Gatehouse, what form this over-attachment took.'

'She made sure in a provocative sort of way that I was very aware of her. Her skirts got shorter, her tee-shirts tighter. She would try to engage me in long conversations whenever I saw her which, at that time, was quite frequently.'

'I believe you lent Mrs Diamond a flat rent-free, is that correct?'

'My Great-Aunt Dolly had just died and left me her flat in Victoria which was very convenient for Tommy's. It seemed ideal for Jane and it meant Lucy could stay with her.'

'What did you think Lucy's intentions were towards you, Lord Gatehouse?'

'To be honest, I don't think she really knew herself. She was very young and very confused.'

'But they were sexual, were they not?'

'Yes, they were.'

A murmur of excitement ripples through the courtroom. This is what the press hounds have been waiting for.

'Please tell us what happened next.'

'I had taken Lucy out for dinner as a kind of sixteenth-birthday present. I felt sorry for her because she was with her mother who was very ill and she was obviously upset by what was happening to Jane. We stopped off at my house in Eaton Terrace on our way back to the flat in Evelyn Gardens as I had stupidly forgotten to bring the present with me that Claudia had chosen for her at Aspreys. When she had opened the present she kissed me but it was not a normal kiss, it was a . . . a sexual one. She tried to put her hands inside my shirt, I had to push her away. At first she didn't believe me, then she came back for more. I think she thought it was a ritual refusal which really meant yes. I explained to her as gently as I could that no meant no, that I was a married man and also a practising Catholic.'

'What happened then?'

'She was hurt at first; she felt a bit foolish, I suppose, but then she became angry. She said she would say that I had attempted to seduce her with presents. I offered to take her home but she refused and left on her own.'

*　　*　　*

There is an adjournment for lunch. There are journalists everywhere, gabbling into mobiles and tapping out copy on their laptops. As I come out of the courtroom, the Gatehouse posse just ahead of me, I look up and see Mac and Lucy descending the rather elegant stairs: 'I always thought she was a lying hussy,' says the dowager duchess in the unapologetically commanding voice in which she addresses dogs and humans alike, 'Gigi's going to expose the whole thing. Thank God Ivar could afford him.'

'She took advantage,' comes Davina's voice, 'Pa was always kind to her and this was how she repaid him.'

'Poppy introduced her into our world,' I hear Sarah say, 'if it weren't for him she wouldn't have become so bloody successful.'

Tom, walking behind his sisters with Caroline, says nothing. He is holding her arm, I notice, but high up under her armpit almost as if she is his prisoner.

I take Lucy and Mac to a little pub on a canal for lunch, somewhere not far from Dumfries.

'I'm worried, Simon,' Lucy says to me, 'the *Fatal Attraction* line seems to be going down rather well. The press are ecstatic.'

'It's a cheap trick,' says Mac. 'They're trying to traduce you as a witness before they've even got on to the murder itself, that's all. Don't worry about it, my dear. I have every faith in Miss Lord.'

Later on, Verona's assistant, Carey, tells me she has witnessed the following scene:

'Please take your hand off my arm,' Caroline is saying to Tom as they walk down the steps of the court, 'I'm not a prisoner. It won't look very good in photographs, I'm surprised you haven't thought of that, Tom dear. You wouldn't want people to think you manhandle me, now would you?'

'Shut up, Caroline,' Tom replies through gritted teeth. 'It's quite bad enough as it is.'

'I must say,' says Caroline in a loud voice, 'your father is a class A liar. I had no idea.'

'Shut *up*!' Tom repeats.

'I don't want to have lunch with your bossy sisters, thank you very much. I'll go somewhere by myself.'

'Where?'

'There must be a pub. This is Scotland after all.'

'Women don't go into pubs in Scotland.'

'This woman will,' says Caroline, turning on her heel.

'Caroline,' Tom says, 'you can't.'

'Try to stop me.'

Simon's Journal – October 18th

Today, the American boy who found the body has given his evidence.

'Please describe to us, Mr Cruickshank,' says Verona, 'exactly what you found on your afternoon ramble last June.'

The boy, for he seems younger than his age of twenty-two, looks pale but composed.

'I was walking in the bog, the Moss, through one of the ancient drainage channels dug a couple of hundred years ago maybe and very overgrown.'

'And what did you see?'

'I stumbled and fell. As I was on my knees I saw a hand protruding from the peat. Naturally, I was intrigued, scared too, but more curious than frightened. I pulled at it, but nothing happened. I began to scrabble at the turf which kind of came away in slices and there she was.'

The courtroom is absolutely silent.

'You mean Katie Gresham?'

'Yeah. Although I didn't know who she was at that time.'

'Of course not. What did you do next, Mr Cruickshank?'

'I was curious to see why I couldn't get the body to move. And then I realized what had happened.'

'And what was that?'

The boy takes a breath before speaking. 'The body was fastened into the peat with clamps, bamboo crooks, driven tight down over each knee and elbow joint. They looked to me as if they had been adapted from shrimping nets or something similar. They were over her breasts too and her abdomen. She couldn't have moved. She was literally pinned down in the marsh like one of those bog people in Jutland who were sacrificial victims. I thought she was one to start with. I couldn't tell how long she had been there as she was naked.'

A murmur of horror swells in the courtroom. Several journalists rush for the door. Pauline Gresham bows her head so that her expression is concealed. Ivar stares straight ahead of him appearing not to notice the commotion all around him. The Gatehouse family do their best to conceal their shock, but Sandy visibly blanches. Waldy, I notice, looks baffled.

The judge calls for silence.

'What did you do then, Mr Cruickshank?' asks Verona.

'I marked the position, and went to call the cops.'

'Thank you, Mr Cruickshank,' says Verona, 'no further questions.'

Now it is Elizabeth Dunbar's turn to come to the dock.

'Did you know at once that the body was that of Katie Gresham?' asks Verona.

'Yes. I was certain that this was Katie before we even got there. My hunch had always been that her body had been hidden somewhere in close proximity to Gatehouse Park. There was to be a search the following week.'

'And what did you see when you accompanied Mr Cruickshank?'

'I saw exactly what he saw. A body pinned into the bog.'

'In your view was she dead when she was laid down in this manner or was it to prevent her from escaping?'

Again, a wave of shocked murmurs runs round the courtroom. Again, the Lady Justice Clerk calls for silence.

'To me, it looked as if she had been pinned down to prevent her from escaping; there were external signs of a struggle – there was severe bruising to the right-hand side of the face and the neck – so she may have been unconscious or barely conscious when she was put in the Moss. However, the forensic evidence will provide you with a precise answer to your question.'

'How do you think the body got there, Miss Dunbar?'

I expect Gigi to intervene at this point for this is after all merely speculation but he is silent. I wonder why.

'I believe she was murdered in the vicinity of the Moss. Whoever committed the crime could have taken the body there by boat and buried it in the depths of the marsh. It was a brilliant hiding-place. It was a protected site. No one ever went in there. The water would have prevented a dog finding her scent. If it had not been for Mr Cruickshank's curiosity, she'd be there still, I daresay, unless we had managed to find her ourselves.'

'Thank you, Miss Dunbar, no further questions.'

'Now, Miss Dunbar,' Gigi is saying, 'you say that the body was pinned down to "prevent her from escaping".'

'Yes.'

'Why do you think that was?'

'Because Katie was not dead when she was placed in her grave.'

'But if Lord Gatehouse had murdered Miss Gresham, surely he would have finished her off first rather than running the risk that she would might possibly come back and tell of her ordeal. Why this refinement? What possible significance could it have?'

'I cannot answer that,' said Elizabeth Dunbar.

'I put it to you, Miss Dunbar, that if this was a crime of passion then Katie would have been well and truly dispatched *before* she was placed in her grave. Don't you agree that it seems peculiar to leave your victim alive?'

'She was more dead than alive when she was placed in the bog.'

'Nevertheless, it is not the action of a man in a rage. Wouldn't you agree?'

'Yes,' said Elizabeth reluctantly.

'You were a girl in Ayrshire when Kettle was abducting young girls,' Gigi continues.

'Yes.'

'And no doubt you were aware that he enjoyed torturing his victims. He enjoyed seeing them beg for mercy, we know that from statements he made to psychiatrists and to clergy in prison.'

'I was aware of that, yes.'

'Therefore, Miss Dunbar, I suggest to you that this killing has all the hallmarks of Kettle's peculiarly refined brand of cruelty. We know he was a highly educated man; this kind of thing was right up his street. And as we have already established, Katie Gresham was much too proud to have begged for anything.'

Pandemonium in the court. The Lady Justice Clerk adjourns for lunch early.

Pauline and Michael leave the courtroom together with their bodyguards. Outside, they are mobbed by reporters demanding to know their reaction to the horrific evidence, but of course they can say nothing.

Elizabeth had told us what had happened to Katie, but hearing it again in court only intensifies the horror. Refined cruelty, hardly describes it. It beggars belief. It was that evidence that had made Lucy certain she was doing the right thing by bringing this case to justice.

'This afternoon, the forensic pathologist, Mr Cameron, will give his evidence,' Elizabeth tells me, 'and then it's Lucy's turn. Miss Lord will want to keep the horror of Katie's death fresh in the jury's mind and then link in what Lucy saw that last night so that they have a complete picture.'

'It's upset you, hasn't it?' she says.

'It would upset anyone. God knows how Pauline deals with it all.'

'Indeed,' agrees Elizabeth.

The courtroom is bursting at the seams for the afternoon session. News of the morning's evidence means that even more journalists and TV crews are being drafted in.

'In your view, Mr Cameron,' Verona Lord is asking, 'was Katie Gresham already dead when she was placed in the bog?'

'The knee joints were severely swollen and bruised and the breasts and lower abdomen were discoloured and bruised which suggests a struggle. In my view the victim was still alive.'

'But there were signs that Katie had been involved in a struggle before she was entombed?' Verona Lord continues.

'She had been involved in a fight with someone who had punched her repeatedly in the head. She had tried to defend herself; her fingernails were broken; she may have been unconscious so that her attacker could have carried or ferried her into the bog.'

'Did you find any material under her fingernails?'

'There was dirt of course and plant material, but the samples were contaminated after so long in the earth and water.'

'No fibres from clothing?'

'There were one or two, but, as I say, after so long in the bog it is impossible to draw accurate conclusions from them.'

'Had she had sexual relations with anyone before she died that night?'

'No, she had not.'

'Which is not to say she had not practised oral sex.'

'Indeed,' agreed Mr Cameron drily. 'But as she was naked we could find no trace of any semen on clothing.'

'I see. Why do you think she was not killed outright by her attacker?'

'I cannot answer that question. All I can say is that such cruelty is exceptional. I have rarely encountered such an example of criminal depravity during the course of my entire career.'

Again, the shocked murmurs. The jury looks stunned. The Asian woman juror is in tears.

Gigi to Mr Cameron: 'You say that there was no sign of sexual intercourse having taken place before Katie was murdered?'

'No.'

'Was Miss Gresham pregnant at the time of her death?'

'No.'

'Was there any evidence of previous terminations?'

'No, none. Miss Gresham had never been pregnant.'

'Thank you, Mr Cameron. No further questions.'

After Gigi has finished his swift cross-examination of Mr Cameron, the Lady Justice Clerk lets us go early, thank God. I know what Gigi's getting at. If they hadn't had sex, what was the point of their meeting? Things could have gone wrong; sometimes it just doesn't work out, but the conclusion he is leading the jury towards is obvious: no sex means the criminal is less likely to be Ivar. Kettle didn't sexually abuse his victims, he got off on torturing them.

Simon's Journal – October 19th

Gigi has led the jury from the story of a pathetic sixteen-year-old with a crush on a man old enough to be her father to the story of Kettle: he has readied them for a script which will have Lucy as the jealous ex-lover prepared to do anything to slander Ivar's reputation. How he will explain away the fact that she didn't confess to what she knew until now remains to be seen, although it is fairly obvious that he will present it as another instance of Lucy's twisted opportunism rearing its ugly head, based upon the discovery of the body.

The stabbing on the London Underground has been ruled inadmissible as evidence just as Elizabeth thought it would be. Gigi will also say that Kettle abducted Katie and killed her before burying her in the peat. He knew this part of the world every bit as well as Ivar apparently. That is the gospel according to Gigi.

'Miss Diamond,' Verona Lord says, 'please would you tell the court your version of how your relationship with Lord Gatehouse developed.'

'I first went to stay at Gatehouse Park in the summer of 1979,' Lucy says. 'Sarah asked me to stay.'

'And you were glad to accept, were you not?'

'Yes. I knew my mother wanted to work and it was easier for her if I was away.'

'But you soon found the family, and Sarah's role in it, quite odd, did you not?'

'Sarah and Tom, her brother, were rebelling against their parents. They – we – drank quite a bit and we smoked joints a good deal.'

'Something you had not done before?'

'No.'

'And how did Lord Gatehouse behave towards you during that first visit?'

'He hardly seemed to know who I was. I was rather scared of him.'

'But when you returned to London with your mother later on in the holidays you began to get to know him better.'

'Yes, that is correct.'

'Please tell the court, Miss Diamond, how Lord Gatehouse got to know you better.'

'He started to come round to the flat he had lent us. Then, on my birthday, he took me out to lunch at the House of Lords. He talked to me as if I were grown-up. He also gave me a present.'

'So, he had changed towards you, would you say?'

'Completely, yes.'

'Please tell the court how Lord Gatehouse came to be your lover.'

'He took me out to dinner. My mother was against it, but I wanted to go. We stopped at Eaton Terrace, the Gatehouses' London house. Claudia – Lady Gatehouse – was there; she was terribly drunk. She became abusive. Ivar asked me to call an ambulance to take her back to The Priory.'

'Then what happened, Miss Diamond?'

'Ivar took me out to dinner.'

'Had he already made a sexual advance towards you?'

'Yes. After Lady Gatehouse had left.'

'Were you surprised by this?'

'No. I think I was expecting it.'

'And what did you do?'

'I responded. I didn't know what else to do.'

'Were you aware that Lord Gatehouse was having a sexual relationship with his daughter, Sarah, at this point?'

'I was aware that there was something wrong between father and daughter, yes.'

At this point, the Lady Justice Clerk is forced yet again to hush the court.

'What happened after dinner, Miss Diamond?'

'Lord Gatehouse took me back with him to Eaton Terrace.'

'Where he seduced you, is that correct?'

'Yes.'

'And did you tell your mother what had happened to you when you got home?'

'No.'

'Why not?'

'I didn't want to upset her.'

'Then you went back to school, is that right, Miss Diamond?'

'Yes.'

'And when did you next see Lord Gatehouse?'

'I was with Sarah and Tom and Katie Gresham in the basement of the house in Eaton Terrace; it was one of the weekends before half-term. We shouldn't have been there. Ivar was furious. He tore into me in front of the others.'

'Not very lover-like behaviour?' suggests Verona.

'No.'

'What did you think about a man who could display such changes of mood?'

'I was scared of him.'

'But would you say you still wanted to please him?'

'Yes.'

'Your mother was very ill by this point, was she not?'

'Yes.'

'So, the next time you saw Lord Gatehouse was at Gatehouse Park at half-term. Is that correct?'

'Yes.'

'And how did he behave towards you then?'

'He ignored me by day but came to my room at night.'

'And you allowed him to do this?'

'I didn't know how to stop him.'

'But you were aware, were you not, that Lord Gatehouse was having a sexual relationship with Katie Gresham at that time?'

'I became aware of that fact on the day of the shoot.'

'And who informed you, Miss Diamond?'

'Tom did. He was very angry with his father.'

'Had you been aware before Tom told you that Lord Gatehouse found Miss Gresham attractive?'

'Yes. I remember him staring at her at the boathouse the first time I went to Gatehouse Park. He looked as if he wanted to devour her. He couldn't take his eyes off her.'

'But Lord Gatehouse continued to come to your room the night of the shoot and again after that, in spite of his feelings for Miss Gresham. Is that correct?'

'Yes.'

'Why do you think that was?'

'Because I was a pushover. Katie was playing hard to get.'

'And still you did not try to prevent him even though you knew that he was sleeping with Katie when the opportunity arose?'

'I didn't know how to prevent him. I was frightened of him. He had a terrible temper.'

'And you didn't want your mother to find out?'

'No I didn't. Or Sarah and Tom. I was ashamed of myself. I felt I had betrayed them in some way.'

'Miss Diamond, on the night of October 27th 1979 did Lord Gatehouse come to your room?'

'No, he didn't.'

'Did you wonder why?'

'I was aware that things had gone very wrong during the

day. Sarah had told me that Lady Gatehouse had asked her husband for a divorce. There had been a scene at dinner too when Tom had stormed off.'

'Why was that?'

'Because his father was chatting up Katie Gresham.'

'So you went to bed, but you got up again. What time of night was that, Miss Diamond?'

'Just after one. I tried to sleep but I couldn't. Then I realized I'd left my book at the bathing hut in the afternoon. I decided to go and fetch it. I knew it was slightly mad but I felt restless and reckless.'

'So you got dressed and went outside, is that correct? How could you see where you were going?'

'I had a torch and there was a bright moon. It was quite easy to see.'

'Please tell the court what you heard and then saw at the bathing hut.'

'I heard the sound of voices. When I crept up on to the verandah and peered through one of the windows I saw Katie wrapped in a towel. She was shouting at Ivar.'

'What was she shouting?'

'She said something like "You'd better watch it, or I'll call your bloody bluff. I'm not frightened of you, Ivar."'

'What else did she say, Miss Diamond?'

'She accused him of sleeping with Sarah.'

'And how did Lord Gatehouse respond to this allegation?'

'He told her that no one would believe her. He called her a teenage fantasist.'

'Thank you, Miss Diamond. No further questions.'

Poor Lucy. My heart goes out to her. What an ordeal.

'Miss Diamond,' says Gigi, 'when you were interviewed almost twenty years ago over the disappearance of Katie Gresham, you said nothing to Inspector Macmillan to suggest that you knew anything whatever about the matter. In the brief interview you had with him you told him that the last you saw of Katie was at the dinner held that night.'

'Yes.'

'Please tell the court about the last time you claim to have actually seen Katie Gresham.'

'I last saw her at the bathing hut at Gatehouse Park.'

'What time would that have been?'

'As I've already said, after one, possibly nearer two in the morning.'

'And what were you doing there at such an unusual time of night?'

'I've already told the court: I left my book there in the afternoon. I couldn't sleep, so I decided to go and fetch it.'

'You were willing to go out into the dark to find your book? Couldn't you have read something else? Gatehouse Park is full of good books.'

'I wanted the book I was reading then.'

'Or perhaps you wanted to see what had become of the man you had a crush on, would that not be more likely?'

'I wanted my book,' Lucy says.

'Tell us what you saw at the bathing hut,' says Gigi.

'I saw Lord Gatehouse and Katie Gresham having a furious row.'

'And what was the substance of this row?'

'She was accusing him of sleeping with his daughter, Sarah.'

'I see,' says Gigi. 'What happened next, Miss Diamond?'

'I saw Lord Gatehouse going towards the table where the hurricane lamps were then I ducked. The next thing I heard was a scream and the sound of breaking glass.'

'You heard but you did not see, is that correct? Why did you duck at that particular point? Why didn't you wait to see what Lord Gatehouse would do next?'

'Because I was scared. I knew how violent Lord Gatehouse could be. I saw what he did to Sarah.'

'So what did you do?'

'I ran back to the house.'

'But you did not actually see Lord Gatehouse strike Miss Gresham.'

'No, I did not.'

'But afterwards you assumed that that was what must have happened?'

'Yes.'

'If that was the case, why on earth didn't you tell the police?'

'Because I was frightened.'

'Frightened of what, Miss Diamond?'

'I was frightened of what Ivar would do to me. I was scared of him.'

'Let us go back then to the dinner at which Katie was last seen. You were, I gather, in the habit of smoking hashish before dinners at Gatehouse Park. It was observed that it soothed your nerves before the social ordeal ahead.'

'It was a ritual practised by Tom and Sarah,' Lucy says. 'I was just joining in.'

'So you didn't inhale?' Gigi says, smiling broadly.

Laughter.

'Silence!' demands the Lady Justice Clerk furiously. 'Really, Mr Graham.'

'I beg your pardon, my Lady,' Gigi bows demurely, not in the least sorry. The Asian woman amongst the jurors has, I notice, laughed even more heartily than the others, perhaps enjoying the inclusiveness of such a global joke.

'So, by the time dinner had begun you were feeling a little more relaxed,' Gigi continues, 'you had several glasses of wine with dinner – the hospitality at Gatehouse Park is legendary – and then you went upstairs to bed. The Balmachie chauffeur, Jimmy I believe, came to fetch Miss Gresham home in Mrs Gresham's Range Rover.'

'Yes, I believe so, although I did not actually see her leave.'

'So, you smoke a joint or two, you have several glasses of wine and then you go to bed. Let me put it to you, Miss Diamond, that you were waiting and hoping that Lord Gatehouse would come and search you out; you were possibly a little drunk; and when he did not you allowed yourself to believe that there was a rendezvous at the bathing hut. You go down there and you peer through the window and what do you see? Lord Gatehouse and your arch-rival, Katie Gresham in a clinch. I put it to you, Miss Diamond, that your story of a row is a fabrication, which is why you did not dare put it forward at the time. Only now, twenty years on, when you are sleeping with Lord Gatehouse's son and heir – a relationship Lord Gatehouse as a devout Catholic is known to disapprove of – do you come forward with this ridiculous story. I suggest that it is all the fantasy of a woman scorned.'

'That's not true,' Lucy says.

Simon's Journal – October 23rd

Verona is doing her best but I can see that it's not going to work. Gigi has stolen her fire somehow; for all the horror of the circumstances in which the body was found, it cannot be proved that it was Ivar who committed the crime. Because Lucy did not see him strike Katie her testimony loses its power. The sadistic detail of the clamped body points more to Kettle than to Ivar; apparently it was the sort of thing Kettle went in for: he had a liking for tethering his girls with handcuffs and gags. He was a university lecturer and he would have known all about those weird Iron Age sacrificial bogs. If it hadn't been for Kettle, I think, then Lucy might have had a chance of nailing Ivar, but the evidence to suggest that Kettle is guilty is too compelling and has been in the public mind for too long. It's as if Kettle's blood-guilt is a magnet that draws forth blame. And he'll go on being to blame for anything terrible that is discovered here for the next hundred years. The jury, I can see, do not wish to be parted from Kettle. And they are in awe of Ivar; he is protected by a caul of respect built up over generations; as much as they want to believe Kettle guilty they want to believe Ivar innocent and Gigi has so cunningly managed to smear Lucy's reputation. Were it not for the fact that she has been sleeping with Tom they might have believed her.

Lucy's Journal – October 25th

Caroline, when drunk, according to my Sunday newspapers, got away from Tom, and told a reporter from the *Sun* that Ivar had made a serious pass at her when she first became engaged to Tom. The headline was CARO IS EARL'S TOTTIE. In the *Sunday Mail*, Dr Jonas Boyd, the *Sunday Mail's* oracle on psycho-babble, describes Ivar as one of those men who attracts unbalanced women: 'The fantasy of a relationship with such a man is not enough,' pontificates Dr Boyd, 'these women need the excitement of a crucifixion in the full glare of public opinion.'

'One of the burdens of modern public life,' drones the *Sunday Times*, 'appears to be the burden of a stalker or fantasist who will go to any lengths to embarrass or harm the victim in question.'

When I get home this evening after a long walk it is almost dark and so wet that I don't immediately realize that someone has thrown dark red paint over the two bay trees that stand outside my front door. There are five messages on the answering machine so thoughtfully provided by Pauline Gresham, four of them calling me a Jewish slag, the other from Simon.

Caroline has vanished from the daily court appearances of the Gatehouse family after that interview in the *Sun*. Nigel Dempster's page tells me that divorce proceedings are now going on in earnest. Charles Butcher, my superior, will be acting for Caroline, according to Dempster. Dempster goes on to add that Father Adrian Hely of the Westminster Tribunal is working overtime on obtaining an annulment to the Creetown marriage, but informs us that it won't render the little Anworth boys, Miles and Sholto (whom I have never met) illegitimate. Well, fancy that: it's that old Catholic magic at work again.

Claudia's attendance record, impeccable to start with, has fallen away. She wasn't there the day I gave evidence. I think she's back on the bottle big time.

The others continue to appear every day with various additions and subtractions: Aunt Marian and her husband, Sir Oliver, did a two-day stint before returning to their garden and their bridge parties in Wiltshire, Hamish Blundell showed up in a post-modern very ironic version of a bookie's suit with the whippet called Hounslow that Sarah had given him. He made a scene when he was prevented from taking the dog into the courtroom, all of which was reported with relish.

Elizabeth Dunbar went postal – as Sarah would say – when she read this in the newspapers.

'We don't stand a chance with all this tomfoolery going on. It completely obscures the seriousness of the crime that has been committed. Mr Blundell and his whippet seem to be more important than what we're really here for.'

'If this were America,' says Simon, 'the whole thing would already have been sewn up in the newspapers, so we'd better count ourselves lucky that we've got the whippet instead.'

I don't think Simon likes Elizabeth Dunbar much and I can't say I blame him. I don't like her much either. She makes very little effort to charm or to reach out to other people but she's tenacious and clever. She'll be an ornament to the new Scotland and Chief Constable of Strathclyde or somewhere by the age of thirty-five.

Simon's Journal – October 26th

Now Ivar's in the dock being questioned by Verona Lord. He's doing well, too well for my liking. Verona is tiny, five-foot-three in her heels and exceedingly slender; she has fair skin and a narrow, delicate, bony face with rather sunken light blue eyes, but her determined manner belies her look of almost tubercular delicacy.

'After Katie Gresham left Gatehouse Park on the night in question, Lord Gatehouse,' Verona is saying, 'please tell the court what you did after that.'

'I went to see if all was well in the kitchen – we had a new temporary cook – and to make sure that the serving staff had been paid and were being taken home in the staff minibus. Then I was going to lock up. I always saw to those kind of details after a big party.'

'And then what did you do?'

'I went to bed as usual.'

'Was your wife awake when you came upstairs?'

'No, she wasn't. In any case we have separate bedrooms.'

'So you cleaned your teeth, undressed, got into bed.'

'Yes.'

'And you didn't go out again?'

'No, I didn't.'

'If that is the case, perhaps you can explain why the door to the flower-room was unlocked.'

Ivar shrugs. 'Everyone makes mistakes. I must have forgotten.'

'And you deny that you had a rendezvous with Katie Gresham at the bathing hut.'

'I deny it absolutely. I was exhausted. All I could think of was going to bed.'

'So when Lucy Diamond says that she saw you there that night she's lying.'

'Yes, she is.'

'And you deny that you ever had a sexual relationship with Lucy Diamond?'

'Look, I . . .'

'Do you deny that you ever had a sexual relationship with Miss Diamond?'

'We slept together once or twice, that was all.' It is obvious

357

that Gigi has instructed him that he must admit to this. 'My wife had been very unwell for a long time. It was not a happy period in my life.'

'So you were having a sexual relationship with Miss Diamond, a young girl then of just sixteen, and at the same time you were also having a sexual relationship with at least two other people: one was your own daughter, Sarah, the other was Katie Gresham.'

'That's not true,' says Ivar but I can tell by the way his eyes flicker he is rattled.

'But your son Tom, also having a relationship of a kind with Katie Gresham, told Miss Diamond that it was true. He was very angry about it.'

'Katie was Tom's girlfriend. She was never mine.'

'So you categorically deny meeting her at the bathing hut on the night of October 27th 1979 for the purpose of having sex with her.'

'I categorically deny it.'

'You also deny that you had any kind of a relationship other than that of a family friend with Miss Gresham, in spite of the fact that Mrs McMin, one of the cleaning staff at Gatehouse Park in 1979, claims in a written statement that you had your hand on Miss Gresham's knee at dinner the night Miss Gresham vanished.'

'That is completely untrue,' Ivar says, but again his eyes flicker.

'No further questions, Lord Gatehouse.'

It's Lucy's word against his. No one saw him, no one saw Katie leave Balmachie, although God knows how they managed not to. Verona has managed to make Ivar look like a liar and a rotter, but she hasn't managed to make him look like a murderer. I suppose I should have known all along that hers was an impossible task.

The prosecution and the defence will now make their closing speeches, the Lady Justice Clerk will give her summing up. It is likely that Ivar's bail will be withdrawn after the jury have retired. I hope they take as long as possible so that he has to spend some time at least in the cells.

Simon's Journal – October 29th

My wish has come true. The jury are spending the night in a new hotel on the bypass; one of those constructions looking like a stack of egg boxes with bedrooms that make even quite healthy, sane people feel like killing themselves. Lucy has been driven home by Elizabeth Dunbar. She says she would rather be alone. In spite of my air of studied calm, I hadn't expected the toll waiting would exact. I try to read but I can't concentrate on anything and find myself staring into space. I am dining alone in my room once more. Pauline and Michael are together downstairs. Michael is twitchy but Pauline is completely calm. I cannot understand how she does it.

Simon's Journal – October 30th

The jury came back in a minibus five minutes ago. We crowd back in to the courtroom. The jury follow and are seated. The Lady Justice Clerk enters, sits, shuffles her papers, clears her throat. Her composure is unnerving. The courtroom is hushed but there is an unmistakable feeling of tension in the air.

The jury answer to their names. The court clerk then asks one of their number, Mrs Patel, for their verdict. The Asian woman, whose face I have come to know so well, has a look of impenetrable wisdom as she stands at the request of the court clerk.

'Ladies and gentlemen of the jury, have you reached a verdict?'

'We have,' says Mrs Patel.

'And what is that verdict?'

'Not proven.'

There is a short moment of absolute silence and then the courtroom erupts. Pauline Gresham puts her beautiful hands to her face in consternation. Michael leaps to his feet glancing round him in a wild, pugnacious way as if looking for someone to punch. Verona, calm as ever, whispers something to her assistant before turning to the papers in front of her. If she is disappointed she does not show it.

Gigi and Ivar shake hands in a restrained way, but do not otherwise touch each other. There is no hugging and crying here. Justice has been done, their demeanour suggests, the natives have been quelled. Again. Business as usual, God's in His heaven, etc. The Lady Justice Clerk does something or says something that I cannot hear. I think she is trying to regain control over her courtroom. I turn away.

Lucy's Journal

Simon says I haven't lost, that I did my best, but I feel defeated and yet also relieved. It is over. I can go home. Home! What is home but the hay-smelling head of my child, the warm arms of my husband. And I think of something my Jewish grandfather told me when I was about Maud's age: how in the upholstered, stuffed front rooms of his youth a corner remained unplastered to remind them that this was not their eternal home. Why do I remember that now? And even as I wonder I know the answer: justice, ultimate justice. If not here, then somewhere else.

EPILOGUE

Outside the courtroom Ivar leaves the loud and congratulatory group of which he is the centre and goes over to the door under the flagpole which is open in spite of the appallingly cold wind. Pauline Gresham is standing on the steps wrapped in her fur waiting for Jimmy to bring the car round. Michael is nowhere to be seen.

'Pauline?' Ivar says, holding out his hand, 'I do hope we can put all this behind us now.'

Pauline turns round fully to look at Ivar. She does not appear to notice his outstretched hand. Her face is very pale under her fur hat.

'I don't think so,' is all she says in her quiet way. 'Please go.'

'Look, I . . .' Ivar, disconcerted, begins to bluster. The wind blows his hair into his face and makes his eyes water.

'Just go, please.'

Pauline turns round, sees her car coming and begins to descend the steps.

A canny paparazzo, spotting that Ivar has left his phalanx of supporters, snaps him as he holds his hand out to the stony-faced Pauline at the top of the steps under the flapping Union flag.

This is the photograph that appears in all the Sundays together with a good deal of surprisingly hostile comment about Ivar. The general opinion seems to be that an acquittal is not enough for him to remain in his much-treasured post of Lord Lieutenant. Ivar is the fourth member of his family to have occupied this post; theirs has been a straight run since Queen Victoria's day, so much so that it was almost an hereditary post in itself. The innuendo about Ivar's relationship with Sarah, although not fully aired in court, has seeped out into the press where unsavoury sexual predilections and practices are hinted at but not fully delineated for fear of libel. Ivar is perceived as a somewhat sinister figure whose easy smile masks a variety of unsavoury characteristics. The profile of him in the News Review section of the *Sunday Times* suggests an Icarus-like figure drawn to danger but not wanting to accept the consequences. It is headed: *The Man who Fell to Earth*.

After the trial, the Gatehouses returned to what certain sections of the press insisted on referring to as their 'family mansion', much to the amusement of the likes of Hamish Blundell, who took to calling Annan House 'Sarah's fm' to the bewilderment of outsiders who did not understand the genesis of the joke, which only amused Hamish even more. Bewildering people was Hamish's stock-in-trade, his forte. But the smile was wiped from his face when Sandy, suddenly remembering he was a man not a mouse, banned Hamish and all his cronies from the fm for good. The tartan upstairs loos would have to be redone; he wanted stripes or chintz, a language he understood; Hamish's post-modern irony left him cold and offended his mother who thought the whole thing a snide comment on her own stewardship of Annan House, not to mention the slight to the hunting Annan tartan which the old duchess was fond of and had had several skirts made from in her time. (She had obviously forgotten that the sacred Annan tartan had been invented, like so many others, by an Edinburgh tailor in 1746.)

Sandy wanted a Rosa not a Hamish, a decorater who mothered him, not some fine-tuned pansy in a bookie's suit who took offence at every second word and who was always sniggering at him behind his back whilst desirous of easy access to his cheque book at the same time. Sarah pleaded with him and threw a series of tantrums that ended with her storming off back to Gatehouse Park with Bob the whippet on the back seat and a badly-packed suitcase in the boot.

Ivar was not remotely pleased to see his difficult third daughter under such circumstances. She was married to Sandy and she should be bloody grateful for the fact; no one else would put up with her, not to mention the fact that Sandy's title was the second or third oldest in Scotland and that he, Sandy, was Hereditary High Falconer to the Palace of Holyrood or some such nonsense. Sarah cried and told her father that he always rejected her just when she needed him most and why wouldn't he support her in her hour of need?

Ivar looked at her in disgust before stalking away across the hall towards the study where, folded carefully into the old dark green blotter with the coronet stamped on it in silver that had belonged to his father and his father's father, lay the letter from the Lord Chamberlain's office or whichever department of the palace deals with such things informing him that 'owing to the unfortunate circumstances in which you have recently found yourself' it would be 'desirable' and pleasing to Her Majesty if Ivar tendered his resignation as Her Majesty's representative in the Stewartry.

Ivar had already heard through the grapevine that his resignation was required. He had been made painfully aware of his fall from grace when he had paid his first visit to the House of Lords since the trial. In the bar several groups of people had fallen silent when he appeared. Buffy Lumley had looked straight through him at the ticker-tape machine; Silas Cripps-Buller had swung away from him in the gents; Tolly Lansdale had got up and walked off when Ivar approached him in the boys' dining-room (where peers dined when they were on their own: it was just like being back at school: same filthy food only one was allowed wine to wash it all down with), and Tolly had been his fag at Eton, for God's sake. As an old Etonian who had been a member of Pop (aka the Eton Society, entrance only granted to super-swells) Ivar knew that Tolly's rejection of him was a death knell. You simply never *ever* cut a member of Pop; not in this life anyway and probably not in the next either.

The most distressing thing of course was that the short list for new holders of the title of Lord Lieutenant should contain the name of that man, the unspeakable parvenu Hergstrom. Hergstrom's father had been a fish-gutter by profession, no doubt a blond lumbering oaf with piggy eyes just like his son. He had been put forward by Sandy for some reason. But when Ivar had remonstrated with him, Sandy had informed his father-in-law in a rather curt manner that Hergstrom was ideal for the job: he had buckets of money (an absolute necessity for the position), a good business head and plenty of time now that he had sold his latest company. Sandy had added cruelly: 'It's time to give someone else a go, don't you think, Ivar? We mustn't be greedy about these things.'

Upstairs, Sarah regressed to a pattern of behaviour formed in her earliest childhood by lying down on her bed wrapped in an old and comforting eiderdown with an emerald green slippery satin cover somewhat faded and threadbare in places but still comfortingly plump. In one corner, there was a Cash's name tape which read 'Sarah Anwoth, Founders House' in small pale green letters. 'SA,' she thought to herself, 'always SA, SA, SA ...' She began to rock to and fro rather as autistic children do, a comforting action which made her feel meditative and calm. It was how she used to deal with it in the old days ... *Don't tell anyone*, he would say, *no one is to know, do you understand?* She would wake in the night and he would be there. And then he would be gone again. SA, SA ... it rhymed with away, away. In the old days, her

Aunt Marian had told her, in the days before anyone in polite society mentioned the word 'sex' in public, SA stood for sex appeal, as in 'that girl has oodles of SA' . . . *Don't tell anyone.* She began to cry and cry and wanted Bob whom she'd left in the car asleep on his hunting Annan rug that Hamish had so sweetly had made up for him. She longed to put her head on Bob's warm mushroom-coloured flank and weep until there were no more tears.

Sarah fell asleep but she was woken by the housekeeper, Josie.

'What is it, Josie?'

'It's your mother, Duchess. I'm sorry to waken you. Your father's away down to the estate office and I canny get her to open her door. I need to take her tea in. She wanted it in the bedroom.'

'Shit,' said Sarah, swinging her long thin legs out from under her comfort blanket. 'Shit, fuck, bugger.'

Claudia's bedroom was on another floor from Sarah's old room. The heavy old door was locked, the keyhole cover firmly in place. Sarah banged and shouted.

'Call the joiner,' she said. 'His number's on the list by the kitchen phone. I'll get hold of my father.'

Claudia, who had been binge-drinking with a vengeance since the trial, had drowned in her own vomit. She had taken too many sleeping pills although whether intentionally or not was never discovered. Her funeral in the Catholic chapel (built by the tenth Earl) on the edge of the village was private; there would be a memorial service at the Brompton Oratory at a date to be advised.

Ivar married again briefly (also in the Oratory – an action deemed 'awfully bad form' by people who knew) a year after Claudia's death to a girl, Perdita something, who was young enough to be his daughter. She was very pretty and very blonde. The marriage lasted nine months, long enough for Perdita to have the child she was carrying at the time of the marriage, a girl called Clementine, now aged five. The grounds given for the divorce were mental cruelty. An annulment was also granted but Ivar did not marry again.

Four years to the day after the discovery of Katie's body, Ivar Gatehouse had a sudden haemorrhage of the brain which killed him as instantly as if he had been shot through the back of the head. He was seventy-four.

Sarah returned to Sandy. They sold the house in Clarendon Road and bought one in Aubrey Walk. Rumour had it that their marriage was falling to pieces. I glimpsed Sarah once more after the trial: she was stalking along Kensington Church Street on a warm spring day wearing the long black coat with the fur on the collar that I remembered from the trial and a cream embroidered pashmina shawl. She was also wearing gloves, but her lips were livid as if with cold. She looked completely dotty; it was there in the walk and the way, on a warm day, she appeared to be dying of cold. Passers-by glanced at her curiously as she passed.

A year and a half after her mother's death she was found dead in her car on a remote road somewhere near where the remains of the girl the police had once claimed to be Katie Gresham were dug up. That girl continues nameless, like those lost soldiers of the Great War, known unto God but not to anyone else, but her mortal remains, together with those of Katie Gresham, are still at the temple on the loch at Balmachie. The black swans are still there too, exotic and sombre in their mourning plumage.

Sandy married again and is now the proud father of twin boys. His new wife, Maddy, is a sensible no-nonsense sort of Scottish girl, good at gardening and plumbing (the kind who regards a cold house as a challenge – 'central heating is so bad for the furniture, don't you know') who is just about to have number three. They are hoping for a girl this time. I saw Maddy the other day entering Peter Jones in Sloane Square like a ship in full sail with the little boys, Alexander and Robert, at heel; they were wearing smart long French navy shorts and tartan puffas; with their tight curls, Roman noses and huge pale eyes they were little replicas of the same rare breed as their father.

Tom succeeded to the title upon his father's death and is now the eighteenth Earl Gatehouse. He continues to work in London but spends an increasing amount of time at Gatehouse Park looking after his estate. After his divorce from Caroline, he eventually married again to a girl called Juliet, a successful dress-designer with her own atelier and clientele. They had a child, a girl and then another girl, so once more there are four children at Gatehouse Park. The boys adore Scotland and spend as much time there as they can with their father. They quite like Juliet (who, after all, is only a wife) and the little girls are no threat. I saw a picture of those boys the other day in *The Tatler*. They were indulging the archaic rituals of their class with a vengeance at a ball somewhere: Sholto, in white tie, was hefting a squealing deb in the air almost over his head, Miles was leering into the camera with a fag in his mouth and his hands round the waist of one of those interchangeable girls called Camilla or Laetitia whose nipples showed clearly through the fabric of her dress. The Gatehouse family saga continues unabated or so it seems. They can take a scandal here or there: the secret of all these families is their ability to adapt and to forget. Sponge-like, they soak up new money and new and pretty girls are drawn to them. A generation on and they will begin to boast about Ivar's villainy.

Pauline Gresham returns to Balmachie House once a year to lay flowers on her daughter's grave on the anniversary of her disappearance. Otherwise, she lives in New York and at the house in Bedford in New York State. She and Michael lead separate lives although they are not divorced. Pauline's work as a goodwill ambassador for the Red Cross means that she travels a good deal. When she is at home she entertains quietly with small dinners for ten or less at the Park Avenue apartment.

After the trial, I went back home to Simon and Maud,

but I gave up my job as a divorce lawyer with Simon's encouragement. I decided that, not knowing what I wanted to do, I would grant myself the luxury of studying for a degree in History of Art at the Courtauld Institute. Paintings had always been my first love. In the end, like my mother, I ended up doing some lecturing and writing. I am now Dr Lucy Diamond. My articles appear in a wide variety of newspapers and magazines ranging from *Country Life* to something as different as *Flesh*. Simon handed over his work in Brussels and came back to London for good.

We decided that we would have another child which we duly did: Natasha Katherine was born a year later. Pauline Gresham agreed to be her godmother.

When I look back on it all now, I see that it was no coincidence that I ended up being a lawyer to the rich and powerful. It was a way of having power over them, a continuation of the life I had first sampled as a girl at Gatehouse Park. I was as intoxicated as an adult as I had been as a girl with the thrill of money and power, only better at denying it to myself. Ever the outsider, I enjoyed my ringside fence and the illusion it gave me of being one of them, but I paid a price for my position in this world to which I did not belong, nearly too high a price as it turned out.

When we last saw Pauline in New York (where I was lecturing at MOMA), she took me aside and told me that she had cancer.

'They've given me a year,' she said, 'maybe longer, maybe less. The truth is, Lucy, they don't know.'

'I'm so sorry,' I said, 'so very sorry.'

'A year is a long time,' she said, touching my cheek with her hand, 'if you know how to live properly.'

'And do you, Pauline?'

'Yes, I think so,' she said in her quiet way. 'I'm not afraid, you know. I want to see her again.'

Our eyes met.

'I will never forget what you did,' she said, 'you know that, don't you. I know what a price you paid for your integrity. I know how it nearly destroyed you.'

'You don't have to thank me, Pauline.'

'Oh, but I do, my dear, I do, from the bottom of my heart.'

Library Media Center
Delav.
Del..... ... . School

Library Media Center
Delavan-Darien High School
Delavan, WI 53115